Wicked Screwed

SIAN CEINWEN

ISBN: 978-1-922559-31-9 (eBook)
ISBN: 978-1-922559-32-6 (Paperback)

Front cover image by Mark Reid at authorpackages.com.
Book design by Lorna Reid at authorpackages.com.

Acknowledgement of Country

I would like to acknowledge the Traditional Owners of Country throughout Australia and recognise their continuing connection to land, waters, and community.

The Whadjuk people of the Noongar Nation are the traditional custodians of the land this book was written on.

I acknowledge that sovereignty throughout these lands was never ceded. I pay my respect to them and their cultures, and to the strength and resilience of Elders both past and present.

Dedication

This book is for you, dear reader, because you deserve *a gangbang* in the first chapter.

While I was writing this book, my watch warned me that my stress was high and suggested that I "might want to take a moment to relax." So consider yourself warned that reading this could be hazardous for your health.

There is an absolutely ludicrous amount of gratuitous smut in this book. When deciding between cutting some smut to end the series as a trilogy or leaving every single filthy scene and making it a 'four-book trilogy' so I could include even *more* smut, I decided to go the latter route.

My thoughts and prayers go out to Lexi. May her pussy recover quickly from the damage that was wrought upon it during this book.

Chapter 1

Insert Squinting Face with Tongue Emoji Here

"I'm going to be sick," I moan as we approach Isaac Meade's office in Nathaniel Walker's G-Wagon.

I'm seated in the back between Logan Ballantine and Ashton Woodford. Nate is driving, and my husband, Dante Sullivan, is in the passenger seat.

"You'll be fine, Angel." Dante turns around to give me a reassuring smile.

"She's going to tell everyone about us." I bite my lip as the fear of being exposed to the world crashes over me.

Logan takes my chin in his hand and turns my face to his. I find myself staring into his beautiful, chocolate-brown eyes as he nods solemnly.

"She probably will. We're going to tell Isaac everything, and he'll work out a plan with us. Okay?"

"Okay," I murmur in agreement.

Logan presses his lips to mine, and I part my lips instinctively. His tongue intertwines with mine, and he uses it with his usual expertise as he kisses me. By the time we part, my breathing is shallow, and my concerns about being exposed are buried under my lust for the man sitting next to me.

"Feeling better?" he asks.

"Feeling horny but still worried. I'm not sure if that counts as better," I say in a thoughtful voice.

"Sounds better to me," Ash says as he pulls me over to him.

He kisses me as well, and he breaks our kiss as Nate pulls into the private parking lot behind Meade Management. Dante called Isaac last night to tell him that the band had something urgent to discuss today, and they organized this meeting.

"Gentlemen. Lexi. It's great to see you," Isaac says as he looks up from where he's seated at a conference table in the boardroom we've been shown to.

"Hi, Isaac." I force a smile at him as I take a seat next to Dante, with Nate to my right.

The guys greet Isaac as well, then get settled around the table. My heart pounds in my chest because I know what we have to tell their manager. What the entire world will likely find out soon. I'm surprised people don't know already because I was expecting the news story to break this morning.

"So, what did you guys need to discuss?" he asks with a pleasant smile at the guys.

Unlike the other times we've revealed this secret, there are no fun jokes about who's going to be 'it.' We decided that Dante should be the one to tell Isaac since he's my husband, and it's expected that Isaac might have questions for him.

"I don't think there's any way to sugarcoat this," Dante says in a somber voice.

He pauses for a second before he continues. Just long enough for me to notice the tightening in his jaw that gives away how tense he is, and I squeeze his hand as he clears his throat before he speaks.

"The guys are all in relationships with Lexi, and Ash's ex-girlfriend has been blackmailing us over it."

Isaac's eyebrows fly up on his face, and his mouth drops open. It's clear that, of all the things Dante could've told him, this was never in a million years what he was expecting. I clutch Dante's hand tightly in mine as I wait for Isaac's reaction.

He collects himself and gives a little shake of his head. "I'm sorry. When you say that they're 'in relationships,' I just want to clarify exactly what you mean by that."

"He means that we're sleeping with her," Nate says.

Isaac's eyes snap to me, then to Dante, and then across to the other guys. "You're joking, right?"

"No, we're not," Dante says. "Do you think that I would joke about this?"

Isaac scans his face for a few seconds, then nods. "I see. Well, your personal life is your business. How it affects your professional life is mine. You said that Ash's ex-girlfriend has been blackmailing you? How long has this been going on, and what is Štěpánka blackmailing you with?"

It's natural that Isaac would assume it's Ash's most recent girlfriend. Štěpánka never had a clue about my relationships, though, because I'd lost all trust by the time Ash started to date her.

"It's not Štěpánka," Ash says quickly. "Cassie."

"Okay, that makes more sense, I guess." Isaac turns to look at him. "Tell me what happened."

"When Nate and Lexi got together, they told all three of us. When Logan and Lexi got together, they told Cassie and me. Cassie didn't take that news well. She thought it meant I was going to sleep with Lexi, too."

"Which you are, aren't you?" Isaac asks.

"I didn't fucking cheat with Lexi. We didn't get together until after Cassie and I were broken up," Ash growls.

Isaac holds his hands up in a placating gesture. "Whoa. I'm just trying to get everything straight so I can figure out what is going on. Cassie didn't take it well. What happened next?"

"She started trying to turn me against the guys, but I guess she was also collecting evidence so she had an ace up her sleeve. After we broke up, she contacted us and wanted us to pay a hundred grand to stop her from going to the media about it."

Isaac groans, "You didn't pay her, did you?"

"We did," Logan admits. "I wrote the first check. Ash wrote the second."

"*Second*?!" Isaac gasps.

"Yeah, she blackmailed us a second time for another hundred grand. Last night she wanted two hundred, and we were going to make her sign a non-disclosure agreement."

Isaac snaps his head back to look at Ash again. "You 'were going to?' That sounds like it didn't end up happening."

"No, it didn't. Which is why we're here. She, uh"—he looks over at me and cringes—"found Lexi and me in bed together. She had a spare key to my apartment that I absolutely did *not* give her, and she let herself in an hour early for our meeting."

"Jesus christ," Isaac breathes.

"We're sorry," I say because I feel like I should apologize for being the cause of all of this.

"Don't apologize. Just—give me a second," Isaac says with a frown at me.

He has a pad of lined paper in front of him, but he hasn't taken any notes. He stares at the blank page as he taps the pen on the pad. The tapping noise fills the silence in the room as Isaac appears to think through what he's been told.

Finally, he looks up at us. "Why didn't you come to me with this?"

"We didn't want anyone to know, and we thought we could handle it," Dante admits.

Isaac glares at him. "What the fuck do you think I'm here for?" He blows out a breath of air and shakes his head. "Sorry, that's not constructive. I'm just frustrated that I'm only finding out about this now. What did she blackmail you with?"

"Two pictures. One of Lexi and Nate hugging, another with Lexi and Logan, uh, when we were at a club together," Dante tells him.

"Hang on. I have the pictures," I tell him.

I open my phone, unlock it, and pull up the messages from Cassie before I slide my phone across to Isaac. He looks at the pictures and tuts as he shakes his head.

"Guys, this wasn't smart." He looks up at us. "These are public places. She had every right to take these photographs."

"I think she also voice recorded us when she came to my place yesterday because I told her she couldn't leave, and she played back a clip of me saying that and said she'd tell people I was holding her hostage. I'm not sure what else she might have recorded," Ash tells him.

I realize with horror that she could easily have the sounds of Ash and me fucking on tape. The thought that she might release it to the world is terrifying. I like it when the guys show me off in public, but having someone do it against my will is violating. I shudder at the thought, and Nate puts his arm around my shoulders as he kisses my cheek while Dante squeezes my hand again.

Isaac takes in these interactions and sighs. "Okay. I'll speak to a lawyer and get some advice. In the meantime, speak to *no one* about this. I'll try to see if there's any whisper of a big Wicked Stallion story in the pipeline." He gives us a stern look. "*Do better.* None of this shit in public." He indicates to the phone.

"We will," I promise as I chew my bottom lip.

Isaac nods. "Good. As I said, I don't care what you do in your personal life. If you're all happy, then great. I'm not sure exactly how we're going to spin this or if it'll affect any of your brand deals and sponsors for the tour, but I'll keep you informed."

A cold chill runs down my spine as I realize that the guys have morality clauses in a lot of their contracts. It doesn't matter that we're all happy. If it seems immoral to the public or the brand, they can be axed in a heartbeat.

We talk with Isaac for about another half an hour, and when the meeting ends, I'm confident he has a plan for what to do. Everything's so up in the air, and it feels like we're just waiting for the other shoe to drop.

"I will speak to the label as soon as I get wind of the story breaking."

He reminds us not to comment on anything and not to trust

anyone, even close friends and family.

"When this does go public, the scrutiny *will* be intense. We may have to look at getting security for you, depending on how it goes."

Dante nods. "I'd already thought that, too. Thank you again, Isaac. We appreciate your support."

Isaac gives him a smile as he shakes his hand. "Hey, it's literally what I'm here for."

As we leave his office, I blow out a breath of air. I walk next to Dante while I hold his hand. Isaac instructed me to ensure I'm not seen anywhere near any of the other guys, and I'm determined to do my best to minimize the damage this does to the band.

We climb into the car, and I get in the back between Logan and Ash again. As soon as we're in the safety of the car, I lean against Ash, and he puts his arm around me before he drops a kiss on the top of my head. Logan holds my hand and brings it to his lips. They're soft and warm against my skin, and I smile at the feeling.

"I love you guys," I say to them, a lump in my throat.

"I'd be concerned if you didn't," Dante says with a laugh, and he turns around to smile at me.

"I just mean that, as much as this sucks, I wouldn't change it for anything in the world if it meant I couldn't be with you all." I shrug my shoulders.

"Alexandra," Logan says, and it catches my attention.

I immediately sit up and turn to look at him. He places his warm palm on my cheek, and his brown eyes mesmerize me as he looks down at me.

"I think I speak for all of us when I say that none of us would want to go back to our lives before. Except for Dante, I guess, since you were already his wife when this all started."

"No, I wouldn't," Dante assures him. "I'm much happier now because you're all happier."

"There you go." Logan presses his lips to mine and explores my mouth with his tongue as he raises a hand to my breast. He breaks our kiss and looks at me again. "We're all happier then, even

Dante. I mean, I personally get to play with the best toy in the world."

My pussy clenches the way it always does when Logan calls me his toy, and wetness pools between my thighs underneath the skirt of my dress. Ash turns his body toward mine and slides his hand up my thigh. I gasp and turn to look into his ice-blue eyes.

"What's wrong, Lexi?" he asks with a grin at me.

"Nothing."

He slides his hand further until he finds my bare pussy, and I moan when his fingers brush against my clit. It's the softest, barely-there touch, and it drives me wild. I spread my legs wider so I can seek stronger contact with his fingers.

Ash dips his fingers into my pussy, then pulls them out and rubs my clit. Arousal swirls through me, and I bite my lip as I look at him while Logan pulls my dress up so we can all see what Ash is doing.

Nate adjusts the rear-view mirror and grins at me. "Let's get home so I can fuck you."

"Sounds perfect," I say around a moan.

Nate puts the car in gear and pulls the car out of the parking bay. I catch Dante's gaze, and his eyes are dark as he watches his friends play with me. Logan pulls my dress down under my breasts and rubs the pad of his thumb over my nipple as he lowers his mouth to my neck. His tongue is warm and wet against my skin, and I moan softly as he trails it up to my ear.

Ash pushes his fingers into me and uses his other hand to pull and tweak my nipple. I'm lost to the sensations they're giving me, and I thrust my hips forward to meet Ash's fingers. The need to come is strong, and my breathing is loud in the enclosed space. I close my eyes and tilt my head back at the same time as I reach my hands out to place them on both Logan and Ash's cocks.

They're both stiff under their clothing, and I rub them through their jeans as I moan, "Yes, Ash. That's so good."

"Yeah? You like this, baby?" He rubs his thumb over my clit as he continues to fuck me with his fingers.

"So much. Oh, god, yes."

Ash lowers his head and takes my breast in his mouth as Logan nips my earlobe with his teeth before he murmurs, "Do you want to come, Alexandra?"

"Mmm," I manage to say with my eyes still closed.

"What do you think, Dante? Should she be allowed an orgasm?" Logan asks.

I open my eyes and pant for breath as I look into my husband's eyes again. Ash is still fucking me, and my entire body is aflame with lust as I wait for Dante's reply.

"I don't know. Isn't she meant to call you 'Sir?'" He raises an eyebrow at me. "Logan asked you a question, Angel. Is that how you respond to him?"

"No, Honey."

Logan nips my earlobe again while he twists my nipple painfully, and I moan as a dart of arousal shoots straight to my crotch. "Good point, Dante. I guess she can wait until we get home."

He wraps his fingers around my chin and turns my face to his. Logan's gaze sears into mine as he looks down at me.

"Don't come, Alexandra."

"Yes, Sir," I pant, and he lowers his face to mine.

Logan holds my face in place as he kisses me. His scent fills my senses, and his tongue flicks out to tangle with mine. Ash swirls his tongue around my nipple as the sound of his jeans being unzipped rings out, and he places his hand over mine before he moves it so he can push my hand into his underwear. I moan into Logan's mouth as Ash's thick cock fills my hand, and I begin to stroke him.

"Mmm, baby. That's so good," Ash moans with his mouth still around my breast.

I can barely focus on any one thing because all of my senses are on high alert. I do my best to keep stroking Ash, but I've stopped rubbing Logan, and he places his hand on mine to move it back and forth. I'm so close to coming and I pant for breath when Logan breaks our kiss and looks into my eyes.

"Don't come, Alexandra," he murmurs.

I'm so close to orgasm, and ecstasy floods through my heated body. I stare into his eyes as I fight to keep myself from tipping over the edge.

"I can't," I whimper. "I need it. I need it. I need it."

"Do you, Angel?"

Dante's voice draws my attention, and I turn to stare at him as I bite my lip and moan, "Yes, Honey."

"Ash, you might need to stop fingering her," he says with a throaty chuckle.

Ash pulls his mouth away from my breast at the same time as he moves his fingers away from my clit and strokes them up and down my labia instead. I moan softly because they're so close but so far from where I want them to be.

"Well, she should probably put her mouth to good use if that's the case." Ash raises an eyebrow at me and indicates to where my hand is wrapped around his cock. "I'd much rather have your mouth around me than your hand."

I don't have to follow instructions or requests from Ash the way I do with Dante and Logan, but I still dutifully lower my head to his crotch. I start by swirling my tongue around his head, and I love it when Ash groans in response. The air is cool on my ass as I bend over, but Logan puts his warm palm on my ass and squeezes it before he rubs it while I start to suck Ash.

"Mmm, such a pretty toy," Logan murmurs.

My pussy clenches as the ache to be filled hits me. Logan reaches down and rubs his forefinger over my nipple as I sink as far onto Ash's cock as I can so his cock makes its way down my throat. I hold myself there for a few seconds before I pull back and swirl my tongue around his head again, then repeat the process. After I've done it a few times, I gasp onto Ash's cock when Logan pushes his fingers into my pussy.

"She's so wet. I've got three fingers in her right now," he tells the guys.

Ash puts his hand on my head and strokes it softly. "It's going to be a struggle not to blow down her throat, but I want to fuck her when we get home."

Logan tweaks my nipple as he continues what he's doing. "She's definitely ready for it. I just needed some lube for my fingers, and my beautiful little slut helpfully has some for me."

Heat rushes to my cheeks at them talking about me in the third person, and Logan calling me his slut almost tips me into orgasm. My pussy clenches, and I moan as I sink down onto Ash as far as I can again. Logan pulls his fingers out of me and pushes them into my ass. I grip Ash's muscled thigh for something to hold onto as my ass is filled. I push back against Logan's fingers instinctively as he fucks me with them while I blow Ash.

I don't know how long we keep going, but I'm surprised when the car pulls into the garage underneath our apartment building. I don't stop what I'm doing, though. Ash groans loudly, and my jaw aches from blowing him for such a long period.

Nate turns off the car, but I'm lost to the lust I'm in, and I don't want to stop. I bury Ash's cock in my mouth and push back against Logan's hand. My pussy aches, and it's so wet that I have to clench my thighs tight together because I'm worried I'll drip pussy juice on the seat of Nate's car.

After a few minutes, Ash murmurs, "I'm about ten seconds from blowing. I think we should stop this and go upstairs."

"I don't know. I'm enjoying the show," Nate says in an amused voice.

Logan slowly pulls his fingers out of my ass. "I'm sure you are, but wouldn't you rather have your cock in her?"

"Let's go," Nate says quickly, and the guys all laugh.

I don't stop blowing Ash, though. I'm so wildly aroused that I just want to suck him forever. He starts to move, but I grip his thigh tighter and push his cock down my throat again, reveling in the moan he makes when I do.

"Stop, Angel," Dante says with a chuckle.

I pull my mouth off Ash and sit up to look at the guys. Dante and Nate are both obviously turned on, and the air is filled with heavy breathing.

"Should we wait a few minutes? I mean, we all kind of have

raging boners right now." Nate grins at the guys.

Ash zips his jeans up and shrugs. "Fuck it. I want my cock in her right now. Let's get upstairs."

He leans over and kisses me as he tweaks a nipple that Logan has left exposed before he pulls my dress back up over my breasts. At the same time, Logan pulls the skirt of my dress back down. As we get out of the car, I see that Nate was right, and all four men have obvious erections.

Our parking space is only a short way from our private elevator to the penthouse apartment we live in, but it feels like it's a mile. A couple drives past us in a Maserati, and my cheeks flood with heat as the woman in the passenger seat turns to gawk at the guys.

I take Dante's hand as we reach the elevator, and he leans down to kiss me as he pulls me into his arms while Nate swipes a keycard against the wall. The doors in front of us slide open, and Dante pulls me inside while he continues to kiss me. He pushes me up against the back wall, his cock hard against me as his tongue explores my mouth.

The other guys never touch me in the elevator because there are security cameras in here, but Dante reaches between us and rubs my clit as he pulls his head back to look at me.

"You're right, Logan. She's wet and ready to be fucked. Aren't you, Angel?"

"Yes, Honey."

The doors open into our apartment, and Dante takes my hand as we exit the elevator. He pulls me over to the dining table, yanks the chair away from the end position, and pulls my dress off over my head before he bends me over the table.

I'm shocked when he drops the dress on the floor, unzips his jeans, and pushes his cock into me. It's so unlike him, and I love that he wants me this badly. The satisfaction of having a cock in my pussy is overwhelming, but I work hard not to react because it's Dante.

"Fuck, yes. I love you, Angel."

"I love you, too, Honey," I say with a small pant as he holds himself deep in me.

"You can react," Dante says as he grabs my hips and starts to fuck me.

I moan loudly, and he chuckles as he bends down and kisses my back before he stands back up to pound into me. I grab hold of the table as I'm pushed against it, the marble top cold against my breasts.

Someone's tongue swirls around my clit, and I gasp at the sensation. I look to my right to see Nate and Ash, both naked and stroking their erections while they watch us. Just knowing that they're standing there to wait for their turn to use my body while I'm being fucked by Dante and eaten by Logan drives me wild. It tips me into the orgasm I've been holding off since the car ride.

My body shakes, and my pussy clenches around Dante's cock as I moan, "Fuck. Oh, fuck. Yes. Fucking fuck."

Logan keeps going, but Dante's fingers flex against my hips, and his cock jerks inside me before he pulls his hard shaft out of me, and I'm left empty.

"Someone else's turn," he says in a husky voice.

Nate immediately grins. "Mine."

He disappears from my field of vision, but it's only a moment before he pushes his cock into me. Dante stands next to Ash and slowly strokes his cock, which glistens with my pussy juice.

Nate enters me, and I moan as I'm filled again. Logan's tongue swipes across my clit, and his hands are warm on my legs while Nate fucks me. I pant for breath as I revel in the ecstasy that washes over me, and another orgasm approaches on the horizon.

Ash walks over to me and murmurs, "You don't seem to be doing anything with your hand right now, baby. I think I could make use of it."

I bite my lip as I lift my hand to his cock to stroke it, and he gets a satisfied smile on his face. I love being used like this, and Logan brings me to orgasm twice before Nate switches out with Ash.

When Ash eventually pulls out, he says, "I'll take over for you, Logan."

"Thanks, bro," Logan says before he nips my clit with his teeth and moves out from under me.

I squeak at the painful sensation, then moan as the pleasure takes over. Ash takes his place, and then Logan pushes his cock into me. I gasp as he thrusts roughly into me, but I love it so much. The entire world is aglow as my men use my body to satisfy themselves and me. Dante moves over to me, and I instinctively begin to stroke his cock while I watch Nate satisfy himself.

"You know, I fucking love watching you guys fuck her," Nate says. "Who needs porn when I get to watch Lexi have her holes filled regularly."

Ash chuckles, and the sound reverberates in my pussy as I tip into orgasm again. Dante switches out with Logan, who I watch as he walks over to Nate and thrusts his tongue into Nate's mouth.

I groan at the sight of them kissing, and again when Logan drops to his knees in front of Nate. He takes Nate's hard shaft in his mouth, and I love the look of pure ecstasy that comes over Nate's face as he looks down at Logan. My pussy clenches around Dante's cock, and Ash's tongue does wonders on my clit as I watch the blow job. I come again, and Dante switches places with Ash.

This continues for a long time, with Dante and Ash repeatedly switching places to fuck or eat me before Nate growls, "Logan, why the fuck won't you let me come? I'm not your goddamn sub."

Logan takes him out of his mouth and grins up at him. "I thought you might want to give Lexi a facial, and she doesn't seem ready to receive it."

"Mmm. Good idea, Logan," Ash says from where he pounds into me from behind. "Maybe, we should all give Lexi a facial. She'd look hot with cum all over her face."

I inhale sharply at the idea and moan softly. The thought of having my face covered in cum causes a spark of electricity to shoot around my body.

Dante moves his mouth off my pussy and rubs my clit with his fingers as he asks, "Do you like that idea, Angel?"

"Yes, Honey," I say with another moan.

Ash pulls out of me, and Dante takes my hand after he stands up. He spins me around and pulls me back against him. His cock is hard against my ass as he reaches one hand down to rub my clit while he twists my nipple with the other.

"What do you think, Nate?" Dante asks as he lowers his lips to my neck.

Nate has his hand thrust in Logan's hair, and he looks up to grin at me. "Fuck, yes."

Dante's lips and tongue are hot on my neck as he kisses me, and I shiver with my nipples stiff and painful as I watch Logan blow Nate. I'm in ecstasy, and Ash moves forward to kiss me as well.

When Ash breaks our kiss, Dante pushes me to my knees in front of himself, and I take him in my mouth at once. Ash moves next to him, and I wrap my fingers around his cock to stroke him. I alternate between the two for a little while before Logan and Nate join them in front of me.

I take Logan's cock in my mouth and move my hand from Ash's cock to Nate's. Ash begins to stroke himself while Logan takes my face in his hands and fucks my mouth. After a while, I switch to sucking Nate, and when I do, Logan crouches behind me.

He reaches between my legs to stroke my clit. "Your pussy is so wet. I think you like the idea of being covered in cum a lot."

"Mmm. Yes, Sir," I moan after I remove Nate from my mouth before I move on to Dante.

Logan rubs me to another orgasm before he stands up again. I take him in my mouth, and I watch as he leans over to kiss Nate. Logan strokes Nate's cock, and I groan as he pleasures him.

"Open your mouth, Lexi," Nate murmurs.

I take my mouth off Logan and open it wide, holding my tongue out while Logan jacks Nate off. After a short while, salty cum hits my tongue, but Logan moves Nate's cock, and the warm stickiness hits my cheek and forehead as well.

Nate pants for breath and kisses Logan again before he looks down at me. "One down, three to go. You already look hot as fuck, though, Sexy Lexi."

I take Ash in my mouth and suck him while I stroke Logan

and Dante. The sticky cum drips down my face, and my pussy aches from knowing that I'm going to be covered soon.

Sure enough, Ash growls, "Stop sucking me."

I move over to Dante at once to take him in my mouth while Ash begins to pump his shaft in his fist.

It's only a few moments before he says, "Look at me, Lexi."

I turn my face to Ash, and he comes on me. I close my left eye as cum drips down my face while Dante and Logan step closer, both stroking themselves quickly.

A glob of cum drips from my chin onto my breast as Logan grunts, "Fuck, Alexandra."

He gives his shaft a few more pumps before he deposits his load on my face, and I stick my tongue out to catch a few drops as he covers me. Dante follows a moment later when he sprays his cum on my outstretched tongue, as well as in my hair and over my face, which causes me to close my right eye as well. More cum drips off my face onto my breasts, and my pussy is drenched as it aches from being used by my men.

"So beautiful," Dante murmurs.

I hear the sound of a camera taking a picture, and I'm sure it's Logan. I know he likes to get pictures of me, and it's hot knowing that he'll have one of me like this.

"Can you open your eyes, Angel?" Dante asks.

I give it a go, and I'm relieved when they don't sting, but I can see a glob of cum on the eyelashes of my left eye.

"Say cheese, Alexandra." Logan grins at me.

I look into the camera lens and say dutifully, "Cheese."

"Spread your legs for me," he murmurs.

I do as told, and a shot of arousal goes straight to my crotch when Logan puts the camera down low to take a close up of my exposed pussy.

"Mmm. Such a juicy cunt," Ash says.

"I think it needs filling," Logan announces as he stands up.

He strides away, and I stay where I am, exposed for the others to look at.

"I'd give you a kiss, but you're covered in cum," Ash laughs, and heat rushes to my cheeks.

"Won't stop me." Nate winks at him.

He kneels in front of me and presses his lips to mine. My pussy aches at the knowledge that he has to be tasting their cum. When he breaks our kiss, he licks my lips, and I groan at how erotic that is.

"Tasty. I'm going to go get cleaned up. Thanks, Sexy. I love you."

Ash thanks me before he leaves as well, and I look up at Dante, who smiles at me. "Are you okay, Angel?"

"Yes, Honey. That was fucking amazing."

"I'm glad."

He looks over as Logan appears, holding a pair of Ben Wa balls that fill his palm, and I gasp at the sight of them.

"These should do the trick. Don't you think, Dante?" Logan raises an eyebrow at him.

"They look very filling. I'll leave you to finish playing with her." He steps forward and drops a kiss on my head at the back, away from any cum. "I love you, Angel."

When Dante is gone, Logan spins the balls in one hand as he looks down at me. My breathing is shallow, and I can't wait for him to push them into my aching pussy.

"Lie on your back and spread your legs, Alexandra."

The marble tiles are cold against my back when I do as instructed. Logan kneels between my legs and pushes the first ball into me. I moan in satisfaction as it stretches me wide. These are bigger balls than I've ever used before, and I love it.

Logan pushes the second one in, then rubs my clit with his fingers. "Is that good?"

"Yes," I moan.

Logan lowers his mouth to my pussy and swipes his tongue back and forth across my clit. It doesn't take long at all before my body shakes, and I come from the stimulation of Logan's skilled tongue and the balls inside me.

He holds his hand out to me. “Come with me, Alexandra. Let’s go have a cuddle in bed together before we make dinner.”

“Um, don’t we need to shower?” I ask as I allow him to pull me up.

“No. You’re going to spend the rest of the night like that. I’ll remove the balls before bed, but you can have a shower after I’ve come inside you tomorrow morning.”

My entire body turns to flames at the thought of eating dinner and sleeping the whole night while covered in the guys’ cum. I almost orgasm again at the thought as one of the balls moves inside me. I’m so satisfied by this experience that even my concerns about Cassie can’t bring me down.

Chapter 2

A Burst Bubble

I wake wrapped in Logan's arms, and I snuggle back against him, his cock stiff against my ass.

"Mmm. Good morning," he says in a husky voice.

"Hi." I can't help but smile as he squeezes me tightly and kisses my head.

"How are you feeling this morning?"

"Looking forward to having a shower," I say with a laugh.

Logan chuckles and squeezes me again. "Well, you know what has to happen before you can have one of those." His hand trails a lazy path up to my breast, and he thumbs my nipple as he says in a serious voice, "I actually meant about Cassie, though."

I sigh and frown at the bedside table in front of me. "I'm not ready for her to go public, but I hate just waiting for it to happen."

"I know how you feel. I just hope that Isaac is able to get some kind of advance notice."

Logan rolls away from me for a second, but then he's back again, and he wraps his arms around me again as he unlocks his phone. My heart pounds in my chest as he checks his email, followed by his messages. There's nothing from Isaac, and his phone doesn't seem to have blown up overnight, which is a relief.

There's a message from Nate, though, and I smile as Logan opens their chat. I can't help but read it since the phone is directly in front of me and their last exchange was a set of 'I love yous' that warm my heart. This morning's message is a little less sentimental and a lot sexier. Nate has sent a picture of his hard cock with an accompanying message.

I had a dream about you, Lexi, and me on a yacht. You were fucking my ass while I fucked hers.

I can't stop the small gasp that escapes me. I don't think I've ever wanted something more. I can picture it in my head, and it makes me horny as shit.

Logan kisses my head again and murmurs, "Do you like that idea, Alexandra?"

"Yes, Sir."

He lowers his hand to the apex of my thighs and rubs my clit. "I can tell. You're already wet."

Logan types a reply to Nate's message as he continues to stroke me.

If you're still hard, you should come and join us. I can't fuck your ass yet, but we can work toward it.

It's not long at all before there's a soft knock on the door as my pussy aches from the desire to be fucked.

"Come in," Logan calls out.

"I was about to come when you replied," Nate says with a laugh as he appears, naked and with a stiff cock.

He slips into the bed in front of me and kisses me, his cock against me, and I assume Logan's hand as well.

"Morning, Sexy Lexi." His beautiful blue eyes crinkle with amusement as he smiles at me.

"Morning, Nate."

I reach between us and wrap my fingers around his cock as Logan pushes his into my pussy. Nate kisses my mouth, and Logan kisses my neck and head. The room is filled with our heavy breathing, but Logan isn't doing anything to try and make me come. In turn, I leisurely stroke Nate and enjoy the feeling of being sandwiched between the two of them like this.

Eventually, Logan says, "Do you think you're ready to try a bigger butt plug, Nate?"

"I think so. I'll never have you fuck me if I don't."

Logan's cock jerks in my pussy, and he asks in a voice laced with lust, "How badly do you want me to fuck you?"

"Well, I'm apparently dreaming about it now, so even my subconscious wants you in my ass."

Nate's cock jerks in my hand, and I love feeling these physical reactions from them to the conversation they're having. I'm so turned on by it. Especially knowing that Nate's been using butt plugs.

"I was thinking..." Logan trails off, then kisses my head. "If you keep plugging daily for another week or two, maybe Lexi could fuck you with a strap-on."

My mouth drops open, and so does Nate's. He stares into my eyes for a few seconds before his eyes become hooded at the same time as the image of me fucking Nate comes into my brain.

"Because we can get them in whatever size we need, it'll be another way for you to work up to taking my cock."

"Are you up for it, Lexi?" Nate asks, and his eyes bore into mine.

The thought of fucking Nate is wildly erotic, and I swallow heavily as I nod at him. "Yes. It sounds like fun."

He presses his lips to mine, and I stroke him faster as we kiss before he pulls my hand away from his cock.

"I'm going to come if you keep doing that," he says with a laugh. Logan slides out of bed, and I must look surprised because Nate places his hand on my face and says, "I think he's gone to get the butt plug. You look fucking hot with cum all over you."

Heat rushes to my cheeks at the reminder that I'm still covered from last night. He pulls my face to his, and our tongues intertwine as we kiss before he breaks it when Logan comes back and Nate raises an eyebrow at me.

"Do you want to do the honors, Sexy?"

I bite my lip and nod. Nate kisses me one more time, then rolls onto his stomach before he climbs onto his hands and knees. I move behind him next to Logan, who hands me a bottle of lube while he holds onto a decent-sized butt plug.

"You've worked your way up already," I murmur to Nate.

"Yeah, I have."

I look at his ass and remember his response to me eating it before. It's not something I even knew I was into until Logan did it to me. I haven't been instructed to do anything yet, so I put the lube down on the bed and spread Nate's ass cheeks. I lick along his perineum before I tongue his hole. He groans, and my pussy clenches as he does.

I squeeze his muscular ass cheeks and gasp into his hole as something hard presses into my pussy. I realize after a few seconds that Logan is fucking me with the butt plug, and I moan into Nate's ass. I reach down and press my thumb against his perineum for a few seconds before I stroke his cock.

Logan rubs my clit while he fucks me with the butt plug, and it doesn't take long before I tip into orgasm. I rest my cheek on Nate's ass while I pant for breath, and my body shakes as the orgasm rolls over me.

As I recover from the intense pleasure, Logan removes the butt plug from my pussy and pulls me upright. He moves hard up against me as he holds the glistening plug between Nate and me. His cock is hard against me as he reaches down to stroke my clit some more while his breath is hot and heavy against my ear.

"You won't even need to lube up the plug because you've already done it with your pussy. Just some lube for his asshole, and it'll slide in just fine. Plug up Nate's ass Alexandra."

"Yes, Sir," I manage to say as arousal swirls through my body, making me foggy.

I open the lube bottle and squirt some onto Nate's ass. I push a finger into him with a sexy groan from Nate as I follow the first finger with a second. I fuck him with my fingers and am surprised by how fucking excited I am to know that I'm going to fuck him with a strap-on soon. I'm so turned on by what I'm doing that I forget Logan instructed me to do something as I keep fucking Nate's ass with my fingers and stroking his cock with my other hand.

He moans, "Yes, Lexi. God, that's so good."

I love it so much, and my hips thrust slightly in time with my fingers as I imagine I'm fucking Nate's ass. I'm lost in the experience as a painful stinging sensation comes from my behind, making me jump.

"I gave you an instruction, Alexandra." Logan smacks my ass again. "Do it now."

"Yes, Sir."

I pull my fingers out of Nate's ass and raise the butt plug to his hole. I push it slowly into him, and he groans as I do. When it's all the way in, I bite my lip as I look at my handiwork. Knowing that Nate is filled with the plug and one step closer to receiving anal almost tips me into another orgasm.

"How is that, Nate?" Logan asks.

"Good," he groans in response.

"Okay. I just need to deal with Alexandra," Logan says in an ominous tone.

Nate flops onto his back and strokes his cock as he looks at us. I catch his eye for a second before Logan pushes me down. My face is against the bed, but I'm still on my knees, my ass in the air. I turn my face to the side so I can watch Nate while Logan positions himself behind me.

"I'm going to spank you, Alexandra. I'm not sure how many times. Your ass needs to glow red for failing to follow my instruction. Count."

Logan brings his hand down roughly on my right ass cheek, and I gasp, "One."

He spanks me harder than usual, and Logan usually spanks me pretty hard. By the time he reaches thirty-seven, I can barely stand it, but I'm also in major subspace. The pain has sent me into next-level ecstasy.

"We'll stop at forty," Logan murmurs as he spanks my left ass cheek.

"Thirty-eight," I gasp as a tear rolls down my face.

He gives the final two hits to my right ass cheek and gets off the bed to retrieve his phone, which he uses to take a picture of me. When he gets on the bed again, he rubs my burning ass gently with his hands.

"Safety light check?" he asks.

"Green," I assure him.

Now that my spanking is over, the pain is tolerable, and my pussy is dripping wet. The need to be filled is intense, and I want one of them inside me right now.

"Climb onto Nate, Alexandra. You can fuck him while I take your ass today."

"Yes, Sir."

When I sink onto Nate, he grins at me. "You feel so fucking good, Sexy."

I lean down to kiss him as Logan squirts lube onto my ass. After a few moments, he pushes his finger into me. I move slowly on Nate while Logan fucks my ass with his fingers. Eventually, he pushes his cock into my ass, and I enjoy the sensation of being filled by both men.

My ass stings each time Logan thrusts forward and presses against my cheeks. It's all so good that I come apart around Nate's cock without any warning. He fucks me through my orgasm and thrusts his tongue into my mouth as he places his hand on the back of my head and holds my face against his.

I've come on his cock twice more by the time Logan dumps his load in my ass. When he pulls out of me, I sit up to ride Nate, who grabs my hips and bounces me up and down on him.

Logan presses against my back and takes my breasts in his hands. "Are you enjoying this, Alexandra?"

"Yes, Sir," I moan.

"Just think about what it's going to be like when I'm in your ass while you fuck Nate."

I moan again as I think about it, and Logan lowers his hand to my clit. "You were the first to tongue his hole, and you'll be the first to fuck him."

I shudder because I know Nate has been with so many women, but I'll be the one who gets to experience this first with him. A first for both of us. I lean my head back against Logan's shoulder, and he kisses my neck while he rubs his thumb across my taut nipple.

"Are you thinking about it, Alexandra?" Logan murmurs.

"Yes, Sir."

He slows down the speed at which he strokes my clit, but I'm still in ecstasy as Nate fucks me, and the friction drives me wild.

He rubs my clit a little faster, and I moan as my orgasm approaches. "My cock will be in your tight ass, while you'll have a cock in Nate's. You'll be able to fuck him and stretch his ass for me." He kisses my neck and adds, "Imagine Nate moaning in ecstasy while you fuck him."

The picture he's painting is so erotic that it brings my orgasm even closer. I bite my lip as I look down at Nate, who looks as turned on by this conversation as I am.

"Once you've broken his asshole in sufficiently, I'll be able to fuck him too. Like right now, his thick, hard cock would fill you, but I'll be buried in his ass while it is."

Nate groans, "Fucking hell."

His cock jerks inside me, and he grips my hips tightly as he pumps a few more times before he fills me with cum. As he does, Logan strokes my clit while he pulls my nipple. The sensation of Nate coming inside me along with what Logan's doing tips me over the edge.

"Oh my god, yes. Yes,"

I moan as my orgasm crashes over me, and I clench my muscles around Nate's cock as my body shakes. I close my eyes as I pant for breath while Logan wraps his arms around my waist, and the room is filled with the sound of Nate and me as we struggle to breathe.

Nate rubs my hip gently with one thumb and gives me a satisfied smile. "I love you, Sexy."

"I love you, too."

"I love you both." Logan kisses my neck. "Alexandra needs a shower, I think."

"I really do," I say with a laugh.

My skin feels tight where the cum has dried on it. As much as the smell turns me on because it's a reminder of what we did, I'm ready to be clean again.

Nate pulls me down to him, and we kiss for a long time, with Logan joining us. By the time Logan takes me into the bathroom, I'm filled with an overwhelming feeling of love and happiness that only increases as Logan carefully cleans every inch of my body and washes my hair.

I come out of the shower smelling of rose-scented shampoo and conditioner. The entire world is aglow as he uses a big, fluffy towel to dry me off.

"How are you feeling?" Logan asks, and he takes my hand to lead me back through his bedroom and into his closet.

"Amazing," I say with a contented sigh as he heads to a drawer and pulls out a pair of briefs.

"I'm glad." He smiles at me in a mirror nearby.

I watch as he pulls on the underwear, jeans, and a t-shirt. He's so beautiful, and I enjoy the show. When he's dressed, we head to the kitchen downstairs and find Nate sitting with Ash at the table eating breakfast.

Ash looks up first, and when he sees my naked form, his eyes go dark. "Morning, baby."

"Morning, Ash."

I let go of Logan's hand and head over to Ash as I greet him. He pushes his chair back from the table as I wrap my arms around his neck and press my lips to his. Our tongues intertwine as I straddle him, and he wraps his arms around my waist. He tastes of coffee and cinnamon, which is intoxicating. When our kiss ends, I'm breathless with desire, and he squeezes me tight before he relaxes his grip on me.

I turn on his lap to face the table and pick up a slice of toast from his plate. "Mmm, this smells good."

I take a bite as Ash chuckles behind me. "By all means, go ahead."

"Don't mind if I do." I turn my head to smile at him as I take another bite.

He kisses my neck and picks up the half-eaten slice I ignored. I revel in the feeling of eating breakfast while wrapped in Ash's embrace, and Logan joins us once he's made some toast of his own. As we talk, though, there's an undercurrent of tension, and thoughts of Cassie come creeping back into my consciousness. My nerves double when Dante comes into the room with a serious look on his face.

"Morning," he greets us in a tense voice.

"Have you heard something from Isaac?" Ash asks immediately.

Dante shakes his head, and Ash blows out a loud breath of air. It's only a stay of execution, though, and I feel sick knowing that the story is going to come out anytime now.

I don't even have work to distract me today, so I make my way through the apartment after breakfast, cleaning it from top to bottom. Nate appears in the bathroom doorway for one of the spare bedrooms as I'm scrubbing the toilet viciously.

"Everything okay, Sexy?" he asks, his voice softer than usual and carrying none of his regular arrogance.

I shrug a shoulder as I bring the brush up under the rim. It was spotless already, but somehow this makes me feel better. I rub around and around the rim, then tap the brush against the side of the bowl and set it aside. As I flush the toilet, I grab a cloth and wipe at the lid with my other hand. I clean all of the outsides of the bowl as well before I sit back and notice that Nate is still there. I stand up, drop the cloth in the sink, then pull off my cleaning gloves and wash my hands before I turn to face him.

"I guess not," I say with a sigh, finally answering his question.

"I can tell."

He strides over to me and pulls me against him. I'm hot and sweaty from all the cleaning I've been doing, but Nate doesn't seem to mind. I wrap my arms around his waist and rest my head against his chest. His heartbeat thuds rhythmically, and it soothes me.

"I don't think I can do this," I whisper.

Everything comes rushing in as I make the admission to him. All of the things I've been avoiding thinking about—the fears about what will happen when our secret is revealed to the world overwhelm me, and I can't stop the tears from falling.

Nate holds me tight and says, "Let it out, Lexi. What are you worried about?"

"The whole world is going to think I'm a slut. As soon as they know, everyone is going to have an opinion. From strangers to family and friends." A cold, sinking feeling overcomes me. "Our families don't even know. I feel like we should tell them, but how do we tell them something like this? Just—"

I inhale a deep breath and let it out slowly as the weight of it all becomes too much. I squeeze Nate tightly as though he's my lifeline and the only thing keeping me from sinking in a sea of worry.

"Everyone will know. I'm the one who's going to be judged the most harshly. It's just how it is. I'm going to be the one who's called disgusting names. I'm the one who people will think has done the wrong thing because I'm the one who's married to Dante. When this goes public, our whole world will change."

Nate kisses my head softly and says in a strained voice, "I know, Lexi. I do. I can't pretend that there isn't a large part of me that's glad Cassie has no idea I'm with Logan as well. I feel bad because I know that would take some heat off you, but then I'd be subjected to that kind of judgment, too. I'm sorry I'm not strong enough to do that."

I'm stunned by his words, and I turn my face up to look into his beautiful blue eyes. "Nate." I shake my head at him. "I would never ask you to go public with your sexuality just to make this easier for me. It's not something you owe to anybody, least of all the public."

"I know." He swallows heavily and looks away from me. "I just feel bad. While this has all been a secret, I didn't need to face the fact that the way people look at me would change if they knew the truth about Logan and me. It's one thing for Dante to share you with us, but add in that we're together as well..."

"It won't change the way the people who love you look at you, though." I reach up and turn his face back to mine. "I don't look at you differently. I love you, and your loving Logan doesn't change that at all. Dante doesn't look at you differently, neither does Ash. It doesn't matter what anyone else thinks. We all love you just the same."

He gives me a rueful smile. "Yeah? Well, I could say the same to you about the world finding out about your relationships. Does knowing that none of us think differently about you make you feel any better about what the rest of the world thinks?"

I cringe at him and shake my head as I give a begrudging laugh. "Okay. That's a fair point." I reach up and kiss his soft lips before I say, "I guess the moral of the story is that we'll always have each other."

Nate raises his hand to my face and wipes at the wetness on my cheeks as he nods. "We always will."

He kisses me, and his tongue intertwines with mine. As we kiss, my concerns fade away because Nate invades my senses and leaves me incapable of worrying about anything. When our kiss ends, I heave a big sigh and rest my head against his chest again.

We stand quietly together, and I think about what he said. I would hate for Nate's sexuality to be exposed to the world as though it's some kind of hot gossip. His relationship with Logan is so beautiful and pure, but I don't think the world will understand that. They'll just see it as tea for them to salivate over being able to tell their friends. Amidst everything, I have to hope that if Nate's sexuality *is* somehow revealed, he has the opportunity to tell people himself and do it in a way that he chooses. Even if I won't get the same chance for my own polyamorous relationships.

I'm running through possible headlines in my head when Nate says, "We can't stop whatever's going to happen, so what can I do to help you relax? Want to watch a movie with me?"

"Sure." I wrinkle my nose at him. "I need to shower, though. I'm kind of stinky."

"I wasn't going to say anything," he says with a laugh.

We head to his bedroom, and I get into the shower. The warm water is soothing, and it eases my aching muscles. After I wash myself, I dry off using Nate's towel and head into his bedroom. He's already sitting on the bed, resting back against the bedhead and flicking through Netflix for something to watch.

I smile as I climb onto the bed next to him. Nate's wearing a pair of sweatpants and a t-shirt, but I'm naked as usual. I've gotten used to being naked in the apartment, but I know it always distracts Nate. I wore clothes when I was cleaning earlier, but Nate eyes my now naked body greedily as I approach him.

"Feeling better now you're clean?" He smiles at me.

"You know I'm dirty as fuck," I tease him, and he laughs.

"Of course you are."

He pulls me into his embrace and trails his hand over my body as he kisses me. His fingers reach my pussy, and he smiles as he slides them through my wet slit, and I moan softly.

"Are we watching this movie or not?" he asks in a husky voice.

"Maybe. Isn't your goal to distract me?" I ask.

"It is." He rubs my clit, and my pleasure builds. "Am I being distracting?"

I spread my legs a little, and he smiles as he pushes two fingers into me, making me groan. "Yes, you're very distracting."

"Good. I guess I'll keep distracting you in that case."

He lowers his mouth to my breast and swirls his tongue around my stiff nipple. I thrust my fingers into his hair and bite my lip as I throw my head back and pant for breath. The sensations of what he's doing flood over me, and I moan in satisfaction.

Nate moves between my legs and spreads them wide before grinning at me. "I think I know another good distraction technique."

He buries his face in my pussy, and I gasp as he uses his fingers to fuck me while he sucks and licks my clit. Waves of pleasure rock my body, and I grind my pussy against his face when I come. My body shakes, but Nate keeps tonguing my sensitive clit. He looks up at me as he raises a hand to my breast. He rubs his thumb across my nipple, sending sparks of electricity shooting throughout my body while he continues his assault on my pussy.

I grasp the bedsheets with my hands to try and get purchase of something as my back arches, and I come on Nate's face again. He strips and tosses his clothes aside before he moves up and over me to sheath himself inside me in one smooth movement.

Nate claims my lips with his, and our tongues dance together as he thrusts into me. I wrap my legs around his waist and fuck him with reckless abandon. I lose myself to the sensations of his cock moving in and out of me along with his lips on mine. He breaks our kiss and holds himself above me to look into my eyes as we fuck.

"I will never get tired of fucking you, Alexandra Sullivan," he growls as he buries himself inside me.

His cock jerks, and he thrusts in and out of me a few more times before he comes inside me. I tighten my hold around him with my legs to pull him in deeper as I come apart around his cock. Nate collapses on me, then rolls onto his side to face me while still buried inside me.

"I love you. You know that, right?" he asks through panting breaths.

"I'm not sure if you've ever told me that before. I'm completely shocked," I manage to laugh back at him.

He kisses me, and we lie in blissful peace with the world glowing around us. I think about what Logan suggested this morning, and I can't help but smile at the thought.

"What's that smile for?" Nate raises an eyebrow at me.

"I can't believe Logan suggested that I should fuck your ass."

Nate grins at me. "I wasn't sure if you would be up for it."

"As if. I almost came just at the thought of it," I scoff.

"What's so hot about it for you?" he asks, sounding genuinely curious.

I think about it and run my hand down his muscled torso

toward the place where we're still connected. Of course, I'm going to be honest with him, but I try to word it carefully nonetheless.

"You've slept with a lot of women." He stiffens a little, and I smile at him. "I'm totally fine with that, but I can't pretend that getting to explore something new with you isn't a part of the excitement. I know it's fetishizing you guys, but seeing you and Logan fucking or doing anything sexual together is hot as hell. I can't even tell you what's so hot about watching two guys for me, but ungh." I bite my lip as I make the sound, and Nate laughs.

"I'm pretty sure I can safely speak for Logan when I say that we don't mind you watching us."

"How did you feel when you watched Logan and Dante?" I ask out of curiosity because we've never actually talked about it.

Nate groans, "Oh my god, it was so fucking hot. I've masturbated while thinking about it." His cheeks flush pink. "You can't tell either of them that."

"Hey, you're not the only one." I wink at him, and he laughs. I can't help but think about Ash, though, and I ask, "Do you think Ash would ever be up for anything like that?"

Nate's cock jerks inside me, and he gets a strange look on his face. "I don't know. I've never asked him about that sort of thing."

Something about his reply piques my curiosity, and I look at his face. The strange look is gone, and his face is completely neutral.

"Maybe I should ask him," I suggest, watching for his reaction.

Nate frowns at me. "Please don't. Ash shouldn't be pressured into doing anything he doesn't want to do. He would've said something by now if he were interested, and he hasn't. I don't want him to feel like we're trying to make him into something he's not."

Guilt washes over me because I know I get pleasure from seeing my men do things with one another. Nate's words remind me that someone's sexuality is their own, and I shouldn't try to force anything for my enjoyment.

I cringe at Nate. "Okay. Fair enough. I won't say anything." I bite my lip and say carefully, "I hope you don't think that's what I was trying to do."

"Of course not." He shakes his head and smiles at me. "I think you were just thinking with your pussy."

I laugh and kiss him before we go get cleaned up. When we get back to the bed, I settle against him, and we finally watch a movie together. It's almost finished when the bedroom door opens, and Logan appears with a serious look on his face.

"Isaac called Dante. A story is being published tonight."

Chapter 3

Revelations III

I'm a complete wreck as we follow Logan downstairs. My whole body is tense, and he looks at me with concern written all over his face. "Do you want to get some clothes on, Lexi?" I chew my lip and nod. "Okay," he agrees with a kind smile.

Logan follows me into Dante's bedroom, where my clothes are kept. Something deep inside me wants privacy so I can fall apart completely, but I suspect that's why Logan stayed with me. He doesn't say anything, though, just leans against the doorframe and watches as I pull on a pair of yoga pants and a top.

He takes my hand in his and gently kisses the top of my head before he leads me to the living room, where the guys are sitting on the sofa. They all have serious looks on their faces, and the mood is somber.

I head straight to Dante, who takes me in his arms when I sit on his lap, and I can't stop the tears from falling as he comforts me. It's a reality now. People are going to know everything.

I wipe my face and look into Dante's beautiful brown eyes. "Sorry. I just—" I take a shaky breath and let it out in a rush. "It doesn't matter. It's going to happen, I guess. So, what exactly did Isaac say?"

"It's coming out tonight on The Gilded Cage's website and it's okay if you're upset, Angel." He kisses me and squeezes me tight.

I think about what I told Nate earlier and turn on Dante's lap to face everyone as I ask, "Is there anyone we want to tell personally?"

My suggestion is met with stunned silence before Ash says, "Fuck. We probably should. How do we explain it?"

Dante's whole body is tense as he says, "Isaac said not to make any statements, so nothing in text. I think we need to tell our families, though." He looks thoughtful for a moment, then continues, "Just say that we're polyamorous and are all in a relationship with Lexi. If they push for more information, tell them what you feel comfortable telling them or not. Explain that a story has leaked, and we don't know what it will be, but it's likely to include a lot of lies. Reassure them that I'm fine with it."

"Oh god," Nate groans. "It's times like this that I'm glad I'm an only child, but my dad is *not* going to understand. No time like the present if we want to tell them before the story goes live." He coughs, and his jaw is tight as he looks at the floor while he says, "If, um, nobody minds, I'd like to keep my relationship with Logan a secret for now."

I glance over at Logan, and the hurt is obvious in his expression, but he's the one who replies, and it's in a level tone. "Of course, Nate. We don't need to tell anybody about us." He stands from the sofa and lifts his phone up. "I guess I'd better go make some calls. My mother will kill me if she finds out about this from social media."

I frown as I watch him stride out of the room, then stand as well. "I'd better go call my parents. I'll be back when I'm done."

I catch up with Logan in the hallway and fall into step with him. His body is tense, but he gives me a tight smile.

"Are you okay?" I ask quietly as we continue toward the staircase to go upstairs.

"I'm fine." He looks at me and then shrugs. "If Nate doesn't want to tell anyone about us, I'm not going to make him."

I don't want to interfere because it's between them, but I can't help but think of what Nate told me earlier.

"I think he's scared of being judged. God knows I am," I say with a sigh.

We've reached the staircase, and I notice Ash and Nate walking toward us. Logan seems to as well because he looks their way, then back at me.

He kisses me quickly. "We'll talk later. I love you, and good luck."

"You, too." I cringe at him because his family is really religious. "I think you'll need it."

"I've been the black sheep of the family since I came out as bisexual. I'm used to it." He grins at me and heads up the staircase as I turn to head to Dante's room.

I sit on the armchair by the window and stare out at Los Angeles as my heart races in my chest. I wish my mom were still alive. I like to think that she would've understood. I love my stepmom, but she doesn't get me like my mom did.

The knot of fear in my stomach grows as I pull up my dad's number to call him. My heart pounds in my chest, and a part of me hopes that he won't answer, even though I know I can't exactly tell him this in a voicemail.

"Pumpkin, it's good to hear from you. What's up?" His voice is relaxed and comforting, like wrapping a warm blanket around me.

"I, um, have something I need to tell you." I consider whether to just tell him but decide to tell them both simultaneously to get it over and done with. "Is Sophie there with you?"

"I'll just get her." I freak out the entire time I listen to him walk through the house and call out for my stepmom. He puts the call on speaker when he finds her and says, "Go ahead, Pumpkin."

I heave a deep sigh before I say, "So, a news story is coming out tonight about us. Most of it is bull crap, but there is some truth to it, and I wanted to tell you before you read about it anywhere else."

I think I'm going to puke. I don't know if I can even voice the words to my parents, but I know that I have no other options.

"I see. Are you going to tell us what it is?" Dad asks when I can't bring myself to say the words.

I want to chicken out. I want to hang up on them. I want to pretend that none of this is happening.

Instead, I steel my nerves and say, "I'm in a relationship with Nate, Logan, and Ash, as well as Dante." Silence greets my confession, and I wish I could see their faces so I could tell what they're thinking. It goes so long that it's uncomfortable, and I ask, "Are you there?"

"Yes, we're here," Sophie says. "I'm sorry, I'm not sure I understand what you mean, though."

"I'm polyamorous, and I'm in love with all of them. I'm in a relationship with them all. Dante's fine with it," I add quickly.

"You're joking," Dad says in a dead voice.

"I'm not." I get cold all over at the sound of his voice, no longer warm and reassuring, and my words are greeted by another bout of silence. "Please say something."

I toy with the hem of my shirt as I wait for some kind of reply, and my dad's voice is cold when it comes through the line. "I'm not sure what to say, Alexandra. What is a man supposed to say when his daughter calls to tell him that she's sleeping with four men? I should've known your marriage was a sham when you did a quickie Vegas wedding without any of your family present."

"*Christopher*," Sophie chides him.

Tears begin to fall as they have a whispered conversation that I can half-hear, and my heart splinters into pieces when I catch the word 'whore' from my dad. I want to die because the shame of it is so painful. Knowing that my own father thinks that absolutely kills me.

"Lexi, are you there?" Sophie asks.

"Yes," I croak out.

She sighs and says, "Listen, sweetie. Your father just needs some time to wrap his head around this."

"What 'this,' Sophie? The fact that his daughter is a *whore*?" I spit the word out with as much venom as I can manage.

"I'm sorry you overheard that. Look, he's overreacting to this news. You said Dante's fine with it, so I'm sure your father will come around."

I wish I were as certain as she seems to be. It feels as though the ground has dropped out from underneath me, and these are just the first people I've told. I'm sure more reactions like this will come when other people find out.

"Yeah, maybe," I say as I slash at the tears falling from my eyes.

There's a long silence again, but I don't fill it this time, and Sophie eventually says, "Well, thank you for calling to tell us. I'm glad we didn't find this out from another source."

"You're welcome." It's all I can manage to say, and I stare blindly out the window, hating everything about this.

"I'll talk to you later. Thanks again for calling us."

I murmur a goodbye before she ends the call, then I drop my phone into my lap as I bury my face in my hands and cry. I love the guys so much, and I shouldn't give a fuck what my dad thinks, but I do. It hurts so much that I can barely breathe.

A part of me is glad that my mom isn't alive. The thought of her saying anything like that to me is unbearable. At the same time, I feel terrible for even thinking that because I wish she were here right now more than anything.

I pull myself together and scroll through the contacts on my phone as I consider if there's anyone else I should tell. Heather Fletcher's name catches my eye, but I can't bear another conversation like the one I just had. I really like her, and if she's going to cut me off because of this, I want to delay the moment when that happens.

Jasmine's name is the next name that comes up as a person I think I should tell. I can't handle having multiple conversations, so I open a group message with her, Vera, and Sherry.

Hey guys. A story is coming out about me tonight. I don't want to talk about it. Most of it will probably be bullshit, but some of it is true.

I sigh as I hit send and then quickly add another message.

Please don't judge me too harshly when you read it.

It's only a few seconds before the message shows as read, and Sherry's the first to reply.

Oh my gosh. I hope everything's okay.

The next reply comes from Jasmine.

Of course, we would never judge you. I'm here if you need to talk.

I quickly reply to them, grateful to have such wonderful employees.

Thanks. I appreciate it. I don't want to talk about it, but I wanted to let you know because…it'll probably be big gossip.

I just can't bring myself to tell them what it is. I know I'm underselling it, but it's all too much. I smile as a message from Vera shows up.

What Jasmine said. I'm here, too, but I understand you don't want to talk about it. I hope you're okay.

I send my thanks through, then lock my phone and stare out the window again. I don't know how long I sit there, with a pit of dread in my stomach, before Dante appears next to me. He crouches at the side of the chair, so he's at eye level with me.

"How did it go with your folks, Angel?"

I snort derisively. "My dad called me a whore. What about you?"

"He did *what*?!" he growls.

"I mean, he said it to Sophie, but I still heard it." I give him a small smile. "Who would've known that she would've been the one who was nice about it. I messaged Jazz, Vera, and Sherry to tell them. They were very nice, though I didn't go into detail. I just told them there was a story coming out and that I didn't want to talk about it."

"Fair enough." Dante grinds out the words, and he still looks pissed.

"Don't say anything to my dad. Sophie thinks he'll get over it.

Maybe I heard wrong. He might not have said 'whore,' maybe he said 'more' or something," I suggest. Dante gives me an incredulous look, and I shrug. "Okay, he didn't, but I just don't want any more drama right now. Please."

Dante's lips are a thin line, but he nods. "Fine. I won't say anything, but you should know that I want to. He has no fucking right to say something like that about you."

Once again, the pain of my father's words slashes through me, but I work to keep my face neutral despite my aching heart.

"Yeah, well, he won't be the only one. You can't be my knight in shining armor against all of them, and we have bigger things to focus on than what Dad said. What about your family?"

"It wasn't great," he admits. "Mom tried to convince me you were cheating on me. I think I got through to her by the end of the call."

I'm grateful he stood up for me, but it hurts to hear that my mother-in-law immediately thought the worst of me. "Add her to the growing list of people who think I'm a slut, I guess."

"She doesn't think that about you. Once I explained that I'm fine with it and we're all happy, she was fine." He pulls me up to stand and hugs me tightly. "Are you okay, though?"

I feel better being in his arms, but the weight of everything that's happening still feels like it will crush me. I can barely breathe through the overwhelming fear of what's to come.

I shake my head, then whisper, "Did we make a huge mistake?"

None of this felt bad or wrong until today. Even when we told Isaac yesterday, he took it in his stride. I was happy in our little bubble and with my relationships, but now I'm second-guessing everything.

Dante lets go of me, takes my hand, and leads me over to the bed. We sit down side-by-side, and he has a serious look on his face as he looks at me.

"Do *you* think we made a huge mistake, Angel?"

I swallow heavily and admit, "I didn't think so. Not until…" I trail off, not wanting to repeat the words again. "I mean, it's going to cause a shitload of problems now. I don't know..."

Dante searches my face for a few seconds, then asks in a solemn voice, "Do you want to end things with the guys?"

An icy coldness grips my heart at the thought. We all bought this place together. We've been so happy here. More than that, even the thought of being without them is painful. Guilt floods through me for even questioning it. I feel like a complete traitor to the men that I love.

"No," I say firmly, with a shake of my head. "I couldn't. I love them all so much. God, I hate this. I hate that I even thought for a second that being with them wasn't right. I hate that my father called me a whore. I hate that everyone is going to think that because they don't understand. I love you all, and we all love each other. You guys are best friends, and we're all fucking happy. How is that so fucking hard to understand?"

I'm breathing heavily, fire in my veins at the unfairness of the people we love and trust not being fully supportive of us, and Dante smiles at me before he kisses my lips softly.

"There you go. I knew you'd get there, Angel."

I know this is hard, and we're only at the beginning, but I wouldn't change any of this for the world, no matter what happens. People won't understand. We'll be talked about and gossiped about, and it's going to be awful, but we'll all be here for you every step of the way. Okay?"

It's a reminder that I'm not the only one carrying this weight. We're all in this together, and the men I love will be right there with me.

I take a deep breath and then nod. "Okay. I love you, Honey."

I kiss him and wrap my arms around his neck as our tongues intertwine. Dante places one hand on the back of my head and the other on my lower back. He holds me against him as I lose myself to this moment with him.

We're both breathless when we break apart, and he smiles at me. "I love you, too."

"Can you not tell the guys what we talked about?" I ask as I chew my bottom lip. "I feel guilty as fuck, and I'd hate for them to think I don't love them and want to be with them."

"Of course. You're just stressed. I know you didn't mean it, and there's no sense in worrying them, as you say." He kisses me again. "Speaking of the guys, let's go back. I told them I'd come to check on you because you hadn't come back."

We find them in the living room, and my heart swells even as my guilt intensifies when I see them. Nate and Logan are sitting next to one another and looking at Logan's phone. Logan has his arm around Nate's shoulders, and I don't know if they've talked, but I take that as a positive sign. Ash is sitting on the other side of the L-shaped sofa and looking at his phone. Maybe it's my guilt that makes me do it, but I stride over to sit next to him.

I link my arms around his as I look at his phone to see The Gilded Cage's homepage displayed there. "Anything?"

"Not yet." He shakes his head, then looks over at me and frowns. "Are you okay?"

"As good as I can be, I guess. My parents didn't take it that well. What about yours?"

"They were a bit shocked but were okay. Ella had about a million questions, and Viv insisted that she could sense some weird energy between us at Thanksgiving."

I can't help but laugh at this. "Well, I mean…"

"What? Just because we fucked in my childhood bedroom during the main course?" He raises an eyebrow at me.

"Something like that." I lean forward and kiss him as I think about that night. "You made me sit at the Thanksgiving table filled with your cum."

He chuckles and reaches between my legs to cup my pussy with his hand as he murmurs, "What can I say? I like it when this cunt is full of cum, preferably mine."

His words remind me of my conversation with Nate, and I'm tempted to ask if he thinks about the other guys' cum often, but I don't want to lead him down that path, so I don't. His hand is warm on my pussy, and he looks into my eyes as he moves his thumb to rub my clit, and I gasp.

He watches me as the pleasure hits me, and I spread my legs a little wider before he stops and says, "Now probably isn't the time."

"Now is *absolutely* the time," I growl at him.

His thumb is still sitting there on my clit, and I desperately want him to go back to what he was doing.

"I'm not sure it is," he teases me as he swipes his thumb back and forth once. "Aren't we waiting for our lives to blow up or something?"

He rubs his thumb around my clit in a circle, and I gasp. "Fuck our lives blowing up or something. Don't stop."

Ash trails hot kisses up my neck as he slides his hand into my yoga pants to find my drenched pussy. "Mmm, so wet as usual, baby."

I look over to where the other guys are sitting and lock eyes with Nate. I can't help but think about our conversation earlier, and I imagine that he's part of this with us, his lips clamped around Ash's thick cock.

The thought tips me into orgasm, and I moan, "Nate."

I freeze as Ash's hand stills, and I feel him look between Nate and me before he chuckles. "Um, I guess you get the credit for that one, bro?"

"Not sure what I did, but I'll take it." Nate shrugs.

Heat rushes to my cheeks, and I'm horrified that I used Nate's name when I came. Ash begins to move his fingers again as he turns his attention back to me.

"Care to share with us what he did?" Ash looks genuinely curious, along with being highly amused.

My cheeks get hotter, but I can't withhold a low moan as he rubs my sensitive clit.

When I don't reply, Logan says, "Answer Ash's question, Alexandra."

I don't want to risk betraying Nate's confidence, so I give an answer that's true, but is also safe. "I was thinking about Nate giving a blow job."

"I see. Does that turn you on, baby?" Ash asks.

I'm mortified at being caught out fantasizing about Nate and Ash, but I nod as Ash brings me closer to a second orgasm. He pushes his fingers inside me and rubs my clit with his thumb again.

"You like the idea of Nate wrapping his lips around Logan's cock and blowing him, huh?"

My pussy clenches around his fingers, and I just nod at him. I can't exactly correct him, and I can't manage any words other than another moan anyway.

"Good to know. Just talking about it makes you hot. God, I love playing with you."

Ash presses his lips to mine, and I part my lips to allow his tongue access to my mouth. Our tongues intertwine, and I'm in bliss as another orgasm comes rushing in.

I'm just about to come again when Logan says in a dull tone, "Fuck."

Ash freezes, and my orgasm disappears at once. He pulls his hand out of my pants and breaks our kiss as he whips his head around to look at Logan.

"It's been posted?" Ash asks, the fear obvious in his tone.

Logan nods. "Yes." He scrolls up the screen and winces. "Fuck. This is so bad."

Ash picks up his phone and refreshes the website. I watch in horror as he pulls up the article. At the top of the page is a picture of me with the guys at the Grammys a few years ago. We're all smiling brightly, happy and excited because it was the first time the band was invited to perform.

ONE BAND, ONE WOMAN: INSIDE THE STRANGE LIFE OF WICKED STALLION

Adored worldwide, Wicked Stallion shot to fame four years ago. In this exclusive interview, we sat down with Cassandra Foster to talk about life with the band and the strange life they lead with all four men in a relationship with one woman.

There's a horrified silence in the room as we read the article, punctuated by occasional gasps or scoffs of outrage from one of us.

It's worse than I imagined. Cassie has detailed every aspect of our lives. She definitely made it sound as though I somehow planned this all along and has painted herself as an unsuspecting victim caught up in my web.

The photos she took of us are the real kicker. I know she would never have been taken seriously by anyone if it weren't for those. They cement every statement she's made as fact, even the false ones.

The article is so long and in-depth that notifications start coming through on our phones before Ash and I have even finished reading it. By the time I'm done and look down at my phone, it's full of notifications from all of my social media accounts.

"I'm going to call Isaac," Dante announces as he stands from the sofa.

I look over at Nate and Logan, where they're sitting together, and they look as shell-shocked as I feel.

"This is so bad." I state the obvious because it's the only thing I can think of to say.

"It really is." Logan looks up at me with a frown on his beautiful face.

"I fucking hate her," Ash growls. "How goddamn *dare* she tell the world that I cheated on her. I would never. Hell, I even asked Lexi if I could date Štěpánka."

His body is coiled so tightly that I know he's ready to explode. I don't blame him because he definitely came off the worst out of the guys in the article. Aside from me, he's the main villain in the piece.

I lean into him and kiss along his angular jaw to find his lips. His body softens a little, and he pulls me into him as I relax into his embrace. I love him so much, and I hate what Cassie's done to him.

"You're a good man, Ashton Woodford. This all started because Cassie didn't know you were after dating you for months. If she'd known that, she would never have had a reason to feel threatened by me."

He stares at me for a few seconds before he finally smiles. "Thanks, Lexi. Look, despite all of this"—he gestures to his phone—"if I could go back in time, I wouldn't change a thing except to dump Cassie the night you told us about Logan."

"Even better, you could never have dated her, and we all could've been fucking for the last decade," Nate says with a wry grin. "I mean, if you're going to go back in time, you might as well fix *all* the mistakes."

Ash chuckles and nods. "Good point."

They continue chatting in a lighthearted way about time travel while Logan types something out on his phone. I look down at my phone and cringe at the notifications on it.

There are so many variations of the question 'Is this true?' that it's astounding. I cringe at some of the names that go back as far as people we attended high school with who have messaged me on social media.

A message comes through from the group chat I started earlier, and I open it to see the new ones. Vera was the first to say something.

I don't know how much of this is true, but good on you. I'll shut any gossip down at the store if I hear it.

The next is from Jasmine.

Lexi said it's not all true, though. This can't possibly be true. It's crazy. Those pictures, though. It looks pretty bad...

I cringe as I read the message, hating the negative connotations, but Vera already called them out.

You're right that it might not be true, but it's pretty rude to say it's crazy.

Ummmm, she's MARRIED to Dante LOL! There's no way this is true. And she cheated with Ash? That's disgusting.

Lexi wouldn't do that. Why even be married if you don't want to be with that person? Marriage MEANS something. It means you love one person and you're going to be with them for the rest of your life. Not that you sleep with an entire band. No way is this true.

Her message is like a punch to the stomach. Something about it reads as unsupportive while seeming supportive at face value. It reeks of her not going to be understanding when I tell her that the main part of the article *is* true.

Erm, tell that to all the divorced people out there. Sounds like toxic monogamy culture to me, but okay.

Sherry joins the conversation with a bunch of crying with laughter emojis in response to Vera's comment, and Jasmine has written another reply, but Ash distracts me before I can read it.

"What's so funny?" he asks.

"Vera told Jasmine that her thinking that getting married means you'll definitely only be with one person for the rest of your life was 'toxic monogamy culture.'" I smirk as I say it.

"Where the lie, though?" Nate laughs.

I look back down to finish reading Jasmine's reply.

It's not "toxic" to think sleeping with multiple men when you're married to someone isn't okay. But whatever.

Three dots show that someone is typing, and as I watch, a message from Sherry pops up.

I'll let you two fight it out between yourselves. Lexi, I'm here if you ever need to talk.

I quickly type out a reply, still stinging from Jasmine's comments.

Thanks, Sherry. As I said earlier, I don't really want to discuss it, but I appreciate the support. I'll see you guys at work.

I close the chat and look up as Dante walks back into the room. He gives us a tight smile and comes to sit next to me on the sofa.

"Isaac's already getting a tonne of requests for statements. He's working with PR from the label to figure out what to do. For now, we have to just say nothing or 'no comment.' Also, expect people at the stores tomorrow, Lexi."

My blood turns cold as I realize that the paparazzi will follow me everywhere now, and I can't help but remember Heather saying she wouldn't wish the media's treatment of her on anyone. I guess I'm about to find out exactly what that's like.

Chapter 4

A Goddess and Her Boy

I wake on Monday morning, wrapped in Ash's arms. His cock is stiff against my ass, and I smile in peaceful bliss for a moment before it falls from my face the moment that everything comes crashing back to me.

Nausea threatens to overwhelm me. I spent the rest of the weekend avoiding my phone and trying to forget the world. This morning, I don't have an option. I have to go to work and face the world. I'm fucking dreading it, so I snuggle back against Ash to remind myself that this is all worth it, and I'm happier than I've ever been.

"Mmm. Good morning, baby." He kisses my neck, and I smile.

"Morning."

Ash slides his hand up to cup my breast as he asks, "How are you feeling?"

"Stressed. Worried. Anxious. Like I might vomit at the thought of going outside. So…totally amazing."

He chuckles as he kisses my neck again. "I'm sure." He gently strokes my nipple with his thumb as he says, "You can call me or message me if you're freaking out."

"Thanks, I appreciate that." I roll over so that I'm facing him and can look into his beautiful blue eyes. "You know I love you, right?"

"I've never had any doubt. I don't expect the world to understand, but I'm glad we have each other now."

Ash presses his lips to mine, and I kiss him back for a while before we part. His cock is stiff against my stomach, and I'm at peace here with him, grateful as ever to have him in my life. The weight of facing the outside world is threatening to crush me.

I'm not sure if some of my concern shows on my face, but Ash asks, "What can I do to help, baby?" He rolls over to pick his watch up from the bedside table and looks at it. "We have a solid hour and a half before you even have to wake up for work." He rolls back, then lowers his hand to my breast again and rubs his tweaks my nipple. "I'll do anything you want."

A dart of arousal shoots to my pussy as I'm distracted by what he's offering me.

"Anything?" I raise an eyebrow at him.

"Anything," he confirms.

The image of Nate with his lips wrapped around Ash's cock comes to mind, and I'm tempted to ask him if that's part of the 'anything,' but I don't.

"Soooo..." I drag out the word as I give him a mischievous grin. "I want full control over you this morning."

My heart pounds in my chest because I've never had this before, and it's thrilling to get the opportunity.

"Okay."

"If we're doing this. I need you to choose a safeword. It should be something you wouldn't say regularly during sex."

Ash smirks at me. "F Major."

I nod as my pussy throbs at his words. Somehow, him having a safeword makes this more real and official. Like I'm an actual Domme or something. It's weird because I've always been submissive with Dante and then Logan, but I get a thrill out of having control with Ash.

I don't even know what to do, so I just say, "Eat my pussy, Ashton." He flinches, and I frown at him. "What's wrong?"

"Cassie always called me by my full name."

"Whoops." I cringe and say, "My bad."

I look at him, sexy as fuck with his blonde hair and blue eyes, full of energy and excitement. I've come across many names used in D/s relationships, and I think a couple could work.

I decide on one to try out. "Eat my pussy, boy."

I'm drenched already from giving the instruction. Ash's eyes widen slightly, and his cock jerks against my stomach as he swallows heavily.

I roll onto my back and spread my legs wide. "I want my sweet boy to lick me until I come on his face. Set a timer on your watch for one minute. If you don't make me come before it goes off, you'll be punished."

Holy fuck.

Even giving him the instruction sends pleasure zinging through my body. I never knew how wildly arousing having this level of control could be.

"Yes, Lexi."

He moves his face over my pussy, and I say on a whim, "Call me Goddess."

An amused grin comes to his face, and he says, "Yes, Goddess."

"Set a timer on your watch. Don't disappoint me, sweet boy."

He has no fucking chance. As turned on as I am and as good as he is at eating me out, Logan has basically trained me to be able to ignore my orgasms for hours when I need to.

Sure enough, I ride the waves of pleasure until his watch rings out with several beeps to alert us that the time is up.

Ash looks up at me with a grin before he composes his features into a contrite look. "I'm sorry, Goddess. I failed to make you come in time."

I don't even know what to do now, and I realize that I probably should've spent that minute thinking up a suitable punishment.

"Bend over the bed," I growl, but then think I sound stupid, so I add in an icy voice, "I'm going to spank my naughty boy like the dog you are."

I surprise myself with the degradation, and I check Ash's face as he takes it in. He looks surprised but not offended, and when he stands, his cock is rock hard.

"Yes, Goddess," he says, and there's no smile this time, just clear arousal in his expression.

He bends over the bed, and I stand up to walk around behind him. His muscled body is impressive, and I get a thrill of exhilaration at the fact that he's mine to do with as I please. I run my hand over his ass cheeks and bite my lip because he's so fucking hot.

I think I should say something, so I murmur, "Such a nice ass. It's a shame we don't have a butt plug in this room so I could fill it." Ash gives a low, sexy moan that surprises me, and I squeeze his cheek before giving it a light slap. "Do you like that idea, sweet boy?"

"I'm not sure, Goddess."

I smack his ass harder. "Don't fucking lie to me." I hit the other cheek as well. "You moaned like you very much want this ass plugged."

I pull my hand back and bring it down as hard as I can, leaving a handprint on his cheek that satisfies me in a way that I had no idea it could. Pussy juice drips down my thigh, and I have to pant for breath. I forgot to make him count, and after I hit his ass a few more times, I realize that I have no idea how many times I've spanked him. My hand hurts, and his cheeks are both red now, but he doesn't seem affected by it other than that.

I spank him a few more times, though, until I notice him jump slightly with each hit. I don't think I've been wetter in my life. I had no idea how fucking hot this would be, and I'm in ecstasy despite the fact that we've done basically nothing. I lean forward and kiss his left ass cheek on the imprint of my hand from my last hit. The skin is hot against my lips, and Ash gives a soft moan when I do.

"Safety light check?" I ask because I'm not sure if that was a moan of joy or pain.

I realize I didn't explain the traffic light system to him, but he's seen it in play with Dante and Logan before, so I hope he knows what I mean.

"Green," he says with a groan, and I smile.

I can't help but think about the moan he made when I suggested plugging his ass, so I kneel behind him and run my finger around his tight hole.

"Yes, this ass would look *very* nice with a plug in it," I murmur.

Ash gives another moan, and I put a little pressure against his hole with my finger to test the waters. I know I couldn't do anything without lube, but when Ash gives a loud groan, I lean forward and push my tongue into him.

He gasps and then moans again, pushing his ass back against my face, and I know he wants this. I reach between his legs and grab his stiff cock to pump him while I tongue his hole. I weigh up the sound of his breathing and the moans of ecstasy to judge when I should stop to ensure he doesn't come and finally pull my mouth and hand away from his body.

"Stand up, boy."

"Yes, Goddess."

He stands and faces me. Now that I can see his face, it's blatantly obvious that he's turned on, even if his rock-hard erection didn't give it away. His eyes have that glazed-over look of someone who is either in or approaching subspace, and I hope I can get him there because I know how amazing it is.

I reach out and stroke his cock slowly, reveling in the low moan he makes when I do. "What to do with my boy now, I wonder." I drop to my knees and swirl my tongue around the head of his cock. "I don't think he should come anytime soon." I wrap my lips around his cock and suck him as I move my lips all the way to the base of his cock, then take him out of my mouth again. "As much as I like my sweet boy's cock, I don't think he's earned my mouth today, let alone an orgasm." I stand and look up at Ash, where he towers over me, and frown at the power imbalance. "On your knees facing the bed, boy."

He blinks at me for a second, then nods. "Yes, Goddess."

Once he's on his knees, I groan at the sight of him. He's absolutely glorious to look at, and I sit on the bed before spreading my legs wide.

"Look at my pussy, boy." His eyes immediately snap to it, and I grin in satisfaction. "I want you to worship it. Crawl to me on your hands and knees, then use your tongue to satisfy me."

"Yes, Goddess."

His reply alone almost tips me into orgasm, and I can barely breathe as I watch him crawl to me. The second his tongue touches my clit, it crashes over me. My body shakes, and I rest on one hand as I thrust the other into Ash's hair and hold his mouth on my pussy as he licks me through my orgasm. I let him go to town on my pussy, and he makes me come twice more. Even after the second orgasm, watching him eat me is so glorious that I don't want him to stop. I'm in such ecstasy from this experience that I think I want him to just stay there all day on his hands and knees, eating me out.

His tongue swipes back and forth across my clit as I float away with the pleasure he gives me, but I pant, "Enough, sweet boy." He keeps going for about another ten seconds, and I snarl, "I told you to get your mouth off my fucking pussy."

He stops immediately and looks up at me, his eyes completely glazed over. "Sorry, Goddess."

"Safety light check?"

"Green, Goddess."

"Good. Then you need to be punished for not following instructions like a good little boy." My jaw tightens as I look at him, and I know exactly what I want to do as I look at the thick cock beneath him. "Kneel and stroke that cock of yours until you're about to come, then stop. *Do not orgasm.*"

"Yes, Goddess."

Ash sits back on his heels and immediately strokes his cock. I spread my legs wide and rub my clit as I watch him. It's amazing to see him bring himself to the edge of orgasm with the grunts and groans he makes before he immediately stops. He pants for breath as he whips his hand off his cock and stares at me.

"Good little boy," I say as I give him a wicked grin. "Do it again."

I come while I watch him do it a second time, relishing in the orgasm I give myself while I deny him his. It's erotic to watch him beat his thick cock into submission, making him edge himself four times while I come again. It's a shorter period each time, though, and I can tell he's desperate to come.

"Stand up, boy."

He sways a little on his feet, and I think I might've left him on his knees too long, but he steadies himself quickly, so I don't do a safety light check this time. I walk around him in circles, trailing my hand over his body and touching any part of him that I so desire. The thrill of the power I have over him is intoxicating. I can use his body in any way I see fit, and I love that fact. His ass is still pink from my spanking, but a part of me wishes it was burning red. He's been so good that I don't have a reason to spank him again, as much as I want to.

I reach his front and take his cock in my hand. He gives a low, sexy moan as I rub my thumb over the head and enjoy the sheen of precum that glistens there.

"Does my sweet boy want to come?"

"Yes, Goddess."

I continue to rub my thumb over the head of his cock, and he shudders as I do. "How badly do you want it?"

"More than anything, Goddess," he murmurs.

"Whose cock is this?" I ask, raising an eyebrow at him.

"Yours."

I release him and give his cock a light slap, unsure if that will be painful or not, but note when he jumps slightly in surprise or some kind of pain.

"Is that how you answer me?" I growl.

"Yours, Goddess."

I can barely breathe. I'm so far gone in the ecstasy of this that I think breathing is just too hard a concept to continue doing it. Nothing matters to me except my pleasure and the pleasure of my sweet boy.

I wrap my fingers around his cock again and rub the head with my thumb. "That's right. This is *my* cock. It is only for my pleasure, and any pleasure it gives you is purely because I deem you worthy, do you understand?"

"Yes, Goddess."

"I think you've earned the right to fuck my pussy with it." I squeeze his cock in warning. "Be careful. I know that I've brought you close to the edge, but so help me, if you come before I tell you that you can, you won't get an orgasm for a week."

I don't know if this kind of play will even continue past this morning, but I mean this with every fiber of my being, and I think Ash knows it because he nods solemnly.

"Of course, Goddess. I wouldn't dare."

"You're damn fucking right. I don't need you to tell me that," I sneer at him. "Now fill my fucking pussy with that thick cock of yours and make me come like a good boy."

I lie back on the bed and spread my legs wide as I say it. Ash strides forward and pushes his cock into me immediately. I groan in ecstasy when he fills me. I pinch and pull my nipples with one hand while I rub my clit with the other as I stare into Ash's eyes while he fucks me.

"Oh fucking hell, yes. Oh fuck yes, Ash," I scream when my orgasm hits. My body shakes, and when my orgasm passes, I notice that his jaw is clenched tight, so I say through panting breaths, "Stop for a second."

He holds himself inside me but stills in his movements. "Yes, Goddess."

I watch for signs that his orgasm has ebbed away, and when his jaw unclenches, I smile at him. "Fuck me again, boy."

He thrusts in and out of me with reckless abandon. I bring myself to orgasm again as I enjoy the sensation of being fucked by this beautiful man. Using his body for my pleasure is exquisite, and when I notice that his jaw is tight this time, I decide that he has well and truly earned the right to come in my pussy.

I let him continue, watching as he struggles to hold his orgasm at bay. I can sense the pressure of it threatening to break him, and I wait until I know it must be nearly unbearable to hold it off. Sweat pours down his face, and he looks like he's about to snap. Ash's entire body seems to glow in front of me, and I don't think I've ever loved him more than I do at this very moment.

"Come for me," I say, my words as sweet as honey because I think I want this as much as he does.

The sheer relief is blatant in his expression, and he fucks me furiously, pounding into me roughly. I grip the bedsheets with one hand as I'm moved back and forth with each thrust. I use my other hand to rub my clit, desperate to come as he does. I bring myself right to the edge and tip over when Ash's cock jerks inside me, and he empties his load in me.

"Oh my god, Lexi," he groans, his eyes screwed shut tight.

"I think you mean 'oh my Goddess,'" I say with a laugh.

He opens them and stares at me in awe. "I'm sorry, Goddess. I've never come so hard before."

I pull his head down to mine and kiss him passionately. I take the initiative and explore his mouth with my tongue as I squeeze his cock with my pussy, and he groans into our kiss.

"You did so well, sweet boy," I murmur as I look into his beautiful eyes when our kiss ends.

"Thank you, Goddess."

I kiss him again, but I feel strange now that my orgasm is ebbing away. I know he needs aftercare, and I need to end the scene, but I'm not sure how. I also have a strange kind of guilt over using his body the way I did. I know subdrop is a thing, but I'm not sure if Domdrop is. I do know that I need to take care of Ash before I take care of myself, though.

"Come with me. I need to clean my sweet boy."

He climbs off me, and I lead the way to the shower, where I

take my time cleaning every inch of his beautiful body. I worship him with gentle touches to thank him without words for the pleasure he gave me. When he's clean, I quickly wash myself before I lead him out of the shower, dry him before myself, then take his hand and lead him back to bed.

We climb into bed together, and I snuggle up against him before I look into his eyes so I can gauge his reaction when I ask, "How are you feeling?"

"Weird," he admits.

I kiss his lips softly, then say, "Me, too."

"Do I still have to call you Goddess now?"

"Shit. No. I'm meant to end the scene. Yeah, you can call me Lexi or baby again." I smile at him. "Sorry. I have no fucking clue what I'm doing or where that even came from."

He chuckles. "Trust me. You might not think you know what you're doing, but that was fucking amazing."

"I guess I've learned a bit from being subjected to Dante and Logan." I place my palm against the side of his face as that strange feeling returns to me. "Are you really okay?"

Ash turns his head to kiss the palm of my hand. "Yes, Lexi. I really am. Are *you* okay?"

"I think so. I definitely enjoyed it, but it's odd being the one in charge."

He kisses me and slides his tongue into my mouth. I relax as we kiss, and my love for him feels more intense than it ever has before.

"If you want to be the one in charge sometime in the future, I volunteer as tribute," he tells me.

"Good to know." We fall silent until my phone buzzes on the bedside table with its normal morning alarm. "I guess I'd better go get ready for work." I kiss Ash again. "Thanks for the distraction. It was very enjoyable."

He runs his hand down my body to rest on my ass as he kisses me a final time. "Anytime, Goddess."

My pussy aches at his words, and heat floods through me. "You were a very good boy."

I slide out of bed and head to Dante's bedroom to get dressed for work. I find him lying up in bed and looking at his phone. He looks tense and worried as I climb onto the bed and curl into him.

"Morning, Angel," he says, and the stress disappears from his expression as he folds me into his warm embrace.

"Morning, Honey."

"It sounded like you and Ash were having fun this morning," Dante comments.

I nod and swallow heavily, unsurprised that he heard us since Ash's room is only down the hall from his. The strange feeling still lingers around me, so I bite my lip and look down at the bed covers when I speak.

"I kind of Dommed Ash this morning, and now I feel weird about it," I admit.

Dante stiffens, but I don't look at him, though I know him well enough to hear the surprise in his voice when he asks, "Really?"

"Yes."

"Did you like that?"

I feel safe and secure with Dante, and I'm calm with him, but I still can't bring myself to look at him when I reply. "Yeah, I did. It was hot, but now it feels…weird."

He takes my chin in his hand and turns my face to his. His eyes search mine as I swallow again and meet his gaze. A part of me feels as though Domming Ash means I'm no longer a good sub. As though liking this side of BDSM is something that should be off-limits to me, and because it isn't, I'm no longer worthy of him and Logan. My heart beats faster in my chest with every moment that Dante stays silent.

"Care to tell me what you're thinking, Angel? You don't have to."

I chew my lip and try to voice my thoughts. "I kind of think that I shouldn't like doing it. I'm meant to be a sub, not a Domme."

Dante presses his lips to mine quickly. "You can switch. I have zero doubt that I could do literally anything I want with you right now, and you would be just as beautiful and submissive for me as you have been for many years." I'm wet at the thought, and I clamp my legs together against the ache between my thighs, which causes Dante to chuckle. "*Zero* doubt. Less than zero doubt, to be honest. Spread your legs for me, Angel."

I do as instructed, and Dante reaches between my legs to find my dripping pussy. I clench my jaw and resist the urge to moan as he rubs my clit, and waves of pleasure hit me.

"See?" he murmurs as he strokes me faster and brings me to the edge of orgasm. "I love to watch you withhold your reactions like this. Such a good angel who follows my rules without even being asked."

He kisses me and thrusts his tongue into my mouth as he brings me to orgasm. I want to scream and wail, but I hold back and do nothing other than kiss him while my body shakes in silent ecstasy.

Dante positions himself over me and pushes his hard cock into my wet pussy. "You can react, Angel." I immediately moan in satisfaction as he fills me, and he laughs a melodic laugh. "Just because you liked what you did with Ash doesn't mean that you no longer enjoy me using your body, Angel."

He's right, and with every thrust into me, he solidifies that knowledge in my mind. By the time he comes buried deep inside me, I've floated away in bliss, and I'm limp with exertion when he pulls out of me.

Dante washes me in the shower and holds me tight with the fluffy towel wrapped around me after he dries me. "Are you okay, Angel?"

"I am." I nod at him. "I think this is exactly what I needed. You've always known me better than I know myself."

He kisses the top of my head and squeezes me tightly before letting me go. "You're my angel. That's my job."

We head back to the bedroom, and as Dante follows me into the closet to get dressed, I say, "I didn't know how to end the scene. I felt so stupid."

"Have you forgotten how many mistakes I made when we were learning?" he laughs.

I turn to blink at him and shake my head. "You were absolutely perfect. I was the one who constantly fucked up with forgetting to call you 'Sir.'"

We came up with our code nicknames because I'd screw up during scenes, so we decided to use our regular nicknames, which would also allow us to use them in public.

"In your opinion, maybe. I made mistakes, though. I'd forget to end scenes in the beginning. I spanked you too hard a few times. You safeworded multiple times. Nobody gets everything right to begin with. We learned together and became what we are now."

"I suppose you're right," I concede.

"You can always come to me for advice if you need it and you two want to keep doing this."

"Thanks, Honey. I really appreciate that."

I'm filled with gratitude for my beautiful husband, who is always supportive of me, so I should've known that helping me with this would be no exception.

He strides over to me and kisses me passionately before giving me a beautiful smile. "I bet if you asked Ash, he'd tell you that you were absolutely perfect, too."

Chapter 5

Manic Monday

Because I had sex with Dante, I'm running late to get to work before the store opens. A million butterflies run rampant in my stomach, and I wish I had more time to get ready. I pull on a smart business suit and do as good a job as I can with my makeup.

"Fuck!" I spit as I smudge the mascara on the skin under my eye.

Dante appears in the closet doorway and frowns at me. "Everything okay?"

"No. I fucked up my mascara, and now I'm going to look like shit, and everyone is probably going to try and take my picture today, and I fucking hate everything," I say in a rush.

He frowns at me and sighs. "Do you want me to come to work with you? I have stuff to sort out, but I can do it from there."

I'm immediately comforted by the thought. Having the support will be nice, and I know I'm not really in a state to drive.

"Yeah, I would." I nod at him.

Dante changes into a pair of trousers and a shirt. As he puts his belt on, I watch him with a smile, grateful to have him with me today. He takes my hand as he leads me out of the closet.

As Dante drives me to the Rodeo Drive store, my nerves mount. I wish I hadn't planned to be at Jasmine's store this morning, and I dread seeing her.

I look down at my phone, which is a mistake because the screen is filled with notifications as usual, including one from Heather.

Can I call you to talk?

I swallow heavily and hit the button to call her instead before I chicken out. I'll understand if she wants to pull her clothes out of my stores.

She answers the phone with a very professional sounding, "Heather Fletcher."

My heart pounds in my chest, and I'm terrified about what she might say to me as I say, "Hi, Heather. It's Lexi."

"Lexi, darling. I'm so glad to hear from you. How are you doing?"

"Not the greatest," I admit.

"I can imagine." She snorts and says, "A little *too* well, to be honest."

I've never spoken to Heather directly about what happened with her. I've always imagined it was a painful topic, even though she gave a prime-time interview about the whole drama, so I didn't want to bring it up.

"How did you cope?" I ask quietly.

"I didn't. Not at first. If you want to know the real truth, Harrison barely coped at all. Our lives were blowing up, and the media was insanely cruel to us." Her tone gets colder as she speaks before she sighs and is silent for a moment. "You don't have to tell me anything if you don't want to, but I just wanted to offer my support. I consider you a friend, and you're welcome to call me any time, day or night, if you need to."

The offer is so generous that I'm overwhelmed with gratitude, and I blow out a huge breath of air. "Oh my god, I honestly thought you might be calling to pull your clothes out of my stores."

"I would never," she assures me. "Aside from the fact that

they're selling well, it's not like you killed somebody." She gives a melodic laugh.

"I don't know. Cassie certainly made me out to be worse than a serial killer," I joke because if I don't laugh, I'll cry.

"She seems like a charming person," Heather says in a dry tone. "I didn't really talk to her the night of the concert, but I did notice she barely cracked a smile all night."

Even though Heather can't see me, I roll my eyes and nod. "Yeah. She was pissed that Logan kissed me in the van on the way to the venue and then was a bitch all night in general."

Dante whips his head around to look at me for a second before turning back to the road, and I cringe when I realize what I let slip.

There's silence as my heart beats a million miles an hour, and I wait for Heather's response to my confirmation that the story is true.

"She sounds like a judgmental cow." Heather makes an 'ohh' sound as though she's just realized something. "Wait, this is the friend who was holding something over your head. Everything makes a lot more sense now."

"Yeah. She blackmailed us for two hundred thousand dollars."

"Holy fuck!" Heather blurts out.

"It's been a total nightmare. I'm headed to Black Lilac now, and I'm dreading what I'm going to have to face there."

"Shit," Heather breathes out. "Do you have personal security to help you?"

I blink in surprise, then tell her, "We've never had bodyguards before. We've never needed them."

"Oh my god, darling. Get them today. If we'd gotten them sooner…" Heather trails off, then says, "No. It doesn't matter. We can't change the past, but we can change the present and, therefore, the future. So get bodyguards today because you'd rather have them in the future than be regretting that you didn't act sooner."

I turn to look at Dante, and the signs of stress are evident in his expression. This has taken a toll on all of us, and our safety is one thing that I would hate to be in question.

"You're right. I'll tell the guys, and we'll look into it today." We're coming up to Black Lilac, and there's a massive crowd out the front, so I tell Heather, "We just got to the store. I'd better go. It looks like a total shitshow."

"I can imagine. I meant what I said. Call me any time of the day or night, and if you need to get away from LA, you're more than welcome to visit me in Chicago."

I'm touched by her offer, and I say, "Thanks. I really appreciate it."

We end our call, and I drop my phone in my lap as the paparazzi take photos of the car. We pull into the driveway that leads to the parking lot behind the store, and I'm grateful when we're hidden from their view again.

"Heather thinks we should get bodyguards, and I think she's right," I say as Dante parks the car.

He gives a solemn nod and turns to look at me. "I think you're right. Maybe just until this blows over, but Isaac suggested that to me this morning as well."

"I think we'll all feel better if we do."

"Yeah, we will. I'll organize straight away," Dante says, and even just the knowledge that we'll be getting security soon is comforting. "Are you ready for this?" he asks as he takes my hand when we're out of the car.

I shake my head. "No, but we don't really have a choice."

He squeezes my hand and lowers his head to kiss me on the lips as I hear the sound of a camera taking a picture. I look up to see two people with cameras snapping pictures down the driveway at the side of the store, and I glare at them.

"Dante! Is it true that your wife is sleeping with the rest of your band?"

He grips my hand tighter as we move toward the store. My stomach is in knots as they continue to snap pictures and call out questions, though they seem smart enough not to move onto the property.

"Lexi? Did you really get together with Nate after you were in the music video together?"

"You don't have a problem with your friends screwing your wife, Dante?"

We're out of their sight, but I can still hear the questions being called out as we reach the door to Black Lilac. Shame washes over me as they ask about our personal lives and from knowing that they're going to take these pictures and share them with the world. We'll be put on display for people to gossip about and have opinions on as though they have any idea about our lives at all.

Nausea threatens to overwhelm me as we finally enter the safety of the store. I don't get much reprieve because we've only just managed to close the door behind us when Jasmine appears in front of me as she walks out of the storeroom to our left.

When she sees me, there's an unmistakable expression of disgust on her face for a moment before she clears it and her face becomes impassive.

"Lexi. Dante," she says by way of a greeting before she turns and walks away from us without another word, carrying a pile of clothes.

I wish I didn't care about Jasmine's opinion of me, but her reaction hurts. I'd guessed that she wouldn't be supportive, but I think a tiny part of me hoped I would be wrong. I lead the way to my office in silence.

Dante and I don't talk as I dock my laptop and turn it on. He takes a seat on one of the chairs in front of my desk and pulls out his phone. I listen as he calls Isaac while I check my emails.

I scroll through my inbox in awe. There are hundreds and hundreds of emails. Requests for comments from news outlets. Emails from Wicked Stallion fans; some supportive, but mostly spewing vitriol at me. Amidst those, a fraction of what is in my inbox are the usual ones from suppliers and other business-related companies.

"What time does the label want us there, and should Lexi come with us?" Dante asks, and my ears perk up. He's silent for a few seconds before he looks up at me and frowns. "That makes sense, I suppose. I don't really like the idea of leaving Lexi here until we've sorted out the bodyguard situation, though."

I take it from his response that Hades Records doesn't want me at whatever meeting they're going to have. Not that I particularly like the idea of being gawked at by everyone at the label's head office anyway.

"Lawyers? Why lawyers?" Dante's voice is strained, and his jaw is tight when he asks the question. "Okay. Well, I'll see you there. Have you told the guys?"

I wait anxiously for another minute or so while they wrap up their conversation before Dante hangs up and I can ask, "What's happening?"

"Hades wants us to come into their office to meet with PR. It's a disaster, apparently. They're going to discuss a plan moving forward. Isaac reiterated not to make any statements to the media. I told him that I won't leave you until you have security, and he's going to organize that for us."

I feel numb as I listen to him tell me this. It's all so surreal. I can't believe that this is what our lives have become. I miss the simplicity of it all from before Cassie started blackmailing us.

"What was he saying about lawyers?"

"Isaac told them about the blackmail, and there's some discussion to be had about how to proceed with having Cassie charged."

My mouth drops open as the realization dawns on me that Cassie's probably fucked herself over even more than us by going public. Maybe not quite, but what she did was illegal, and I find myself eager for her to wear an orange jumpsuit.

Rage at the unfairness of the situation, at the fact that Cassie was so greedy that she blackmailed us. That she probably sold our story to the media for a fucking fortune courses through my veins.

"Good. I hope they do fucking charge her. She deserves it," I spit.

Dante looks up at me, his expression as dark as I feel. "She does. I guess we'll see what the lawyers have to tell us."

There's a knock on the door to my office, and butterflies tumble around in my stomach as I call out, "Come in."

"Hi, Lexi."

It's Jenna, one of the sales assistants, and I can't help but notice her eyes flicker to Dante as she enters my office. When she looks back at me, a rush of shame floods over me from knowing that she's no doubt read all about my sex life online.

"Um. Jasmine said to ask you if you could maybe call the police. It's getting kind of crazy here."

I hate this so much. I just want peace and quiet, but I stand and nod as I head toward the door.

"Has something happened?"

"Well, there are those people outside," she says as Dante and I follow her toward the store. "Some of the customers have had trouble getting inside. A lot of people are coming in just to ask if you're here, and some have been very rude. It's pretty bad."

I can hear the commotion as soon as we get near the store. It's packed, and the girls are trying to assist people, but we've never had this many people in the store at once. There's a line of customers waiting to pay, so at least some people do seem to want to actually shop, but there is a group of about fifteen women standing and talking at the side of the store.

Jasmine looks up and catches my eye, then quickly looks away. I don't have time to focus on how that makes me feel as I stride over to the group.

"Excuse me. Is there something I can help you with?" I ask as politely as I can.

A few of them quickly turn and flick through some clothes on nearby racks, but at least five of them stare at me with defiant looks on their faces.

"Is it true you're sleeping with all of Wicked Stallion?" a brunette woman asks as she glares at me.

"Are you here to shop for clothes? I'm very sorry, but we have a capacity limit for the store, so if you're not here to buy clothes, I will need to ask you to leave."

"Oh my god, Dante is *right there*," a blonde woman whispers to her friend, but she's not quiet enough for me to not hear.

"How could you cheat on your husband?" the first woman snarls, looking openly hostile now.

My jaw tenses, and it takes everything in me to stop myself from reacting. I narrow my eyes at her but work hard to keep my voice level when I reply.

"Yeah, I'm going to need you to leave now. I'll be calling the police to escort you off the property if you don't leave." I turn to the store and yell above the noise, "*Attention, everyone!*" I wait as the store slowly falls silent and people turn to look at me. "*If you are not here to shop, you need to leave. This isn't a museum. It's a store. My employees don't deserve to be harassed, so I'll be calling the police to come arrest anyone who is loitering. Thank you.*"

I turn back to the group in front of me, and one of the women says, "Let's go."

She and the three people standing next to her follow her as she walks away from us. A few other people leave the store, but the brunette woman smirks at me.

"I'll wait for the cops, I guess." She looks over to the rest of the group. "I think it's true. What kind of skank sleeps with four men?"

"*And* she cheated on Cassie with Ash," another one of the group chimes in.

Shame washes over me along with indignation at the accusation. I know that I can't make any kind of statement about it as much as I desperately want to defend myself.

I stare at them as I breathe heavily for a few seconds, fighting the feelings inside me, then grind out, "Leave my store. I'm calling the police."

I spin on my heel and stride over to the counter where Jasmine is serving a customer along with one of the sales assistants.

"I'm calling the police."

"That's what I *said* to do," she snarls. "I didn't need you to come in here and cause a scene."

I'm cut by her response, and the customers in front of us quickly look away as heat rushes to my cheeks at being spoken to this way by my oldest employee.

"Okay, well, this is *my* store. I wanted to see what was going on for myself before I called the police. I'll be in my office. Let me know when they get here."

I turn and head out of the store, ignoring the chatter around me as I walk away and fight against angry tears. Dante has disappeared, and I find him in my office, on the phone with Isaac.

"Okay. I'll be able to leave as soon as they get here in that case. Thanks, Isaac. I'll let you know when I'm leaving." He looks up and sees me, his expression immediately turning to one of concern. "I have to go. I'll talk to you later."

He hangs up the call as he stands and drops his phone on the desk. I close the door behind me, and he pulls me into his arms. I can't stop the tears that fall as everything crashes over me.

"Oh, Angel. I'm sorry. I'm here for you, and we'll get through this, okay?"

I can't even make myself respond in any way. I cling to him as he holds me safe in his warm embrace. After a little while, I take a deep breath and wipe away the tears as I pull back from him.

"What did Isaac say?"

"He's organized bodyguards for us. They're going to come here, and yours will drive you home. Mine will follow me back to the apartment, and then we're all going to Hades for the meeting."

I nod and move behind my desk. "I have to call the police and get them here. Then I'll be organizing security for the stores. It's impossible out there."

"Yeah, I saw. I'm sorry, Angel," he says quietly.

I blow out a breath of air and shrug as casually as I can manage. "It's not your fault, Honey."

The next two hours are a blur as I call the police, who come to clear away the paparazzi from the front of the store. The rude customers disappear while they're doing that, but it's to no avail because, less than thirty minutes later, Jenna appears at my office door again.

"Um. The people out the front are back again," she says with a cringe.

"Fucking hell," I growl.

"Let me deal with them, Angel."

I shake my head and remind him, "You're not allowed to make any statements."

"I know. I won't say anything. I'll just tell them we're calling the police again."

I chew my lip and consider his offer. Our bodyguards haven't arrived yet, and I've organized a security guard for each store, but the company hasn't sent the employment contract through to me yet, and they won't be starting until tomorrow.

I don't want to risk one of my employees potentially getting hurt by them, so I nod. "Fine. See if you can get them to leave without me calling the police again."

Dante leads the way to the store this time. It's just as full as it was earlier, but everyone seems to be putting on the pretense of shopping for clothes now. A few whispered conversations take place as Dante strides toward the shop door. I stop at the display near the entrance and hover there as Dante pulls the door open.

"Dante! What do you say about the story published by The Gilded Cage last night?"

"Is it true that your wife is sleeping with your whole band?"

"Give us a statement, Dante. If it's not the truth, tell us what is."

The questions come hard and fast, but Dante manages to keep his cool, though I can see that every muscle in his body seems to be tense.

His voice is calm and cool as he says, "We won't be making any comments. I'm just here to ask you to please leave, or we'll have to call the police again, and I don't want to do that."

"Tell us if the story's true, and we'll go away," a reporter nearby with a British accent tells him.

The guy looks to be in his early forties, wearing a suit, with a microphone in his hand and a camera guy next to him.

Dante gives a casual laugh. "You'll go away when the police come to move you on, no doubt."

"But wouldn't it be better to just give us a statement, Dante?" the man says with a charming smile. "Then we can all happily go about our day."

"No comment." Dante's voice is cold now.

"Come on. The whole world was told how your wife is having sex with four men. You deserve to tell us your side of the story. So tell us. Is it true?"

"I said I wasn't going to give a comment. Now I'm going to call the police."

Dante starts to turn back to the store, but the guy says, "All we want to know, Dante, is if you watch when your friends fuck your wife. Are you into some kind of cuck fetish? Because that's what we all think it must be."

Dante catches my gaze, and I see the moment the anger takes hold. He spins back to face the reporter before I can stop him, and fear floods through me that Dante might be about to make a huge mistake.

"No fucking comment," he snaps.

I know the reporter can tell he's gotten under Dante's skin, but I'm at a loss as to how to put a stop to this without making it any worse. I'm helpless, and I watch in horror as the guy smirks at him.

"Ooh, you seem sensitive, Dante. Did I touch a nerve? Maybe Lexi will share with us. We've heard she likes using her mouth." He looks past Dante to leer at me. "Hey, Lexi? Tell us all about how much you like screwing four guys!"

Dante steps forward and goes toe to toe with the reporter. He's so tall that the guy is forced to crane his neck up to meet Dante's gaze.

"Keep my wife's name out of your *fucking* mouth," Dante snarls. "Our relationship is none of your business. We have no fucking comment, and the only reason I won't knock you out for that is because I don't want to be charged with assault."

"So *now* you're protective of her? But you're fine with letting her get railed by three other guys?"

I know this is going to end badly, and I have to stop it. I've never seen Dante this angry, and I'm worried that he's going to actually hit the guy. I rush out and grab his arm to pull him back toward the store.

"Honey, please come inside," I beg him.

He turns to look at me, and something inside him changes. His body relaxes a little, and he nods as he keeps my gaze.

"Come on, just tell us if you're really the Wicked Stallion bike before you go," the guy calls out again. "You know, everyone's had a ride!"

Shame rushes over me, but I cling to Dante's arm, and we continue inside. I let go of Dante's arm, and he puts it around my shoulders as he leads me back through the store. He holds me tight against him, and my cheeks burn as we pass through the customers and my employees, all watching us. I'm shaking as we reach my office, and Dante holds me tightly against him. I don't cry, but I think the shock of everything has set in.

"Do you need me to get you a glass of water or something, Angel?" he asks into my hair.

"Maybe," I tell him.

He kisses my head and leads me over to the chair behind my desk. "Sit here. I'll be back in a minute."

I look down at my phone, and amidst all of the notifications on the screen, I see that I have a video message from Logan.

I open the message and smile at Logan's beautiful face on the screen.

"Hey, Lexi. I tried calling, but you didn't answer. I just wanted to tell you that I love you and stay str—"

"Who are you talking to?" Nate asks from off-screen.

"Lexi. Say hi." Logan turns the phone to show Nate dropping onto the sofa next to him.

"Hi, Sexy Lexi. Oh, it's a video?"

Logan laughs. "Yeah, it is. I thought she might need to hear from us, and I couldn't get through. We should record it again, though."

"What? So we can pretend we're perfect. I think Lexi knows we're not. Hey, Ash!" he calls out. "Come tell Lexi she's amazing."

"You really are," Logan says as the camera turns to focus on him.

"You're amazing, Lexi," Ash says, his face appearing over Logan's shoulder. "Why am I telling her something she already knows?" He gives the screen a cheeky grin. "I can't stop thinking about this morning."

"What did you do this morning?" Nate asks as Logan pulls the phone back so I can see all three of them.

"What do you think?" Ash smirks at him.

Nate turns to look at the screen quickly. "I want to do that, too!"

"I bet you do," Logan laughs. "This is getting long. We should probably send it now. I love you, Lexi Sullivan."

"Love you, too," Ash adds.

"Fuck you tonight, Sexy Lexi. Oh yeah, I suppose I love you as well." Nate gives a cheeky grin to the camera as the video ends.

It means so much to receive this message when it's been such a hard day, and I'm glad I got the unedited version rather than something they'd planned perfectly. Tears are falling again as I type out a reply because I feel so loved and cherished by them.

I love you all. I always will.

Chapter 6

A Formal Dinner

By the end of the day, I'm exhausted and stressed. Dante left after lunch when my new bodyguard, Darren Wyatt, arrived. He's already been a godsend, taking over monitoring the store for people who were loitering, and the LAPD ended up leaving two officers at the front of the store after we called them a third time. I feel bad for taking up their resources, but at least they kept the paparazzi away this afternoon.

I've hidden in my office for most of the day because whenever I have gone into the store itself, it caused issues. I tense as my phone rings, but I relax when I look over and see Dante's name on the screen.

"Hi, Honey. You're finally out of the meeting?"

"Yes. Clive is driving us back to the apartment from Hades now."

I met his bodyguard, Clive Martin, briefly before he and Dante left to pick up the guys for their meeting at the label.

"Okay. I'll be leaving soon. We're just closing up the store, and then I'll be on my way. How did the meeting go?"

"I'll tell you about it when you get home. It wasn't great. I fucked up with that reporter, and Hades is pissed."

I cringe because I've been avoiding reading anything online, but I've still seen a couple of headlines in my notifications.

"Damn. I'll leave as soon as I can. I love you."

"Love you, Angel." The sound of Logan's voice comes from the background, and Dante chuckles. "Logan says you can wear clothes tonight if you want to."

"He's nice like that," Nate calls out, and I laugh.

"I'll think about it. Love you all." We end our call, and I drop my phone on my desk, then jump when I look up and see Jasmine standing in the doorway to my office. "Holy shit, Jazz. You scared me."

She's got a strange look on her face, but I sense her distaste as she asks, "Can we talk?"

My stomach drops as I realize she must have overheard the end of my phone conversation. I nod and watch with trepidation as she walks to stand in front of my desk.

She drops a piece of paper in front of me. "My two weeks' notice."

"You're quitting?"

I spin the piece of paper around to read what she's written. It doesn't say a lot, just that she's giving her notice and will finish her employment two weeks from today.

"Yes. I'm sorry, but the store is clearly going to become too stressful to manage. After today, I don't wish to continue my employment here."

Both Vera and Sherry told me the other stores were just as bad today. Me not being there helped, though, since the paparazzi left those stores after they figured out I'd come here.

"It's only that? There's nothing else behind this?"

I know I shouldn't ask the question. I know that I don't want the truth, and I should just accept her lie. However, a masochistic part of me needs to hear her say what I'm pretty sure is the real reason she wants to quit.

"Of course it is. What other reason could there be, Lexi?" she asks too innocently.

I snort in derision. "I don't know. Should we talk about the things you said in those messages last night?"

My blood heats a little as Jasmine looks at me for a few seconds before narrowing her eyes at me. "Fine. You're right. It's not just the way the store was today. I would probably have given you my notice even if it hadn't been like that. I'm guessing the story is true?"

I know that I'm not meant to make any statements, but at this point, Jasmine could do some tell-all interview if she wanted to anyway.

"Not all of it, but I suspect the part you're concerned about is true. As you saw today, Dante and I are still very much together and love each other."

"Even though you're cheating on him with his friends?" Her lip curls in distaste.

Disappointment cuts through my anger because as much as I don't want to care about Jasmine judging me, this still hurts.

"It's not cheating if Dante's fine with it," I point out.

"Ash had a girlfriend."

"No, he didn't. He and Cassie were broken up before anything happened. She lied about that."

"But not that you're sleeping with the entire band?" she demands.

Suddenly, I get a bad feeling about this conversation. Even though I've basically said as much to her already, I don't want to say those exact words aloud. I also don't want her in my store after today to talk to any of my other employees or the paparazzi.

"I accept your resignation, and I'll pay you out your notice period, so you don't need to come in for the next two weeks. Collect anything you need to take with you. I'll organize your final pay while you do that."

"I'll take that as a yes," she says, her voice cold.

My jaw tightens, and I ignore the nasty feeling in my stomach as I say, "Go, Jasmine. Get your shit together and leave. I've accepted your resignation, and I don't want you in my store anymore."

I'm on edge, waiting for her response. I don't want to hear

another word out of her mouth, and I'm grateful when she walks away. I spend the next ten minutes calculating her final pay and transferring it to her account. She doesn't say anything when she goes, just walks past my office with her tote bag packed full of stuff.

I walk through the store and check it's all locked up, but Jasmine clearly did that before she came in to quit. I check the staff room and her locker, but it doesn't seem like she took anything that wasn't hers. I drop onto one of the chairs in the staff room and put my head in my hands.

The sad feeling that's been creeping at the edges of my consciousness all day takes hold. I don't know how many more people I can take treating me like shit because of it. Dad, my mother-in-law, Jasmine. I know it's just the beginning, and it's only been a day.

God, it fucking hurts so *much.*

I take a few deep breaths and remind myself that the people who matter support me. I pull my phone out of my pocket and open my chat with the store managers from last night. I remove Jasmine from it before I send a message.

Jasmine just quit. I've paid out her notice period, so I won't be at the store tomorrow, Vera. I'll need to cover Jasmine until I can get a new manager.

I start collecting my things, and Vera's reply comes through as I switch off the lights.

No great loss, to be honest. I wondered if she would after last night's messages. You need people in your life who will support you, not be a raging bitch.

I've always appreciated Vera's candor, and it's nice to know she doesn't have the same opinion of me as Jasmine.

True. Thanks for your support.

Sherry's reply comes through just after I send mine.

Vera's right as usual. We're here for you, and we can handle the stores for however long you need to be at Rodeo Drive. Whatever you need from us. Just let us know.

I send through my thanks and head to the small staff kitchen where Darren is waiting for me.

"Are you ready to leave, Mrs. Sullivan?"

I nod my head. "Yes, I am. I just wanted to check everything before I left."

"I overheard your manager say she was going to quit, so I watched as she collected her things. She didn't take any merchandise that I saw."

"I know. I checked, but I appreciate that."

I follow him out to a big, black SUV as I send a message to the guys to let them know I'm on my way home. When we leave, a few of the paparazzi snap pictures of the SUV as we drive past them now that the police have left. We drive in silence to the apartment, and Darren escorts me upstairs. I thank him for his service and organize for him to come back early enough for me to open the store tomorrow morning.

The sound of the guys talking comes from the direction of the living room, and I consider Logan's offer of wearing clothes tonight. I'm torn because it's been such a long day that I'm exhausted, but I also desperately want some sense of normalcy in all of this. My 'normal' these days is to be naked in the apartment, which may or may not lead to sex. I know that if I leave my clothes on, they'll take it as a sign that I'm off-limits tonight.

I make my way to Dante's room and set my handbag there before I strip off my clothes. I even open a drawer to pull out some sweatpants before deciding that I want to just ignore everything tonight. I don't want to wallow in the drama of it all. We'll still have to talk about what happened in their meeting, but maybe I can just forget everything after that.

I find Nate, Ash, and Dante in the living room while the smell of food being cooked wafting from the kitchen tells me where Logan is.

"Hi, guys," I say, and they look up to see me.

All three have the same darkening expression of arousal when they see that I'm naked.

"God, you're so fucking sexy," Nate says.

"She looks like a goddess to me." Ash looks at me, and heat rushes to my cheeks as I catch his eye and remember this morning.

"An angel for me," Dante adds.

"Some kind of celestial being," Nate laughs as I walk toward them.

Ash is the closest, so I sit on his lap to kiss him. He raises his hand and thumbs my nipple as our tongues intertwine. His cock stiffens underneath me, and I wrap my arms around his neck, luxuriating in the feeling of being with him. It's a reminder that today's drama was for a good reason because I found love with these men, which is worth anything the world wants to think of me.

I break our kiss and press my forehead to Ash's. We both pant for breath as he looks back at me with his crystal blue eyes.

"I love you, sweet boy." I test out the nickname to see his reaction to it.

He smiles at me and says quietly, "I love you, too, Goddess."

I hug him, place my lips next to his ear, and whisper, "Want to discuss this later, or is now okay?"

"We can talk later." He kisses my neck softly, then whispers in my ear. "I liked it. I've been hard all day whenever I've thought about it. It was a real problem at Hades."

He's fully hard underneath me, and I grin as I tell him, "It seems like a real problem now."

"Logan will probably kill us if we have sex now. Dinner is almost ready," Ash points out.

"Fine," I say in a sulky voice before I kiss him a final time and slip off his lap to sit on Nate's lap.

He immediately wraps his lips around my breast, and I moan. My legs are spread because I straddled him, and he reaches between them to rub my clit. He looks up at me, amusement and arousal in his expression as he pleasures me. I thrust my fingers into his hair while he uses his other hand to pull and tweak the nipple that isn't in his mouth.

My orgasm approaches rapidly, but Dante says, "Do you want her to come now, Nate?"

He halts in his movements and pulls his mouth off my breast before grinning at Dante. "She is pretty close." He slows the tempo at which he rubs my clit and looks at me. "Do you want to come, Lexi?"

"Yes, Nate," I moan.

He continues to rub me slowly and trails kisses up my collarbone and neck to my ear, where he murmurs, "We should wait until after we've eaten. Logan's worked really hard to make us a nice dinner to enjoy."

"You make a good point, Nate," Dante says slowly. "We should enjoy dinner, and I think Lexi needs to get her mind off things. I'll be back in a minute. I need to talk to Logan."

He strides out of the room, and Nate chuckles. "Scared, Sexy Lexi? You know it's trouble for you when those two team up."

I shake my head and bite my lip as I let out a low moan because he's rubbing me faster again. "No. Whatever it is will probably take my mind off things, as Dante said. I would like to know what happened at your meeting, though."

Ash groans, and I turn to look at him. "They're absolutely furious. Said it casts them in a bad light. PR said not to make any statements for now, so they're pissed that Dante said anything to that reporter. There's also some rumor that an interview with Cassie will be announced tomorrow for later this week. I fucking hate her so much."

"Don't we all," Nate grumbles. He stops rubbing my clit and wraps his arms around me in a hug. I lean back into his embrace as he says, "Anyway, that was basically it, but the lawyers are going to liaise with the LAPD about what Cassie did. We'll likely have to go in and give statements sometime this week, including you."

I nod because I figured that would be the case if something went ahead, but it doesn't stop the knot of worry in my stomach. "Fuck. This is so awful."

Nate squeezes me and kisses my neck as Ash moves over so he's right next to us on the sofa. I lean across and kiss Ash as well before Nate passes me over to him, and Ash holds me tight while I kiss him.

"You've got us, remember. Try not to think about it. We can't do anything tonight, and stressing about it won't help," Ash says.

"Easier said than done," I moan.

"I think I know how to make you forget about it, Angel." Dante's low voice comes from the entrance to the living room. "Come here." I slide off Ash's lap and walk over to Dante instinctively. "Follow me," he instructs.

My nipples harden, and my pussy aches as I trail Dante to the dining table. I'm curious about what he has planned for me and what he talked to Logan about, but I'm already wet just from the anticipation of it all.

Dante moves the chair out from the end of the table, places his hands on my waist, and lifts me onto the table. "Spread your legs, Angel." I do as I'm told, and Dante gives me an appreciative look. "Good girl."

He steps forward between my legs and trails his fingers up and down my wet slit, unbearably slowly. I work hard to resist the temptation to moan aloud. It forces me to internalize the sensation and focus solely on what he's doing to me.

He pushes two fingers into my pussy as he watches me intently. I have to breathe faster, but it's the only giveaway of the pleasure he's giving to me.

"Is that good, Angel?" he asks.

"Yes, Honey," I breathe.

He uses his thumb to rub my clit, and the pleasure becomes so intense that my orgasm rapidly approaches. I can barely breathe because I'm sure I'll moan, and Dante smiles at me.

"Okay, you can react for the rest of the evening, Angel."

I moan as he brings me to the brink of orgasm, but he pulls his fingers out of me and gives me a wicked grin.

"You can react, but you can't come until after we've had dinner."

I blink at him, then moan softly as my orgasm recedes. He chuckles and presses his lips to mine. His tongue makes its way past my lips, and he explores my mouth while slowly stroking my clit. He brings me to the edge of orgasm again before he stops abruptly.

"Lie down, Angel."

"Huh?" I ask in confusion.

"On your back in the center of the table," he informs me.

I follow his instruction and find myself staring up at the light fitting above me, so I have to close my eyes. I feel the light get dimmer through my eyelids before I'm pulled slightly up the table.

"You should be able to open your eyes now, Angel," Dante tells me.

I'm no longer directly under the light, which Dante has dimmed to its lowest setting, and I can indeed open my eyes again.

"I want you to be able to see tonight, or I would've just blindfolded you," he says with a grin.

I watch as he moves the dining chairs to the side of the room before he walks back over to me. He leans over the table to kiss my lips, and his tongue flicks out to part my lips. He trails his hand lightly over my skin as he kisses me. His touch makes a fiery path on my body, setting my nerve endings alight as I lose myself to what he's doing. He breaks our kiss and follows a similar path with his lips, stopping at my breast to swirl his tongue around my nipple and causing me to moan in ecstasy.

I don't know how long Dante continues this tease. It could be minutes or hours, but eventually, he makes his way down one side of my body and up the other to reach my head again.

I look into his beautiful face as he says, "I think dinner might be ready. Wait here, Angel."

He walks away, and I'm left lying naked on the cold, hard table, looking at the ceiling. I'm still in ecstasy, and the anticipation of what's to come builds around me as I wait for Dante or one of the other guys to appear. My heartbeat finally starts to return to almost normal when Dante comes back to the dining room with

Logan. They're each carrying a tray with food on it, and I'm mildly confused.

Logan stops by my head and smiles down at me. "Hello, Alexandra. You look very beautiful this evening."

He drops his head to kiss me, and as he kisses me, I gasp when something hot touches my stomach. Logan breaks our kiss to give me a wicked grin. As he steps down toward my body, something is placed on my stomach again, and I catch sight of Dante placing roasted vegetables on me.

"We seem to be out of plates this evening, so we need something to serve our dinner on," he tells me, and I shiver as Logan begins to place hot bite-sized pieces of steak around my breast.

"It's a good thing we have you, Alexandra. So useful."

They continue to lay out the hot food on me, but it's not so hot that it burns me, and I wonder if Logan let it cool in the kitchen before bringing it out.

"Did you make gravy?" Dante asks Logan.

"Of course." He holds out our silver gravy boat to Dante. "Do you want to do the honors while I get the wine?"

Dante takes the gravy from him, and as Logan walks away, he warns me, "This will be hot, Angel. Let me know if it's too much. Hold your palms up."

I turn my hands over, and Dante pours some gravy on my left one. I stiffen at the sting of the hot liquid but adjust to it after a second. It's much like having candle wax poured on, and I nod as I look up at him.

"It's fine. Please don't put it anywhere too sensitive."

"Of course."

I gasp at the stinging sensation as he drips gravy around my body, starting at my chest. It's hot and wet as he takes the path around my breasts but stops when he reaches my pubic bone. Every nerve ending in my body is set alight by the experience, and I completely give myself over to whatever he plans to do with me tonight.

Dante steps back and looks at me, his voice heavy with lust as he says, "You're so beautiful, Angel."

"I love you, Honey," I respond through heavy breaths.

I turn my head to watch as Logan comes back with glasses and a bottle of red wine, trailed by Nate and Ash. Their response to the sight of me is amazing to see. Nate's jaw drops slightly open, and Ash immediately reaches down to adjust his jeans.

"Holy shit. This is even better than I imagined when you told me what you guys had done," Nate says as he walks over to me. "You look so fucking sexy."

He drops his head and kisses my lips as I listen to the other guys move around the table. His tongue dances with mine, and I'm lightheaded when our kiss ends.

"Dig in, guys. We were going to have steak for dinner, but I cut it into bite-sized pieces for obvious reasons," Logan chuckles. "I can't guarantee it'll taste as good this way."

I gasp as someone picks up a piece of hot food from my thigh, and my skin is suddenly exposed to the cold air of the room. It's dragged along my skin through what I assume is some of the gravy.

After a moment, Ash says, "Mmm. Best steak I've ever tasted."

"I'd better have a try," Nate informs us all.

He, too, picks up a piece of hot meat. This time, it's from my stomach, and he dips it in the gravy as well. I'm able to watch as he places the piece of meat in his mouth, and I don't think watching someone eat has ever been more erotic for me.

"Very tasty," Nate agrees.

Logan pours out glasses of wine, and I watch as the men pick up pieces of food off me to eat. I'm in sensory overload. Sometimes I can see where they're going to touch me. Other times I can't, and I'm in complete ecstasy.

Dante picks a piece of meat up from my chest and drags it over my nipple, causing me to moan before pulling it through some gravy and moving up to my head.

"You need to eat, too, Angel," he murmurs.

I open my mouth and allow him to feed me. The steak is

delicious, and even though I can recognize that it's colder and slightly more rubbery than it would be had I been eating it regularly, I can't help but agree with Ash's opinion of it being the best he's ever tasted.

As I'm chewing the steak, Logan leans down and takes a piece of roast potato in his mouth. He kisses my stomach with his lips in the process, and I moan in delight at the sensation. He trails his tongue along my skin and through some of the gravy before he lifts his head, and my pussy aches with desire.

"How did you come up with this idea, Dante?" Ash asks as he casually takes a sip of some wine.

Dante is still standing by my head, and he strokes my hair softly as he smiles down at me. "Lexi and I have talked about doing something like this in the past. It would've been a much smaller meal, of course."

Nate takes a leaf out of Logan's book and picks up a piece of steak with his mouth, distracting me for a moment as Dante asks, "Are you enjoying yourself, Angel?"

"Uh-huh," I tell him through a moan. "This is amazing."

"Is it what you imagined?" Dante asks the question as he drags another piece of food across my nipple before putting it in his mouth.

"Better," I assure him.

I could never have known how good this is—not knowing where I'll be touched next. The sensations of the hot food and the cold air, along with mouths and hands on my body. Watching these beautiful men use me as a dinner plate. Being fed the delicious food that Dante places in my mouth whenever I finish a mouthful. It's beyond amazing.

As they eat their fill, the touches change. Instead of simply picking up the food, the mouths and hands linger on me. Nate takes a sip of his red wine, then takes my breast in his mouth. His tongue is wet and warm against my painfully hard nipple. Someone else trails their tongue along my side, down to my pubic bone, but stops just before they reach my pussy, and I groan, desperate for them to continue further.

Dante brings a roasted carrot to my mouth, but I shake my head at him. "I'm full. Thank you."

He smiles at me, then pops it into his mouth. As he chews it, he gently strokes the side of my face, and I lean into the palm of his hand. After he swallows, he leans down and kisses me, tasting of the honied carrot that Logan cooked.

I'm unable to focus on anything other than the touches that I receive, and I've floated away in complete ecstasy by the time the men finish their meal.

"Time for dessert," Logan announces in a husky voice. "I think ice cream would be a good choice. Don't you, Dante?"

Dante runs his thumb over my nipple and nods at Logan. "A very good choice. I'm pretty sure we're out of bowls, though."

"What a shame," Logan says, and we all laugh.

I'm dripping wet and eager for the sensation of the cold ice cream against my skin. I can barely breathe through my desire to be fucked as it is, and I'm sure that it will happen soon. I'm just going to experience some sweet, sweet torment first, and I'm ecstatic for that to happen.

Nate's the first to take his clothes off as Logan walks away toward the kitchen. I moan softly as he pulls his shirt over his head, then drops his jeans to reveal his stiff erection.

"Oh, it's like that, is it?" Ash asks with a grin as he looks at Nate's cock while Nate strokes it.

I can't help myself as I look at Ash watching Nate, and I envisage him reaching over to take over stroking Nate's cock for him. The thought sends a dart of electricity straight to my pussy.

Nate grins back at Ash. "Well, I mean…" He nods to Ash's crotch. "You know we're going to fuck her, right? Might as well be comfortable for dessert."

Ash is already unzipping his jeans, and he laughs. "Thank fuck. It's been killing me since I walked in here. I was just waiting because I didn't know if we were allowed to get naked."

"You're allowed to do whatever you want, Ash. It's just Lexi that has rules," Logan informs him as he re-enters the room with a tub of ice cream, an ice cream scoop, and a wet towel.

Ash turns back from tossing his shirt aside, fully naked, with his cock jutting impressively in front of him, and he catches my eye. "If you say so."

I bite my lip as I remember this morning, and even though I'm in subspace right now, an added layer of ecstasy is the thought of Ash being here with me from something I've had him do for me.

I don't have time to think about it because Logan reaches my side. He wipes my body down with the warm, wet towel before setting it aside and scooping some ice cream out of the tub. He drags the back of the cold metal scoop around my nipple, and I gasp before he drops the ice cream in the valley between my breasts.

He drops several scoops of ice cream on me before he announces, "Enjoy. I'll be back."

He takes the towel and ice cream with him as he leaves the room. Ash is the first to eat some ice cream. He chooses a scoop that Logan placed near my hip bone, and I moan as his tongue and lips make contact with me.

Dante places his finger in the scoop between my breasts and then pushes it and some of the ice cream between my lips. It's sweet and cold, and I suck his finger as though it's his cock. He pushes a second finger into my mouth and then a third while he watches me with dark eyes.

He continues to fuck my mouth with his fingers while he lowers his head to eat the ice cream between my breasts. Logan returns and joins in with the others.

It isn't long before the ice cream is gone, and somebody pushes their fingers into my pussy. I moan in ecstasy as a tongue flicks across my clit as well.

Logan kisses me expertly as the mouth on my pussy disappears and, through my lust-filled daze, I hear Dante say, "Dinner is over, Angel. You can come now."

He lowers his head again and eats my pussy until I come. I writhe in ecstasy as he takes me over the edge while the other guys take turns either kissing me or playing with my breasts. Dante gives me another orgasm, and my body shakes as waves of pleasure rock me.

As I pant for breath, Dante kisses my clit before he says, "Mmm. So tasty, Angel."

He stands and pulls his top over his head before he folds it and sets it on one of the chairs at the side of the room. He removes his jeans and underwear, then folds them and puts them on top of his shirt before he comes back to the table. He climbs on the table and holds himself over me, the heat from his body almost as hot as the lust in his eyes.

"Do you know how badly I want to fuck you, Angel?"

"Almost as badly as I want you to fuck me, Honey?" I ask, and he chuckles.

"Something like that."

He sheaths himself inside me and fucks me slowly. Ash kisses me and plays with my breasts, but I break our kiss to look over when Nate speaks to Logan.

"You're wearing far too many clothes right now."

Logan chuckles. "Am I?" He pulls his shirt over his head and tosses it aside. "Better?"

"Not quite." Nate drops to his knees in front of Logan, and I moan softly as he says, "I'll help you out."

Ash stops playing with my breast, and I glance to my right to see him watching the two of them as well. He resumes playing with my breasts while Nate pulls Logan's stiff cock out and wraps his lips around it as Logan groans. I love watching Nate blow him and the sensations of being fucked, Ash's touch, and the erotic show they're putting on send me over the edge again in no time.

My pussy clenches hard around Dante's cock, and he groans, "Fuck yes, Angel. Come for me."

He fucks me hard through my orgasm, and by the time Logan comes down Nate's throat, I'm screaming in ecstasy. Dante buries himself in my pussy and empties his load a few moments later. I love the feeling of being filled by him, and when Nate swirls his tongue around the head of Logan's cock to swallow every drop, I almost come again.

Dante pulls himself out of me as Nate stands up to kiss Logan, and he climbs off the table as Ash climbs on to take his place, pushing his thick cock into my full pussy.

"Want me to go get some lube?" Nate murmurs to Logan.

"I got some earlier," Dante tells them. "When I first spoke to Logan, I figured we might end up needing some."

He pulls a tube out of a drawer in the buffet at the side of the room and tosses it to Nate, who grins. "Thanks for thinking of me."

Dante laughs. "It wasn't specifically you, but you're welcome."

Logan leans over and kisses me as Nate begins to prepare his ass. "Do you want to watch Nate fuck me, Alexandra?"

"Yes, Sir," I moan.

"Do you like watching us fuck?"

Ash's cock jerks inside me as he thrusts roughly into me, and I gasp, "Very much, Sir."

"Did you like seeing me come down Nate's throat and watching him suck me dry?"

"Oh god, yes," I assure him.

Logan reaches between Ash and me to rub my clit as we fuck. "I'm sure you do. Probably as much as I'm enjoying watching Ash stuff his fat cock into your tight pussy. Just knowing that he's stretching you and will soon be filling you with his cum is fucking hot."

"Jesus christ," Nate moans from behind him. "You're going to make me come before I can even get inside you, Logan."

Ash grins down at him. "Do you like that, Nate? Do you like hearing about my cock splitting Lexi's cunt in half? Do you want to know how fucking tight and wet she is and how I'm going to come deep inside her when you're in Logan's ass?"

I have no fucking clue what is going on right now and who exactly is teasing who, but I'm beyond any kind of rational thought. I reach up and grab onto Ash, digging my fingers into his back as I come hard on his cock.

"Fucking fuck, fuck, fuck, fuuuuuck!" I yell as I come.

Logan looks down at me. "Good girl, Alexandra. Come on Ash's cock." Nate stands up and pushes his cock into Logan's ass, and Logan says, "Yes. Come around Ash's big cock while Nate fucks me with his."

Logan tweaks and pulls at my nipples, and I'm dead. This is so fucking erotic that I can't even handle it. Dante gently strokes my head as he watches on, and I look into his beautiful brown eyes.

"She feels so good when she comes," Ash tells them. "Just think about it, Nate. Think about how Lexi's cunt felt just now as she came around me. She obviously loves being fucked, but I think she loves watching you fuck Logan just as much."

Nate groans and stares over at Ash as he pounds into Logan's ass while Logan takes my breast in his mouth. "Are you trying to kill me?"

"Just trying to help you come," Ash says with an innocent smile.

The words alone are enough to tip me into another orgasm. I'm not sure if Ash has any idea of the double entendre he just made, but the thought of Ash helping Nate to come is enough to drive me wild.

"You're a little *too* helpful, thanks," Nate growls, and he's gripping Logan's hips so hard as he fucks him that his knuckles have turned white.

Logan lifts his mouth and grins at Ash. "It's working for me. I don't think Nate's fucked me this hard in a while." He grunts as Nate thrusts forcefully into him and breathes out, "Much appreciated."

Ash fucks me with a similar rhythm to how Nate is fucking Logan and grins down at his friend. "You're welcome."

He comes buried deep inside me while panting for breath and then holds himself there as he watches Nate finish fucking Logan. I love the feeling of his thick cock being inside me while I watch Nate blow his load. When he does, the room is filled with the sound of our panting breaths, and it feels as though the world is aglow.

Nate leans forward and kisses Logan's back. "I love you."

"I love you, too," Logan murmurs with a dazed smile.

'I love yous' are exchanged between me and everyone before Ash pulls out of me and climbs off the table. I get lots of kisses from the guys before Dante picks me up and carries me to his bathroom.

"How are you feeling, Angel?" he asks as he stands me up in the shower.

"Absolutely wrecked," I answer honestly. "But also *so* fucking good."

He smiles at me. "I'm glad about the last part."

Dante washes me gently, and after the shower, we get into bed together, and I snuggle up next to him, completely satiated.

"Oh my god, that was so much more intense and amazing than I ever imagined," I tell him.

"I'm glad. I thought it might help to keep your mind off things tonight."

I realize that I haven't looked at my phone or thought about everything that's going on for hours. Even now, lying in bed, I can't bring myself to worry about any of it.

I'm just a limp bundle of complete bliss, and I smile into the darkness as I tell Dante, "Mission accomplished."

Chapter 7
Daddy Dante

I wake on Tuesday morning in Dante's arms, familiar and warm. My worries are back, but I'm grateful that I got an escape from them last night. I snuggle back against Dante, and he squeezes me tight before he kisses my neck.

"Morning, Angel."

"Morning, Honey," I say with a contented sigh as I revel in being in his embrace.

"How are you feeling?"

"Stressed. Nate and Ash said there's some big interview with Cassie coming up."

He sighs, and I feel him nod his head behind me. "Apparently so. The lawyers at Hades are going to try to get a gag order to stop her from speaking. They're going to argue that it could impinge upon the blackmail case if there is one."

I frown as I take this in and roll over to face him. "Is it likely that'll work?"

He shrugs. "I don't know. It's possible, but it's hard to say. They honestly didn't seem hopeful, but it seemed like standard procedure to try."

"I don't want her to talk about us any more than she already has," I say with a sigh.

"I know, Angel." Dante kisses me softly. "They might not be able to stop her, but at least they're going to try."

"I don't want to go to work," I admit. "I hate that so much because I love Black Lilac, but the thought of going back there again today is awful, even though I know I have to. Jasmine quit last night."

Dante's eyebrows raise. "She did?"

"Yeah. I would've told you, but somehow, I got distracted last night and never got around to it." I smirk at him, remembering how good last night was.

"I wonder what ever could have distracted you?" he chuckles, and I laugh as well. He kisses me again and says solemnly, "Unfortunately, I don't have any solution for Jasmine quitting. Hopefully, you can find a replacement before her two weeks are up."

I cringe and shake my head. "I paid her out and told her not to come in. I didn't want her in the store after some of the things she said to me."

The pain of the way Jasmine turned on me stings, and Dante frowns as he takes in my reaction.

"Oh, Angel. I'm sorry that happened."

I shrug. "You win some. You lose some. Sherry and Vera have been really supportive. I'm just going to stay at Rodeo Drive instead of visiting their stores until I get another manager. I'm pretty sure they can handle it."

"Maybe it's a sign you can stop micromanaging the stores?" Dante raises an eyebrow at me and gives me a small smile.

I feign indignation and tell him, "*Me?!* Micromanaging? Just because I visit every store multiple times a week?"

"Yes, you," he laughs. "I mean. They're your stores to run however you like, but you know they've been able to run fine without your daily oversight for a while now. Maybe it's time to consider if you want to open another store or do some other venture as well?"

I blink at him because he's right as usual. I've been so involved in Black Lilac that I haven't really stepped back and looked at the big picture. I go to the stores every day, but I don't normally have to do a lot. The only time I'm really needed is if we have some big shipment or event happening.

"I'll think about it," I concede. "At the moment, I really do need to be there because Jasmine left."

"True." Dante kisses me. "Whatever you decide to do, you'll have my full support. I'm always here for you, Angel."

I wrap my arms around his neck and kiss him, thrusting my tongue into his mouth to deepen our kiss. Dante reaches behind himself to take each of my hands in his, then rolls me over and pins me to the bed. I pant for breath as I look up into his beautiful brown eyes, and the pressure from his hands holding mine down on either side of my head is enough to get me wet.

"What time do you need to be at work?"

"I have to open the store," I tell him and wrinkle my nose at him.

"Then, by my calculations, I'd better make use of you quickly," he murmurs. I moan softly at the way he phrases it, and Dante raises an eyebrow at me. "Did I tell you that you could have reactions this morning, Angel?"

"No, Honey."

I bite my lip, and my body is already aflame because I know I'm going to get a punishment. His cock is stiff against me, and I'm eager for him to use me and give me a few moments more of distraction before I have to face the day.

Dante lowers his head and kisses my neck. He lets go of my hands, but I don't dare even attempt to move them as he begins to kiss his way down to my breast.

He swirls his tongue around one of my painfully stiff nipples when he reaches it, and I have to focus on my breathing to prevent myself from moaning. Dante looks up at me, his eyes heavy with lust, before continuing his path down my body.

When he reaches my pussy, I'm wildly aroused and desperate for an orgasm. His breath is hot on my most sensitive area, and I need nothing more than for him to lower his head the last inch that will bring his mouth to my clit. To my dismay, he raises his head and gives me a wicked grin as he looks at me.

"You're going to worship my cock, but I'm going to tie you up and blindfold you so that you don't get to fully enjoy it. The pleasure is only for me."

I moan softly as Dante's weight disappears from the bed, and I watch him walk away. He comes back a few moments later and grabs my wrist after climbing on the bed. My heart pounds in my chest as he buckles a leather cuff on my wrist. He puts one on my left wrist as well, then clips them together before he shackles me to a tie-down point at the head of the bed.

He places a blindfold over my eyes, and the world becomes dark. "So beautiful. So vulnerable. I can do anything that I want with you. I love that so much." His voice is a low, seductive rumble as he trails his hand over my body. "You can have reactions now, Angel."

"Thank you, Honey." I'm so relieved because my sensations are so heightened with the removal of my sight.

I gasp when Dante lowers his head to my nipple and swirls his tongue around it before his tongue is gone. His fingers gently stroke my side, and I jump when he suddenly tweaks my other nipple roughly. I don't know where or when he's going to touch me next, and I'm in ecstasy, being wound as tight as a spring with each passing moment.

Dante rubs my cheek softly with his hand and murmurs, "Good girl, Angel. I'm going to fuck you now. Don't come until I tell you to."

"Yes, Honey," I breathe through my ecstasy.

Dante moves up to the bedhead and unshackles my hands. He leans down to put his face near mine and takes my chin in his hand, holding my face in his warm hand as he kisses me deeply.

"On your hands and knees," he instructs when our kiss ends.

I do as I'm told, and I hear the sound of Dante moving before I sense him near my face. I moan softly, accurately predicting what he's about to say.

"Worship my cock, Angel."

I open my mouth dutifully, and he pushes his cock past my lips. I take him as far as I can, sliding down to the base of his erection and touching my nose to his stomach. Dante gives a soft groan, and he places a hand on my head to stroke it as I blow him.

It's thoroughly enjoyable to listen to him as I give him head. He's so sexy when he moans his satisfaction as I swirl my tongue around the tip of his cock that my pussy aches to be filled. I need him to fuck me, but I don't know if he'll even do that, and knowing that I'm surrendering myself to Dante's wants and needs is amazing.

"You'd better stop, Angel. I need to fuck you now if you want to have time to eat breakfast before you leave."

I reluctantly take my mouth off his cock, even though I know that he'll be fucking me with it in a few moments. Dante chuckles and places his palm on the side of my face for a moment before he moves away from my head.

He settles behind me and pushes two fingers into me before saying, "Mmm. So wet and ready for me." He pumps his fingers in and out faster, and I moan as he asks, "Do you want my cock?"

"Yes, please, Honey."

He uses his other hand to rub my clit and says, "Come for me, Angel. Then I'll give you my cock."

It takes approximately two seconds after that for my orgasm to rush over me. Dante knows exactly how to work my body in such a way as to give me pleasure, and I moan his name as I come, my body shaking as he continues to finger me until my orgasm passes.

Dante pulls his fingers out of me and then says, "Very tasty."

I love knowing that he's tasting my juices on his fingers, and I pant for breath as he chuckles. He places his hands on my hips and finally pushes his cock into me.

"Oh, god, Angel," he says with a sexy groan, and I clench his cock tight with my internal muscles.

He begins to move in and out of me, and I love it. Not having my sight for this only heightens the experience of Dante fucking me. He holds himself deep inside and reaches underneath me to rub my clit.

"Come on my cock," he instructs.

I focus on the sensations he's giving me and moan as the pleasure builds inside me. Dante's breath is hot on my back, and I close my eyes tight as my orgasm crashes over me.

I can barely hold myself up with my arms as my body shakes in ecstasy, and I moan, "Oh, yes, Honey. Yes. Oh god, yes!"

He kisses my back, then grabs my hips and fucks me until he buries himself deep and groans when he comes inside me. We stay there for a moment, both panting for breath, before Dante pulls out and unshackles me. He pulls off the blindfold, and I blink a few times before his beautiful face comes into focus.

"Hi, Angel." He presses his lips to mine, and I inhale his scent before he takes my hand and leads me to the bathroom.

He kisses me and holds me close as he washes me. I'm completely blissed-out by the time we're finished, and I get dressed for work quickly, so I have enough time to make some toast to eat before I leave.

Dante takes my hand in his as we head toward the kitchen. We find Nate and Ash sitting at the dining table, talking in solemn voices. They look up and smile at me as we approach.

"Morning, guys," I say as I give them a hug.

"I'll go make you some breakfast, Angel. What do you want?" Dante asks.

"Jam toast and cranberry juice are fine. Thank you, Honey."

I take a seat next to Ash, and he gives me a tight smile. I notice that both he and Nate wear signs of stress. Their bodies are coiled tightly like a spring, and Ash's hair is messy. Even as I watch him, he shoves his hand through it and gives a small sigh.

"What's up?" I ask with a frown.

Ash looks at Nate quickly, then back at me. "Cassie's doing an interview on Sunday. It's all over the internet."

"Shit," I gasp. "Can I see?"

Ash unlocks his phone and slides it over to me. On the screen is an article from a well-known gossip site.

WICKED STALLION TRUTH TO BE REVEALED IN INTERVIEW

We can confirm that Cassandra Foster, the ex-girlfriend of Ashton Woodford from Wicked Stallion, will be giving an interview on Sunday night to Grant Stan from Backline.

The trailer for the interview was uploaded to the show's YouTube channel and shared on their social media accounts this morning. The interview looks explosive as Cassandra tells all about her time with the band and their alleged relationships with Lexi Sullivan, wife of bassist Dante Sullivan.

According to Cassandra, the band 'share' the woman who—

I snort in derision, and I can't stomach reading the rest of the article, so I slide the phone back to Ash. "Ugh."

"That about sums it up. Isaac sent us all an email. Hades PR is in overdrive, but they still don't want us to say anything publicly. They're working behind the scenes and think it's best for us if we don't make any kind of statements. We also have to go to the LAPD on Thursday to make statements about Cassie, and then they'll decide if they're going to press charges if we don't want to do it."

I stare at him as I consider the situation. "*Should* we press charges?"

"We were just talking about that," Nate says. "We're going to see our lawyer today, not just go on what Hades' lawyers say."

I nod and say thoughtfully, "That makes sense. We need to protect ourselves first and foremost."

Ash reaches over and puts his arm around my shoulders before he pulls me into him for a hug. "Exactly. I have no doubt that Hades will be protecting their interests before ours, so we should do the same."

He kisses me passionately, and I sink into his embrace, warm and comforting. He's still kissing me when Dante appears with my breakfast.

I break our kiss and smile up at my beautiful husband. "Thank you, Honey."

"You're welcome." He sets a plate of toast and a glass of cranberry juice in front of me before he heads back to the kitchen.

"I'm going to go shower," Nate announces as he stands from the table and walks over to pull me up from my seat. He wraps his arms around me and holds my body against his as he looks down at me. "Have a good day at work, Sexy."

He drops his head and captures my lips with his. His tongue slides into my mouth, and I wrap my arms around his neck as I kiss him back. He tastes of coffee, and I assume he and Ash must already have eaten.

His cock is stiff against my stomach when we break apart, and he gives me a sexy smile. "I'll let you eat your breakfast. I'll enjoy you tonight, though."

"Is that a promise?" I grin at him.

He drops his head and kisses me again, then says in a husky voice. "Of course it is. I've just started using a bigger butt plug. One step closer to you fucking me."

I moan softly at the thought, then add, "And one step closer to Logan fucking you, too."

I reach between us and rub his cock as he laughs in response, "Precisely." He grabs my wrist and pulls my hand away from him. "If you don't stop, your toast is going to get cold, and you'll be late for work."

"Sounds like a plan." I remember that Jasmine quit last night, and I groan, "Ugh. I need to open the store. *Fine*. We can fuck later."

Nate and Ash laugh as I take my seat again, and Ash asks Nate in a curious voice, "You use butt plugs?"

"Yeah, I do." He smiles at Ash from where he's still standing behind my chair. "It's how you work up to actually receiving anal."

I'm reminded of our sex session yesterday morning, and I ask

Ash, "Is it something you'd be interested in trying?"

Ash's cheeks flush pink as I take a bite of my toast, and he darts a glance at Nate before he shrugs. "I don't know. It was pretty hot when you ate my ass, but I probably would've found anything at all that you suggested to be a turn-on."

Nate chuckles and shakes his head at me. "You're just out here determined to be the first person to eat everybody's ass, huh? I thought I was special."

He clutches his chest as though he's mortally wounded, and both Ash and I laugh at him.

"What can I say? I like what I like."

I wink at Nate, and he leans down to kiss my neck before he says in a husky voice, "Hey, I didn't say I was complaining. Have a good day at work, Sexy."

Ash and I watch Nate leave, then I look toward the kitchen, but there's no sign of Dante coming back, so I turn back to Ash.

"Is what we did yesterday morning something that you might want to do again?" My heart beats faster in my chest, and I realize how much I want to explore BDSM with Ash.

"I haven't been able to stop thinking about it, so yes," he admits. "How does it all work?"

I take a sip of my juice and think back to when Dante and I first started our kink relationship. We'd been together for about five years before I admitted to him that it was something I'd always been intrigued by.

"When Dante and I started, we just did scenes at first. We weren't full-time immediately." I laugh and shake my head. "Remember your twenty-third birthday party?"

Ash's eyebrows raise, and he nods. "Most of it. I got pretty drunk."

"I didn't." I grin at him. "It was one of our first experiences with kink in public. Dante would only let me drink water the whole night as punishment for something I did. I can't even remember what now."

"I remember you not drinking," Ash gasps and then laughs.

"We all thought you must be pregnant."

I burst into laughter. "Yeah, I kind of figured that. Anyway, it was shortly after that that we decided to go full-time. Every kink relationship is different from any other relationship. So we can decide together what we want to do, and we'll only ever do things that you're comfortable with."

"I think I'd like to try something like what we did the other morning again, but…"

"But what?" I ask when he trails off and doesn't continue.

"I don't think it's something I want to do with the other guys or even have them know about. Just until I get my head around it a little more and see how I feel about doing anything around them."

I cringe and admit, "I did tell Dante yesterday morning. I'm sorry. I just needed to talk to him about what happened because I was trying to figure out if it was even something I should've liked doing."

Ash frowns and nods. "I'm okay with you telling Dante. Did you like doing it?"

He has a slightly worried look on his face, and I place my palm on his cheek as I smile back at him. "I did. A lot. That was part of my confusion because I've always been a sub. Dante was very reassuring."

"Dante was very reassuring about what?" Dante asks as he walks toward us with his own breakfast.

Ash and I both jump, then turn to look at him. I'm not sure exactly how much Ash wants to say, so I let him speak instead of saying anything myself.

"Lexi and I were just talking about what we did yesterday morning," Ash tells him.

"Ohh." Dante sets his plate down next to me. "Yeah. I told Lexi that being a switch is totally fine. I'm kind of fascinated by the idea of Lexi as a Domme, to be honest."

My pussy aches because I have a vision of being Dommed by Dante while I, in turn, Domme Ash, and the idea is wildly erotic for me.

"We're going to try it again sometime, so maybe in the future, you can watch if you want to. I was saying to Lexi that I'd appreciate it if we kept this between us for now, just while I'm getting used to it. I hope that's okay."

Dante nods and smiles at him. "Of course. It's not my information to share. Whenever you're ready, you can tell them."

I finish the rest of my breakfast quickly and kiss Ash and Dante before heading back to Dante's bedroom to finish getting my things together to go to work. My phone is full of notifications, and I ignore them as I slip it into a pink Chanel handbag that I sling over my shoulder.

I find Logan coming downstairs just as I'm about to go upstairs to say goodbye to him before I leave.

"Hi, Lexi." He gives me a sexy grin, looking as good as ever, wearing jeans and a t-shirt that both show off his body nicely.

"I was just coming upstairs to see you," I laugh. "I'm going to work. Jasmine quit last night, so I have to open the store."

"Oh wow. Everything okay?" he asks. I shrug as casually as I can, but the hurt of her quitting and why she did it must show on my face because Logan immediately frowns. "Why did she quit?"

"Basically the same reason that Cassie was uncomfortable with our relationship. She thinks I'm a slut."

"She *said* that?!" Logan growls, his face absolutely thunderous.

"Not in as many words. I was paraphrasing, but she might as well have."

He stares into my eyes for a few seconds, then pulls me tightly into his arms. Logan doesn't say anything and just holds me against him, his face buried in my hair. With the comforting sound of his heart beating in his chest sounding in my ears, it's so calming being with him that it eases the pain of what Jasmine did. Once again, I'm reminded of how much I love the men I'm with and why it's worth all of the judgment in the world to have them in my life.

"I know you have to go, but you can call me any time you need to. We have meetings to go to today, but I don't give a fuck who I'm in a meeting with. I'll always answer your call, okay?"

I smile into his chest and say, "Okay. I love you, Logan Ballantine."

He pulls back a little, places his hand under my chin, and tilts my face up to look at him. "And I love you, Alexandra Sullivan."

He lowers his head to kiss me thoroughly. He's as skillful with his tongue as ever, and by the time we break apart, we're both breathing heavily.

"I'll let you go to work now, Alexandra," he says with a wicked grin at me. "Call me if you need me."

I reach up on my toes to kiss him quickly again. "I will. Thank you, Sir."

I meet Darren in the entry near the elevator, and I'm floating on air as I head down to the parking garage to get into the black SUV. As I follow Darren across the parking garage, I smile to myself and think about how lucky I am to have the guys.

My nerves and worry return with a vengeance on the drive to work. Being in peak-hour traffic, with a bodyguard behind the steering wheel, reminds me that so much has changed. I would normally travel to work a little later than this and avoid the traffic, on top of driving myself.

It also reminds me of Jasmine's resignation, which then reminds me of Cassie's upcoming interview, which reminds me of her previous interview. By the time I reach Black Lilac, I feel sick, and the paparazzi out the front of the store makes it a thousand times worse.

"I hate them so much," I tell Darren, and he gives me a tight smile in the rearview mirror.

"I know, Mrs. Sullivan. I'll deal with them when we get inside, and I'll make sure they stay away from you today."

I'm relieved to hear that he has a plan, or at the very least, he sounds confident that he's capable of doing this, which is better than nothing.

"Thanks."

I unlock the store, get the money for the tills out of the safe, and then set everything up to open. As I do, Darren heads out the front of the store, and I listen as he reminds them that loitering is illegal and threatens to call the police. They move away from the entrance but only go so far as to hang out in front of the store next to ours, and I cringe because I don't want to cause trouble for our neighbors.

About ten minutes later, Jenna shows up, along with two other sales assistants who work here.

I approach them as they're putting their things away in the staff room. "Hey, guys. Before we start work today, I'd like to have a short meeting in the kitchen. Come join me there when you're ready."

I smile at them before I turn and head to the kitchen. I'm nervous about telling them Jasmine quit. I know that it's going to cause them to gossip, and I'm not sure how exactly to approach the situation.

When they're all seated in front of me, I smile at them. "Okay, I just wanted to let you guys know all at once that Jasmine quit last night."

There are audible gasps before Hannah says, "You're kidding."

"No, I'm not. So until we get another store manager, I'm going to be here daily." I sigh and frown at them. "I'm sure you've seen the stories out there about me."

Their eyes widen, and I can sense that they want me to tell them it's true, but I don't think it's appropriate to talk about it with my staff, even if Hades hadn't told us not to tell anyone.

"I'm not going to go into any details regarding that, but I expect that the paparazzi will continue to hang out at this store since I'm here. I also think that me actually being *in* the store will also continue to cause issues, so for the most part, I'm going to try to stay out of sight. Jenna, as Jasmine's second in command, I'm hoping that you'll be willing to step up and help out until I find someone to fill her role."

She sits a little straighter in her seat and nods. "Of course, Lexi. I'm happy to do whatever you need me to do. I'm sorry this is happening to you. It must be really stressful."

"It is," I admit. "But I appreciate all of your support so much. Anyway, we'd better get the store open and let the masses in."

The ladies head into the store, and I go to my office, where I finally look at my phone. I cringe at all the notifications on there. There are so many of them, and some make me feel sick. News articles about us, people messaging me or commenting on my posts. Amidst them all, I see one from Sophie, and my heart pounds in my chest as I remember the last time we talked and what my dad said.

Hi, Lexi. Just wanted you to know I'm thinking of you. I hope you're okay. We love you.

It's weird because Sophie never really texts me. We talk, but it's normally stuff about what she should get Dante and me for Christmas or what I'm bringing for Thanksgiving dinner. We've never had the kind of relationship where we just chat via text.

I hesitate with my thumb over the screen for a minute before I hit the button to call her, and she answers after a few rings. "Lexi. It's good to hear from you. How are you doing?"

"About as good as can be expected," I tell her honestly. "How are you and Dad?"

"We're good," she says, but I can sense the hesitation in her voice.

"I'm guessing Dad hasn't come around yet," I say, unable to keep the hurt out of my voice because it's painful as fuck and feels like my dad doesn't love me anymore.

"It's only been a few days. Give him time, sweetie." She sighs and then says, "We saw that Ash's ex-girlfriend is giving some kind of interview on Sunday."

"Yup. Can't wait," I say, my voice dripping with sarcasm.

My nerves have doubled, and I kind of regret this phone call. I appreciate Sophie's support, but I feel so much worse than before I called her. All it's done is remind me of all this shit.

"Is there anything I can do to help?" she asks.

"I appreciate it, but not really. Hey, look, I'm at work, so I should probably go. Thank you so much for supporting me, and"—

I hesitate for a second—"tell Dad I said hi, I guess."

"I will. Keep your chin up. I'm sure this will pass quickly. You know how the news cycles are."

"Thanks."

We end the call after that, and I'm left thinking about Sophie's words. I'm not entirely sure that she's right about this. Objectively, this news is salacious as hell and makes for excellent headlines. Any time the guys are in public, especially if I'm with them, pictures of us will make the media a fortune.

I suddenly feel like I'm nothing more than a commodity, and it sucks.

Chapter 8

Never Read the Bottom Half of the Internet

By Thursday afternoon, when Darren escorts me to the SUV at the back of Black Lilac, I'm so stressed that I think I might snap. The paparazzi scrutiny has only gotten more intense over the last two days. Cassie's interview is being promoted everywhere, and I feel like I can't breathe from the weight of everything.

"Thanks," I mutter to him under my breath as he holds the door open for me.

I'm very aware of the cameras snapping pictures of me down the alleyway next to Black Lilac. I don't even bother trying to get them to stop now. It's a lost cause. I breathe a sigh of relief when Darren shuts the door, and I'm safe inside the car.

He drives down the alleyway, and the paparazzi crowd around us, snapping pictures as we pass them. I want to give them the finger, but I don't. I'm a very good girl, and I haven't said anything to them.

It's so hard to keep my silence, though. To read the awful things being said about me online and not respond in any way. None of us has posted anything, but I've spent hours scrolling through, which is what I do now as Darren drives me to the LAPD headquarters.

I see plenty of gossip accounts, but I come across Heather's face as I'm scrolling. She's posted a video to the official Serenity account with a tour of her factory floor where women are making her clothes. My jaw drops at this inside look behind the scenes of my favorite fashion label, and I can't resist commenting.

Holy crap, @serenityclothesofficial. This is amazing to see. Thank you so much for sharing with us!

Almost instantly, people start making comments in reply to mine.

Are you really sleeping with all of Wicked Stallion, @lexisullivanofficial?

Is it true you're in a relationship with four guys?!

I hate you @lexisullivanoficial! You should die for cheating on Dante!

Your a digusting whote!!!!!

I hope you know how gross you are, @lexisullivanofficial.

I can't wait to see Cassandra Foster tell us EEEEEVERYTHING! Spill the tea, sis!

My finger hovers over my comment, and I consider just deleting it, but comments start disappearing in front of my eyes as I watch. Anything nasty disappears. I see a couple more show up, but they also disappear after a few seconds. In another moment, a pinned comment appears.

I will not stand for bullying or harassment on my account. If you have something nasty to say to someone, just don't. I will be blocking anyone who posts those types of comments. - Heather Fletcher

My phone rings, and Heather's name is on the screen. I blink at it for a few seconds before I answer the call.

"Hi, Heather."

"Are you okay, darling?" she asks immediately.

Shame floods through me that she saw the kinds of things they were saying about me. It's so embarrassing for someone I admire so much to see me being slut shamed by the world.

"I guess. Thanks so much for that. You didn't have to do it."

"Of course I did," she tells me earnestly. "I've been there, and I know how much it sucks. My receptionist is currently sitting on the account and monitoring that post for me. She'll delete and block anyone who's an asshole."

I can barely stand her support, and a tear rolls from my eye as I croak out, "Thank you."

"Oh, you're crying. You poor thing. I know how hard it is to ignore what's being said about you. If I were you, I know that I would've sat there reading those comments for hours and feeling shit about myself. I didn't want that for you."

I hesitate for a second, unsure if I should ask the question or not, but then I go ahead. "Did you do that?"

Heather sighs heavily and is silent for so long that I think she might not be going to answer me, but she says, "Yes, I did. I spent hours some nights just trawling the internet to read all the terrible things people said about me. They were nastier to me than they were to Harrison, you know. Said just the most absolutely awful and disgusting things about me and how I deserved everything I got because I supposedly cheated on him with Sebastian."

I listen, astounded to hear the background of the story, knowing that I would never ever tell Heather how closely I followed it online at the time. I devoured every morsel we were fed and theorized with Jasmine about what had happened. My guilt over that is immense now that I know how it feels to have the entire world talking shit about you.

"That must've been terrible." I cringe at the thought.

"Yeah, it was. Harrison and I have some pretty amazing friends, though. Without them, I never would've gotten through it all—hey, have you got anything planned for this weekend?"

She abruptly switches topics, and I'm slightly confused by it. "Not really. Probably just hide out at home with the guys and feel bad about myself."

Maybe Nate will be ready to try anal. That would probably keep my mind off things. I can't help but smile to myself at the thought, and I'm eager to see if he is.

"You're coming to Chicago," Heather announces.

"What? No. For the weekend? I mean, I could. I'd have to book a flight today, I guess," I rattle off stupidly in reply to her suggestion.

"I'll organize it. You can come on a private jet to keep you away from everyone. I think that getting away from LA will do you wonders."

I'm still a bit stunned by her idea and unsure if I want to do it. "I'd have to check with the guys…"

"Naturally. Trust me. Sebastian took me away from Chicago on one of the worst days for Harrison and me. Getting away from where I normally was really helped."

I'm morbidly curious which day that was, but as nice and friendly as Heather is, I definitely don't want to push her for any more information than she's willing to give. I have to admit that the idea of being away from LA is definitely an attractive one.

"It sounds good. I'm seeing the guys in a little bit because we have a meeting with the LAPD about Cassie blackmailing us. So, I'll let you know after that."

"Of course, darling. Just let me know, and I'll organize everything."

I'm overcome with gratitude to have such a wonderful friend in her, and I say, "Thank you, Heather. You're amazing."

"I certainly like to think so," she says with an amused laugh.

We end our call, and I look down at her name on the screen with a smile before sending a message to the group chat I have with the guys.

I'm almost there. Where are you guys? Heather invited me to visit her in Chicago this weekend. What do you think?

I watch as three dots come up to show that someone's typing. After a minute, a reply from Ash shows up.

Yeah, we're here. Chicago sounds good, but I'll miss you.

I quickly type a reply.

I don't have to go if you guys don't want me to.

It isn't long before a message from Dante appears on the screen.

We don't own you, Angel. You can do whatever you want. Do you want to go to Chicago?

I consider the question, and I think my only reservation is that I'll be away from the guys. It's not like I've never been apart from them before, but I'm worried about being away from them with everything that's happening. I suddenly realize that I have a bodyguard now, and I look up at Darren in the driver's seat.

"Hey, Darren. If I were to go to Chicago this weekend, would you come with me? How does that work?"

"Yes, Mrs. Sullivan. If you travel, I'll generally go with you."

I frown as I think about it. "What about your family? Do you have a family? I'm so sorry. Am I prying?"

"It's fine," he chuckles. "Yes, I have a wife. We don't have any children, and she's used to me traveling for work."

"Okay. Cool, then. Heather's invited me to go to Chicago for the weekend, so I'm just trying to figure out if I should take her up on the offer."

I look down at my phone and type a reply, even though we're pulling into the parking garage for the LAPD.

I think so. I just checked with Darren, and he can come with me, so it should be safe enough. Heather said she'd organize a private jet. How fucking wild is that?

We've flown in private jets before, but it was always for some reason. Some brands or promoters had organized it. It's not something that I'd ever just book for a weekend away.

As I get out of the car, a message from Nate shows up.

Fancy. Private jets are nice.

It's only a few seconds before Ash sends a message.

Yes, we all know you're rich as fuck. Doesn't your grandpa own about fifty private jets?

I laugh aloud at Ash's message because it's true. Nate's family is pretty rich. He got his estate in Napa as a birthday present for his twenty-first birthday. Well, not so much a present as it was held in trust until then.

No. Only five. He called my parents last night to say I'm being written out of the will. Apparently, Gramps reads Loose Lips.

I goggle at the message as Darren escorts me into the building. The guys are standing nearby, and I stride over to stare at Nate.

"Is that true?"

He shrugs. "Probably. I don't see why they'd lie about it. I mean, I was joking about Loose Lips. Gramps is too important to read celebrity gossip accounts on Instagram."

Guilt washes over me that this has caused something so huge to happen. I'm horrified to be the reason behind it, and the thought of Nate's family talking about me and seeing me as the hussy who is worth disinheriting him over is awful.

"You don't seem fazed," Ash comments.

"I mean, he can't take Napa from me. We earn plenty with the band, and we have our apartment. I don't actually give a fuck if he wants to be an asshole and leave me out of the will. Anyway, Mom said she supports me, and that's really all I care about." Nate looks at me and smiles. "She said she's always liked you, and as long as I'm happy, she's happy."

I have the strong urge to hug him, but I know we're in public, so I probably can't.

"I love you, Nate," I say under my breath.

We wait for another five minutes for Isaac to arrive with our lawyer just before PR from Hades arrives with their lawyer. We're taken through the building and into a conference room. A few people in the room seem important, but a black man sits at the head of the table, wearing a highly decorated uniform.

I actually know who he is simply because I followed what happened to Heather so closely.

So I'm not surprised when he starts the meeting by saying,

"Good afternoon, everyone. I want to thank you all for coming. My name is Aaron Hamilton, and I'm the Chief of Police for the LAPD."

He looks around the room, and his eyes land on us. He scrutinizes me closely but doesn't say anything, and his expression gives away nothing of his thoughts.

"I've been briefed on the situation, and we wanted to have a preliminary discussion about what has happened before we move forward more formally with any charges."

I'm sitting between Isaac and Logan, so I reach for Logan's hand under the table. He glances over at me and squeezes it quickly. Aaron runs through a lot of the information that the guys got from our lawyer on Tuesday before he asks for our version of events.

"So, Mrs. Sullivan, you were the one who she initially threatened with the pictures?"

I nod and bite my lip. "Yes, I was. She sent me a text and told me she wanted Ash to call her." I turn to look at him, sitting between Nate and Dante.

"Okay. What happened next?"

I remember the day Cassie sent those pictures and tell him, "I was with a friend, and I said I needed the bathroom. I called Cassie, and she said she wanted to meet up."

The meeting drags on as they get as many details as they can from us about every aspect of Cassie's blackmail. I cling to Logan for support throughout it, and he strokes my hand with his thumb under the table, which is soothing. It's embarrassing baring as much of our lives for the people in this room as we need to. By the time we get to how Cassie discovered us, my stomach is in turmoil.

"So, can you tell us about the final meeting with Miss Foster?" the police chief asks.

I'm grateful when Ash speaks up, so I don't have to. "Lexi and I got there early. I was moving house, so we did some packing…"

I watch as he trails off, and I think that's when he realizes what he's going to have to tell them next because he looks at me, and his jaw tenses.

"You did some packing, and then what happened?" Aaron prompts.

I turn to look at him, then say bluntly, "We had sex."

I keep my eyes on Aaron Hamilton because I don't want to see anyone else's reaction to my words.

He simply says, "I see, and after that?"

"Cassie walked in on us," I tell him.

He frowns and looks back at Ash. "She still had a key?" He looks down at a notepad in front of him. "I thought you said that your relationship had ended months prior to that."

"She said that she was planning to return a key I'd given her," Ash says darkly. "I never gave her any fucking key, that's for goddamn sure."

Aaron looks at someone in a police uniform next to him, and they have a hushed conversation before he looks back up at Ash. "Would you swear to that in a court of law?"

"Absolutely," he tells him.

"Okay." Aaron writes something on the notepad and then looks up at me. "Continue, Mrs. Sullivan."

Between us, Ash and I relay the horrible last meeting that we had with Cassie. Aaron reviews his notes and then asks a few more questions before he dismisses us after telling us that they'll look into it and we'll hear from them.

As we walk through the building toward the elevators that will take us to the underground garage, I become hyperaware of all the people looking at us. I know that none of them know what we revealed in the meeting we just had…yet. It's uncomfortable, and there's something about it being police officers and people who work for the LAPD gawking at us that is incredibly strange.

I'm grateful when the elevator doors close in front of us, and we're hidden from their stares. When we get to the cars, I see two of the black SUVs parked a few spaces away from the one Darren drove here.

"Can we all go in one car?" I ask as Darren, and I stop in front of ours.

Dante looks around at the bodyguards who have been trailing us since we left the meeting.

Clive shrugs his shoulders. "It's up to you, Mrs. Sullivan. Three of us can go in the other SUVs, and two of us can come with you for protection."

"Cool. Yeah, we'll do that."

Logan gives me a wicked grin as we approach the door to get in. "You can go in the back with Ash, Alexandra."

I can't help but laugh as I'm reminded of the day we drove to the airport with Ash. So much has changed since then, and I have absolutely no reservations about getting into the back seat with Ash today.

"Of course, Sir," I mutter under my breath in the hopes that neither Darren nor Clive will hear me.

I climb in first, and Ash follows, settling himself on the seat right next to me. He smells of the cologne that he wears, and he casually rests his hand on my thigh. I love that it's so normal now, and he does it without thinking.

Once we're on our way, the guys talk in the seat in front of us about the meeting we just had. Even though I'm not sitting next to them, it's comforting just to have them here with me. I rest my head on Ash's shoulder, and he kisses the top of my head.

I sit up and away from him as we near our apartment. Sure enough, there's a throng of paparazzi crowded around the entrance to our parking garage. The SUV's windows are tinted pretty darkly, but I don't want to risk it.

Ash gently strokes my thigh with his hand, and I try to focus on my breathing as we make our way through. Flashes go off constantly as Darren steers the car toward the garage. A few paparazzi members get in front of the car to take pictures, and Darren comes to a halt.

"Move!" he growls even though I'm not sure they can actually hear him.

While we're stopped, other people with big cameras come right up to the car's windows and start snapping pictures. My heart pounds in my chest as I hold my head forward and let my hair fall around my face, horrified that it's come to this.

"Just move," Darren says, sounding even more annoyed, and after a few more horrendous moments, the car starts moving again.

By the time we get upstairs, I'm exhausted from the whole experience of the day. I instantly relax once we're safely inside our home, though. Dante sees the bodyguards off, and once they're gone, I strip off before we head to the living room. Nate and Ash sit on the sofa with a gap between them that's big enough for me to sit in. I choose instead to lie on my back with my head resting in Nate's lap and my legs stretching out over Ash's.

"It's like that, is it, Sexy?" Nate asks with a laugh.

"I'm wrecked," I tell him.

"Yeah, me too," he says and places his hand on my breast to slowly stroke my nipple with his thumb.

"Do you think they'll charge her?" I ask as Dante sits in an armchair across from us, and Logan drops onto the sofa next to Nate.

"I fucking hope so," Ash says darkly.

I look over at him, and my heart breaks a little for him. I can see the hurt through the anger, and I remember that he did love Cassie once. Not only did she betray us, but she has the entire world thinking that he's some kind of cheating scumbag. I hate that they think this about him when he's such a beautiful, loyal person. I have the strong urge to comfort him, so I sit up and throw my arms around his neck.

He jumps and looks down at me with an amused grin on his face. "Hi."

"I love you, Ash."

"Good to know. I had some serious doubts that you might not. I can't even tell you what a relief it is to hear you say that," he jokes.

The guys laugh along with us, which lightens the mood a little.

"If you guys are okay with it, I'd like to spend tonight with Ash," I tell them.

"Since when do you make big announcements for your

bedtime plans, Sexy?" Nate raises an eyebrow at me.

Heat rushes to my cheeks because he's right that I never do this. I just really want to explore things with Ash, and I'm hopeful that I can at least get his mind off things for a little while, the same way Dante did for me on Monday.

"Since tonight, I guess." I give Nate a chagrined smile. "Are you okay with that?"

"I guess I'll have to be. Maybe Logan will comfort me since you'll be leaving me all on my lonesome," he says with a dramatic sigh.

"Sorry, I'm spending the night with Dante," Logan teases him.

Dante laughs and nods. "Yup. It's true. Definitely not a lie at all."

"Fine. I'll just sit alone in my room and jerk off while thinking about my partners fucking other people, I guess," Nate says with a fake pout.

"Oh, wait a minute. It's Thursday, isn't it?" Dante looks at Logan, who nods. "I'm washing my hair tonight. Maybe you can spend it with Nate after all."

We burst into laughter, and it's nice to just relax with the guys. I can't help but think about the time that Dante blew Logan after that joke, though. It makes me think of Nate's conversation about Ash, and I desperately want to ask if he would ever do that. The thought of Ash giving someone head is so fucking hot that my pussy aches.

The guys are talking casually, but I'm so lost in the erotic thoughts I'm having that I don't actually know how many times Dante calls my name before I hear him.

"Huh?" I ask stupidly.

"I asked if you decided about Chicago." He smiles at me.

"Oh. Yeah, I think I'll go if you guys are all fine with it. I should actually tell Heather."

"Good thinking, Angel," he chuckles.

I retrieve my phone, then take my seat back next to Ash on the sofa and send a text to Heather.

I'm in for a weekend trip to Chicago.

I look up at Dante and say, "Yeah, I think it'll be good to get my mind off things and that stupid interv—ah, shit. The interview. It's on Sunday. I want to be with you guys when that happens."

I choke out the last few words, and Nate throws his arm around my shoulders before pulling me into him. "Get Heather to fly you back on Sunday afternoon. You can be back in plenty of time and be distracted until then. It's a win-win."

I tilt my face up to his, and he kisses me deeply when I do. When our kiss ends, I grab my phone and send another text to Heather.

I just need to be back in LA for the interview on Sunday night. I want to be with the guys for that. I hope you understand.

I set my phone aside and relax into Nate's embrace. Occasionally, he kisses me or rubs his thumb over my nipple, and he's slowly working me up. We order Thai food for dinner rather than having to cook anything, and when Dante and Ash go to meet the delivery driver, I look up at Nate.

"So, you've been using a bigger butt plug?"

He nods and immediately reaches between my legs to begin stroking my clit when he replies. "I have. You're very wet, Sexy Lexi. Does that turn you on?"

"Fuck, yes," I moan softly as I close my eyes to focus on the pleasurable sensations he's giving me.

"I've ordered your strap-on," Logan tells me, and my eyes fly open to stare at him.

"Really?"

Logan nods. "Yup. It should be here by the time you get back from Chicago. I didn't want to go into a sex shop to get one right now."

"Solid life choice," Nate laughs and leans over to kiss Logan, even as he continues rubbing my clit.

I watch them kiss and see Logan slip his tongue into Nate's

mouth. It tips me into orgasm, and I moan loudly as waves of pleasure rock my body one after the other. Nate breaks his kiss with Logan and turns to capture my lips with his as he strokes my clit until I stop coming.

When my body stops shaking, he says in a husky voice, "God, you're so fucking hot when you come." He pushes a finger into my pussy, and I pant for breath. "Just thinking about Ash fucking you tonight is enough to make me hard. Lucky fucking asshole."

"Which one of us? Me or him?" I tease Nate.

He gives me a sexy grin and brings his lips to my ear. "Both. You're both fucking lucky."

I shiver as his hot breath tickles my ear, and Nate pushes a second finger into my pussy. We're interrupted by a cough from the entrance to the room, and I look up to see Dante and Ash there.

"Dinner's ready," Dante announces.

Nate pulls his fingers out of my pussy, and heat rushes to my cheeks when he raises them into the air. "Mmm. So wet." He gives me a wicked grin, then looks up at Ash. "Want to taste, Ash?"

Ash looks surprised, and my mouth drops open a little because if I thought that I was turned on before, I wasn't half as turned on as I am now. Ash looks at me, and his eyes darken before he nods.

As Ash walks toward us, Nate chuckles. "The first day Logan fucked Lexi. I lured him in like this with how good she tastes."

I swear to fucking god that I lose the ability to breathe by the time Ash reaches us. He leans down and takes Nate's fingers in his mouth to suck my juices off them. He keeps my gaze the whole time he's doing it. I try to swallow, but my mouth is completely dry.

When Nate takes his fingers out of Ash's mouth, he asks in a seductive voice, "How does she taste?"

Ash finally breaks our eye contact to grin at Nate. "As good as ever. I wish my tongue was in her pussy."

"Do you want to eat dinner first?" Dante asks, sounding amused. "It's getting cold."

"Sure. Lexi's pussy will taste just as good after dinner, no doubt."

I'm tormented throughout dinner with visions of what happened between Ash and Nate. When Logan first did that to Nate, it was hot because I knew there was a possibility they might end up doing it for real. With Ash…it was just *so* fucking hot, even though I know there isn't a possibility it might happen.

A part of me wonders if I could order him to do it under a kink relationship, but I know I would never abuse my power over Ash like that. It would have to be something he actually wanted for me to order him to do it.

I can't help but think about how good it would be if he did.

Chapter 9

This Chapter Is All Sex

By the time Ash and I make it to his room after dinner, I'm wound so tight that I can't help but spring at him the second his bedroom door is closed behind us.

I smash my lips against his and kiss him passionately. Then I remember that I'm meant to be a Domme for him. Dante and Logan are *far* more restrained than this. I break our kiss and pant for breath as I look at Ash.

"Are you ready for this?" I ask through heavy breaths.

"Is this an answer?" Ash indicates to his obvious erection.

I raise an eyebrow at him. "We haven't technically started the scene, but just so you know, that would warrant punishment if we had."

"How com—ohhhhh. Yes, Goddess."

"Good boy," I tell him. "We can consider that the start of this scene. Now take off your clothes. I want to see my sweet boy naked."

He strips quickly and tosses his clothes to the side of the room. His cock is stiff and juts out in front of him. I walk around him in circles, taking in every inch of his muscled form. I get the same thrill of excitement at him being mine to play with as I did the other day.

I wish I'd brought some kind of implement to spank him in here with me, though, so my hand doesn't hurt if I do it. He's looking at me expectantly, and I know I need to do something with him.

"What's your safeword?" I ask.

"F Major," he replies at once.

"And the traffic light system?" I remember to reinforce that one this time.

"Green means fine, yellow means it's getting too much, and red means stop."

I nod, satisfied that he's gotten it right and is prepared for this. "Correct. On your knees, boy."

"Yes, Goddess."

It is intensely satisfying to see him drop to his knees, and now I know why Dante does it to me so much. There's something about the immediate following of my order that arouses me.

I walk over to stand next to his bed, then turn to look at him before sitting on the edge of it and spreading my legs wide.

Ash stares at me with obvious desire in his eyes as I order, "Crawl to me and worship my pussy."

I almost lose it when Ash drops his palms to the floor and begins to crawl across the room to me. As soon as he reaches me, he clamps his lips around my clit and sucks it. I moan in ecstasy as he flicks his tongue across the sensitive nub and thrust my hand into his hair, holding his mouth against me as he eats me out.

My pleasure builds as he continues what he's doing. He lifts a hand from the floor and pushes two fingers inside me. I'm not sure if I should tell him off, but I suppose this counts as worshipping my pussy since I use my hands when I do it to Dante and Logan's cocks. It's satisfying as hell to have his fingers in me while he uses his mouth on my clit, too. I know I'm going to come very soon, and it's almost strange to be in a BDSM situation but have all the control over whether or not I come.

"Mmm. Make me come, sweet boy. I want to come on your face," I tell Ash.

He groans into my pussy, and it reverberates against my clit, sending me over the edge. I close my eyes and throw my head back as my orgasm hits me. It's so good, and Ash flicks his tongue across my clit faster as my body shakes from the pleasure.

"Oh god, yes. Yes. Fuck yes," I scream as I come.

Ash pulls his head back, and when I open my eyes and look down at him, he's watching me come. I realize that it's my job as his Domme to train him to follow my instructions to the letter, and I frown at him.

"Did I tell you to stop, boy?" I growl. "When I tell you to worship my pussy, you do it until I tell you to stop."

"Sorry, Goddess," he says before quickly diving back into my pussy.

My orgasm has well and truly finished, though, and I'm mildly annoyed at him because I know I could've ridden his mouth to another one. It's still good to have him eating me, but I watch him while considering how I'll punish him for what he did. I'm actually excited to punish him, and it makes me wonder if there's something wrong with me.

I revel in the pleasure of him eating me and knowing that he has to do anything I say is bringing me rapidly toward another orgasm, so I decide to make him give me another one before I punish him. I give myself over to the sensations he's giving me as he pushes his fingers in and out of me again, using the same technique as before to push me back over the edge. He doesn't stop when I come this time, and it's exquisitely painful to have him go to town on my sensitive clit as my orgasm passes.

For a few moments, I revel in the feeling and in Ash following my instructions better before saying, "You can stop now."

He immediately pulls his head back and his fingers out of me, panting for breath as he looks up at me, his face glistening with my pussy juice. I take his face in my hand and kiss him passionately, taking pleasure in tasting myself on his tongue.

"Good boy," I tell him.

I grab his hand and lift it to my face, taking the fingers he used to fuck me in my mouth. I suck him as though it's his cock, and when he groans, I ache to have his cock in my mouth instead. I look down at it, and it's so beautiful. Thick and hard, ready for me to play with it.

I remove his fingers from my mouth and smile at him. "Did you like that, boy?"

"Yes, Goddess."

"Just like when you tasted me from Nate's fingers earlier." I can barely get the words out through my arousal at the memory, and Ash's cock jerks when I say it.

"Fuck, that was hot. Sucking my Goddess's juices off someone else's fingers was *so* good."

"Good to know." The idea of involving Nate in our play like this drives me wild, but it also reminds me that I still have to punish Ash, and the thought of Nate gives me an idea. "I still need to punish you for failing to follow my instructions. I want you to stay here on your knees. I'll be back in about five minutes."

If it were Dante or Logan with me, they would leave the room without giving me any time frame, but I remember that in the beginning, Dante would let me know how long he'd be gone, so I give Ash the same accommodation.

I leave the room and quickly head upstairs. I make my way to Logan's room and knock on the door.

"Come in," he calls.

I open the door and can't help but smile at the scene in front of me. Logan and Nate are lying together in his bed. Nate has his arm around Logan, and the TV is paused in the middle of some show they must be watching together.

"Mmm. You look good, Alexandra," Logan murmurs, his eyes darkening at the sight of me.

"Sorry, Sir. I'm in the middle of something with Ash," I laugh. "I just came to ask if I can borrow something."

His eyebrows raise, and he says, "Sure, Lexi. What's up?"

I appreciate the token of him changing my name, and it touches me that he makes that definition to put us on an even level.

"So, Nate's worked his way up to bigger butt plugs. Um, I was wondering if you've still got any of the smaller ones and which one would be the first one you'd suggest using."

Heat rushes to my cheeks, and I'm not sure if Ash would be embarrassed knowing that I asked them, but Dante and I got rid of all the tiny butt plugs I began with years ago.

Logan and Nate look at each other for a second, then turn back to me, and Nate asks, "You're going to use butt plugs with Ash?"

"I'm not sure how much he wants me to tell anyone, but it's something we're trying out, yeah."

"Okay. Give me a second," Logan says.

He hops up off the bed and heads into his bathroom. I can't help but notice that Nate's cock is stiff in the sweatpants he's wearing. I climb onto the bed, and he wraps his arms around me.

I stroke his cock and ask quietly, "What's up, Nathaniel Walker?"

"Me, obviously," he chuckles.

"Do you like seeing me naked, or do you like hearing about Ash using butt plugs?" I raise an eyebrow at him.

"I *definitely* like seeing you naked, and I'm going to plead the fifth on the stuff about Ash."

I can still hear Logan moving around in the bathroom, and I'm curious about this, so I ask, "Are you attracted to Ash?"

Nate darts a glance to the bathroom then looks back at me. "I mean, yeah, he's obviously hot. Logan knows I think that. Ash is straight, though. We've done a shitload of stuff in front of him, and he's never shown any interest, so I would never want to try and lure him into something that he didn't want."

"He sucked your fingers earlier," I point out.

"Yes, and I almost fucking came in my pants." Nate grins.

"Well, just so *you* know, he told me that he liked doing that." I slip my hand under the waistband of Nate's sweatpants to stroke his cock properly, and he groans. "He's waiting for me in his bedroom, naked and hot as fuck," I murmur.

"Are you trying to torment me, Sexy Lexi?"

"Yes. Yes, I am."

I kiss Nate and slip my tongue into his mouth, enjoying our kiss before there's a cough from nearby. I break our kiss and look up into Logan's amused face.

"I've got our three smallest butt plugs and some lube." He holds the three plugs up. "You could try the smallest one, but honestly, I'd just skip it and start with the middle one. Also, probably try a finger or tongue first like you did with Nate to gauge how he likes that if you haven't already."

I continue to stroke Nate's cock while I listen to Logan, and Nate's pants for breath are so hot.

"Awesome, thanks," I say to Logan.

I can't exactly tell him that this is a punishment for Ash, so it's not so much about whether he likes it or not. Though, I will stop if he doesn't.

I look into Nate's sexy face and say, "I'll leave you with Nate, Logan. I think you guys will have a good time tonight."

"I'm sure we will," Logan agrees.

I kiss Nate quickly, then stop stroking his cock and squeeze it once before pulling my hand out of his pants. I walk over to Logan, whose cock is clearly erect in his sweatpants as well, and I kiss him quickly before I take the butt plugs off him.

"Have a good night, Alexandra," Logan says as he hands the items over.

"You, too, Sir," I murmur huskily.

I'm in a high state of arousal as I head back downstairs. I can't help but think about the conversation I had with Nate about Ash. I know he doesn't want me to push Ash on his sexuality, and I definitely don't want to do that, but I desperately want to know if there's some chance he'd consider doing something.

Dante's straight but has both given and received head from Logan for me. If Nate is actually attracted to Ash, I don't want to push anything. No matter how hot I find it, I'd hate for it to fuck with Nate's head. As I push open the door to Ash's room, I decide to keep my fantasies to myself because it's the safest course of action.

I find Ash kneeling exactly where I left him, and I almost groan aloud because I know what it's like to be left naked and aroused while waiting for my Dom to come back to me.

"You're such a good boy, waiting so patiently for me," I tell him, unable to keep the arousal and excitement out of my voice.

He doesn't turn to look at me, and I walk over to the bed to sit in front of him again. His cock is ramrod stiff, and I'm pleased that this clearly turns him on. I hold the butt plugs up in front of me and give him a wicked grin.

"I think the best punishment for you today isn't a spanking. I'm going to plug that ass of yours so you can understand that you're mine to do anything with that I want to do. Do you understand?"

"Yes, Goddess," he says in a husky voice.

"I borrowed these from Logan. He used them on Nate, but Nate has graduated to bigger ones."

Ash's cheeks flush pink, and he asks, "You told them you were going to use a butt plug on me?"

"I had to, unfortunately. I didn't tell them why, however. Just that it's something we're exploring. I certainly made it seem a lot more mutual than the fact that I'm going to put something in your ass as a punishment, so you know better than to get your mouth off my pussy before I tell you to," I say, and my arousal is so high that I have to work to control my breathing.

Ash doesn't say anything in response, but he swallows heavily as he looks at me and his cock is still stiff, so I assume he's okay with all this.

I smile encouragingly at him. "That being said. You don't have to do this if you don't want to. You can use your safeword or even just tell me to stop or not do it, and it won't happen, okay?" Ash nods. "I will never ever punish you for using your safeword. I will never even punish you if something I want to do sexually is something you don't. So tell me now if the plug is something you don't want, please."

"I want it, Goddess," he murmurs.

"Good. Bend over the bed, boy. I'm going to fill your ass."

I move off the bed as Ash stands up and walks over to it. He bends over, resting his torso on the mattress, presenting his ass to me.

I run my hand over his ass with a groan. "Such a nice ass. I assume you've never had anything in it before."

"No, Goddess."

My pussy aches, and I give his ass a light slap, then grab a handful of his flesh. "Well, you will today. Let's see how well you take your punishment. You'll need some lubrication first, though."

I place a hand on either of his cheeks and spread them before I press my tongue to his flesh. He gasps, and I'm pretty sure he wasn't expecting me to do this. I've learned a lot from Logan and Nate, though, and I put pressure on his perineum as I tongue his hole, ecstatic when it elicits a groan from Ash.

I'm pretty sure he'll take the butt plug fine, and I wonder vaguely if I might get to fuck him with a strap-on sometime as well. I imagine both Nate and Ash bent over a bed while I fuck them in turn, and I can't help but moan at the thought.

I reach between Ash's legs with my other hand and wrap my fingers around his cock to jerk him off while I eat his ass. The room is filled with our moans and pants for breath. I can barely stand how erotic this is, and I desperately want Ash to fuck me, but waiting for it is almost as much fun as doing it. Especially knowing what comes next.

I pull my head back and look at Ash's ass, wet with my saliva, and I stroke him for a few more seconds before I stop. He groans when I stop, and I grin because I know exactly what Dante or Logan would do about that.

"Did you just complain about me stopping, boy?"

"Yes, Goddess," Ash admits.

I smack his ass as hard as I can. "You're mine to play with, and I do whatever I want to with you. It's your place to enjoy whatever pleasure I give you when and if I decide to give it." He doesn't respond to this, and I smack his ass again. "What do you say?"

"Yes, Goddess."

I'm completely high on the ecstasy of this experience, and I wonder if this is Domspace because I feel like I'm flying with how aroused I am, and we're nowhere near done. I pick up the lube and squirt some onto Ash's ass. He jumps when the cold lube touches him, and it amuses me. I rub the lube around his hole before carefully pushing my pinky into him.

He groans, and I ask, "Is that okay?"

"Yes, Goddess."

"Good," I murmur.

I continue to push my pinky in and out of him a few more times before trying with my pointer finger. Ash gasps and then moans straight after. I rub his red ass cheek with my left hand while I fuck his ass with my right one.

After about a minute, I add some more lube and fuck his ass a few times more with my finger before I pull it out and pick up the smallest plug. Even though Logan said to start with the middle one, that was for plugging, and I want to try fucking Ash with it.

I push the plug into him slowly, and it slips in easily. "How's that?"

"Good, Goddess."

I pull it out slowly, then push it in again. I'm fascinated by watching it and hearing Ash's response. He groans loudly, and I begin to move the butt plug in and out faster. After a few minutes, I'm straight-up fucking him with it, and I'm so aroused that my pussy juice is running down my leg.

Both Ash and I are panting loudly as I fuck him. I've reached that high level of ecstasy that I normally only get to through BDSM scenes with Dante and Logan. The entire world is aglow, and my entire body is alight with arousal.

I pull the butt plug out and set it aside before picking up the next size. I add a good amount of lube to the new plug before I press it against Ash's asshole and push it slowly into him.

"Is that a bigger one, Goddess?" he asks through a groan.

"Yes, sweet boy. How does it feel?" I ask, even though I'm

pretty sure he's okay with it.

"So good, Goddess," he tells me.

"Good."

I'm so glad he's enjoying this as much as I am. I had intended to plug him with this one, then finally have him fuck my pussy with it in, but it went in so easily that I can't resist pulling it out again.

I slowly move it in and out like I did with the last one, and Ash seems fine with it. He's more than fine with it by the way he moans and slightly pushes back against it to get it into him faster. It isn't long before I'm fucking him with this one as well.

I move my hips in time with the plug and go back to my fantasy where I'm fucking him with a strap-on. I reach between my legs and rub my clit while I do it. I can't help but imagine Nate with us as well. Maybe with him in my ass while I fuck Ash…or vice versa. I come at the thought of it, and I hold the butt plug in Ash's ass while my body shakes from the intensity of the pleasure flooding my body.

When my orgasm passes, I open my eyes and stare at Ash's plugged ass in front of me. I groan in satisfaction at my handiwork, and I suddenly get why Logan takes pictures of me all the time. I'd like nothing more than to be able to have a photograph of this beautiful sight to commemorate the occasion.

I retrieve my phone and make sure it's off silent when I take the picture because I know that always drives me crazy.

"Such a beautiful plugged ass, sweet boy."

I toss my phone down near his face with the picture open on the screen, and Ash looks at it before moaning.

"Do you like seeing your ass stuffed full of a plug?" I ask him.

"Yes, Goddess. It feels so good, too."

"I know it does. I think you can take more, though." I wiggle the butt plug inside him. "This seems too small."

I pull it out and set it next to the first one as I pick up the last one Logan gave me. It's not huge by any means, but it's big enough that I'll be impressed if Ash can actually handle it on his first attempt. Not actually seeing it probably helps. I watched the first few times Dante tried butt plugs on me, and it screwed me mentally. I have to make sure not to mention the size until it's already inside him.

I squirt a *lot* of lube on Ash's ass and push it inside him with my finger. I can already tell that his ass has relaxed and stretched a bit from what I've been doing compared to when I had my finger in him before. When I'm satisfied that he's ready, I pick up the final plug and attempt to push it into his ass. As it approaches the widest point, Ash's ass clenches tight, and I can feel the resistance to it going in any further.

I halt with it there to let him adjust and say in a soothing voice, "It's okay, sweet boy. You can do this. Just relax and let it in."

"Yes, Goddess," he breathes.

It takes a few seconds, but the resistance against me disappears, and I push the butt plug in the rest of the way.

"Safety light check?"

Ash moans softly and says, "Green, Goddess."

"Good."

I trail my hand back and forth over his ass cheeks as I bite my lip while looking at him. I don't think I've ever seen a sexier sight than this. I can't resist grabbing hold of the butt plug and giving it a small tug.

Ash groans, "Oh, yes, Goddess."

My eyebrows raise at his response, so I pull it back, noting that he stiffens as it reaches its widest point. Once it's out, I push it back in again, and Ash doesn't resist at all this time. He stays relaxed, giving nothing but soft moans as I pull and push the butt plug in and out of his ass. I desperately need to know how far I can take this, but I'm aware that his ass is going to be sore after this as it is.

A part of me wants to go to Logan and get an even bigger plug or to fuck Ash's ass more roughly with this one, but I don't want to risk hurting him. The slow fucking of his ass with this bigger plug is more than satisfying enough for me.

I reach between his legs to stroke his cock again, and I do it in time with the plug. It's slow and exciting, and the pleasure swirls around us. Every one of Ash's moans gives me an intense satisfaction like I've never experienced before. Knowing how much he's enjoying this, that I'm able to use his body to give us both so much pleasure, drives me further into ecstasy. Eventually, I leave the plug buried in his ass and step back from him to look at it.

"You're so beautiful and all mine to do with whatever I want," I tell him in a husky voice to an answering groan from him. "What I want right now is to finally have your fat cock in my pussy. I want you to fuck me while your ass is filled with a butt plug that Logan thought would be too big for you."

"Do you want to get a bigger one, Goddess?" Ash suggests, and I almost explode at his eagerness.

"No, sweet boy. You've done very well, but trust me when I say that you'll be feeling the after-effects of this later. Every time your ass aches, you can think about the fact that you need to follow instructions better."

"Yes, Goddess," he says in a dutiful voice, and the idea that he'll be thinking about me as his Goddess every time his ass aches makes me incredibly happy.

I think about the best way to fuck him so that he'll feel the plug while I do, and I decide to make him lie on his back. It should put some pressure on the plug and remind him that it's there.

"Get on your back on the bed, boy. I want to ride you."

Ash does as I've instructed, and his cock is ramrod straight, pointing toward his stomach. He looks so beautiful, and I'm more than ready to have him fill me. I climb onto the bed and straddle him before lowering myself onto his cock. I push him between my folds but hold him there instead of dropping myself all the way down.

"Do you want to fuck my pussy, sweet boy?"

"Yes, Goddess," Ash moans.

I give him a wicked grin and tell him, "Beg for it."

I can barely catch my breath as Ash looks back at me. We're both so ready to fuck that holding off from that is amazing. I know that I'm torturing myself as well, but it's part of the fun. I also want to hear Ash tell me how badly he wants this.

"Please let me fuck you, Goddess. I need my cock inside your cunt so badly that it hurts. I can feel your wet juices sliding down my cock, and I know how good you're going to feel when I'm inside you. I need you to fuck me until you come on my cock, and I blow my load inside you. It's the only thing in the world that I want right now. Just you."

I hold his gaze as I slide myself down, so he's buried all the way inside him. "Like this?"

"Oh god, yes. Fuck, you feel so good, Goddess."

I begin to move up and down on him, doing it at as slow a pace as I can manage. I can see in Ash's eyes how much he needs me to fuck him properly, but it only makes me hold off longer.

"Do you like fucking me with your ass full?" I ask as I raise one hand to my breast to tweak and pull my nipples while I lower the other to my clit to rub it while I fuck him.

"Yes, Goddess."

"Did you like me fucking your ass with the plug?" I ask, knowing he did but wanting to hear him actually say it.

"Oh god, yes. It was so fucking good, Goddess."

"I'm going to fuck Nate with a strap-on soon. Do you think you might like to work up to receiving anal from your Goddess?"

His eyes are clear, and heat rushes to his cheeks, so I know he's telling the truth when he admits, "Yes, Goddess."

His answer tips me into orgasm, and I rub myself faster through it as I close my eyes and envisage it. I also think about Ash receiving anal from Nate. I imagine how erotic it would be to see Nate stuff his big cock into Ash's ass. My pussy clenches around Ash's cock, and I hold him deep inside me while I ride out my orgasm.

When it passes, I open my eyes and look down at Ash, who is watching me with a dazed look on his face. I can tell he's in subspace, and I'm so happy for him.

"As a reward for telling the truth, I'm going to let you have an orgasm now, sweet boy," I murmur, my voice sweet because I'm so pleased with him.

I begin to fuck him much faster. I know exactly how Ash likes to be fucked, and I give that to him. He groans loudly as I ride him, and when I notice he's getting close, I bury him in me and begin to grind myself on him, not pulling off him anywhere near as much and driving myself back to the edge with him.

When he comes, the feeling of his cock jerking as he empties himself inside me sends me into another orgasm with him. I fuck him roughly until we both come out the other side, and I can stand it no longer, so I flop onto him, with both of us panting heavily for breath.

Ash's heart pounds in his chest, and he wraps his arms around me as we lie together to recover. When I can finally breathe again, I lift my head to smile at him.

"How was that?"

"Amazing, Goddess."

I kiss him slowly, and my love for him is so intense that my heart feels like it might explode in my chest. We stay together on the bed for a long time before I kiss his chest and raise myself again.

"Let's go get cleaned up, sweet boy," I say with a smile.

I lead the way to his bathroom, where I remove the butt plug and wash him clean, taking my time to worship his body in thanks for the pleasure he gave me. I try to put all of my love for him into this act, and he still has that glazed look in his eyes, so I hope he's still on a high, but I do know I need to help him come down so he doesn't crash.

I quickly clean myself and then dry us both before leading him back to the bed. We climb under the covers, and I pull him over so his head rests on my breast.

I gently stroke his hair as I say, "That's the end of our scene. How are you feeling?"

"Good," he murmurs. "So incredibly good."

"Was there anything you didn't like? Anything you wished I'd done differently?"

He shakes his head, and I feel him smile against me. "No. You were beyond perfect. Is it always like that?"

"Pretty much. It can be really intense sometimes, but it's so good. It takes a lot of trust, though." I swallow against a lump in my throat and choke out, "I can't even tell you how honored I am that you trust me that much, Ash."

He moves up to kiss me passionately, and our tongues dance together for a while before we part again.

"Of course, I trust you that much, Lexi. I'm excited to do more of that with you. It was *so* good."

He yawns, and I laugh. "Tired?"

"Just a little." He nods.

"How's your ass?"

His cheeks heat, and he says, "Yeah, it's sore. I'm glad you didn't get a bigger plug."

"I was pretty sure you'd deeply regret it if I did, and I didn't want to hurt you."

"Thank you." He kisses my lips gently, then murmurs, "And my aching ass is indeed a reminder that I need to follow my Goddess's instructions better."

I moan softly at his words. "God, you're so fucking hot, Ash. I never knew I wanted to Domme someone before, but I fucking love doing it so much."

"How do *you* feel about that? You said you were conflicted before."

I consider the question, and I know that if I'm honest with myself, it was getting Dante's permission to enjoy it that allowed me to actually do that without guilt. Which probably tells me a lot about whether or not I'm still a sub for him.

"I've come to grips with it. I mean, I'm still learning how to do it as we go, but I know that I was still in complete subspace on Monday night, so my concern that doing this with you might mean I'm not still a sub was unfounded."

"What exactly is subspace?"

I smile at him. "I'm hoping that you've experienced it. It can be different for people because everyone's different, but for me, it's basically when I kind of float away. Nothing matters except what's happening and the sensations of what we're doing. I've completely given myself to my Dom, and they have total control. It feels so fucking good." I give a small sigh as I think about it.

"Oh, fuck. There's an actual name for that feeling?" Ash looks at me in complete awe, and I nod. "I think I got it both times. More just now because I was more comfortable with it, but god." He shakes his head. "It was like being high, but I hadn't taken any drugs. Better than any drugs I've ever had to be honest."

I smile at him because I know he gets it. "It really is."

"Is this why you do it full time?" he asks.

"I'm not in subspace 24/7," I laugh. "But yeah. There's just something about giving over control to another person that excites me. Knowing that Dante or Logan can do anything to me whenever they want is an incredibly good feeling. It means that basically anything can be sexual, even everyday tasks. I love it. And consensual non-consent, oof!" I fan myself.

He gives me an odd look, then asks, "Like in the car that day?"

"Yeah. You have no idea how badly I wanted Logan to make me fuck you, but I was also mentally fighting it, *really* hard. I'm glad he knew not to push me that far because what we did as it was ended up being super intense."

"I got that." He cringes.

"The point is that I used my safeword, and Logan respected it. It was partially my fault for not safewording earlier. Don't ever be afraid to use your safeword, okay? I won't be angry. All that matters is you and how you're feeling. I want you to feel safe and secure at all times." He yawns again, and I smile at him. "You're tired. Let's get some sleep, sweet boy."

"Okay, Goddess," he replies with an answering smile.

I turn the light off, and we snuggle up together in the darkness. Ash's arms are warm and comforting around me, and I start to drift off to sleep when his voice sounds out in the darkness.

"Would you go full-time with me?" he asks.

I seek out and find his lips so I can kiss him to take the sting out of the reply that I know I have to give him. "I wish that I could tell you yes, I really do, but I have to say no."

"Oh," he says, sounding disappointed.

I hate having to deny him this, but I need him to understand why. I want it so much, but I know I can't commit to it.

"It's definitely something I would love to work up to with you, but I can't Domme you safely from subspace." I kiss him again, then continue, "Because I'm full-time with Dante and Logan, I couldn't trust myself to be completely in control of you at all times."

"Okay." He sounds a little less disappointed, at least, and he falls silent for a while. "So there's no way that you could ever even consider being full-time with me, then?"

My heart pounds in my chest, and I consider what he's asking. The idea is fucking hot. We could be out somewhere, and I could tease him all night long while also being teased by Dante and Logan. I can only see one way that it could possibly ever work.

"It would have to ultimately involve one of my Doms basically being in control of you, too. I could Domme you, but they would have the final say. It would mean that if I were too far gone, they would be able to guide you through the scene."

"Oh. I see."

I stroke his muscled chest with my thumb and kiss it softly. "I'm sorry I can't be everything that you want."

He pulls me tighter against him and kisses my head. "You *are* everything that I want, baby."

His switch to the regular nickname brings with it a touch of sadness. I like being his Goddess more than I care to admit to myself.

Chapter 10

The Chapter Formerly Known as the Hottest Chapter in the Book

"All ready to go, Alexandra?" Logan's low voice comes from behind me, and I jump about a mile.

I left Jenna to close up Black Lilac today, so I could come home early to pack for my weekend away. I was also more than ready to get away from the store with the week I've had there. This might have been the worst week of my life, and I'm so grateful to Heather for inviting me to visit her for some time away from LA.

"Oh my god, you scared me. Almost. I'm just packing the last of my things, and then I'll be all set to go to the airport later."

He walks further into the closet and leans against a chest of drawers as he watches me with an amused grin on his face. "I see. Are you going for the weekend or a month?"

I put the last of my things into my suitcase and check it against my list. Even though I'm only going for the weekend, Heather's a fashion designer, and I feel the need to take an outfit for basically any possible occasion.

I look up to give Logan a cheeky grin. "As if I could possibly be away from you for a month. Who would deny me orgasms? I'd masturbate every chance I got."

"You woke up and chose violence today, huh?" he laughs.

I stand and walk over to press my body against his. "I mean, I'm going to miss you while I'm in Chicago. I don't see a reason not to play with fire before I go."

Logan wraps his arms around me and lowers his mouth to mine. I part my lips to allow his tongue access to my mouth, and he kisses me with his usual skill as he slides a hand down to my ass. He pulls me harder against his growing erection, and I'm excited to play with him before leaving for the weekend.

He ends our kiss and looks into my face, his eyes full of lust as he slips his hand underneath the waistband of my trousers. He seeks out and finds my wet clit with his fingers and begins to rub it slowly.

"You're very wet. Do you want me to make you come, Alexandra?"

"Yes, Sir," I pant in response.

"Did you tell me that you would masturbate every chance you got if you weren't in the same city as me?"

I can't help but smirk as I tell him, "I did, Sir."

"It seems to me like you're begging me to tell you that you can't come until you're back in Los Angeles again. Is that the case?" he growls, and it's sexy as fuck.

"No, Sir," I object, though the idea of being edged for the entire weekend is pretty goddamn hot.

He strokes me faster, and I can feel my orgasm building. I moan softly as it approaches, and I'm so close that I know it's going to hit me any moment.

Logan stills completely in his movements, and I gasp as my orgasm disappears, even though I should've predicted he would do this. "You should consider yourself lucky that my plans for you this weekend involve you coming for me, Alexandra."

"Huh? What plans, Sir?" I blink up at him, my arousal making it hard for me to focus.

He grins at me and rubs my clit again. "I'm sure you'd like to know. All in good time. Right now, I want to play with my slut toy."

He knows how much I love hearing him call me that, and I moan loudly as my arousal builds again. Logan once again brings me to the brink of orgasm before he stops, and I groan. Logan watches me as my breathing returns to normal, and he raises a hand to my breast to stroke my painfully hard nipple through my top as he waits for my orgasm to disappear.

When it has, he drops to his knees in front of me, and I gasp as he undoes the button of my trousers. Logan pulls them down to my ankles along with my panties, then slides his tongue through my wet slit. When he reaches my clit, I moan in ecstasy.

Logan grips my hips and holds me still while he slides his tongue back and forth across my clit. I'm in such pleasure that I have to grab hold of the clothes rail with one hand and Logan's shoulder with the other to stay upright.

Sure enough, he brings me right to the edge of orgasm again before denying me again by taking his mouth off my pussy. He looks up into my eyes. Even if I couldn't see how hard his cock is in his jeans, I'd be able to see in his eyes how incredibly turned on he is.

"Very tasty, Alexandra," he murmurs.

He stands and captures my lips with his. I can taste myself as he takes my hand and places it against his cock. He rubs himself through his jeans with my hand as he breaks our kiss and looks down at me.

"See how much I like playing with my toy?"

I can barely breathe as he continues to use my hand to pleasure himself. I love it so much, and I almost come when he calls me his toy.

Logan lets go of my hand and says, "Pull your pants up and follow me, Alexandra."

I quickly do as asked and scurry after him. He leads the way upstairs, and when I realize he's taking me to the sex room, my pussy aches with desire. I follow him inside, and he takes my hand to lead me to a chair at the side of the room.

He runs the back of his hand down the side of my face and

says in a low, seductive voice, "I'm going to do whatever I want to you, and you are *not* allowed to come, Alexandra. Do you understand?"

"Yes, Sir," I tell him, but I'm so worked up that I'm not sure I'll be able to manage it.

Logan starts by pulling my top off over my head, exposing my breasts with their stiff nipples displaying my arousal for him. He lowers his head and swirls his tongue around one of them, and I moan in satisfaction. He takes it between his teeth and pulls his head back, causing me to gasp in pain before he releases it and swirls his tongue around it again. The pain is replaced by intense pleasure that goes straight to my pussy, and I bite my lip as I watch him do it again.

I'm completely lost in how good this feels, and by the time Logan turns his attention to my other breast, I'm so aroused that I know my panties have to be completely soaked. When Logan's done torturing my breasts, he drops to his knees and pulls my trousers off before setting them aside.

"These panties are basically ruined," he murmurs, confirming my suspicion as he strokes back and forth along them.

I swallow heavily and pant for breath. His touch is torturous, so good but also frustrating due to the fabric separating his fingers from me. I need him to touch my clit underneath my underwear, but he looks up at me and smirks as he continues to torment me by not doing anywhere near enough to satisfy me.

When he finally hooks his fingers in the waistband of my panties and pulls them down and off, I moan in satisfaction.

Logan stands up with my panties in his hand and raises an eyebrow at me. "You know, you're being very noisy today, Alexandra. Open up."

I open my mouth, and I don't realize what he's going to do until he does it, and I almost orgasm when Logan stuffs my wet underwear into my mouth because it's so hot. I can taste myself along with having the strange texture of the fabric in my mouth, and he pushes me down onto the chair.

It's got a curved back, and as I settle against it, Logan moves behind me and grabs two straps that he pulls forward. He raises my legs in the air and hooks one around each of my ankles, spreading me wide, then he takes my hands and pulls them above my head. He gets two more straps from behind me to restrain my hands, and I'm left in a position that allows him to totally use my body, with my underwear in my mouth as a gag. I'm in such ecstasy from this that I can barely breathe.

Logan steps back and pulls his phone out of his pocket. "You look so fucking good right now, Alexandra. My slut toy, ready and waiting to be used." I give a muffled moan, and Logan chuckles. "What was that? I couldn't quite hear you."

He snaps a picture of me, and I moan again, more loudly this time but still muffled through the fabric in my mouth.

"Ohhhh, I get it now. You said you want me to stick something inside you."

He gives me a wicked grin as he pulls his top off over his head. He drops it on the pile of my clothes, then strides across the room to a chest of drawers, wearing only his jeans and looking hot as hell. He comes back with several sex toys, and I moan at the sight of them. He turns a vibrator on and presses it against my clit, causing waves of pleasure to rock my body.

He holds up a thick dildo and grins. "Is this more Dante, Nate, or Ash, I wonder? I should get them to do models of their cocks so I can fuck you with them in here."

I groan at the erotic thought of Logan using a model of one of my other partners' cocks to fuck me with as he pushes the dildo into me. He's still holding the vibrator on my clit, and I'm rapidly approaching orgasm. I remember that I can't have one, so I do my best to hold off, but it's so hard. My body shakes with the intensity of trying to avoid it, and Logan pulls the vibrator off my clit, but continues to fuck me with the dildo.

"Good girl, Alexandra. You know not to come."

He puts the vibrator back against my clit, and the sensations flood my body as he brings me near to orgasm again before he stops. He stops fucking me with the dildo, sets the vibrator on the floor, and steps back to look at me.

"A very nice toy. I think it's important to remember who you belong to while you're in Chicago, though."

He strides back over to the drawers and comes back with a permanent marker, as well as a candle and a lighter. He sets the candle and lighter down but steps between my legs as he reaches down to the dildo in my pussy.

He jiggles it a little, then says, "Good girl keeping that safe in your pussy for me." He trails the capped marker around my nipples, causing sparks of electricity to shoot to my pussy. "Who do you belong to, Alexandra?"

"You, Sir," I try to say, but it's muffled from the panties.

"I didn't quite hear you." He smirks at me and pulls the panties out of my mouth. "Try again."

I breathe in the fresh air heavily as I pant for breath, then answer dutifully, "You, Sir."

"That's correct."

Logan stuffs my panties back in my mouth, and my pussy aches because I love how he's using me today. I've floated away to subspace, eager for him to continue the beautiful torment he has in store for me.

"What if you forget that while you're away, though, hmm?" He taps my clit with the marker, and I jump at the slight sting. "You could get very forgetful with the timezone change and all." He taps my clit again, and I groan. "I think I know exactly how to make sure your memory of that fact is kept fresh."

He taps my clit a final time, then uncaps the marker and holds the lid in his mouth as he puts the pen to my chest, underneath my breasts. In the position that I'm in, my breasts are in the way, and I can't see what he's writing on me, but just being written on is enough to send me wild.

I try to figure out what letters he's drawing on me, but I'm so turned on that I can't focus enough to work them out. He draws them quite large from the feel of it, and there are two lines of lettering.

He caps the pen and looks at my chest with a sense of pride about him. "Very nice. I don't think you'll forget now." He looks at me, his eyes filled with lust as he says, "Now. What else can I do with my toy?"

He kneels in front of me before he pulls the dildo out of me and puts it down next to him. He runs his fingers up and down the outside of my pussy, spread wide in front of him, and heat rushes to my cheeks as he inspects me.

"So pretty." He picks up the candle and sniffs it. "I think this could have a better scent."

He pushes the bottom end of the candle into me, and I almost die from how fucking good it feels. It's nowhere near as big as the dildo was, so it's not the physical sensation that's so erotic, but everything from him saying he's scenting the candle down to being fucked with an implement drives me crazy.

"Mmm, yes, Alexandra. Get your pussy juice all over this candle so it can smell like you when I burn it. I want your scent in the air as I drip wax all over my toy."

I'm gone. So far gone that I can't resist the orgasm from crashing over me when Logan rubs his thumb across my clit. I give muffled moans over and over as I come, and Logan watches me, continuing to rub my clit until my orgasm has passed.

"Naughty girl. You know you'll pay for that, right?"

I nod my head and mumble the obligatory answer into my panties. Logan pulls the candle out of my pussy and holds it up in front of me. I can see how it glistens with my juices, and I pant for breath as Logan raises an eyebrow at me.

"This has a nice amount of your pussy juice on it now, but it needs to be completely covered." He uses his hand to rub the liquid all over the candle, and I groan at the humiliation of him doing it, which heats all of the blood in my body to boiling as I watch him. "Much better," he murmurs before he picks up the lighter and lights the candle. "Smell it, Alexandra. Does it smell like you?"

Logan brings the candle near my face, and the heat and smell both hit me at once. I can smell my juices on the candle, though

I'm not sure I can smell them in the smoke from the flame. I nod my head, though, and Logan sniffs the candle as well.

"Yes, it does." He tilts the candle and drips some wax onto my stomach. "I'm going to do your stomach, your breasts, and your pussy today, Alexandra. Ten drops on each area. Nod if you understand me." I nod, and he says, "If you need to stop, click your fingers. Do it now so that I know you can in this position." I manage to click my fingers, and the sound rings out in the room. "Very good girl."

I soak in his praise, enjoying it even though clicking my fingers is such a small task. Logan tilts the candle and drops a second drip of wax onto my stomach. I jump again at the stinging pain, but I know this is nothing compared to what's coming. By the time he's done the tenth drop on my stomach, I'm panting for breath and dreading my breasts. I know it's going to hurt way more.

Sure enough, even though Logan drops the first lot of wax on the fleshy skin of my upper breast, it still stings way worse than my stomach. He's done five drops when he first hits one of my nipples. I squeal in pain into the panties in my mouth before it recedes into the usual incredibly pleasurable feeling that floods my body. He splits the next four between my two nipples before moving down to my crotch.

At first, Logan drips the wax across my pubic bone just above my pussy, and I jump and squeal at the pain. He rubs my clit with his fingers, and the pleasure mixes with the pain, causing major confusion for my senses.

He drips the next lot of wax down the side of my pussy and once again rubs my clit after. He continues this sweet, painful torture, and when he's done seven drips around the outside of my pussy, it aches painfully. I'm also pretty certain where the next drips are likely to be.

Logan lowers his head and swirls his tongue around my clit until I'm so close to orgasm that my pussy clenches around thin air, and my need to be filled is almost unbearable. That's when he lifts his head and drips hot wax on my clit. I scream into my panties and jump as far as I can in the restraints.

Logan rubs my clit with the hot wax and murmurs, "Good girl. You're being a very good girl. We're almost done. Just two more."

I nod and pant for breath as I mentally prepare for the next drop. When it comes on my clit again, I scream because it's even more sensitive now. I feel like my entire body is on fire, and my eyes roll back in my head with the pain and pleasure when Logan rubs my clit again.

He halts his movements and asks in a concerned voice, "Safety light check?"

I open my eyes and try to say, "Green."

It's muffled, but Logan nods when I say it and again holds the candle above my clit. I close my eyes again so I can focus on the painfully pleasurable experience. It means I don't have a warning before it happens, though, and I'm startled by it when the wax hits my clit. It's incredibly painful, but the exquisite pleasure that comes afterward makes it worthwhile.

Logan rubs my clit before I open my eyes and watch as he unbuckles his jeans then drops them to the floor with his briefs. He strokes his erection as he looks at me.

"I know just what this pussy needs," he murmurs before he buries his cock inside me and holds himself there as he looks at me. "Don't think I've forgotten that you need to be punished for coming before I told you to, Alexandra." My pussy clenches around his cock, and he laughs. "Does my naughty toy like being punished?"

I nod and moan loudly. He begins to move slowly in and out of me. "I know it does. I also know the perfect punishment for my toy today."

He holds himself inside me again, and I realize at the last second what he's going to do when he reaches up to tickle me. I squeal and writhe against the restraints as my pussy clenches hard around Logan's cock.

He doesn't stop, though, continuing to tickle me without giving me any relief. I have absolutely no control over my body as he tickles under both of my arms. I thrash against the restraints, my panties muffling my uncontrolled laughter until tears roll down my cheeks and Logan finally stops tickling me.

He wipes a tear from my cheek. "Safety light check?"

"Green," I mumble into my panties.

"Are you sure?"

I nod, and Logan moves in and out of me again. Every now and again, he tickles me, and he alternates it with stroking my clit until I'm about a millisecond away from coming. I don't know how long this torture continues, but I'm delirious with lust by the time he comes inside me.

Logan rubs my clit as he continues pumping in and out of me, and it's an immense relief when he growls, "Come now, Alexandra."

I lose myself to the orgasm he's denied me for so long, and my muffled screams fill the room as I come apart around his cock. My orgasm keeps coming, and it's so intense that my body shakes against the restraints holding me back even when it's finished.

Logan strokes my sensitive clit as he watches me, his cock still hard inside me, despite the fact I felt him empty his load.

"Come again, Alexandra," he says.

"I can't," I say into the panties with a shake of my head.

"Yes, you can," He rubs me faster. "You *will* come for me again, Alexandra, or you won't be let out of here. I will keep you in these restraints all weekend and video call Heather to show her exactly why you can't go to Chicago."

The humiliation that comes with imagining that scenario tips me over the edge, and I scream again as another powerful orgasm crashes over me.

"There you go. That's my good girl. Milk my cock of every last drop of cum. I want to make sure you're completely filled before you leave me for the weekend." He reaches up and runs his finger over whatever he wrote on my chest. "Not that you'll forget."

When my orgasm ends, Logan holds my hips and keeps himself inside me as he looks into my eyes. "You're so beautiful, Alexandra."

He leans down to kiss me, long and slow, as his cock begins to soften inside me. After he pulls out of me, he pulls up his briefs and jeans, then zips the jeans up.

He leans down, picks up his phone before unlocking it, and grins at me. "I need a picture of my used toy." He snaps a photo of me, my cheeks burning as he does. "And I definitely need a closeup." He squats in front of me and snaps another picture. "Mmm. It's very hot to see my cum dripping out of you, Alexandra."

He does something on his phone, but I don't know what before he pulls the panties out of my mouth. I can breathe freely again, and I'm still wildly aroused despite the painfully intense orgasms I just had.

Logan unties me, then grabs my clothes and takes me to his bedroom to wash me in the shower. By the time he's finished, I'm completely blissed-out and with a smile on my face.

"Can you please pass me my clothes? I'll go to Dante's room to get dressed so I can get a pair of panties."

Logan gives me a wicked grin. "No, you won't. You're wearing these. You can change when you get to Chicago."

"I can't do that," I tell him, my cheeks burning at the humiliation of possibly wearing my saliva and pussy juice-soaked panties.

He raises an eyebrow at me. "Yes, you can, and you will if you want an orgasm at all this weekend."

"Yes, Sir," I say and dutifully accept the dirty panties.

I pull them on, and they're wet against my pussy, which is sore and sensitive after the scene we just had.

"Good girl," Logan purrs as he takes my chin in his hand and slips his tongue into my mouth. He kisses me thoroughly and pulls me against him. "Come with me, Alexandra." He leads me to the bed and says, "Let's have a cuddle before you get dressed again."

He strips quickly before joining me in bed, where he holds me safe and secure in his arms for the longest time. I love the feeling of his warm body next to mine and, occasionally, he'll drop a soft kiss on my head. I'm at such peace that I start to drift off, lying in bed with him.

"Sorry, Lexi, but you're going to need to leave for the airport soon," Logan eventually says quietly.

I sigh and turn my face up to his for him to kiss me, then say, "Fine. I guess I'll get ready to go."

I slide out of bed, and Logan does the same. "Wait a minute. I'll come with you." I start to pull my trousers on as he gets dressed, but he grins at me as I pick up the trousers and shirt that I picked out so I'd look stylish when Heather meets me at the airport. "Don't get dressed yet. Do it in Dante's room."

I raise my eyebrows, but he doesn't give any further information. He gets dressed while I wait, and I trail him back to the closet in Dante's room with my packed suitcase.

Logan picks up a shopping bag that I didn't notice when he came in to talk to me before. "I had Killian go out to buy something to take to Chicago with you."

When he pulls two vibrators out of the bag, my cheeks burn with embarrassment from knowing that his bodyguard purchased these for him.

"Why two, Sir?" I frown in confusion because both vibrators seem to be exactly the same.

"So you'll be able to charge one and wear the other." He grins at me.

He pulls one of the vibrators out and shows it to me. It's flat and a pretty teal color. There are several buttons on it, and Logan turns it on its lowest setting before he hands it to me.

There's a low, rumbly vibration coming from it as I hold it on the open palm of my hand, and I look up at Logan. "It's fairly quiet."

"Precisely." He grins at me. "Unless you're in a completely quiet room, I don't think anyone will be able to hear it. When you're somewhere private…"

He turns it up to its highest setting, and it starts moving off my palm, so I have to grip it to hold it still.

Logan grins at me. "We can have a lot of fun with you. These are synced to my phone, and I just need to sync them to yours. Then we'll be able to control it while you're in Chicago."

My body heats as he explains it to me. The thought of being in Chicago and Logan turning the vibrator I'm wearing on without warning is incredibly erotic. I hand my phone over, and he syncs both vibrators to it, then hands my phone back.

"Pull down your dirty panties, Alexandra." Heat rushes to my cheeks at the reminder as I pull them down, and Logan turns the vibrator on before placing it against me. "How is that?" he asks, all of my senses filled with him along with the pleasurable vibration on my clit.

"Good, Sir," I tell him, and he smiles before turning the vibrator off.

"Excellent." He pulls my underwear up and shows me a small, round magnet. "This goes on the outside of your panties to keep the vibe in place."

He snaps the magnet against the outside of my underwear, and the panties drop slightly with the vibrator's weight as he does. I pull them back in place, and my breathing is shallow because I'm back in a high state of arousal just from this.

"Get dressed, Alexandra."

"Yes, Sir."

I pick the clothes up from the dresser where I dropped them and pull my trousers on. As I'm pulling the top over my head, the vibrator in my panties turns on, and I gasp in surprise. Logan turns it right up, and I moan loudly as I adjust my top.

Logan turns the vibrator off and says in a husky voice, "Just checking that works. I've set it so that it doesn't go to sleep until it's been out of use for four hours. The app will send you a notification when it's running out of battery and needs to be charged. At that point, you'll need to switch it for the other one and connect to it on the app as well."

I nod my acknowledgment of his words, and he pulls me against him for a hug. He presses his lips against mine and kisses me passionately. As we pull apart, he grins wickedly at me.

"You didn't even look in the mirror before you got your top on, Alexandra."

I blink at him for a second, then my mouth drops open because I'd forgotten that he wrote on me during our scene. He was careful when washing me not to scrub my chest so the writing would remain there.

I stride over to the mirror, lift my shirt, and take in my appearance. There I am, Lexi Sullivan, hair a complete mess, lips swollen from kisses, looking freshly fucked, and wearing dirty panties. With two words scrawled across my chest…

LOGAN'S
TOY

Chapter 11

The Sub Club

When I discover the plane has wi-fi, I connect to it at once, and I'm scrolling through my social media feed, trying to ignore the shit being said about me when the vibrator first turns on. It's very quiet, but I can just hear the rumble over the noise of the plane's engine.

I glance over at Darren. He's sitting about ten feet away near the window on the other side of the plane, so I doubt he can hear anything. Logan did say that I could disconnect the vibrator any time that I absolutely can not have it turn on.

The vibrations start making a strange pattern, rumbling with an odd rhythm. When they get a little more intense, I quickly stand up and glance over at Darren again.

"I'm just going to have a lie-down," I tell him.

He nods at me, and I rush away from him toward the bedroom at the back of the plane. I'm still a little bit stunned that this plane has a bedroom. The ones I've been on in the past only had seats or sofas.

I almost slam the door behind me in my haste to get to safety as the vibrator cranks up, and I give a soft moan once I'm hidden away. I lie on the bed and allow the vibrations to do their magic on my clit.

The pattern is still strange, though, and I wonder what exactly Logan is doing. I can't quite get to orgasm because they don't stay in a standard enough pattern to stimulate my clit the right way. I'm sure Logan is doing this on purpose, and when the vibrator turns off after a few minutes, I groan in frustration.

I lie where I am, panting for breath as my pleasure recedes. My phone dings beside me, and I look down to see a message from Nate in our group chat.

Did you enjoy that, Sexy Lexi?

I blink at the message, then heat floods my cheeks as I realize that Logan has handed his phone to Nate to play with me.

That was you?

I desperately want to stroke my clit, but when Dante found out about the vibrators, he told me I'm not allowed to touch myself this weekend. So I have to rely on them giving me orgasms. Which, of course, makes it hotter.

The vibrator switches on at a high speed and intensity. I gasp and moan as quietly as I can. Even though I'm safely ensconced in this bedroom, I don't really want Darren to hear me. It switches off again before I can even really enjoy the sensation, though, and another message comes through from Nate.

Does that answer your question? Did you enjoy our song?

I don't understand what he means, so I text back quickly.

What do you mean?

When Logan told me it vibrates in time with music, I just HAD to use Heavenly Promises.

I bite my lip and moan, both from the memory and because the vibrator turns on again. When it makes the strange vibration pattern this time, it's just as unsatisfying sexually as it was the first time, but I love it so much more. I know the song so well that I can recognize the rhythm now, and I send another message to the chat, hoping that it sends quickly.

Isn't it right about now that you make me come?

The message shows as having been read, and the vibrator turns up to a far more satisfying tempo and doesn't stop. I open the camera app and start recording a video.

"Yes, Nate. Make me come. Please make me come, just like you did when we recorded the music video." I'm right on the edge of orgasm now, and nothing stops me from tipping into the abyss this time. "Oh my god, Nate. Fuck yes. Fuck, fuck, fuck. Oh, yes."

I stop recording when my orgasm ends, but the vibrator continues rumbling against my sensitive clit. I pant for breath as I fumble to send the video to the group chat. It sits in the chat showing as sent for a few seconds, and I'm left with no recourse but to enjoy the sensations of a second orgasm before the video shows as read, and a short while after that, the vibrator finally stops.

I'm panting heavily for breath when my phone rings, and Nate's name shows up on the screen.

"Hi," I say through panting breaths.

"Was that good for you, Sexy?" His voice is low and husky. "Because I'm sitting here with a painful erection, and I'm probably going to have to get Logan to sort me out."

"Holy fuck," I gasp. "I came twice, and the vibrator kept going. I thought I might die if you didn't stop."

Nate chuckles, but Logan's voice comes through the line. "Sorry, Alexandra. I should've thought of that. I'll make sure that if any of us is planning to make you come, we're in constant contact with you while we do. If you're not in contact with us, you have my permission to remove the vibrator from your clit or disconnect it if it gets too much."

I'm grateful to have this tiny bit of control because I would never do either of those things without his permission.

"Thank you, Sir."

We end our call, and I lie there panting for breath until I collect myself together enough to freshen up in the bathroom before I head back to the sofa. I'm hyper-aware of the feeling of my dirty underwear against my skin, and I can't wait to put on a clean pair in Chicago.

I'm wired from the orgasm and from knowing that the vibrator could start rumbling against my clit at any moment. It certainly adds a level of excitement to my Chicago trip that I never expected. I scroll through social media and come across a new article about us.

WICKED STALLION INSIDE SOURCE SPEAKS OUT

The entire world was shocked last weekend when Cassandra Foster, ex-girlfriend of Ashton Woodford from Wicked Stallion, revealed to the world the band members are all in a single relationship with Alexandra Sullivan, wife of band member Dante Sullivan.

An anonymous poster on Reddit has confirmed this to be the case. On Thursday afternoon, user throwawayimnotdumb posted:

"Yeah. It's true, and she's admitted it to people. She has no shame about it. So disgusting."

My heart pounds in my chest as I read the article. Surely, this has to be someone we know, and there are very few people who would be able to confidently make that kind of statement.

The hurt that someone we know would talk to the media is intense, and despite knowing better, I continue to read.

We reached out to the Reddit user, who agreed to speak to us on the condition of anonymity. The person was able to provide proof to us that they indeed have a connection to the band.

When speaking to us, the person said, "Everything Cassie said about them all being with her is true. I don't really believe that she cheated with Ash, though. It doesn't make it any less gross."

My whole body goes cold as I read it. I hate this, and I can barely stand the shame I feel at this article, there for anyone in the entire world to read. Just knowing that people are going to be reading and discussing this is awful, along with the betrayal of whoever spoke out.

It could be Jasmine, but what if it isn't? What if someone we still trust is spilling our secrets? It makes me want to crawl into a hole and hide there for the rest of my life.

I wipe away a tear rolling down my face and lock my phone instead of reading any more of the awful article. I stare blindly out the airplane window for the rest of the flight to Chicago, completely numb.

A huge part of me regrets this trip. I just want a cuddle from the guys, and I can't have that. I don't want to be 'seen' in Chicago with Heather Fletcher. Hell, I barely know her. We have bonded over the past few months, and we talk all the time, but now I'm going to stay in her apartment, which suddenly feels awkward.

I sigh heavily because I am still grateful for Heather's friendship, and if there's one thing I'm sure of, it's that Heather Fletcher is the last person who would ever sell someone's story to the media. So at least I know I can trust her, which is something.

The only distraction I get from my thoughts is when the vibrator runs on a low rumble for about five minutes. I don't hear from the guys, so I don't know who did it, and that's incredibly hot.

I'm left with just my thoughts after that, and by the time we land, I'm in two minds about asking Heather if I can just go home tonight or tomorrow. If only because I doubt I'm going to have a good time, and I don't want to be a wet blanket on her weekend.

When she greets me at the private hangar where the plane landed, she has a bright smile on her beautiful face.

"Darling, hi!" Her face falls as she gets closer. She throws her arms around me and says quietly, "Oh, dear. I know it's hard, but I'm going to get your mind off it, I promise."

Darren is wheeling our suitcases behind me, and Heather is so positive and friendly as we get into the black SUV her bodyguard drove her in that I can't bring myself to ask her to let me go home.

As the car takes off, she smiles at me. "I've got an amazing weekend planned for us. Harrison's going out tonight, so we can have a girls' night. I figured you probably didn't want to go to Club Delirium with the others because there will be a million people taking pictures."

She rolls her eyes, and I can't help but laugh as I nod. "Yeah, that doesn't sound even the least bit enjoyable right now."

"Exactly. Then tomorrow, we're going to get the fuck away from the city. We're going to go to Sebastian's estate in Galena and spend the night there. It's so pretty there and completely private, so there's no concern about anyone finding you."

I'm touched that she's thought this through so thoroughly. It's actually a huge relief to be here in Chicago with the paparazzi thinking that I'm home in LA.

"Thank you, Heather," I choke out.

She smiles at me. "Anytime. I just want to help you forget everything as much as possible."

We stop in front of a restaurant called Giovanni's, and for an awful moment, I think that Heather might have gotten us reservations.

My heart pounds at the thought of possibly being seen, but she says, "Would you mind going in to pick up my order, Cal?"

Callum Archer turns to smile at her. "Of course not, Mrs. Fletcher."

Darren waits with us in the car, and it's still weird having a bodyguard. Someone who's just always there, hanging around you. Callum comes back with a bag of food that smells absolutely amazing.

"What did you order?" I ask after I inhale deeply.

"Arancini." She gives a dreamy sigh. "It's the *best*."

"I can't wait to taste it. I'm starving."

I'm very aware of the bodyguards in the car with us, so I ask Heather about how Serenity is doing because I don't really want to talk about anything more personal in front of them.

What if *Darren* is the one who talked to the media? The thought leaves a pit of dread in my stomach, and I don't have any idea who I should trust.

"If we have time, we can drop by on Sunday on the way to the hangar," Heather says, and my attention snaps back to her.

"To Serenity?!" I gasp.

"Sure." She smiles at me.

"Holy shit, yes."

"There. Something to look forward to," she says with a laugh.

"To think I was going to ask you to send me home when I first arrived," I admit.

She sobers and nods. "Yes, I thought you might. You looked very upset. Did something else happen?"

I glance at the bodyguards in the front seats, and she follows my gaze before looking back at me, and she nods imperceptibly.

"You don't have to tell me if you don't want to, of course," she says casually.

"I'm not really feeling up to talking about it."

"Of course. I don't want to pry. How was your flight here?"

Heat rushes my cheeks as I think about it, and I'm grateful that Heather won't be able to tell how badly I'm blushing in the semi-darkness of the car. "Yeah, it was good. Flying on a private jet was perfect. No stress and no people gawking at me."

"I'm glad."

After reaching her apartment building and heading up to her apartment from the underground garage, Heather smiles at the two bodyguards.

"Cal, would you mind taking Darren to the hotel I booked for him?" He nods, and she turns to me. "Lexi, are you comfortable with Harrison or me driving to Galena instead of us having the bodyguards take us?"

"You said it's safe, right?"

"Yup. Completely gated." She rolls her eyes. "Absolutely ridiculous, to be honest, but he and Lita live there now, so I suppose it's worthwhile. He has full-time security because he's so worried about safety. Basically, you're safer there than here."

"Okay," I laugh. "Yeah, I'm fine with that."

"Awesome. Well, Cal, if you can pick Darren up from the hotel on your way here on Sunday, you guys can have the weekend to yourselves." She smiles at Darren. "Your room is totally paid for, and you can charge anything you want to the room."

"Wow. Very generous, Mrs. Fletcher. Thank you."

Heather takes the bag of food off Callum and lets them out before she turns back to me. "I'll show you to your room, and you can get yourself settled while I dish up our dinner."

"Thank you."

I follow her to a room with a large bed and big windows that show the pretty lights of Chicago. I open my suitcase but figure I might as well not bother putting much away since Heather said we're staying somewhere else tomorrow. I chuckle as I hang up a few delicate dresses because there's *no way* Dante would stand for an open suitcase in the room if he were here.

When I'm done, I immediately grab a pair of panties and rip off my trousers and the dirty panties I'm wearing. I put both into a sectioned-off area of my suitcase for dirty clothes and slip the clean underwear on with a sigh of relief. I make sure to clip the vibrator in place again before I pull on some black yoga pants and a loose blue top.

I check my reflection in the mirror just to make sure that Heather won't be able to see the outline of the vibrator in my underwear. I'm satisfied that unless she suddenly decides to actually gaze at my crotch, that won't happen.

I quickly head out to the dining table and sit down with the amazing-smelling food in front of me.

I take a sip of the glass of red wine Heather sets in front of me. "Mmm. Very tasty."

"Yeah. I don't pay much attention to vintages, but Harrison does." She shrugs. "I just think it tastes good. He says some bullshit about the top notes or something." When I laugh and shake my head in response, she raises an eyebrow at me. "What?"

"I don't know. It's just weird hearing you swear and not give a shit about the vintage of a wine."

She bursts into laughter. "Yeah, I'm probably not as classy as people think I am just because I design clothes."

We talk about her label for about ten minutes, and when there's a lull in the conversation, Heather picks up her glass and takes a sip before she looks at me.

"Do you mind if I ask what upset you on the trip here?"

I wrinkle my nose at her. "Some article where someone who knows us has given a statement. I have ideas about who it could be, but I'm not sure, and it makes me not trust anyone."

"You think it might have been me?" she asks, sounding hurt.

"God, no. I know you would never do that. Of all the people—I mean, I know I can trust you. No, I didn't think it was you," I say in a rush. She doesn't respond to what I say, taking another sip of her wine instead, so I continue, "I mean, I was wondering if it might have been one of our bodyguards, or my employees, or someone from Isaac's office, or a family member. I just wanted to be home safe with the guys. I promise it wasn't about you."

"That makes sense. You can go home if you want to. I really won't be offended," she offers.

"No, no. You've planned this awesome weekend, and I'm having fun. It probably *is* what I need to get my mind off it, anyway." I roll my eyes as my phone lights up with a message from someone I worked with at an office job years ago before the guys were famous. "I love how many people want to 'reconnect' with me lately."

I hold up the phone to show it to Heather, and she snorts when she reads it.

Hey, Lexi! OMG, it's been SO LONG. We should catch up sometime soon.

"A close friend, I assume?" Heather says in a dry tone.

"Naturally," I can't help but laugh. "Basically my best friend ever, don't you know."

"Yeah. I got a lot of those, too. I blocked so many people because I just couldn't deal with their shit. People who I pretty much hadn't heard from since they sent a similar message after the guys first got famous."

I grin at her. "Yes! I didn't even realize it until you said that, but yup. Some of these people *did* message me when they realized I was now friends with famous people."

I look down as another message comes through, and Heather

says, "That's it. Hand over your phone, woman."

"Huh?"

"I'm taking it off you. It's no good for your mental health."

I clutch it tighter and say, "Noooo!"

"Yup. Give it to me."

Heather holds her hand out, and I laugh as I hand it over to her, only to cut my laughter short when I realize with horror that I can't give her my phone for the weekend.

"Oh, shit. I can't, actually."

She looks surprised and asks, "Why not?"

"There's an app on there that I have to be able to use." Heat rushes to my cheeks as I say it.

She smirks at me and says, "I see. Want to tell me the name of this important app?"

"Not really."

"I bet you don't." She tilts her head to the side and says casually, "If I had to guess, I'd say that Dante has a matching app on his phone."

"Hah. You'd be wrong, then."

Her eyebrows raise, and she says, "Oh, really? I was sure you were talking about an app that controls a vibrator remotely."

"It is."

My cheeks heat again, and I can't meet her gaze as she says, "Ohhhhh." I focus intently on cutting a bite of arancini, and Heather asks, "Which one?"

"Logan," I admit and finally meet her gaze.

She bursts into laughter, and I'm horrified at her reaction until she manages to calm herself down. "Oh my god, darling, I'm so sorry. I'm not laughing at you. It's just that I never would've asked you that. I was waiting until you felt comfortable saying anything about your relationships. I was asking which brand of vibrator you have so I knew which app you were talking about."

I blink at her for a second as she gestures to the phone in her hand, then groan as I laugh and hit my forehead with my palm. "Shit. Way to out myself, I guess."

"So we *will* talk about that now that you've told me." She smirks at me. "But what's the brand of vibrator?"

I tell her, and she faces the phone at me, then takes it back when it unlocks.

"Hey!" I object with a laugh.

"Isn't technology great?" she says as she does something on my phone before handing it back. "I've created a Chicago focus for you."

I look at the screen, and the only thing I can see is the vibrator app. My email, messages, and phone app at the bottom of the screen show no notifications for new items, whereas I had plenty a few minutes ago.

"Whoa."

"It'll allow messages and calls from Dante, Logan, Nate, and Ash as well as notifications from the vibe app, but no one else unless there's someone you want to add." She smiles at me. "You don't have to leave it on if you don't want to, but it might help."

I look down at my phone, no longer as dark and menacing as it's seemed this week since the only people who can contact me are safe. I add Vera, Sherry, and Jenna to the list in case anything comes up to do with Black Lilac, then set my phone aside.

"Thanks."

We finish our dinner and make our way to the living room, Heather bringing the bottle of wine with her and me carrying a second one.

We sit on the sofa facing each other, and as I settle in, Heather holds up her glass. "To an awesome weekend."

"To an awesome weekend," I agree and clink my glass against hers before taking a sip.

"Okay…I've waited as long as I can, but you admitted it. I don't believe for a second that you and Ash cheated on Cassie, but the rest of it is true?"

"Yeah, it is." My cheeks heat, and I can't help but smile at the thought of the men I love. "Go on. Ask anything you want to know. I might as well tell you."

She laughs and says, "Okay. So I read the article." She wrinkles her nose and adds, "I felt bad for reading it, but I didn't believe it at first and wanted to see what shit they were talking about you so I could call and tell you to ignore it." She takes a sip of the wine. "Buuuuut then there were those pictures, and it kind of made a few things make sense for me. So then I was just pissed at that bitch for giving the interview."

"I appreciate the loyalty," I say and tip my glass toward her.

She clinks hers against mine. "Anytime. Fuck bitches. Anyway, I figured if it were true, then I'd just wait for you to say something." She gasps, and her eyes widen. "Oh my god, I hope you don't think I invited you here to get you to tell me."

I laugh and shake my head. "No. I wouldn't have thought that until you said it. *Did* you invite me for that?"

"I promise I didn't."

"Good," I say before I take another sip of my drink, even though I didn't really think she did it for that reason.

"So the timeline is what she said, though? You hooked up with Nate during 'Heavenly Promises,' then got together with Logan, and then Ash?"

"Basically," I admit. "I mean, I didn't get together with Ash until—" I'm cut off by the rumbling sound of the vibrator, and I groan. "Oh, fucking *really*?" Heat rushes to my cheeks as Heather bursts into laughter. "I'll be back," I say as I start to stand.

"By all means, don't leave on my account." Heather grins at me and takes a sip of her wine.

"I have no idea if they'll make me come or not," I tell her.

My phone rings, and I remember Logan saying they'd make sure they were in contact with me if they made me come.

"Hello?" I answer the phone.

"Are you having a good evening, Angel?" Dante's husky voice comes through the line in time with the vibrations increasing in speed.

"Um, yes. I'm drinking wine with Heather right now, and she can hear the damn vibrator. I forgot to disconnect it."

It switches off as Dante chuckles. "Whoops. Sorry, Angel."

"Aww. I was looking forward to dinner and a show," Heather calls out.

Heat rushes to my cheeks as I mumble, "I'll be back in a bit."

"Have fun," she laughs, and I spin on my heel to rush out of the room.

Dante changes it to a video call when I reach the bedroom I'm staying in, smiling at the screen after a few seconds. "Hi, Angel."

The guys are sitting in our living room as the vibrator starts rumbling again. The vibrations increase in intensity, and I watch Dante look down at Logan's phone before they increase again. Nate and Logan are sitting next to Dante, so I assume Ash is holding Dante's phone.

"Do you like that, Angel?"

"Yes, Honey," I pant as he increases the intensity of the vibrator again. "Good girl."

It's not long at all before I'm moaning loudly and about to come. Just as I'm going to topple into the abyss, the vibrator slows down again, and I groan.

Nate smirks at me on the screen. "Orgasm denial. Oof!"

"I could hardly let her off that easy," Dante tells him.

I moan softly because, even though the vibrator is still running at a slow speed, I'm rapidly approaching orgasm again.

"There's nothing better than edging Lexi," Logan says in a low, sexy voice.

"Indeed," Dante agrees, and the vibrator increases again. "I just need to be careful when I turn the vibrator on, apparently."

I love having people watch me, and I can't help but imagine what would happen if the vibrator accidentally got turned on in front of Heather and her friends tomorrow.

"Or don't," I say with a laugh.

Dante chuckles. "Do you like the idea of me turning the vibrator on when you're having breakfast with Heather and Harrison, Angel?"

I moan softly at the erotic idea of it and imagine sitting at the table eating breakfast with them when the vibrator turns on without warning.

"You could even tell her she had to sit there and pretend it wasn't happening," Logan adds in a husky voice.

I have to pant for breath at the erotic images in my head of being forced to sit still and make polite breakfast conversation while they brought me to orgasm in front of Heather and her husband.

"You do like that idea. Don't you, Angel?"

"Yes, Honey," I admit, heat flooding my cheeks at the embarrassment of telling them how turned on I am by the thought of it.

"Alexandra is a good girl. We could make her come in front of them over and over all weekend, and she would take every orgasm we offered. Wouldn't you, Alexandra?" Logan stares at me through the screen with an almost uncomfortable intensity.

"Yes, Sir," I manage to breathe out.

"Lift your shirt and show the guys your chest," he says.

I hesitate, and the vibrator slows right down when I do. Dante doesn't even need to tell me that this is my punishment for not immediately following Logan's orders. I stand from the bed and walk into the en suite bathroom, the vibrator still on its lowest rumbly setting as I do.

I switch to the rear-facing camera as I stand in front of the mirror and lift my shirt to reveal the words on my chest.

"Logan's toy?" Nate turns to grin at him. "That's fucking hot."

"Well, she is." Logan shrugs. "I thought she might forget."

"Lexi *is* very forgetful," Dante smirks back at him.

"What do you think, Ash?" Nate asks with a grin.

I lock eyes with Ash, and I'm flooded with memories of our last scene. I wish he were here with me, so I could make him bury his cock in my pussy, which is so painful from the need to be fucked that it hurts.

He looks at me and smiles. "I think she's the sexiest woman in the world." I have to pant for breath as he jokes, "Oh, about the writing? I just wish it said 'Ash's Goddess,' too."

"Next time, grab a permanent marker and mark her up before she leaves the city, then," Logan gives him a nudge.

Dante increases the intensity of the vibrator again, and I give a loud moan as the sensations from my clit rock my body.

I catch sight of Nate looking intently at the screen with his hand moving out of the frame. I'm pretty sure he's jerking himself off, though he might be doing it to Logan, I can't tell.

It's enough to tip me over the edge. Everything about this has been crazy hot, and it all combines to send me into the orgasm that's so close, and I have to grip the vanity to stay upright as it hits me.

"Oh, fuck yes," I moan and close my eyes.

My blood is on fire from the ecstasy, and my body shakes as the vibrator rumbles against my clit. The intensity of the orgasm is incredible, and knowing that all four guys are watching me contributes to that. When my orgasm passes, I pant for breath and open my eyes as the vibrator switches off.

"How are you feeling, Angel?" Dante asks.

"Amazing," I murmur.

"Okay. Do you need a private call with me?"

"Yeah, that would be good. I love you guys," I tell the others.

They say their goodbyes and I wait as Dante makes his way to the bedroom.

"Was that good for you?" he asks.

"Oh my fucking god, yes," I admit.

"I wish I was there to cuddle you right now."

"Me, too. I miss you already."

"You know how much I value consent. I would never involve Heather or Harrison in our play without it, so I'm sorry I turned the vibrator on in front of Heather," he says in a solemn voice.

"I'll apologize to her. That orgasm was worth the embarrassment, though."

"I'm glad to hear it," he says with a smile.

I spend about fifteen minutes talking to Dante, and my heart rate returns to normal as I do. The conversation moves on from sex to Heather's plans for the weekend.

"She's taking me to Sebastian Fox's estate. There's no way I can have the vibrator on around her friends." I chew my bottom lip.

"Do you want to take it off for the rest of the weekend?" Dante asks.

"No, it's fine. I will definitely take it off whenever we're around Heather's friends tomorrow," I laugh.

"Okay, Angel. Well, whenever you need to take it off is fine. As long as it's still connected, we'll be making sure to use it at least once every four hours to keep the connection going."

"Apparently, it's a three-hour drive, and I'm going in the car with both Heather and Harrison."

"I guess you'd better not forget to let us know before you leave then, Angel. I'd hate to accidentally turn it on while you're in the car with them," he murmurs. "Otherwise, I'll have to call Harrison and get his consent to turn it on to refresh the connection."

"Of course. I won't forget, Honey," I say in a slightly breathless voice because the thought of it being turned on during the drive is both terrifying and exciting.

I flop back on the bed after we end the call and take a few deep breaths as I fight the arousal from the idea of being caught out with the vibrator. I make my way to the living room to find Heather sitting on the sofa, looking at her phone.

She looks up and grins wickedly at me. "Did you have fun?"

"Yes. Yes, I did," I laugh as casually as I can while I pick up my wine glass again and take my seat back opposite her.

Heather frowns at me. "I was thinking when you were in there having your mind blown. You said Logan had the app. I thought Dante was your Dom?"

"He is." I nod my confirmation. "Logan's my Dom as well."

She goggles at me for a moment before she asks, "You have *two* Doms?"

"Yes."

"Wow. Lucky girl. I'm jealous." Heather laughs, then says,

"Though, I might die if I had a second Dom. Harrison is more than enough."

"Oh my god. Logan is seriously the fucking king of orgasm denial, too. He will edge me for, like, a whole fucking weekend," I groan.

"Sounds like a good time." She winks at me, and I laugh.

"I thought it was going to be weird when I came back out," I admit as I take a big swig of my wine.

"What? Just because you got off in my spare bedroom?" she asks with a cheeky grin.

Heat rushes to my cheeks because it's partially that, and it's also partially because I fantasized about being made to come in front of her and her husband at breakfast tomorrow.

"Yes, because of that," I say casually.

"Nah. You wouldn't be the first of my friends to fuck in my house." She pouts dramatically. "You got your orgasm, but I have to wait for Harrison to get home so I can fuck him to get mine."

"Lucky you. He'll be home tonight. It's two days before I'll get fucked."

"Yeah, but when you do, won't it be by four men?" She grins at me.

I smirk at her. "That's true." I shake my head. "I can't believe I had an orgasm in *Heather Fletcher's* apartment."

"Oh, for fuck's sake, do *not* say my name like that ever again," she laughs. "It's weird. I'm just a person, and we're friends."

"Are you this open about sex with all your friends?" I ask, kind of curious now if she is because she's being so casual about it.

She bursts into laughter. "Well, there was that one time that Sebastian and Hayden listened to Harrison and me fuck…"

"*Excuse* me?" I gasp.

"Yeah, Seb had the suite next to ours, and when we walked in, they gave us a standing ovation."

Heat floods my body at the thought, and I can't stop myself from saying, "Fuuuuuck, that's kind of hot."

"I know, right?" She grins at me. "Exhibitionist kink?"

"Of course. The guys showed me off to Logan a few times, next minute…" I trail off in a suggestive tone.

"They're doing a lot more than showing you off to him?" she finishes in an amused tone.

"You could say that." I shake my head and admit, "They threatened to turn the vibrator on at breakfast tomorrow, and I just about lost my shit."

Heather raises an eyebrow at me. "In front of Harrison and me?"

"Yes," I admit, my cheeks absolutely burning from embarrassment now.

Heather bursts into laughter. "Yup. That's fucking hot. I'd come in a heartbeat if Harrison did that to me. Even if he just threatened me with it."

I'm relieved that she doesn't think I'm weird because we talked about her and Harrison while Dante played with me.

"I'm so glad that you *get it*," I tell her honestly.

"Oh, man. I'm just excited to meet someone who's in the scene. I've told you shit that I would never in a million years tell Ariana, and she's my best friend." Heather shrugs.

"You gotta be part of The sub Club to be cool, I guess," I tell her.

"Precisely."

I grab the wine bottle to top up our drinks and raise my glass once I've refilled them. "To The sub Club!"

Chapter 12

Fresh Connection

I wake in a state of high arousal sometime around three in the morning with a gasp. I'm wet as fuck, and the vibrator is rumbling against my clit. I lie there, panting for breath, and I wonder how long it's been going.

I roll over and fumble around to grab my phone off the bedside table to type a message in our group chat.

Who's there?

My phone begins ringing, and Logan's name is on the screen. I lie back against the pillows in the darkness of the room as I answer the call.

"Good evening, Alexandra," he says, his voice the usual low, seductive tone that sets my pussy on fire.

"Don't you mean good morning, Sir?"

The vibrator speeds up, and I moan down the phone line.

"I suppose I do," he says, sounding amused. "I just called to make sure the vibrator stays connected overnight."

"Of course you did," I say sarcastically without thinking.

Logan chuckles. "You must be tired, Alexandra, to think that's the way you should speak to me."

"Sorry, Sir." I cringe because he's completely right.

The vibrator slows right down to a rumble, and he says, "I'm not sure I'll be giving you an orgasm tonight, Alexandra."

"Please, Sir," I beg around a moan.

"Maybe. I'm lying here in the dark with a very hard cock. Why don't you tell me all the things you could do about my problem while I decide."

The vibrator starts rumbling fast, then stopping, then rumbling fast again, setting my nerves on edge.

"I could worship your cock, Sir. I could spend an hour on my knees in front of you, just satisfying you until you blew down my throat."

"That would be a nice start," he admits, his breathing coming harder and faster, with the distinct sound of him stroking his cock in the background.

"Or you could tie me up on something like the stockade and use whichever hole in my body you wanted."

"Mmm," he murmurs. "That sounds very good. I think I would spend a long time with my mouth on your pussy first." The vibrator speeds up and becomes more intense, with no pauses now. "My tongue flicking back and forth on your clit until you were in complete ecstasy. I wouldn't let you come, of course." He chuckles, and I moan as my pleasure builds.

"I know how much you love to tease me by withholding orgasms, Sir."

"I do. One of my favorite things is to watch you work hard to hold it back. To make you enjoy the pleasure longer and not just give in to what I could so easily give you." The vibrator speeds up again, and my orgasm rushes in. "Like right now. I expect you're coming very close, but you know not to come. Don't you, Alexandra?"

"Yes," I pant a few times, trying to focus on replying as well as not allowing my orgasm to hit me. "I do, Sir."

He's silent for a few moments while I moan down the line to him before the vibrator slows down again. "Very good girl. After I was done eating my toy's sweet pussy, I would push my cock into you and fuck you until I came inside you."

"Yes, Sir. Oh god, that would be so good."

"Then, when I was done, I would leave you tied up there. I would tell the guys that you were free for them to use however they wanted for the next twenty-four hours." I gasp at the thought and moan as the vibrator speeds up again. "Do you like that idea, Alexandra?"

The thought of it almost tips me into orgasm, and it takes me a few moments to be able to compose myself enough to answer.

"Fucking hell, yes. Being used for twenty-four hours would be amazing."

"Dante did say he thinks you'd be capable of it. You're a very good toy, and I think that would be the perfect use for you. Think about it, Alexandra."

I envisage it, being tied in the sex room and left there for a full day. The guys coming in to take turns with my body. Maybe some of them coming in together, two, three, or all four at a time as well.

"I'm going to come, Sir," I moan.

"No, Alexandra," Logan growls. "Make sure you don't. Stay where you are in this ecstasy for two minutes, and I'll allow you to come. If you come before, you'll be punished, and you won't like it."

My eyes roll back in my head, and I focus on nothing but the pleasure flowing through my body. I can barely keep my orgasm at bay, but Logan slightly lowers the vibrator's speed, which helps. I'm still incredibly close to the edge, especially as I listen to his moans and pants, along with the sound of him jerking himself off, but I can just prevent my orgasm from coming.

By the time some beeps sound out from Logan's end of the line, I'm delirious with lust. My clit is on fire, and my body is a bundle of nerves full of nothing but the desire to come for him.

"You are the perfect slut toy, Alexandra. Come for me. I want to hear you come."

I don't have to be asked twice. Logan doesn't even get a chance to change the speed of the vibrator at all, and I simply explode into a thousand pieces as my orgasm hits me.

"Oh fuck yes, Sir," I moan. "God, yes. That's so good." I pant for breath, and my body shakes while the vibrator continues to rumble against my clit.

"Mmm. I love the sound of you coming, Alexandra. I want to hear it again."

The speed of the vibrator increases against my sensitive clit, and I squeal as it does. I adjust to the sensation, but I know that it's not going to take long at all before I'm going to be losing my mind again.

Sure enough, my second orgasm hits me hard and fast, but this time Logan moans down the line, indicating that he's coming as well. It drives me wild to listen to him masturbating, and I wish I were there with him.

"God, Alexandra. I'm coming right now and pretending that I'm doing it deep in your tight, wet pussy. I love that you've come twice for me, and I wish I could be inside you while you're doing it. When you get home, I'm going to fuck my toy over and over to make up for not getting to do it this weekend."

I snap my legs shut around the vibrator, but I have no control over it, and it keeps going against my clit.

"Do you like that idea?"

"Yes, Sir. I want you to fuck me."

"Of course you do. Whose toy are you?"

The vibrator speeds up again, and I can barely form the words, "Yours."

"What does your chest say?" he asks, amusement clear in his voice.

"Logan's toy," I tell him and saying it is enough to get me close to a third orgasm. "Oh fuck, Sir. I love being your toy. I love fucking you. I love you writing on me. I love you using this vibrator on me. I wish you were here in Chicago, fucking me with your cock buried deep in my pussy.

"That's it, Alexandra. Come for me, toy," he growls.

It's enough to tip me into the abyss, and I pant, "I'm fucking coming. Fuck, Sir. Oh, fuck, yes. Oh my god."

When my orgasm finishes, I lie there panting for breath, and the vibrator finally turns off to my absolute relief. Logan is silent for a few seconds, with nothing but the sound of me trying to catch my breath coming through the line.

"You're such a beautiful sub, Alexandra. Thank you so much for that," he says in a sweet voice.

"You're welcome, Sir." I smile into the darkness. "I wish I were there so I could clean you up with my tongue."

He chuckles. "That would be nice. I'll take your tongue over a tissue or water any day. I wish you were here so I could clean you up and bring you back to my bed to sleep with me."

"Mmm," I say as a powerful wave of tiredness hits me, making me yawn.

"Get some sleep, Alexandra. I'll stay on the line until you're asleep."

He begins to sing "Between Whispered Words," a Wicked Stallion ballad that has always been one of my favorites, and it's one of the few songs that Logan sings lead on. I fall asleep with a smile on my face, feeling completely satiated, and with Logan's sweet voice in my ear.

I wake late the next morning, and the sun is streaming in the windows of the room. I yawn and check my phone, still lying next to me from when Logan called last night. It's almost ten in the morning. The time difference plus the late-night orgasms made me sleep in.

I snap a picture of myself lying in bed, looking a complete mess with bedhead, and send it to our group chat.

I'm living my best life.

I get up and shower before I get dressed and snap the vibrator in place against my crotch underneath the jeans and tight blue t-shirt I've decided to wear today for the drive to Sebastian's estate.

I check my phone and see replies from the guys. Ash replied first.

Good morning, beautiful. You look heavenly.

My pussy clenches at the underlying message that I read between the lines of his text, and it's just as good as if he'd called me Goddess. Dante was the next to respond.

I couldn't agree more. Morning, Angel. What time are you leaving for Galena?

Nate has replied to this message.

You're going to Seb's place? I went there once with Hayden. You'll have fun, Sexy Lexi. Super secluded. Not a reporter in sight.

I quickly type a reply.

Sounds absolutely perfect. I think we'll be leaving soon, Honey. I've slept in SO late because someone called me in the middle of the night.

As I head out of my bedroom toward the kitchen, my phone buzzes, and I look down to see a message from Nate.

And yet you didn't wake up when I used the vibe on you this morning when I joined Logan in bed.

I groan aloud at the thought of them in bed together, Nate using the vibrator on me while they fucked.

Missed opportunity. I'd better stop being rude and go see my hosts.

I slip my phone into my pocket and find Heather and Harrison sitting on the sofa in the living room. Harrison is playing a video game on a console hooked up to the big screen in front of them, and Heather is lying on her back, using his lap as a pillow as she scrolls through her phone.

"There you are," she says with a grin.

"Morning," I say with a yawn. "Hi, Harrison. Good to see you again."

He quickly glances over me and smiles before looking back at the TV. "Hi, Lexi. Sorry, I'm in the middle of a timed race."

"All good," I laugh.

"I was going to come in and wake you up if you weren't awake in fifteen minutes." Heather gets up and walks toward me. "I'll make you some breakfast, and then we can leave. I thought you might sleep in because of the time difference, so I told Seb we wouldn't be there until after lunch."

"Thank you. I'm so sorry for sleeping in." She leads me toward the kitchen, and as soon as we're out of earshot of Harrison, I add, "Logan woke me up at three a.m. to give me not one but *three* orgasms with the vibrator."

"What a dick. I do like middle-of-the-night orgasms, though. There's nothing better than being woken up being fucked." She fans her face as though she's hot, and I laugh.

I follow her into their kitchen as I ask, "Ooh. Do you guys have a CNC agreement?"

"Yup." She nods. "He only uses it for stuff like that, though. We haven't ever done sharing like you guys. I assume you and Dante have one. That's how Nate happened?"

"Basically." I smile at the memory. "I think he just wanted to see what would happen when we filmed the 'Heavenly Promises' music video, but the next day he invited Nate around to our place, and that was that."

"What about Logan? Also, cereal or toast?" she asks.

"Granola is fine if you have it and a coffee, maybe?" She nods and moves toward the pantry while I lean on the kitchen bench. "Logan and I have a CNC agreement. The first time he used it with Ash was a disaster." I cringe. "I safeworded. It was a whole thing because he'd only just broken up with Cassie, and I thought I shouldn't want him."

She raises an eyebrow at me as she sets a bowl and a container of granola on the bench. "If he was single, what was the problem?"

"Well, she was going to be sitting next to him on the flight home, and it was on the drive to the airport for a start," I admit, and Heather's mouth drops open.

"Oh, so it was *that* fresh."

Shame washes over me at how quickly I got involved with Ash

after he dumped Cassie. "Yeah, it was. Also because she accused me of wanting that and said it was what I would do. I swear, I wasn't even interested in him until she dumped him, which he only did because she called me a slut for sleeping with three men."

Heather blinks at me for a second, then starts laughing as she shakes her head. "Wait, let me get this straight. This bitch was *so* insecure that she basically manifested Ash and you fucking by doing everything she could to drive him into your arms?"

When she puts it that way, I can't stop myself from laughing, too. "Pretty much. Holy shit. I've never thought of it that way."

"I have no doubt that you wouldn't have gotten together with Ash while he was in a relationship," Heather says as she gets the milk out of the fridge. "You're a good person, Lexi." She smiles at me as she pours some granola into a bowl. "Don't let what anyone wants to say about you get into your head. From what I can tell, you guys are all happy, and people are just jealous."

"'Toxic monogamy culture' is what Vera called it," I say with a laugh.

Heather chuckles and nods. "Yup. Sounds about right. People think the way they want to live is the way everyone should live, and instead of just minding their own business, they want to give their two cents."

She rolls her eyes as she slides the bowl of granola across to me with a spoon, then turns to head over to a coffee machine. As I start eating my breakfast, I think about what she said and can't help but sigh because it reminds me of my dad.

"I can ignore what most people are saying, but did I tell you my dad called me a whore?" My voice cracks on the last word.

Heather gasps and spins to face me. "He didn't."

"He did." I take a mouthful of food and stare into my granola bowl as I chew it.

"Wow, that fucking sucks. I'm sorry. I don't even know what to say to that because I'm pretty sure nothing I can say will make that better."

I look up when her voice changes, and I can tell she's turned back to the coffee machine so I can swipe at the unshed tears in my eyes, but I don't say anything because my throat is still closed over.

"Harrison's family was really angry at him. They knew why it happened, and they were still angry. It took a while for us to get to a point where we were all comfortable again. I'm not glad he had the accident, but it did put a lot of things into perspective." She turns back to me with a cup of coffee in her hand. "He's forgiven them, and so have I, but those things were still said. Some wounds don't fully heal, so even though the relationship has been mended, they still come to your mind occasionally."

She takes a sip of her drink and looks thoughtful for a moment, then smiles at me.

"I guess what I'm saying is that it might never be the same, but hopefully, you can get past this if you want to. Even though he can never unsay those words."

"My step-mom, who has been surprisingly supportive, has told me to just give him time. I could really use the support now, though, you know?" I swallow heavily, my voice getting croaky again.

Heather puts her mug of coffee down and comes around to my side of the kitchen bench to give me a hug. "I know. Trust me. I know. I'm here for you, though. You'll get through this, and at least you have the guys to support you."

"Yeah, I can't imagine going through this shit without them." I cringe and wrinkle my nose at her. "Sorry. I guess you had to."

"I did. I had good friends, though. So did Harrison." She gets a soft smile on her face. "None of them took sides. They were all just amazingly supportive of us both the whole time, and, honestly, it's in the past. I can't pretend that seeing what you're going through hasn't brought it to my mind a lot more lately, but for the most part, I don't even think about it anymore unless someone or something reminds me. We're happy, and it's a part of our past that I've come to accept. All that matters is that both Harrison and I are happy and healthy."

"I hope there comes a day when I can get to that point."

I sigh because I have my doubts. The fact is that Heather and

Harrison *are* past it, but our scandal is something that will always be scandalous on some level. Ten years down the track, I will still be with the guys, and it will still be far outside of society's norms.

Heather takes a sip of her coffee and gives me a chagrined smile as she says, "Okay, eat up so we can get going. I fear that I'm being unsuccessful in keeping your mind off things right now."

I can't help but laugh. "Good point. No more drama talk."

"If you need to talk, you can, though. I'll be here to listen."

"Thanks."

I finish eating my breakfast while we talk about Serenity and Black Lilac. I avoid the topic of Jasmine and the way the paparazzi have been hounding me all week or that I'm glad to be well away from the stores for the first time since I opened them. When I get back to my bedroom to grab my suitcase, I check my group chat and see a reply from Logan.

You wouldn't want to be rude, Alexandra. I would've thought you would just say 'thank you for the orgasms' and not complain about being woken up.

I can't help but laugh when I read it as well as Nate's response.

I get the feeling Sexy Lexi would get a spanking for that if she were here, and I'd have to pop some popcorn to enjoy while I watched if that happened.

I know exactly what to reply with, so I shoot back my own message.

Thank you for the orgasms, Sir. I'm about to go for a three-hour-long drive. *hint hint*

My heart races as I wait for a response because I don't really want it turning on in the car, as hot as I find exhibitionism to be.

Noted, Alexandra.

I'm zipping up my suitcase when it turns on. It does a short vibration that's so short I don't even have time to truly appreciate the sensation when it stops. I wait for it to start again, but nothing happens, and I frown.

Who was that?

I wait for a response, and it's Nate who replies.

Logan gave his phone to Ash to use. He took it off into his bedroom.

After a few seconds, Ash sends a message through.

Yup. It was me.

I'm typing a reply to ask if he's planning to keep going when my phone rings and his name is on the screen.

"Hi, Ash," I say with a smile. "Are you just trying to tease me or something?"

"Good morning, Goddess."

A dart of arousal floods through my body, and I inhale sharply. "Tell me why you're not using the vibrator properly, boy?"

I'm surprised by how excited it makes me to switch into this Domme/sub relationship with Ash.

"I'm sorry, Goddess. I didn't feel right having control over you."

Interesting.

I didn't think about how the new dynamics of our sexual relationship might play out in relation to stuff that Logan had planned for me. If it continues, we're going to need to come clean with Logan and Nate, but for this weekend, I think I have a solution.

"I see. Well, Heather and Harrison are waiting for me at the moment, so I don't really have time for an orgasm anyway. However, the next time Logan gives you control of the vibrator, take his phone somewhere private and call me. Do you understand, sweet boy?"

"Yes, Goddess," Ash says, his voice full of lust.

"I love you, and I look forward to you using the vibrator to make me come. If you're a good boy, I might even let you come as well. Or I might just tell you that you're not allowed to come until I'm back in LA."

Ash groans softly and says, "I'm so hard right now."

"That's what I like to hear. I want you to stroke that thick cock of yours. Let me listen as you do it, but *do not* come. No orgasms until I talk to you next, and I'll decide if you've behaved well enough to earn one."

Ash moans, "Yes, Goddess."

I can hear him stroking himself, and I wish I were there to watch. I envisage him kneeling in front of me and jacking himself off. I listen eagerly as he does it and wish I could give myself an orgasm, but I'd have to get him to use the vibrator because of Dante's instruction. So, instead, I simply allow my arousal to envelop me as I listen to my sweet boy pleasuring himself.

Eventually, he moans, "Oh, fuck, Goddess." The sound of him masturbating stops immediately, and he says through panting breaths, "I stopped, Goddess. I was so fucking close to coming, but I stopped."

"Good boy," I coo in a soothing voice. "You've done very well, and I'm pleased with you. I look forward to Logan giving you control of the vibrator sometime soon."

I talk to Ash for a few minutes afterward until it seems like his breathing is back to normal, but I have to change my underwear before I head out. They're wet from my call with Ash, and I want to be comfortable on the drive to Galena.

I smile at Heather and Harrison when I find them back in the same position they were in earlier. They look so comfortable and relaxed together. It's obvious how in love with one another they are as Harrison absentmindedly strokes Heather's head, and she gets a smile on her face as she looks at her phone.

"Hey, guys," I say, stopping at the entrance to the living room with my suitcase beside me. "I'm ready to leave."

Heather jumps and looks up at me before smiling. "Cool. We can get going then. We'll be a bit later than expected, but that's okay."

I frown at them as they start to leave the apartment. "Don't you guys need a suitcase?"

"Nah. Harrison's had clothes in his room at Sebastian's since they recorded *Games We Play* there. We visit so often that I have stuff there now, too."

"Oh, makes sense," I say as Harrison locks the apartment door behind us.

We head down to the parking garage and pack my suitcase into the back of Harrison's black Tesla.

"Duck your head when we leave, Lexi," Harrison warns me. "Occasionally, some paparazzi will hang around here."

I do as told, but I can't relax until we're safely on the interstate toward Sebastian Fox's estate. I'm a little nervous about spending time with Heather's friends, but I'm hopeful they'll all be as nice as she and Harrison have been. If they aren't, I suppose it will be better than being hassled by the paparazzi in Los Angeles. At least, I hope it will be.

Chapter 13

I'm Just Like You

It's a bit over three hours later when we pull onto a private road that leads up to a big estate with massive wrought-iron gates barring entry. The gates have words on them in large gold script.

Maison De L'amour Et De La Musique

"Whoa," I say as we pull up to a security guard booth in front of the gates.

Heather turns in her seat to grin at me. "Right? It's ostentatious as fuck. Seb's so over-the-top."

Harrison speaks to a security guard who opens the gates and lets us through. As they swing open, I look at the rolling green fields ahead of us before we drive along a tree-lined road up to a big house.

Harrison uses a remote to open a door for the garage, then parks his car next to a red Ferrari that I recognize as Sebastian's from pictures I saw of him in it with Heather.

We enter an entryway, and Heather calls out, "Hello?"

"We're in here," a woman's voice calls, and we follow it into a living room strewn with colorful toys.

Sebastian Fox is sitting on a sofa next to his fiancée, Lolita Ciccone, with his arm around her shoulders. On the television in front of them is a children's show, and playing on a rug is a little girl with her black hair tied back in a small ponytail.

"Hi, guys," Lita says as she looks over at us.

The little girl looks up, and her face splits into a smile, her bright blue eyes full of delight as she runs over to Harrison with a cry of, "Unca Harra!"

He laughs and picks her up to cuddle her. "Hi, Mira." She wraps her arms around his neck, and he kisses her cheek. "How are you, baby girl?"

"Tell Uncle Harrison about your new fire truck, Mira," Lita says with a smile.

"Fuck!" Mirabella says.

I can't stop the snort of laughter that escapes me, and Heather chuckles as well.

"Fire truck, Mira," Lita corrects her, and I don't know how she manages to do it with a straight face.

"Fuck!" Mirabella repeats.

"A new fire truck, you say?" Harrison asks with a grin as he sets the little girl down. "Where is it, Mira?"

She takes his hand and leads him over to a wooden fire truck. Harrison kneels on the floor next to her, and they start to play together.

"Mira's *obsessed* with it, and we think it's funny as fuck the way she says it," Sebastian laughs.

Heather walks over to hug him and Lita while I hover at the entrance to the living room, unsure where I really fit in this picture until Heather turns to smile at me.

"Guys, you've met Lexi Sullivan before. She's Dante Sullivan's wife, and..." she trails off and frowns at me for a second.

I realize that she's probably trying to figure out how to explain my relationship with Wicked Stallion. It's always been clear-cut before. Dante's wife. Friends with the rest of the band members. However, if I'm not willing to tell people I'm in a relationship with the others, am I diminishing their position in my life to meet society's standards?

I know this isn't the time to figure it out, so I finish her sentence for her with, "And visiting Heather in Chicago this weekend to get away from Los Angeles."

"Oh, yes, I read those articles about you." Lita says it very matter-of-factly. "People must be going crazy trying to get pictures of you with the guys."

I blink at her for a second because I wasn't expecting one of Heather's friends to outright say they've read the articles about me. "Um, yeah. They have been."

"Sorry to hear that. It sucked when I was pregnant with Mira." She nods to the little girl. "They followed us everywhere. It was the worst."

"Well, at least they can't get to us here, princess." Sebastian pulls Lita closer to him for a hug, then he smiles at me. "I'm Sebastian Fox. This is my fiancée, Lita Ciccone. That's our baby girl, Mirabella, but we call her Mira, and you already know Heather Fletcher, who is apparently terrible at introductions."

He smirks at Heather, who laughs. "I was getting around to it."

"You were taking your sweetass time, Lover," he teases her, causing my eyebrows to fly up into my hairline.

It's such a strange nickname, especially in front of his fiancée, who is sitting right next to him on the sofa and doesn't bat an eyelid at it.

"Shut up. Anyway, can someone show Lexi which room she's staying in tonight?"

Sebastian shrugs and stands up. "Sure. Follow me, Lexi."

"I'm just going upstairs with Seb and Lexi, Honey." Heather smiles at Harrison. "You're clearly very busy right now, anyway."

He looks up from where he's currently following Mirabella's fire truck with a wooden ambulance while making the sound of the siren, and he grins at Heather. "Okay, Angel."

We head back into the entryway, and Sebastian carries my suitcase upstairs, which I thank him for. He leads us to a room, and I leave my suitcase in the room again because I figure there's no point in unpacking for a single night.

"I'll just freshen up, then come downstairs," I tell them with a smile.

After Heather and Sebastian leave, I quickly remove the vibrator from my underwear, grateful that nobody turned it on while I was downstairs. I put it on charge and disconnect it from the app before sending a message to the group chat.

Arrived safely at Sebastian's estate. I've turned the vibrator off for now. It'll be back on later.

I head back downstairs, and I reach the living room as everyone else is leaving it.

"Oh, where are we going?" I ask them.

Sebastian is carrying Mirabella, and he smiles at me. "I'm taking Mira upstairs to put her down for her nap while you guys have some lunch."

"Heather said you haven't eaten since breakfast," Lita says as we follow her through the house to the kitchen.

"True, but I had a very late breakfast because I'm still on California time."

"Yeah, but Harrison and I ate at a normal breakfast time." Heather nudges me with her elbow.

Heat floods to my cheeks. "Oh, damn. Of course you did. Sorry!"

"All good," Harrison says, giving me a good-natured smile.

Lita makes us sandwiches, and it's almost strange to sit at the ornate dining table eating something so simple, but I don't comment on it. For the most part, I let the conversation happen around me.

Sebastian comes back from putting Mirabella down for her nap, and we've been sitting there for about another twenty minutes when two people appear in the doorway.

Heather looks up and exclaims when she sees them, "Hayden! Tati!"

She jumps up and throws her arms around the tall man with brown hair and eyes, who is smiling as he hugs her back. "Hi, Heather."

"Hi, Tati," Heather says as she moves on to a tiny woman with long, ice-blonde hair and blue eyes.

"Hey," she says.

Heather turns back toward me and smiles. "Lexi, this is Hayden and Tati Vega. Guys, you've met Lexi Sullivan before. She's visiting me from Los Angeles this weekend."

I wave at the newcomers, and when they come to sit at the table with us, Tatiana sits next to me. I smile at her before I finish the last of my sandwich.

"Any idea when Gabriel and Ariana will be here? I should text Ariana and find out where they are," Heather says to Sebastian.

He shakes his head. "Gabriel said that Carys has an ear infection, so they can't come."

"Oh, that's a shame. I'll have to go see her tomorrow afternoon after I drop Lexi at the airport."

When we've finished eating, Lita takes our plates away, and Sebastian asks, "Who wants to go for a swim?"

"I'm down," Tatiana says.

Hayden grins at her and says, "Me, too."

Heather and Harrison agree, then everyone looks at me, and I shrug my shoulders. "Sure. Sounds like fun."

We traipse upstairs to get swimsuits on, and I'm grateful I brought a bikini with me so I can go swimming. It's not until after I've stripped off and actually pulled the bikini on that I catch sight of myself in the mirror and groan.

LOGAN'S
TOY

Despite the fact that the sight of those words from Logan claiming me as his sends a shot of arousal zinging throughout my body, there is *no way* that I can go swimming like this.

I grab my phone and snap a picture that I send to our group chat.

This could be a bit of a problem.

I wrap a big, fluffy towel around myself and then head out of the room. I hover in the hallway because I'm unsure which room

Heather and Harrison are in, nor which room Sebastian and Lita's baby is sleeping in, so I call Heather from my phone.

"Lexi?" she answers, sounding confused.

"Yeah. Um, could you come to my room for a second?" I beg her. "I don't know where your room is or if Harrison's decent, and I didn't want to wake Mira up."

Heather's head pops out of a doorway a few rooms down the big hallway. "I'm here."

I walk over to her, and she waves me into the room. Harrison is standing nearby, shirtless and wearing swim trunks low on his hips. He gives me a smile, and heat rushes to my cheeks because there's no way that I can explain my issue in front of him.

"What's up?" Heather asks.

"I was wondering if I could borrow a swimsuit," I ask.

"Sure." Heather gives me a bright smile, and I trail her to a closet nearby.

She opens a drawer and pulls out a blue bikini with white stripes, and I shake my head. "Sorry. It's very nice, but I was wondering if you have a one-piece I could use."

"Oh. Nope, sorry. I only wear bikinis." She grins at me and says quietly, "It's a Harrison rule."

I cringe and say with a sigh. "Okay. I won't be able to go swimming with you guys."

"Huh? Why not?"

I'm so fucking embarrassed, but I know that if anyone will understand, it's Heather. I'm clutching the towel tightly around me for modesty, but with my back to the room Harrison's in behind me, I feel safe enough to open the towel for Heather.

She looks at my body for a second before she bursts into laughter. "Holy fucking shit, Lexi. You can't go swimming like that."

"Right?!" I groan.

She's laughing so hard now that she has tears in her eyes. "I'm sorry, but that's hilarious. You have the best Doms ever. Harrison needs to up his game. He's never made me travel somewhere with writing on me. Come with me, and we'll get you sorted. Lita will almost certainly have a one-piece bathing suit for you to wear."

We enter the bedroom with Heather still chuckling in amusement, and Harrison asks, "What's so funny, Angel?"

She grins at him, then looks at me. "I don't know how much Lexi's comfortable telling you."

"Logan wrote something on me before I left LA," I tell him with my cheeks absolutely burning from embarrassment. "I need to wear a one-piece, but I packed before the writing happened, and I didn't think about it until I got my swimsuit on."

"I see." Harrison chuckles, clearly amused by my predicament.

"Don't go getting any ideas," Heather says with a grin.

He raises an eyebrow at her. "I'll get all the ideas I want, Angel. I think you'll find you can't stop me."

"Yes, Honey," she says so quickly that my gaze flickers between them.

"Holy shit," I say slowly before I can stop myself. "Dante and I do that, too."

They both look at me with wide eyes before Harrison asks a little too casually, "Do what?"

"Use our pet names in front of people, but it's actually a Dom/sub thing. You can't tell me that's not what that was."

Heather grins at me. "Our friends have figured it out."

"I probably wouldn't even have commented or noticed if we didn't do it as well," I laugh.

Heather takes me by the arm and guides me toward the door. "I'd appreciate it if you didn't say anything in front of my friends."

"Of course not," I say with a gasp. "I would never. The sub Club has to stick together."

She grins at me. "Exactly."

Heather makes a 'shh' sound and puts her finger to her lips as we pass what I assume is Mirabella's room. She quietly raps on a door, and Sebastian opens it a few moments later.

"What do you need, Lover?" he asks Heather.

I can't help but look over at his fiancée, who is sitting on the end of the bed, but she still doesn't seem fazed at all by it.

"Lexi needs to borrow a swimsuit off Lita." Heather pushes past Sebastian, who steps aside and lets me past him.

"Why me?" Lita asks as she looks up at us.

"I was hoping you have a one-piece I could borrow. Heather only has bikinis."

"Oh, sure. Not a problem," Lita says to my relief.

Sebastian laughs. "I don't think I've ever seen Heather wear anything other than a bikini. Do you even own a one-piece swimsuit, Lover?"

"Nope. Never have. Never will." She shakes her head.

"What about when you're old and in a nursing home?" He raises an eyebrow at her.

"God, no. I'll probably insist on skinny-dipping because I'll be too old to give any fucks by that point."

We all laugh as Lita hands me two swimsuits. "I'm not sure which one will fit or which you'll like better."

"Thank you so much," I say, grateful as hell that she had something I could borrow.

"Not a problem." She smiles at me.

"We'll see you guys downstairs," Heather says as we leave the room.

"Thank fuck," I breathe quietly as we head back toward our rooms.

"If I don't get written on in the next week, I'm going to be quite sulky," Heather says with a fake pout.

"It's *so* fucking hot, and from what Harrison said to you"—I fan myself dramatically—"he seemed into the idea."

We're out the front of their room, and she grins at me. "Yup. Now to see if I can goad him into giving me a spanking later."

"Do you like playing with fire?" I laugh.

"Yup. Don't you?"

"Of course." I'm still laughing as Heather enters their bedroom, and I continue to mine.

When I get inside, I glance down at my phone to see a reply from Nate.

Looking hot, Sexy Lexi. Are you actually going swimming like that?

I laugh as I write my reply.

Fuck, no. Heather's friend Lita loaned me a one-piece to wear.

I strip the bikini off and hold up the two swimsuits. I think the black one would probably hide the writing better, but it's a bit too loose on me when I put it on, so I put the red one on instead. It's a bit sheer in places, but it fits much better, and the writing looks like I might just have a tattoo on my chest. I snap a pic and send it to the guys.

Fit to go swimming in polite company.

It takes a few seconds, but Logan replies to my text.

Very beautiful, Alexandra. I like that I can still see that you're mine, but no one else should be able to read the words.

When a text from Nate comes through straight afterward, I groan aloud.

I can personally confirm that he likes the look of you, Sexy Lexi.

A dart of arousal shoots to my pussy because it makes me think about all manner of things they might be doing to one another today. I'm also excited that when I get back to LA, Nate and I are going to try pegging. I lock my phone and head out of my room with my pussy throbbing.

"Nice," Heather says with a smirk as she looks at me. "I think that swimsuit becomes a little see-through, though."

"I was hoping it would just look like a tattoo." I cringe.

"I'm sure it'll be fine," Harrison says with a reassuring smile. "Just put a towel on as soon as you get out of the pool."

I trail Heather and Harrison to a big indoor pool downstairs, where we find Sebastian, Lita, Hayden, and Tatiana already in the pool. Lita has a monitor near the edge of the pool that I assume is to keep an eye on their little girl.

The pool area is magnificent and rivals Nate's one in Napa. It's lit with underwater lights at the edges, and I recognize the Cruise Control symbol tiled into the bottom of the pool. There's a spa at the side of the room with steps to get into it from the pool and an impressive gym that overlooks the pool area behind a door. With the massive floor-to-ceiling windows showing the gray sky outside, the heat in the room is disconcerting.

When I walk down the steps into the pool, the temperature is beautiful and warm, causing me to smile in satisfaction. "Ooh, toasty."

"Lita likes it warmer than I'd have it," Sebastian says with a grin at his fiancée.

"It's not me." She shrugs. "It's Mira. If it's any colder, she ends up shivering like mad after about ten minutes."

"Whatever the reason. I love it." I smile at the couple.

We hang out in the pool for a while before I end up in the spa, which is even warmer and more enjoyable than the pool, with Heather and Tatiana. Harrison and Hayden go to make everyone cocktails, and I'm sipping a margarita when I smile at Tatiana.

"So everyone knows Heather has been friends with the guys forever, but how did you meet Hayden?"

Tatiana grins at Heather, who turns to me. "She was his bodyguard."

"I'm sorry, *what?!*" I choke on my drink and have a coughing fit for a few seconds.

Heather pats my back as she and Tatiana laugh. "Tatiana's a certified badass."

I look at the tiny woman and shake my head. "I did *not* expect that answer."

"I wasn't technically his bodyguard. I'm in the business of specialist security. I'm semi-retired now, though." She looks over at Hayden, where he's hanging out in the pool with the others, and smiles. "I only take certain contracts now. If something particularly intrigues me, I'll take the contract, but I'm a lot choosier these days.

I don't really want to take some of the risks I was willing to take in the past."

"She's going to give me another niece or nephew soon, I think," Heather teases her.

Tatiana rolls her eyes and I laugh, "What about you, Heather? When are you and Harrison going to have babies?"

"Babies? Me? God, no. I'm far too busy for crotch goblins. Don't get me wrong. I love babies for *other* people. Personally, I just love being able to play with them and have all the fun, then hand them back for all the hard bits." She grins at me. "I happen to know that Hayden's always wanted babies, though. That's why I tease Tati about it."

"She's very worried about my 'old eggs.'" Tatiana smirks. "Just because I'm turning forty soon."

Heather makes a ticking sound, and Tatiana nudges her with her arm.

"That's not old. My aunt had my cousin at forty-six." I shrug.

"Exactly," Tatiana says. "I have no qualms about turning forty. I bet Heather will have a mid-life crisis when she does."

"Luckily, that's a good six years away, so I don't have to worry." Heather wipes her brow as though she's relieved, and we all laugh.

"I'm not looking forward to turning thirty later this year," I cringe.

"Oh, please," Heather says. "I'd love to be turning thirty again." Her smile slips, and she adds, "Okay, maybe not. Maybe, I'll just be grateful I'm not old like Tati."

Heather gives her friend a cheeky grin, and Tatiana raises an eyebrow back at her. "Did you forget the part where you told Lexi I'm a certified badass, Heather Fletcher? I might be old, but I'm *definitely* not too old to drown you in this hot tub and make it look like an accident."

"Have I told you how glowing and *young* you look, Tati?" Heather says innocently. "Not a day over twenty-five. Younger than Lexi for sure and probably the most beautiful woman I've ever come across." Heather puts her hand to her mouth and stage whispers to me, "*I'm not one hundred percent sure she wouldn't do it. I do know she's capable of it.*"

Tatiana laughs and pretends she didn't hear the last part. "That's better."

"Anyone want their drink topped up?" I ask after I take a sip of the last of my margarita.

Tatiana nods, but Heather's drink is almost full, so I take the two glasses over to a jug on a table at the side of the room and pour us fresh glasses, smiling at the people in the pool as I walk back to the spa.

By the time we've finished in the pool, had dinner, and watched a movie in Sebastian's theater room, most of us are ready for bed. The others because it's almost midnight and me because I'm nowhere near tired, but I'm hopeful that when I connect the vibrator in my bedroom, someone will use it on me at some point.

When I place it in my panties and connect it again, I message the group chat.

Safely in my bedroom for the night. Vibrator is connected.

Nothing happens for a while, not even a text, and I think nobody's going to use it until my phone starts ringing and Ash's name is on the screen.

"Hello, sweet boy," I answer his video call, smiling at the sexy man on the screen.

"Evening, Goddess. Sorry for the delay. We were playing poker, and it was a few hands before Dante saw his phone. I asked Logan if I could take the app and folded pocket aces to come to play with you."

I chuckle. "That's quite the hand to fold."

"You're worth it," he says with a grin.

"Damn straight I am. Show me your cock, boy. Is it hard for me?"

He moves the phone to show me his stiff erection, and I love that he's hard for me already. I don't tell him to do anything, and I'm pleased when he doesn't make any move to speak or touch himself.

"Very nice. Turn the vibrator on, boy."

"Yes, Goddess."

It switches on but doesn't change from the lowest setting, and I smile. "Turn it up. I want you to watch me while I come. Flip the camera on the call so I can watch your cock while I come."

He does as instructed, and I'm very aware that he's watching me, but I'm entranced by watching his cock. When I bite my lip and moan, his cock jerks. I love seeing his reaction to watching me, and it mixes with the pleasure flooding through my body.

"Mmm. I like that, boy. I wish you were here with me. I would have you worship my pussy." His cock twitches again, and he groans. "Do you like that idea?"

"Yes, Goddess," he pants.

"I do, too. I can practically feel your face buried in my pussy. Your tongue on my clit and maybe your fingers fucking me if I felt like having you do that. I could do anything with your body." I moan as my orgasm approaches, and I say, "Turn the vibrator up and stroke yourself, boy. Do *not* come. I want to watch you do it while I have an orgasm."

I can't withhold a moan as he wraps his fist around his cock and begins to pump it. The rumbling from the vibrator increases against my clit, and it doesn't take long before I'm lost to the orgasm that hits me.

"Oh fuck, yes, boy." I almost fuck up and call him 'Ash' but catch myself in time. "That's so good. I'm coming."

My body shakes as I orgasm, and I watch Ash pumping his swollen cock in his fist as it passes. I don't tell him to turn the vibrator down because I want a second orgasm, so I just enjoy the sight in front of me as well as Ash's pants for breath and groans while I writhe from the intensity of the vibrations against my sensitive clit.

I already know what I'm going to do, and it excites me to see how Ash responds to it. So when my orgasm is nearing again, I moan before I give Ash an instruction.

"I'm going to come again, boy, but you don't get to come until

I'm back in the apartment."

He gives a soft, disappointed groan, and his hand stills for a moment on his cock before he continues pumping it, but slower than before.

I look directly into the camera and raise an eyebrow at him. "Do you understand?"

"Yes, Goddess."

"Who do your orgasms belong to?"

Even asking the question is wildly erotic, but I tip into orgasm when Ash answers, "You, Goddess."

"Yes, boy," I moan. "That's right. Fuck, yes. Your orgasms are fucking mine. I get to come, and you don't, but you'll come tomorrow when I'm home with you. I'll watch while you blow your load after waiting over half a day for it."

My body is shaking again, and I close my eyes as I imagine Ash coming in my mouth, on my chest, in my pussy. Just knowing that he has to wait for it because I told him to drives me wild. I know that when I let him come tomorrow, it's going to be a fucking huge orgasm for him.

When my orgasm has passed, I open my eyes and look at the screen. "Turn the vibrator off and get your hand off *my* cock, boy." He does both things, and his cock remains in the frame, stiff as hell. "So pretty. I wish I had my lips wrapped around it right now." It jerks, and I smile. "I want you to send me a picture of your cock any time you get an erection."

"Yes, Goddess," he says dutifully.

"Switch the camera again so I can see your face." He does as I said, and I smile at him. "You were a very good boy. I look forward to rewarding you tomorrow."

"Thank you," he says.

I tilt my head at him. "How do you feel?"

"Horny as fuck, Goddess."

I smirk at him. "That's how I like you. I know this is going to be hard, but trust me when I say that orgasm denial makes it so much more worthwhile when you finally get one."

"I hope so," he groans. "I'm not sure how I'll lose this erection."

I remember what I was thinking about earlier and realize that making him wait to orgasm is coming close to a full-time kink relationship.

I frown and sigh. "So, I think we probably need to involve Dante in our relationship if you're okay with that. I don't want you to make any decisions right now because you're not in the frame of mind when we've just played. Me banning you from orgasms is coming close to full-time kink. It certainly extends our scenes beyond a definitive start and end point, so for your safety, I think we need to involve Dante."

"I see what you're saying."

I'm not sure how he's going to react to this, so I take a deep breath and add, "We probably also need to consider telling Logan and Nate since you didn't want to use the vibrator on me without my permission. I think that Logan will understand, and he'll be able to accommodate you in his plans."

Ash is quiet when I finish talking, and I don't pressure him to respond.

Eventually, he says quietly, "I don't know. I guess I'm a little bit embarrassed, if I'm honest."

"Okay. Why is that?"

He looks away from the screen. "I guess because I like giving you control so much. At one point, I wanted to be your Dom, but I like this even more than the night you gave me full control. I don't want the guys to think less of me because I'm not 'manly' or something."

His cheeks flush pink, and I think I might love him even more for being so honest with me. I know this is his issue to deal with, but I know the guys will never judge him for this as well.

"Ash, look at me," I say, and he turns his face back to the screen. "Dante and Logan are both into kink. They're hardly going to judge you for liking what you like." He opens his mouth, and I shake my head, cutting him off before he can say Nate's name. "And Nate wouldn't, either. He was so scared about telling you he's bisexual because he thought you might judge him."

"What the fuck? Of course, I wouldn't," Ash says quickly.

"Precisely. So what makes you think that he'll think less of you for liking what you like sexually? At the end of the day, I wouldn't be with any of you if you were the type of person who might be like that. Nate loves you, and so do Dante and Logan. None of them are going to think less of you for this."

He's quiet again for a little while, and he says, "Okay. I'll think about it."

"You don't have to do it. Maybe the Dante thing because that's important for safety, but if you still want to keep it from Logan and Nate, I'll be completely fine with that."

He smiles at me. "I love you, Goddess."

"I love you, too, sweet boy."

Chapter 14

Well, That Happened.

Logan wakes me twice overnight to 'refresh the connection' of the vibrator, which I switched out with the charged one before bed.

He doesn't give me an orgasm, though, and I fall back asleep both times in a state of high arousal. I wake to a picture of Ash's stiff cock, and I groan when I see it along with the message he sent.

I dreamed about you, Goddess.

I bite my lip and send a reply through.

Very pretty cock, boy. I look forward to sucking it dry when I get home.

I spend a few minutes messaging back and forth with him before heading downstairs for breakfast sans vibrator but horny as hell.

We leave Galena late on Sunday morning, though, and Heather has to take me straight to pick up Darren at the hotel before she takes us to the private hangar to catch my plane back to LA.

"You'll have to come back, and I'll give you a tour of Serenity next time," she says as she gives me a hug.

"Okay. Sounds good."

Dante uses the vibrator on me on the plane, but he also doesn't give me an orgasm. "You're almost home, Angel. It will be much more satisfactory to watch you come in person."

Between the vibrator use and the three more pics I've received from Ash, I'm more than ready to fuck someone or everyone by the time Darren has escorted me upstairs and left our apartment. I'm about to strip my clothes off when Ash appears nearby.

"Hey, I've been thinking about what we talked about, and I want to talk with the guys."

"Okay," I say with a smile. "I'll stay clothed for now, then."

"Good. You're very distracting when you're naked."

I walk over to him and wrap my arms around his waist. I breathe in his scent and sigh, glad to be back in his arms again. A sense of peace and security washes over me, despite my arousal. Everything is right again now that I'm back in the arms of one of my men. Just knowing that I'll be seeing the others soon makes me feel better, too.

"I'll get Logan and Nate if you want to take your suitcase and put your stuff away."

I grin at him. "Sure. You know how Dante is."

When I get to Dante's room, he's not there, so I quickly empty my suitcase, taking the shortcut of dumping all my clothes in my hamper even though I didn't wear about ninety percent of them. I head out of the room and find Dante in the office as the sound of Ash, Logan, and Nate's voices ring out from upstairs.

"Hi, Honey," I say with a smile as I wrap my arms around him from behind.

"Hello there, Angel." He grabs my hand and pulls me around him as he spins his chair so that I land on his lap, then raises an eyebrow when he sees me. "You're wearing clothes."

"Yes, I am. Ash wants to have a conversation with everyone, and I thought it would be best if I were clothed."

"Ah. Fair enough." He kisses me and wraps me in his warm

embrace for a few moments before he ends our kiss. "I guess we should go, then."

I hold Dante's hand as we walk toward the living room where we find the others, but I let go as I stride quickly toward Logan and Nate, sitting on the sofa together. I straddle Nate and wrap my arms around his neck before smashing my lips against his. He kisses me back, and Logan strokes my leg, which has landed on his lap.

"Did you miss me, Sexy Lexi?" Nate asks with a laugh.

"Yes," I say through panting breaths, but I remember that we need to have an important conversation, so I turn to smile at Logan.

Before I can say anything, he places his hand behind my head and pulls my face to his. He parts my lips with his tongue and kisses me skillfully while he raises a hand to my breast and thumbs my hard nipple through the fabric. Nate is hard underneath me, and I'm so wet as I moan into Logan's mouth.

He breaks our kiss but leaves his hand on my breast as he looks into my eyes. "Is there a reason you're wearing clothes in my apartment, Alexandra?"

"Yes, Sir," I manage to say. "Ash and I need to talk to you guys, and I didn't want to be a distraction."

He chuckles and tweaks my nipple painfully before he pulls his hand back. "I think you'll find you're plenty distracting either way, Alexandra, but I'll allow it."

I climb off Nate's lap and walk over to sit next to Ash. I grab his hand and smile up at him reassuringly.

"I'll let you take the lead. Tell them whatever you feel comfortable telling them," I say in a quiet undertone to him.

He smiles and swallows heavily before he looks over at Logan and Nate. "So, um, Lexi and I have kind of started doing BDSM stuff."

Logan looks over at Dante, then back at us. "Okay. If you want my permission to Dom Lexi, you don't need it, and I'm sure Dante feels the same way."

I squeeze Ash's hand for comfort as Logan replies. I should've known that would be the natural assumption, given I've never shown any desire to be anything other than a sub to Logan.

"Thanks, but it's not like that. Lexi's, um, been a Domme for me."

Logan and Nate's eyebrows fly up, and Logan looks at Dante again before looking back at me.

"Really?" he asks, his surprise evident in both his tone and expression.

"Yeah. It turns out I like having control sometimes. Go figure," I say casually. "Dante knows because the morning it first happened, I freaked out a little bit because I've never been a Domme before."

"Wait, how long has this been going on?" Logan asks.

I look back at Ash, and he says, "Just this week. At first, I was just trying to distract Lexi. I wasn't sure if I wanted to do it any more than that, but we tried it again, and I really like it."

Logan looks between Ash and me a few times, then smiles. "Okay. Well, good for you guys. Why the big talk?"

"Lexi said I can't go full-time with her because she's full-time with you and Dante," Ash says.

"I also said that I wouldn't go full-time so soon as well," I jump in quickly to add this, and Logan nods.

"Both things make sense. Lexi can't Domme from subspace." Logan looks over at Dante, then back at us. "So you want to know if one of us would be willing?"

"Huh?" Nate asks with a frown.

I smile at him because he's never really understood the dynamics of the kink relationships he incidentally participates in.

"Ash wants me to Domme him full-time, which I can't commit to unless someone who isn't a sub at all is willing to have the final say, or it's not safe. If Ash and I are both subs in a scene, I could instruct him to do something. If I go into subspace, I can't be counted on to watch and make sure he's safe. Someone else needs to do that to ensure his safety."

"Ohhhh," Nate says slowly. "Gotcha."

"I was thinking maybe Dante," Ash says.

"Sure. I don't mind. I half expected this question when Lexi came to me all excited and confused about the idea of Domming you."

"You've always known me better than I've known myself," I laugh, and Dante grins at me.

Ash turns back to Logan. "Nothing against you, Logan. I just…you and Nate are together, and I didn't want to do anything that might interfere with that."

"I wouldn't be jealous." Nate shrugs. "In fact, wouldn't it be better if both Dante *and* Logan agreed to it? Or are you just never going to have sex with Lexi if Logan's there and Dante's not?"

My jaw drops open because, considering Nate's the least experienced in this, he thought of an aspect that none of us did.

Logan looks from Nate, over to Dante again, and then back to Ash. "Nate makes a good point. I'm willing. My only concern when I realized what you were asking was whether or not Nate would be comfortable with it."

He smiles at Nate, and Nate presses his lips against Logan's to kiss him. They kiss for long enough that I'm turned on again, and I love how comfortable they are in front of us all now.

"I'm totally fine. Kind of curious to see Sexy Lexi bossing Ash around, to be honest." He smirks at us. "Not gonna lie, it sounds pretty hot."

I'm surprised by the way Ash's breathing quickens at Nate's attention, but he says casually, "It is. My Goddess is the sexiest woman in the world."

"Wait, wait, wait. *That's* what's behind all those 'goddess' comments you've been making?" Nate gasps.

Ash nods, and I'm satisfied from the turn this conversation has taken that I can reveal things to them now.

I look very obviously at Ash's crotch, where there's a telltale bulge in his jeans, and I place my hand on it to rub it through the fabric. "Your cock is hard, boy. I believe you owe me a picture of it."

"Yes, Goddess," he says.

He glances over at the other guys, his cheeks flushing pink, but he pulls his phone out of his pocket and unzips his jeans to pull his cock out. It's fully erect now, so I know he's turned on, and my pussy aches, along with my stiff nipples, as Ash snaps a picture of his cock. He sends it to me, and my phone dings in my pocket.

"Very nice," I tell him as I pull my phone out and set it aside. I wrap my fingers around his cock and begin to stroke him. "I'm looking forward to making you come."

"Please, Goddess," he murmurs.

"You've waited very patiently, haven't you?" He nods. "Well, you can wait a little longer, I think." Ash groans, and I wrap my lips around his cock, swirl my tongue around the tip, then pull my head back to grin at him. "If you're a good boy. You can come in one of my holes."

I look back at the guys, and I'm interested to see the different responses. Dante is watching intently, and I assume he's watching to see how I behave in this different role. Logan and Nate both have stiff cocks; while Logan looks interested in what's happening, Nate is straight-up turned on, and I can tell. He keeps darting glances at Ash's cock, but then looking away as if he's trying not to get caught staring at it.

"I believe I said that I was going to make you worship my pussy when I got home?" I raise an eyebrow at him.

"You did, Goddess," Ash says, and his cock jerks.

"If he's going to worship your pussy, Alexandra, then you might as well take your clothes off since you're in my apartment," Logan says in a husky voice.

"Yes, Sir." I stand and pull my top off over my head, then grin as I hand it to Ash. "Hold this, boy. You can put my clothes away for me."

"Yes, Goddess."

He dutifully takes my top from me, and I have to withhold a groan of satisfaction. Four sets of hungry eyes watch me as I remove each item of clothing. My need to be fucked grows with each piece I take off. By the time I'm naked and Ash is holding all my clothes, I'm delirious with lust.

"Take those and put them in my hamper, sweet boy," I say, placing my hand on the side of his face as I do. "Come back naked."

Ash kisses my palm, then leaves the room, and I turn back to the others.

"Enjoying yourself, Angel?" Dante asks.

"Yes, Honey."

"This is fascinating," Logan says. "I never would've predicted it for either of them, but it clearly works. I can see that already."

Dante nods, and I laugh. "Trust me. I'm the *most* surprised. You should've seen my freakout when it first happened. I thought it meant I couldn't be a sub anymore."

"Is that what you thought?" Logan shakes his head. "Spread your legs wide, Alexandra." I immediately follow his instruction, and all three guys laugh. "Yeah, I think you're fine."

"She's more than fine," Nate says, looking up from my pussy as he does.

Ash appears at the entrance to the living room, and I smile at him. "Very good, boy. Come here and worship my pussy."

I love doing this in front of everyone. I love them seeing me as a Domme, and I'm very proud of Ash when he immediately strides over to me and gets on his knees. He buries his face in my pussy, and I moan in ecstasy. I thrust my fingers into his hair and pull his face harder against my clit. I ride his face for a while before I notice Nate slowly stroking his cock.

Dante and Logan both have erections but haven't given in to the temptation to do anything about them yet, so I ask Nate through panting breaths, "Do you want to come to join us?"

"I thought you'd never ask."

He grins at me as he stands and strips naked. His muscled body is glorious to behold, with his large cock jutting out in front of him below his toned stomach.

When he reaches us, I raise an eyebrow at him. "Do you want your cock in my mouth, or do you want to help Ash eat my pussy?"

Ash's tongue halts on my clit, and he looks up at Nate out of the corner of his eye. I wait to see if Ash will continue his movements, but he doesn't.

"I love eating your pussy if Ash is willing to share," Nate says.

Ash lifts his head and grins at Nate. "Of course."

I glare at Ash. "Boy, when I tell you to worship my pussy, you don't take your mouth off it until I tell you to stop."

"Sorry, Goddess," he murmurs before diving back into my pussy immediately.

"As punishment for that, you don't get to come until everyone else in this room has. Do you understand?"

"Yes, Goddess," he says, and his reply is muffled because he keeps his mouth on my pussy when he says it.

"You may lift your mouth from my pussy, only if it's to share it with Nate. Your job is to ensure there is a tongue on my pussy at all times until I say otherwise. If Nate stops eating me out, your tongue had better be there, or you won't get an orgasm at all tonight. Do you understand?"

He gives another muffled reply into my pussy, and I moan as Nate leans down to kiss me while he plays with my breasts.

"Holy fuck, this is hot," Nate says as he gets on his knees next to Ash. "I'm kind of tempted to see if I can trick Ash into getting screwed out of an orgasm."

Ash nudges Nate with his elbow but doesn't take his mouth off my pussy, and Nate laughs. I watch Nate slide his tongue up and down my outer lips while Ash keeps tonguing my clit.

Their tongues are so close to each other's, and I don't know why this is so hot, but it fucking is. Probably because I want to see Nate and Ash hook up so badly. Nate finds my hole and sticks his tongue into my pussy. The two men are so close as they eat me out in tandem that I can barely stand it.

Nate slides his tongue up to my clit and pushes Ash aside just before their tongues touch, then flicks his across my clit. I gasp and thrust my fingers into Nate's hair. I grind my clit against his tongue, my orgasm so incredibly close, but I force myself to hold it off just to preserve this moment with these two men.

It takes everything in me to stay where I am and not come as

Ash takes over on my clit from Nate. Ash's tongue chases Nate's over my clit, and they're so close, I can't tell whether or not their tongues touched. Either way, it sends me over the edge.

Ash sucks on my clit as I tip into orgasm, and Nate lifts his head to watch me. "Fuck yes, Sexy. Come for us. You're so fucking hot."

"God, yes, Nate. Mmmm, yes." My body shakes, and I look down at Ash. "Lick my clit, boy. Give your Goddess the orgasm she deserves."

He does exactly that, and Nate moves up to kiss me while he plays with my breasts until my orgasm has passed. When it has, he thrusts his cock into me without warning. Ash is still sucking my clit, and I look down into his eyes as Nate pumps in and out of me.

I desperately want Ash to lick Nate's cock, but I know I can't make him do it, no matter how close it is to his mouth. Nate's cock glistens with my pussy juice each time he pulls out of me, and I can't help but notice how Ash watches him fuck me.

"Do you like watching Nate bury his thick cock in my pussy, boy? You may answer."

"Yes, Goddess," he admits, his cheeks flushing pink as he looks up at Nate.

"Hey, no need to be embarrassed." Nate gives him a reassuring smile. "If you recall, I just about busted a nut watching you fuck Lexi the other night." He thrusts roughly into me. "Watching your big cock disappear into her tight pussy was hot as fuck."

I want to wrap my legs around Nate's waist, but I leave them spread so Ash can maintain his view. I decide not to order his mouth back on my pussy, though, so I can see what he does.

He watches Nate fuck me for a short while, then tongues my clit again. He flicks it up and down my pussy, in a longer vertical path each time, coming ever closer to the point where Nate and I are connected. I see the moment his tongue makes contact with Nate's cock, and Nate gasps.

"Is that okay?" Ash asks in a strange voice.

Nate immediately turns to look at Logan, who smiles, before

he looks down at Ash with pure lust in his gaze. "Yes."

"I just wanted to taste my Goddess on you."

"Of course," Nate murmurs as he continues to fuck me.

I'm fucking dead. I've lost control of this scene, not because I'm in subspace, but because these two men have so completely surprised me. Ash seems to have taken this as the green light to lick Nate's cock whenever he chooses to do so. Each time he does, both Nate and I groan in ecstasy. When he's not licking Nate's cock clean of my juices, Ash is doing wonders on my clit.

Nate stops fucking me as quickly, and the licks from Ash become more obvious, more intentional. Nate pulls all the way back and holds himself there while Ash slides his tongue up and down his shaft, and I almost lose my fucking mind. Nate slowly buries his cock in me, then pulls it out again equally slowly, and Ash's tongue trails his shaft as he does.

When he reaches my entrance, Nate continues moving and pulls his cock all the way out of me. I watch in awe as Ash doesn't hesitate to continue his path to the head of Nate's cock. He swirls his tongue around the tip before he opens his mouth and wraps his lips around it. I immediately come at the sight of it. The orgasm I've been holding back hits me, and I moan as my body shakes.

Ash seems totally focused on his task, and he sucks Nate for a few seconds before he sinks onto his cock and presses his nose to Nate's stomach. Nate groans, and his eyes close as he throws his head back in ecstasy.

"Fuck, Ash," Nate moans.

I don't know what this means. I don't know what any of this means. I'm in a daze of love and lust, but a part of me suddenly worries that Ash will regret this. Did I bring this on by ordering him to share my pussy? My concern that I have completely fucked up as Ash's Domme is intense. Even if they're both enjoying this, I need to shut it down, just in case. They can always do this another time if they want to.

"Stop, boy. Get your mouth off Nate's cock," I say sternly.

Nate's eyes snap open, and he glares at me while Ash pulls his mouth off Nate and looks at me in a complete daze.

"What the fuck, Lexi?" Nate growls.

I look between them and say, "I need to be sure he wants to do this, Nate."

Nate's expression turns to one of horror as he looks down at Ash. "Oh, shit. Fuck."

"Huh? Why do you think I didn't want to do it?" Ash asks me.

I smile at him. "Because you've never shown any interest in being with Nate before, and we've made a lot of big decisions today. I just want to be sure you're making one like this with a clear head and not because you're in subspace. If you want to suck Nate's cock, you can feel free anytime. Just not tonight, okay?"

Ash's cheeks flush pink, and he blinks up at Nate for a few seconds before he says, "Okay."

I'm not sure how to handle it from here, so I look over to Dante and Logan for guidance. Logan looks absolutely stunned, but his cock is rock hard in his jeans.

It's Dante who provides the guidance I need right now without me having to ask. "I think Ash has probably well and truly earned his orgasm. Don't you, Angel?"

"Yes, Honey." I look down at Ash and tell him, "Come fuck me, sweet boy." He moves into the position Nate previously held and pushes his cock into me. I look up at Nate, who has a strange look on his face. "Do you want to fuck my mouth, Nate?"

The strange expression clears, and he nods as he steps forward. He pushes his cock between my lips and fucks my mouth. I do my best to make up for what I did by stopping Ash, and it isn't long before both men are groaning.

When Ash comes inside me, I come with him, my pussy clenching repeatedly around his cock as Nate fucks my mouth. Ash pants for breath when he's done and stares at me, looking stunned.

I realize that he needs aftercare, but this scene is nowhere near done. I remember the first time I fucked Logan in Napa and tap Nate's hip to get his attention. He pulls his cock out of my mouth, and I smile up at him.

"Sit on the sofa with your back against the end and your legs going down the sofa, sweet boy," I say to Ash. He does as instructed, and I sit in his lap, grab his arms, and pull them across my torso. "You can cuddle me while Nate fucks me. You did so well, sweet boy. I love you."

I lean my head back against his shoulder and kiss his cheek. He gives a satisfied sigh, and I revel in the sound of it as I lift one leg over the back of the sofa to spread myself wide for Nate. He claims my lips with his as he pushes his cock into me, and I love being fucked by Nate while Ash holds me tight in his arms.

He looks into my eyes while he fucks me and says in a husky voice, "I love you, Lexi."

The look in his eyes is one of gratitude, and I hope this means he's forgiven me for stopping Ash. I'm in complete bliss as Nate fucks me while Ash holds me tightly. I place my hands over Ash's and softly stroke his arms with my thumbs. By the time Nate comes, I'm in some kind of version of subspace that is familiar yet different. It's a combination of the love and lust and the strange new experience I've had tonight.

Nate kisses me deeply as he holds himself inside me before he pulls out when he ends our kiss.

I'm left in Ash's warm embrace, and I look at him. "How are you feeling, sweet boy?"

"Perfect, Goddess." He smiles.

"Will you be okay if I fuck Logan and Dante?"

Ash nods, and I turn to look at the other two. They look at each other, and something passes between them.

"I'll go get the lube," Logan says, and Dante nods.

"Come here, Angel," Dante says.

I walk over to him, my pussy dripping with cum and juice, and I clench it tight to try and avoid making a mess.

"Straddle me."

"Yes, Honey."

I climb onto him and lower myself onto his cock. I ride him until Logan comes back with a bottle of lube.

"Hold still, Angel," Dante says.

I pause in my movements with him buried deep inside me, and Logan's tongue flicks over my asshole. I moan as he rims me while Dante rubs his thumb across my clit and when I come on Dante's cock, Logan squirts some lube on my ass.

When he's finished preparing my ass, Dante says, "Sit on my cock so Logan can fuck your pussy, Angel."

I climb off him and turn around to sheath his cock in my ass. I pant for breath as he enters me inch by inch until he's buried inside me. Logan takes my legs and puts them over his shoulders before he pushes his cock into my pussy. I gasp at the sensation of being filled by them and lose myself in everything. Dante thumbs and pulls my nipples while they fuck me in tandem, and Logan rubs my clit with his thumb.

They make me come on them over and over before they have their own orgasms. I've lost track of how many I've had and can't even tell which of them comes first, but eventually, I'm filled by both Dante and Logan, who collapses on me, panting heavily for breath. Dante kisses my neck while Logan captures my lips with his. I don't know how long we lie together in complete ecstasy before Logan's weight disappears and he pulls out of me.

"Thank you, Alexandra. That was amazing."

"You're welcome, Sir."

"Hop up and come with me, Angel," Dante says, then looks across the room. "Ash, you'd better come with us."

I look over to see Ash and Nate sitting stiffly next to each other on the sofa, and I worry again that I fucked up. Ash and I follow Dante to his bathroom, where he washes me and holds me under the spray while I hold Ash's hand. When I'm done, I turn to Ash and give him the same treatment, except when he's clean, I pull him into my arms and kiss him softly before I just hold him for a long time.

Dante kisses my head. "I'll be in the bedroom."

Once we're alone, I look up at Ash. "How are you feeling?"

"I don't know," he says honestly.

"I'm sorry if I pushed you to do something you didn't want to do."

Ash stares down at me and shakes his head. "No, Lexi. It wasn't something I didn't want to do. It was something I was scared to want to do. I've been curious for a long time. Even back when Logan came out to us years ago. I was curious, but thought it was something I shouldn't want because I knew I was straight."

"So was Nate," I point out.

"Yeah. When they told me about their relationship, I was even less likely to try anything because I didn't want to cause trouble between them." He's quiet for a moment, then he says, "When you told me to share your pussy, I don't think I've ever been more excited. Then when I was licking you while Nate fucked you, I told myself that it was okay to want it because my Goddess told me to do it. I fucking wanted it *so* bad, too. When Nate pulled out of you, I finally got to satisfy a desire I've had for a long time."

I don't point out that I didn't tell him to lick my clit when Nate was fucking me because I'm curious how he rationalized it for himself.

Ash looks into my eyes. "Thank you, Lexi. I don't know if I would've gotten the courage to try it otherwise, but I also love you for stopping it. I understand why you did it, and I appreciate your concern."

"I love you, too, Ash. Your safety, including your mental wellbeing, is the most important thing to me in all of this. Well above any sexual desires I might have."

I pull his head down to mine and kiss my sweet boy, stunned and amazed at how lucky I am to have him like this.

"I'll tell you the same thing I told Nate and Logan. If something happens between you two, I'm okay with it. No outsiders, but I would never deny you guys any sexual pleasure from one another."

"I don't know what will happen, either. I guess we'll have to talk, but that's good to know."

I grin at him as I remember something Logan said to me once. "Unless I've banned you from having an orgasm, boy. In that case, you can pleasure Nate all you want, but if I find out you've convinced him to give you an orgasm when I've said you can't have one, you *will* regret it."

Chapter 15

Liar, Liar, Pants on Fire

When we get out of the shower, I follow Ash to his bedroom, where he gets dressed as I lie back on his bed. He pulls his shirt over his head, and I smile at him.

"Come lie down with me, sweet boy." Ash comes, and I cuddle him against my breast, then kiss his head. "You don't have to make any decisions right now, but do you have any idea what you want to do?"

He sighs and frowns at me. "I think we need to talk to Logan and Nate about what happened."

"I'd say that's a discussion that needs to happen. Are you ready for that?"

"I think so." He kisses the swell of my breast. "I know my Goddess will be with me, which is nice."

I turn his face up to mine. "I won't be there in that capacity. Anything between you and Nate or you and Logan is between you guys. I don't interfere in Logan and Nate's relationship, so it'll be the same for you."

"Oh. Okay."

He looks a little hurt, and I feel bad because I think he sees this as a rejection.

"Hey." I kiss his lips softly. "I'll always *be* your Goddess. Sometimes I just won't be acting in that role. It doesn't change the fact that you're my sweet boy, and I'm your Goddess."

He kisses me, our tongues dancing together before we lie in silence for a while. The sound of his breathing is soothing and I stroke his head, gently running my fingers through his hair.

"This is all so complicated sometimes," he says, breaking the silence.

I think about all the different dynamics of my relationships and nod. "It is. Does that worry you?"

"Not particularly. Before we got together, it was part of what concerned me. I didn't know how we would all work with the different relationships, plus Logan and Nate being together. What if something happens with them?"

I frown and then shrug. "If Logan and Nate ever break up, we'll work through it. I can't see it happening, but it wouldn't affect my relationship with either of them if it did. It might affect group scenes, but that's it. I would still love them both as wholeheartedly as I do now. The only way that would change would be if one of them cheated on the other. For that to happen, they'd have to cheat on me, too, so I sure as shit wouldn't be okay with it."

"I suppose that makes sense."

We fall into silence again, and I doze off, content with Ash being here with me. I don't know how long we've been lying there when Ash speaks again.

"I guess we should go talk to them, then."

My eyes flutter open, and I look down at him with a smile. "Okay."

I don't get dressed, but I do slip Ash's terry-cloth robe on before we head upstairs to see Nate and Logan. We hear voices coming from Nate's room, and I knock on the door, Ash clutching my hand tightly.

"Come in," Nate calls.

I open the door and smile at him, where he's relaxed on the bed, watching TV. His eyes flicker to Ash, then quickly back to me.

"We were wondering if we could talk to you and Logan."

"Sure. Logan's in the office, I think."

I head to a room a few doors down and find Logan in the upstairs office. He agrees to talk with a good-natured smile and makes us all coffee before we sit down in the living room upstairs to have a conversation.

"What did you want to talk about?" Logan asks as he takes a sip of his coffee, even though I know he already knows.

"About what happened," Ash says.

Nate stiffens, and his eyes are downcast. "I'm sorry, Ash. I shouldn't have done that."

"No. That was fine. I liked it. It was more about if you want to do it again and if Logan would be okay with it."

Nate's eyes snap up to meet Ash's, and his eyebrows fly up as he does.

Logan looks between them and shrugs. "I could hardly stand in your way. It would be a bit hypocritical to be fine with Nate fucking Lexi but not you, Ash." He smiles at Nate. "We've discussed it anyway, and I've told Nate I'm fine with it. I love you both and just want you to be happy. If this gives you happiness, then go for it."

Nate leans across and kisses him. He places his hand on the back of Logan's head and holds him there as they kiss.

When they part, Nate murmurs, "I love you."

"I love you, too."

Both men look over at us and smile before Nate says to Ash, "What if I spend tonight with you and Lexi in your room? I know I liked having Lexi with us when Logan and I first spent the night together." He chuckles and grins at me. "You're quite the safety blanket, Sexy."

"Happy to help." I look at Ash. "What do you think?"

Ash doesn't respond immediately but frowns. "Is it too soon? This is a lot to take in."

"We don't have to. It was just a thought," Nate quickly backtracks. "We can just see if we want to do more stuff like today but without Lexi stopping us if you want."

"Maybe. Can I think about it? I'll see how I feel at bedtime, if that's okay?"

"Totally fine." Nate gives him a reassuring smile.

I sip my coffee, and an awkward silence falls. It's strange because it's never been like this between us.

"So tell us about your trip to Chicago, Lexi. How was it?" Logan asks with a smile.

"Good. Heather had it totally planned out, so I never even saw the paparazzi the whole time I was there. Sebastian's place in Galena is gorgeous. Very peaceful, and we just hung out. Went swimming." I grin at them as I remember borrowing a swimsuit from Lita. "Then just hung out the rest of the time. Their little girl is totally adorable. Heather was going to take me to Serenity, but unfortunately, we ran out of time. She did invite me to come back, and she'll give me a tour next time, so that was nice of her."

"Sounds like you had a great time," Nate says.

"Yeah, I did. It was good to get my mind off things."

As soon as I say it, everything that's happening at the moment comes rushing back. I've been distracted since I arrived home, but now that I have a moment, I realize that it's only a few hours before Cassie's big interview.

"What do you think Cassie's going to say that she hasn't already?" I ask the guys.

Ash squeezes my hand. "Probably nothing that she hasn't said, but they can put a face to the name, make her seem sympathetic, get people talking even more about us." He sighs. "Maybe we shouldn't watch the interview. We're just going to feel like shit if we do."

"I want to watch it," Logan says. "I'd rather know what was said than be unprepared."

"Fuck. Good point." Ash cringes.

Logan looks at his watch. "I'm going to go make dinner so we can eat before it airs."

I'm left alone with Nate and Ash. There's a weird silence in the room, and I can sense that Nate is waiting for Ash to break it.

I smile up at him and suggest, "Why don't you go get your guitar, Ash? I need some distraction, and I love it when you guys play music."

He perks up at the idea and nods. "Sure. That's a good idea."

Nate and I watch him walk away before he turns to look at me. "You love it when we play music?"

"It's not a lie." Heat rushes to my cheeks, and I move over to sit next to him on the other sofa. "Are you okay?"

"Why wouldn't I be okay, Sexy?" He looks down at me, his ice-blue eyes piercing into mine.

"Because a lot of stuff has happened, and I want to make sure you're feeling okay about it all."

"Ohhhh," he feigns an enlightened tone. "Do you mean because Ash sucked my cock?"

I raise an eyebrow at him. "And?"

He uses his finger to hook my hair behind my ear, and my skin tingles where he touches it. "And I liked it a lot. Is that what you want to hear?" He trails his finger down my neck and chest to follow the path of the robe's neckline. He pulls it back with his index finger, exposing my breast with its rock-hard nipple, and says in a husky voice, "It certainly seems like it."

"Am I interrupting?" Ash asks with a laugh, sounding almost back to normal as he appears, holding his acoustic guitar.

I stare up at him, and it takes me a second to recollect myself before smiling at him. "Not at all. Nate was just telling me how much he loves to sing for me. He can sing while you play."

Nate takes my nipple between his forefinger and thumb to tweak it as he grins down at me. "Yeah, that was totally it." He kisses me while he plays with my breast, then breaks our kiss and pulls the robe closed again. "Okay. Music time."

"Music schmusic," I object, and Nate laughs as he sits back up and away from me.

Ash is back on the other side of the sofa, and I look over to see him looking at us with clear arousal in his expression. I don't want to push him on anything sexual right now because it really has been a lot, so I smile at him.

"What are you going to play for me, Ash?"

He looks between Nate and me for a few seconds, then smirks at us and plays the chords for "Heavenly Promises." Nate and I laugh, but he cuts his laughter off as his cue to begin singing the first verse hits.

He puts his arm around me and pulls me into him as he sings. I relax into Nate's embrace and close my eyes as they play what I definitely think of as 'our song.' When it finishes, Ash immediately moves into another of their ballads. His voice joins Nate's for each chorus, and they harmonize so well together, even without the other two guys.

I'm able to fully relax as I sit and listen for what might be minutes or could be hours. I lose count of the number of songs they sing to me, eventually moving into more upbeat songs once they've run through all their ballads. I'm fascinated by watching Ash play. His fingers strum the guitar, and I watch as he moves them when he changes chords. Meanwhile, Nate's voice is smooth and low, sexier than ever. He strokes my arm gently as he sings, and I'm not sure I've ever felt this level of peace and satisfaction.

Eventually, Ash stops playing and looks up past Nate and me. Nate sings the end of a line before he cuts off and looks around.

"Dinner's ready," Dante says with a smile.

I'm so relaxed that my entire body feels like a marshmallow, and I float over to put my arms around my husband's waist. He wraps his arms around me and smiles down at me.

"Hello, Angel." He ducks his head to kiss me, and I reach up to wrap my arms around his neck when he does. "Dinnertime," he reminds me before he kisses my head and lets me go.

We have enough time to eat dinner and clean up before the interview airs, and the tension creeps back into my body as we do. By the time I take a seat between Dante and Ash on the sofa in front of the television, I'm wound as tightly as a spring.

I clutch their hands as Grant does the intro for Backline. He gives a basic rundown of the situation to explain to the viewer who will be on the show tonight, and I think I might be sick.

It cuts to what looks like a casual living room with two armchairs, but I know it's a set because I've seen videos online behind the scenes of the show. It's weirdly bizarre to be sitting here and watching an episode dedicated to what should be our private lives.

Cassie sits casually in an armchair across from Grant, wearing a baby blue dress and her hair in loose waves. Grant's in jeans, a collared shirt, and dress shoes. He looks casual enough to be accessible to the viewer but classy enough to be the host of a show like this. He starts with a rundown of how I got together with the guys, and Cassie lies about Ash cheating on her with me.

"We do have a collection of photographs of Lexi with the band where it certainly seems that way," Grant says after Cassie accuses me of having wanted this all along.

I watch in horror as he picks up a stack of printed-out photographs and casually hands them to Cassie as though he's handing over family photos to look at. An overhead camera cuts in, showing the audience the pictures that Cassie is flicking through. It cuts back and forth between shots of Cassie and Grant talking, but whenever Cassie looks down at the photos, the overhead camera cuts in.

"I hate to say it, but that's a fucking clever tactic. It feels like we're looking down with her," I mutter.

"Don't you love watching this show, Lexi?" Nate asks with a grim smile.

I give a mirthless laugh. "I used to."

The photos are from the first time the guys were ever spotted in public after becoming famous, through to Dante and me out the front of Black Lilac this week. Cassie doesn't hesitate to give her opinion on them, even though she didn't even know us when the earlier pictures were taken.

"See how she has her arms around Ash's neck in this picture?" Cassie asks as she turns a picture from at least two years before she met us to face Grant.

On cue, a camera from behind him gives us his perspective of looking at it before going back to the two of them in the frame as he nods.

"She was always hanging all over them all like this. Just touching them and looking at them. I told Ash it was inappropriate, but he brushed it off. I guess we know why, now."

"Get fucked," Ash growls and turns to me. "She didn't have a problem with you until Logan. I mean, she did say she was a bit uncomfortable with Nate, but she was pretty supportive. Even said to me that you two were obviously in love. After Logan…" He rolls his eyes. "Fucking bitch."

I lean up and kiss him. "I know."

I turn back to the screen to endure the rest of the torturous interview. Cassie and Grant casually sip coffee as they finish going through the photos. When they've sufficiently broken them down, Grant sets his coffee cup down and looks across at Cassie.

"So, the recordings…"

Cassie shrugs, seeming slightly defensive before visibly relaxing and giving a tinkling laugh. "As I said, I started tallying my receipts when I suspected Ash was cheating on me."

"*Fuck off!*" I can't help but yell at the screen, rage coursing through my veins. "She knows *full well* that she recorded those *after* you'd fucking dumped her!"

Ash squeezes my hand, and Logan says, "I know this sucks, Lexi. We know the truth, and we will get through this, okay?"

I manage to nod at him and give him a tight smile. "Of course we will."

"So, you didn't release all your 'receipts' at once." Grant pulls a phone from his pocket and unlocks it, then says, "You graciously offered to let us exclusively release some things that have never been released before."

"That's correct," Cassie says with a smug smile before she clears it quickly.

"It has to be you at the apartment, Ash," Nate says.

Ash cringes as he nods back at him. "Probably."

"So, when I heard these, I'll admit that they definitely shocked me." Grant shakes his head. "I think hearing these was probably the most damning evidence you have."

He's teasing the audience, and I want to puke knowing that people around the world will be on the edge of their seats right now, waiting for this reveal.

"Let me play some voice recordings that you have. Now, legally, I obviously need to say that we haven't verified the authenticity of these recordings. So this is all hearsay, and we will leave it up to the viewers to come to their own conclusions. I'm very interested in getting *your* thoughts, though, Cassie."

He sets the phone down on a coffee table between them and presses the screen before my voice rings out.

"Fuck you. I have to speak to the guys, though. You know that."

I gasp as I recognize the conversation from the last time she blackmailed us.

"I thought you would."

I blink in shock as my voice comes next because I wasn't expecting it.

"Are you jealous, Cassie? Do you wish it was you getting fucked by the gorgeous men of Wicked Stallion?"

Grant steeples his fingers and looks at Cassie as I say numbly, "What the fuck?" I miss the question he asks her because I'm so thrown, and I whip my head around to look at Ash. "That's not how the conversation went."

"She's doctored it. Or the show has," Dante says gruffly.

"Isn't that slander? Is that even legal? Is she allowed to record me?"

Logan frowns. "Recording is only legal in California if both parties consent. I'm not sure if chopping it up and releasing it is slander. We'll have to ask the lawyer."

I turn back to the interview as Cassie is saying, "I definitely had my suspicions. I was living with Ash, and I came home early one day, which was when I found them in bed."

"And that's when you got this next recording?"

"I read she'd apparently claimed that in one of the online posts," Logan scoffs as Cassie nods and Grant leans forward to the phone again.

"What the fuck are you doing in my apartment?"

Ash sounds out of breath, probably because his face had been buried in my pussy when she appeared.

"You're the one who gave me the key."

This time, I'm unsurprised that she's chopped up the conversation to make us out to be the bad guys.

"Wait. Where are you going?"

I can hear the sheer terror in my voice, but I can also tell that from an outsider's perspective, I sound guilty as fuck.

"I think I've seen enough."

Again, without the context of her calling me a whore and the fact that she broke into the apartment, she sounds exactly like the hard-done-by cheated-on girlfriend she claims to be.

"Get the fuck out of my apartment, you bitch. Lexi is a thousand times the woman you could ever hope to be."

I cringe and squeeze Ash's hand as I look up at him. His face is thunderous as he watches this character assassination take place.

"Go fuck yourselves."

The sound of a key being thrown to the floor sounds out before the slamming of a door. There are some rustling noises, and then she makes a small shriek.

"You can't leave, Cassie."

"You're fucking her!"

Cassie couldn't modify this, and she sounds just as sure and confident as she did when she yelled it at him that day. I don't think that anybody else in the world will take note of that fact. They'll bury it under the weight of the apparent evidence that she was betrayed by Ash.

"You're not leaving."

I cringe at Ash's words because it sounds awful without people hearing the entirety of what happened that day.

"Move out of the way and let me out of your stupid apartment."

The recording ends, and there's a shocked silence in the room around me. My heart pounds in my chest, and I can't even understand all of the different emotions I feel right now. It's a combination of rage, sadness, disappointment, shame, but most of all, guilt that I'm the reason the world will think so badly of Ash after tonight.

There's silence for a few moments on the screen as Cassie dabs at her eyes with a tissue before Grant asks in a solemn voice, "Are you okay, Cassie?"

"No." She sniffs and shakes her head. "I don't think I've ever been more scared than I was that day. I just wanted to spend time at home with my boyfriend, and he was having sex with another woman. Then, when I dared to confront them, I was abused, and Ash wouldn't let me leave. It was terrifying."

"Do you need to take a moment?" Grant asks solicitously, and Cassie nods.

She stands and walks away off-screen. The fourth wall is broken, and the cameras are pulled back to reveal more of the set as producers come rushing in, their conversation heard clearly over Grant's hot mic.

"What do we do?" the first asks.

"I don't know. I don't want to push her if she's really traumatized," Grant says, sounding concerned.

"I'll go make sure she's okay," a second says and takes off in the direction Cassie disappeared.

"Um, this is fake as fuck," Logan says as he shakes his head.

I've seen stuff like this happen before on the show, and I never realized it, but he's right. They're a little *too* concerned, and their voices are stilted as they perform their lines.

"I mean, *I* was scared listening to it," the only female producer says. "I can only imagine how she feels reliving something like that."

Grant frowns as he nods up at her. "I'm sure. Oh, she's coming back. Okay, be prepared in case she needs to halt the interview entirely. I'm sure it's hard for her to do this, so I'll keep her as comfortable as I can so we can get as much of the truth out there as we can."

The producers nod, and a couple of them move across the screen to ask Cassie how she is, but her mic is switched off, so we can't hear the questions except through Grant's mic, and they're inaudible. She nods, and a woman comes in and makes a show of fixing Cassie's hair and powdering her nose before everyone leaves the set.

The camera returns to just the two in the picture with the usual framing of a living room with two armchairs and no sign of it being a TV show.

"How are you feeling?"

Cassie dabs at her eye and sighs. "I'm okay. I'm so sorry for that. I didn't mean to cause a scene." Her voice is perfectly shaky, and she says, "It was hard to listen to."

"I'm sure. If you don't want to talk more about that day, as I'm sure you don't, let's talk more about everyday life for Wicked Stallion both before and after this development with Lexi."

We sit and watch the rest of the interview in silence. The credits roll as Logan picks up the remote and switches it off when it ends.

My mind is a whirling mess as I think through what we just witnessed, and I stare at the blank TV screen while I try to process it.

Finally, I say in a deadened voice, "So, that happened."

Nobody replies to my comment. I don't know whether I want to cry, scream, or yell, but I don't have the emotional resources to do any of them.

"We should call Lewis to ask about the legality of that shit," Dante says.

"They would've had their lawyers check it, but it's worth running it past him. Isaac as well. No doubt Hades will be furious," Logan agrees.

The next few hours are a blur as the guys talk to their team. I message back and forth with Heather, as well as Vera, Sherry, and Jenna, who are all super supportive. I don't put anything in writing to my management team and just tell them the audio was doctored, but I'm open with Heather about everything.

The guys move in and out of the room as they take calls, but I stay where I am, and they alternate sitting with me. Eventually, I give a big yawn and am more than ready for bed.

Dante is next to me, and he kisses my head. "Tired, Angel?" I nod, and he kisses me again. "Go to bed, then."

I kiss his lips and say, "Okay."

I find Ash and Logan talking in low voices as Logan looks at his phone at the dining table, and I walk over to give them each a kiss and a hug.

"I'm going to bed." I smile at Ash. "Is it okay if I sleep in your bed tonight?"

I think he needs it. His hair is a mess from running his hand through it, and he definitely copped the worst of it in the interview.

I'm pleased when he relaxes a little at the suggestion. "Of course, baby."

Nate is in the downstairs office, and I knock once on the door before I enter to get his attention in case he's on a phone call.

He looks around and smiles when he sees me. "Hey, Sexy. You look wrecked."

"I am. I'm going to bed. I'll see you in the morning."

He comes over to pull me into his arms before he claims my lips with his. He holds me tightly against his body as he kisses me, and I relax into him.

"Sweet dreams, Lexi. I love you."

"I love you, too."

I kiss him again before we break apart, and I walk slowly to Ash's bedroom, my heart heavy with the weight of what happened tonight but also full of the love I have for the four men of Wicked Stallion.

Chapter 16

Gotta Add Twenty-Four Words

I hang Ash's robe up in his bathroom before climbing into bed. I'm still reeling from the interview, but it doesn't take long for me to fall asleep. I wake in darkness as Ash slips quietly into bed behind me.

He wraps his arm over me and pulls me against him before he kisses my neck. I softly moan as I snuggle against him, but to my surprise, a cold breeze blows over me as the duvet in front of me is lifted.

Someone else climbs into the bed and presses their lips to mine. I realize by his scent and taste that this person is actually Ash as I kiss him back, and I have a suspicion about who's behind me, but I want to know for sure.

I break our kiss and ask, "Ash?"

"Yes," he confirms.

"Who's behind me, then?"

"You can't guess, Sexy?" Nate asks before he kisses my neck and slides his hand over my stomach toward my already drenched pussy.

"I didn't think…" I trail off, not really able to form much coherent thought as Nate strokes my clit.

"What didn't you think?" he asks, his voice a low rumble

before he nips my earlobe with his teeth.

I moan softly, and he presses his stiff cock against my ass.

"Come on, Lexi," Nate chuckles as Ash places a hand on my breast and begins to play with it. "What didn't you think? Tell us."

"Um."

I moan again and spread my legs wider for him. He pushes two fingers in and out of my pussy a few times, then rubs his wet fingers back over my clit again.

"She seems confused, Ash."

Ash chuckles and tweaks one of my nipples. "I think you could be right."

Ash clamps his lips around my other breast and swirls his tongue around the nipple.

"Is something making it hard to focus, Sexy?" Nate asks before kissing my neck.

I lean back against Nate and push my chest forward into Ash's touch as I finally unscramble the words in my brain. "I thought Ash wasn't sure about tonight."

His mouth comes off my breast, and he finds my lips to kiss me before he says, "I wasn't. After everything—I just needed something good."

"Oh, and being with just me isn't good?" I tease him.

"No! I'd never say that. I just meant—"

"Calm down, sweet boy." I use the nickname without thinking, and heat floods through my body as I do. "I'm joking. Thank you for having me here for this."

Nate pushes his fingers into me again and says, "No, thank *you*, Lexi. Because I'm going to fuck you as your payment for getting a first-class seat."

"Is that so?"

I laugh as I roll over to face him. I reach up in the dark to find his face but end up kissing his chin instead, and we burst into laughter.

"Smooth moves, Sexy."

"It's not my fault. Can we turn the damn light on, please?"

"No," Ash objects quickly from behind me.

I start in surprise at the volume of his voice and roll back over to face him.

"Are you okay?" I ask, finding his head in the dark and stroking his hair.

"Yeah, I just…can we maybe turn the bathroom light on and just leave the door ajar?"

Nate's the one who answers. "Of course we can, Ash."

He slips out of bed, and after a few seconds, there's a click of the light switch being flicked. A low light comes from the bathroom door, which is slightly ajar. It's enough for me to be able to see Ash's face, and he smiles at me.

"Sorry," he says.

"Hey, nobody wants to be blinded by the overhead light in the middle of the night," I joke, and he chuckles.

I wrap my arms around his neck and kiss him. He reaches between my legs and finds my wet clit as Nate slides in behind me again. Nate's cock is hard, and I press my ass against him while I kiss Ash.

Both Ash and I are breathing heavily when our kiss ends. I look into his beautiful face, so honored to be here with him but curious about what will happen.

"Is there anything you want to do tonight, Ash?" I ask, and Nate stiffens behind me.

Ash's cheeks flush pink in the dim light, but he admits, "I want to try sucking Nate's cock again."

Nate inhales a sharp breath of air as his cock jerks against my ass, and I roll over to face him. I take his cock in my hand and slowly pump his shaft as I look into his eyes.

"Do you want that, too, Nate?"

"Yes," he murmurs, looking past me at Ash, his eyes full of lust.

I kiss his neck and then up his jaw to his lips, where I take the bottom one between my teeth and tug at it. Nate moans and reaches down to place his hand over my breast and skirt his thumb over my nipple. I release his lip to moan aloud as Ash moves closer to me.

I stroke Nate faster and ask, "Do you like the idea of Ash wrapping his lips around your hard cock the same way he did earlier?"

"Yes." Nate tweaks my nipple.

I reach behind me to wrap my fingers around Ash's cock and stroke him as well. "Tell me how much you liked it."

"Oh, god. It was so good. Your pussy was so tight and wet, then whenever I pulled out of you, Ash's tongue was on my cock."

As Nate says this, Ash's cock jerks in my hand, and I love that he's so obviously turned on by the memory Nate is recalling.

"It was so hot, and when he took my cock in his mouth, I don't think I've ever been more satisfied in my life. Seeing Ash wrap his lips around me was amazing, and when he took me all the way in his mouth, I almost blew down his throat."

Ash's breath is hot on my neck as he pants for breath, then brings his lips down on my skin, and I shiver as he kisses behind my ear.

He reaches over me and places his hand over mine on Nate's cock. Nate gasps and stares down at Ash's hand. He strokes Nate by proxy using my hand before I test the waters. I move my hand slightly, so Ash's hand touches Nate's cock a little, and both men groan in unison.

I can help but chuckle. "Are you two enjoying this?"

"Ash is stroking my cock, Sexy. I think you know my answer."

"Well, he's not really yet, but I can fix that."

I slowly slip my hand out from under Ash's, giving him plenty of time to pull his back if he doesn't want to do this. He doesn't, though. He wraps his hand more firmly around Nate's cock, and Nate stares down at what's happening, a look of pure awe on his face.

"Do you like stroking Nate's cock?"

"Yes, Goddess," Ash murmurs.

Fuck.

I'm not sure what to do about that. We're technically not in a scene right now. I remember Ash saying that he felt freer to want what he wanted within the confines of our kink relationship.

"Nate, are you okay if I Domme Ash tonight?"

He groans but grins at me as he nods. "Yes, but I would probably say yes to anything because I can't fucking believe Ash is giving me a hand job right now."

One of the hottest things about getting together with the guys was hearing about all the times they'd fantasized about me, so I decide to ask Ash.

"You're doing so well, sweet boy," I encourage him. "Tell us, have you ever thought about Nate sexually before?"

Ash's cock jerks against my ass, and his hand freezes. There's silence in the room as Nate stares at me intently, looking aroused and curious.

"Yes," Ash finally admits.

"Tell us the kind of thoughts you've had about him, and keep stroking his cock while you do it, boy."

Ash immediately returns to stroking Nate but doesn't answer at once. I know this request will come with many emotions for him, so I'm patient as I wait, but also wildly aroused and eager to know the truth.

"I've thought about blowing him," Ash admits quietly. "There was this one time on our first tour." Ash's breathing quickens, but he slows the tempo as he strokes Nate. "We went to the hotel gym and worked out together. The changeroom didn't have private showers, so we showered next to each other."

"I remember," Nate murmurs, his voice full of lust.

"I tried not to watch you wash, and we made jokes about how many fans would wish they could take either of our places. When I got upstairs, I couldn't get the image of you naked out of my head."

My pussy aches listening to him. It's such a pure and honest retelling, and something about the idea of him having harbored this kind of desire for years is erotic, while also being sad that he didn't feel safe enough to indulge in it until now.

"I masturbated while thinking about you for about a month after that before I convinced myself to stop because it was wrong."

"It wasn't wrong," Nate says in a low voice.

"It felt wrong. You were my bandmate, and I was straight. It didn't matter that the thought of you got me hard. I knew I shouldn't be thinking that way about you, so I put it out of my mind."

I have a lump in my throat as I listen, horrified that he rejected his desires so intensely, and I can't resist asking, "Was that the first time you'd thought about a man that way?"

"No. When Logan came out, I thought about kissing him a lot. Then, I wondered what it would be like to give him head. I told myself I was just curious because Logan had come out, so it was normal to wonder about myself."

"Ugh. I hate that word. Who's to say what's 'normal,' anyway?" I roll my eyes.

"I've always thought you were hot," Nate tells him. "In an objective 'that's an attractive man' kind of way." Ash and I laugh. "But after I realized I was bi, I suddenly had my eyes opened to men as sexual creatures. Dante blowing Logan was about the hottest thing I've ever seen because Logan's amazing, and there was something taboo about Dante doing it because I'm pretty sure he's straight."

I've stopped stroking Ash's cock because I'm so fascinated by the conversation taking place, but I start up again when I realize, to a soft moan from Ash behind me.

"After I started seeing you naked on a regular basis, though"—Nate smirks—"it was pretty hard to resist thinking about you sexually. I didn't want to push you to do anything sexual because I'd hate for you to resent me. I don't ever want you to do something you don't want to do, Ash."

Ash doesn't respond immediately, and I don't interject because this feels like a conversation they need to have between them. I place my hand on Nate's chest and gently rub it for comfort. He smiles at me and kisses me softly.

"When you asked me to suck your fingers, I almost died," Ash admits. "You were so casual about it as though it was nothing, and you said Logan had done it, but I was really turned on. I've had so many fantasies about sucking someone's cock, so I pretended it was yours." Nate gives a soft moan as Ash strokes him faster again and continues, "When I found out that you were working up to doing anal, I kept thinking about what it would be like if I was the one fucking your ass."

"Why didn't you say something if you wanted to do it so badly?" Nate asks.

"Basically, because you and Logan are together." I feel Ash shrug behind me. "I didn't want to get involved and risk fucking anything up between you or us or this whole thing."

"Are you attracted to Logan, too?" Nate asks.

I try to detect if there's any jealousy attached to the question, and I can't quite tell. He sounds mostly curious, but there is a strange note to his voice that I don't fully understand.

"I mean…yes and no, I guess. I would be willing to try sexual stuff with him, but I'm more attracted to you, and I'm glad you're here."

Ash pulls his hand back and rubs his thumb over the head of Nate's cock, eliciting a groan from him. I have a strong urge to direct Ash to suck Nate now, but I want to be sure they've finished their discussion and cleared the air first.

Nate swallows heavily and looks past me at Ash again before he says solemnly, "I'm glad you're here, too. I feel weirdly honored that you're doing this with me. That's probably how Logan felt when I kept practically begging him to suck my cock and then for me to suck his."

I can't help but laugh as I remember it. "I think Logan has probably never been more stunned than the day you asked to return the favor." Nate turns his gaze to me and grins as I add, "It was hot as fuck, too."

"Do you want to see Ash suck my cock, Sexy?" I bite my lip and nod as he grins at me. "Well, I'm led to believe that you're the one who can make that happen."

Arousal floods through me from the knowledge that I have this power over Ash. That on my directive, he's going to give his first actual blow job after years of not allowing himself to want it.

"Take your hand off Nate's cock, sweet boy."

He does as instructed and drops his hand between Nate and me. I sit up out of Ash's arms and move out of the middle of the two men, leaving them lying in bed facing each other. My heart races as I look at them, staring at one another, cocks hard, and with so many truths out in the open.

"Can you lie on your back, Nate?" When he does, I add, "And move over closer to Ash?"

Nate does it, and when he settles him on his back, he's so close that Ash's cock is touching his thigh, and I groan at how hot it is. I want to ride Nate's face while Ash sucks him, so I move up toward Nate's head. I stop when I reach his torso because I realize that it would prevent him from watching Ash, which would be unfair.

Both men are obviously waiting for my next instruction, but Nate wraps his hand around my legs and softly strokes up and down my inner thigh while he waits. I moan when his fingers brush against my pussy, but I force myself to focus through my lust and look at Ash.

"Worship Nate's cock, boy. Take him in your mouth and suck him the way you know you want to, but also because your Goddess desires it for you."

Nate toys with my pussy lips, stroking them incredibly softly, but it doesn't matter how badly he teases me because my arousal is at fever pitch watching Ash move down to position his face over Nate's cock.

Ash wraps his hand around the base, and I groan in tandem with Nate as Ash wraps his lips around it. Not just because it's erotic as fuck to watch, but because Nate pushes his fingers into my pussy without warning as it happens.

Nate fucks me with his fingers, and I rub my clit as I watch Ash move his mouth up and down on Nate's cock. When Ash moans, it's so arousing that it tips me into orgasm.

"Fuck yes, Nate," I gasp as I ride his fingers.

He fucks me harder and says, "Come for me, Sexy. Come for

me while Ash sucks my cock." He knows what seeing this does to me, and even as my orgasm passes, I'm back in a state of high arousal as Nate looks down at Ash. "Mmm, yes. Your mouth feels so good, Ash."

I groan as Ash looks up at him with obvious lust but doesn't stop sucking him, and I make a mental note to watch for signs of distress from Ash. I told him to worship Nate's cock, so I don't want him to do it so long it hurts him, but so far, he seems to be experiencing nothing but enjoyment from it.

Nate turns his gaze back up to me. "Your pussy is so wet. I can tell how much you like this." He makes a 'come here' motion on my G-spot, and I close my eyes as I pant for breath when another orgasm comes closer. "Hey," Nate says in an amused tone. "Don't close your eyes. Look at what Ash is doing. Don't you want to see him suck his first cock?"

My eyes snap open, and I look down at Ash, as beautiful as ever, using his hand to stroke Nate's cock while he blows him. Ash's cock is rock hard as well, and I imagine him using it to fuck Nate. I get an image in my head of Nate on his hands and knees, with his face buried in my pussy, while Ash grips his hips and thrusts his fat cock into Nate's ass.

It tips me into the orgasm that has been hovering nearby. "Oh god, Ash. You're so fucking beautiful." As my orgasm passes, I remember with horror that I'm meant to use his nickname during a scene, adding, "I love watching you blow Nate, sweet boy."

Nate pulls his fingers out of me, and I move down to his cock. I get a close-up view of Ash's big, soft lips moving up and down on Nate, and I'm so close to coming again just from this.

"Do you like this, boy?" Ash nods his head but keeps his mouth on Nate, and I grin. "Does your jaw hurt?" Ash shakes his head, and I raise an eyebrow at him as I wrap my hand around his cock and begin to slowly stroke him. "It will. If you need to stop, tap me anywhere on my body, do you understand?" Ash nods his understanding, so I turn to face Nate and say, "Fuck his mouth."

Ash's cock jerks in my hand, and I grin in satisfaction as I turn back to watch. Nate puts his hands on the back of Ash's head and begins to thrust his cock into Ash's mouth. I've been on the receiving end of a face-fucking from Nate before, and I can tell he's going easy on Ash, which I'm glad about. He's barely thrusting his hips, but it's enough for it to be clear who's in control, and I love it.

"Yes, Ash. Take my cock. Let me fuck your mouth like your Goddess told me I could," Nate groans.

Ash makes a muffled sound on Nate's cock, but his cock jerks in my hand, and he doesn't look distressed, so I chuckle. "I'm sorry, boy. We couldn't quite understand you."

His cheeks flush pink, but his cock not only jerks in my hand, but he also begins to slightly thrust his hips into my hand as I stroke him.

Humiliation kink.

I can't help but note the reaction, so I add, "Try again, boy."

"Thank you, Goddess," he says.

The words are not at all clear because his mouth is still full of Nate's cock, so I grin wickedly at him. "You want me to spank you? Okay."

His eyes widen, and he moans onto Nate's cock as I move around behind him. Nate's eyes follow me as I pull my hand back to smack Ash's ass.

I lean around and put my face near his as I instruct, "Count, boy. I'm going to spank you five times."

"One," comes the muffled reply, and Ash's cheeks flush pink again.

I smack his ass as hard as I can, and he jumps forward, his nose hitting Nate's stomach when he does.

"Two."

By the time I've spanked him five times, my pussy is dripping juice down my thigh. I move over next to Nate's cock and in Ash's line of sight.

"Look at your Goddess's pussy, sweet boy." His gaze moves to my pussy, and he groans onto Nate's cock. "It's wet for you. Do you want to taste it?" He nods, and I say, "Get your mouth off his cock, then." Ash does as instructed, and as he starts to move toward me from his position, I shake my head. "No. Stay there. I said you could taste it, but I never said it would be from the source."

I straddle Nate and hold my pussy above his cock, right in front of Ash's face. I rub my clit as I look down at him, then take his chin in my hand and tilt his face up to look at me. He has a faraway look in his eyes, and I frown.

"Safety light check."

"Green, Goddess."

"Are you sure?" I ask because he looks pretty dazed.

"Yes, Goddess. Please don't stop."

I run my thumb over his bottom lip and smile at him. "I didn't plan to."

I let go of his face, and his gaze snaps back to my pussy as I drop onto Nate's cock. He's so hard, and his cock stretches my pussy nicely. Being filled is amazing, but I know this is a feeling I'll have to wait a little longer to indulge in properly.

Nate puts his hands on my hips and pumps in and out of me as he strokes my hip with one thumb. "You feel fucking good, Sexy."

"I'm only giving him a taste, Nate," I warn him.

"Noted." Nate fucks me faster. "Enjoy it while it lasts."

I laugh as I reach my hand down to rub my clit. Ash licks his lips as he watches me. His mouth is so close to me that his breath is hot on my pussy. I put my hand behind his head and pull him even closer, so there's barely even half an inch between his lips and my clit.

"Watch Nate fuck me, boy. Watch his cock get wet with my juices and know that you're going to be the one who cleans him for me." Ash's cock jerks, and I smirk at him. "You like that, don't you?"

"Yes, Goddess," Ash admits.

"I'm not done with your mouth tonight, sweet boy. I'm going to get a lot of use out of it, and so is Nate. Then, when we're done with your mouth, we'll move onto your cock." He moans softly, and the sound is incredibly satisfying. "That's right. Maybe, I'll allow Nate to have the enjoyment of blowing you. Not for your pleasure, but for his, because your body is mine to use, and tonight I'm gifting your body to Nate." I watch for his response to this because we don't have a CNC agreement in place, but Ash moans loudly. So I climb off Nate and tell him, "Clean Nate's cock, boy."

I look down at Ash's cock, and pre-cum oozes from its tip. I squeeze it firmly, and he jumps before relaxing again. As he does, Nate begins fucking his mouth again, slightly rougher than before, and Ash grips Nate's thighs as he does.

I rub the sticky liquid over the head of his cock with my thumb, then move up to Nate's head and say, "He's enjoying being used, Nate. His cock is literally weeping with joy,"

I place my thumb near Nate's face, and he locks eyes with Ash as he sucks it before he says, "Tasty. I'll have to suck him dry later." Ash groans onto Nate's cock, and Nate laughs. "Seems like he likes the idea."

"I think he does. You can do whatever you want with him, though. He's a good boy. He'll do everything you ask."

"Good to know." Nate slows down the pace at which he fucks Ash's mouth and says through panting breaths, "I am going to have to stop now if I don't want to blow my load down his throat."

I laugh and turn to Ash. "Stop sucking Nate, sweet boy."

Ash pulls his mouth off Nate's cock, and I lie back next to Nate and spread my legs. "While Nate calms down a little"—I smirk at Nate—"you can worship my pussy, sweet boy."

I catch sight of a look of pure lust on Ash's face before he dives between my legs. I moan as he swirls his tongue around my clit. I buck against his mouth as he pleasures me, sparks of electricity shooting from my pussy and darting through my body until every one of my nerve endings is on fire.

I pant for breath as Nate rolls onto his side to face me and raises a hand to my breast. He presses his lips to mine and teases my mouth open with his tongue. The pleasure of Ash eating me out while Nate kisses me as he caresses my breasts, on top of everything I just witnessed with them, causes me to come once again.

I break my kiss with Nate and lift my head to look down at Ash when it hits. "Yes, sweet boy. Make your Goddess come with your mouth. Just like that, yes. Oh, fucking hell."

"God, this is fucking good. When you're done, I might fuck his mouth again."

Ash moans into my pussy when Nate says this, and I laugh through my panting breaths. "I think he likes that idea. Make me come again, boy, and I'll let Nate fuck your mouth. If you can't make me come in five minutes, you don't get his cock in your mouth again tonight."

Nate grabs his phone to set a timer, then grins down at Ash. "You'd better fucking make her come, or I'm gonna be pissed. I want your mouth on my cock again."

He starts the timer, and I don't think Ash has ever been more determined to make me orgasm. I manage to hold off for three minutes, but I'm perilously close by the fourth. Ash flicks his tongue back and forth across my now very sensitive clit and fucks me with three fingers.

"Thirty seconds, Ash. I need you to make her come soon because I want to fuck that hot mouth of yours."

To my surprise, Ash promptly nips my clit with his teeth, and the sudden pain followed by the intense pleasure after as he goes back to licking it tips me over the edge.

"Holy fucking shit!" I scream as my orgasm hits.

My entire body shakes, and my eyes roll back as I'm engulfed by waves and waves of pleasure.

"I can't," I pant. "I can't fucking—oh, fuck. I can't. Fuck. Oh my god."

Ash doesn't lift his head, and he continues his assault on my clit as I lose myself in the ecstasy rocking my body. I can barely stand the pleasure, and it's exquisitely painful because my clit is even more sensitive now. I revel in the feeling of it, though, and place my hands on the back of Ash's head to push him more firmly against my pussy. I ride his face the short time it takes to come again before letting go.

"Stop, boy."

He immediately lifts his face, and I groan at the sight of him. He has that dazed look that I've come to realize means he's in subspace. His face is covered in my pussy juice, his hair is a complete mess, and his cock is rock hard.

"Come to me, sweet boy," I say, moving away from Nate and patting the space between us, my love for Ash overwhelming me as he approaches. "Lie with us," I murmur in a husky voice I don't recognize as my own.

Ash lies on his back in between us, and I look over at Nate, who looks wildly curious and aroused as he stares at him.

"Look at what a mess Ash has made of his face, Nate," I say, noting when Ash's cock jerks.

"It is covered in pussy juice." Nate chuckles, and Ash's cheeks flush pink. "I wonder what it tastes like," he says in a faux thoughtful voice.

"There's only one way to find out. You should kiss him."

Ash inhales sharply, and his eyes widen before they quickly become hooded, and he stares up at Nate, looking eager to be kissed. Nate lowers his head to Ash's and kisses him. The satisfied moan that comes from Nate drives me wild. He reaches down and wraps his hand around Ash's cock as he kisses him, stroking him slowly and eliciting a guttural groan from Ash.

I reach between my legs to rub my clit, lost in the pleasure of watching them, as Nate lifts his head and looks down into Ash's eyes. "Do you like that?"

"Fuck, yes, Nate."

"Good to hear. Don't come, okay?" Ash nods. "I still want us to fuck Lexi."

"I'll let you know if I'm going to come."

Ash reaches up and pulls Nate back down to him, which surprises me. A part of me wants to punish him for taking control of anything at all, but I remind myself that what's happening right now was initiated by Nate. I might have said I was handing Ash to him, but this is between them right now.

They kiss for a long time, with Nate jerking Ash off until he warns him that he's going to come. Nate slows down the speed at which he strokes him, and they continue to kiss. Ash wraps his arms around Nate's neck, and I love them both so much that I'm sure my heart is going to explode from how full it is.

Eventually, Nate breaks one of their kisses and smiles at Ash. "This is fucking amazing."

"It really is. I can't believe this is happening."

"Are you okay with it all?" Nate asks, a frown on his face.

Ash pulls Nate back to him as they kiss for about another thirty seconds before Ash says through panting breaths, "Fuck, yes. I'm okay with all of this. It's the hottest thing I've ever done."

"Of *course,* I'm the hottest thing you've ever done," Nate says with a smirk, and I can't help but laugh.

The two men jump, and Nate looks over at me. "I'm sorry, did you two forget I was here?"

I grin at Nate, and his cheeks flush pink. "We could never *really* forget you, Lexi."

"If you say so. I think Ash has blinded you with his amazing cock."

Nate strokes him slowly and looks at Ash. "I can't wait to get it in my mouth, but I think I've brought you too close too many times. So maybe you should suck my cock again while you calm down."

"I'm not sure that's going to have the desired effect," Ash laughs as he reaches between them to stroke Nate's cock. "Getting to suck your cock is basically one of my biggest fantasies being fulfilled, but I'm not about to say no."

Nate rolls onto his back, and Ash takes his cock back in his mouth again, with a long groan from Nate. He sucks him again as Nate reaches over to pull me closer.

"Sit on my face, Sexy," Nate growls. "I want to eat your pussy while Ash blows me."

He doesn't have to ask twice, and I straddle him before I lower myself to ride his face, Nate unintentionally fulfilling my wish from earlier. Nate wraps his arms around my thighs and holds me down on his face as I watch Ash suck him.

It's not long before I come because I'm crazy aroused now, and my clit basically only needs to be touched to set me off at this point. I don't count the number of times my body shakes, and I come on Nate's face because they're too numerous, and I can't focus enough to keep track.

Eventually, though, Nate places his hands on my waist and lifts me off his face enough to say, "You're going to need to stop, Ash. I don't want to come yet, and your mouth is so fucking good that I'm going to blow."

Ash lifts his head, and his cheeks flush pink as he says, "I know you don't want to do it tonight, but, um, is that something you would consider doing sometime?"

I move off Nate so he can properly see Ash, and his arousal is obvious as he asks in a husky voice, "Blow down your throat?"

"Yeah."

"Anytime, Ashton Woodford. Literally." Nate smirks at him. "Middle of the stage during a concert? Yes. Live TV during an interview? Yes. Visit to the White House in front of the President? Yes. Any. Time."

"Good to know," Ash murmurs.

"Can I suck your cock now?" Nate asks.

"Of course. If you still want to fuck Lexi, I don't think you'll be able to do it for long, though." Ash flushes pink again. "I'm so fucking close to coming right now."

Nate moves over to him and kisses him. "I just want the chance to try it. You can always blow down my throat some other time, too."

Ash lies down next to me, and I immediately kiss him, thrusting my tongue into his mouth before I break our kiss to watch Nate as he wraps his lips around Ash's thick cock. Ash groans as Nate blows him. I watch in pure ecstasy as Ash experiences his first blow job from a man. He stares down at Nate in complete awe, and I rest my head on his chest, holding him tight as he does.

After about a minute, Nate takes Ash's cock out of his mouth and strokes it slowly with his hand as he looks up at him. "You don't have to be gentle with me. I've sucked plenty of cock. Well, one cock," he amends with a grin. "But I've sucked it a lot. You can be rougher and properly fuck my mouth if you want."

"Okay," Ash says.

I move off him as Nate sinks onto his cock again. Ash places a hand on either side of Nate's face and fucks his mouth. Like...*really* fucks it. Nate gags on his cock occasionally, and I'm driven further into lust whenever he does, fucking my pussy with my fingers in time with the way Ash fucks Nate's mouth. He doesn't do it for anywhere near long enough before he stops, though, and I'm disappointed because I was enjoying it so much.

He pulls Nate's head up and pants, "You've gotta stop. Now."

Nate blinks at him a couple of times, and I recognize just how far gone he is with us into the state of arousal we've all reached tonight.

"Sure. Let's fuck Lexi." He turns to look at me. "Get on his cock, Lexi. Time to pay for your ticket."

These words are so arousing, and the thought of using my body for payment to Nate causes me to moan as I climb over Ash. I start to lower myself onto him, but Nate shakes his head.

"Not like that. Lie on your back on him so that he can fuck you from behind, and I can lick your clit."

I can barely manage to hold off coming as I follow Nate's instructions, and when Ash's cock is buried in my pussy and Nate lowers his mouth to my clit, I explode into orgasm. Nate continues to swipe his tongue across my clit while I come on Ash's cock. Ash takes my breasts in his hands and kisses my neck as he fucks me slowly through my orgasm.

Once it's passed, Nate lifts his head and moves over me to kiss me. I wrap my arms around his neck and kiss him back, then gasp as I experience a painful stretching in my pussy.

I stare up at Nate, and he says, "You can take it, Sexy. You can take us both at once."

I'm done for.

They move slowly in and out of me together. It's a mixture of pain, pleasure, excitement, and sheer lust from how good it is to have two men in my pussy at one time. I had no idea it could be like this.

"Your cock feels so good against mine in her pussy, Ash," Nate says, and Ash grunts underneath me.

Nate leans back and holds my hips as he continues fucking me while he looks down at my pussy. "God, this view is fucking phenomenal. Lexi's pussy stretched tight around our cocks. I'm going to fucking come."

His cock jerks inside me as he orgasms, but he continues to slowly fuck me, rubbing my clit as he does. Eventually, he squeezes his eyes shut tight, and I can tell he's in pain, but I don't say anything because I know he'll stop if he really needs to.

He doesn't.

He keeps going for another short while until Ash groans, "Fuck, Goddess. I'm coming. I'm coming inside your cunt, Goddess."

Nate opens his eyes and stares down at us, watching Ash come, and he rubs my clit and says, "Come for us, Sexy. I want to feel your pussy come around two men at once."

Ash is still spilling his seed in me when my orgasm hits. Nate pushes his cock as far into me as he can manage, and Ash holds me tight against him but reaches up to pull and tweak my nipples as I come.

"You're so beautiful when you come like this, Sexy. I love you. I love that you're filled with both Ash and me. I love this, and his cock feels so fucking good against mine with you coming around us both." He rubs my clit slowly in circles until my body stops shaking.

As I lie on top of Ash, with two cocks stuffed into my pussy and filled with cum, I'm stunned into silence. I've just had the most mind-blowing experience of my life, and I don't think I'll ever forget this night.

"Holy shit," I eventually say. "There's no way I'm not going to mess up the sheets when you guys pull out of me."

Both of them laugh, and Nate leans down to kiss me before he says, "If you mess up the sheets, we can all just go sleep in my room tonight, and they can be washed tomorrow."

Sure enough, the moment Nate pulls out of me, cum starts dripping out of me and onto Ash's cock.

"God, you two look so fucking hot," Nate groans. "But yeah, we're going to have to go to my room."

I climb off Ash, and we rush to the bathroom to minimize the amount of mess we make on the way. Nate already has the water in the shower running from both of the double shower heads, and it's beautifully warm.

I pull Ash under the spray while I kiss his soft lips, and Nate watches as I clean Ash's beautiful body from head to toe. I kiss Ash's skin as I clean it until, eventually, I kiss his lips and hold him tight under the spray.

I press my lips to his ear and ask quietly, "Do you want to talk in front of Nate or in private?"

"I'm fine to talk now," he says with a smile.

"How are you feeling?" I ask. "That was…" I blink a few times as I try to process it myself. "A lot."

"It was really good, though," Ash says, then looks at Nate. "How was it for you?"

I turn to look at Nate, and he grins. "Top five sexual experiences of my life."

"That's saying something," Ash teases him.

"You should be honored." Nate looks down at Ash's cock and says, "Your cock is amazing."

"I could say the same thing," Ash says with a suggestive grin.

I wash quickly and then dry Ash off as Nate dries himself before we follow Nate to his room. We climb into his bed and end up the same way this night began, with me squished in between Nate and Ash.

"Thanks for tonight, it was absolutely amazing."

"Thank you both," Ash says in the darkness. "Especially you,

Goddess." He kisses my lips softly. "You gave me permission to want what I wanted, and I felt safe with you the whole time."

"Do you need me to be there the next time you and Nate do anything? I'm okay either way."

"If Nate wants to do stuff with me, I don't need you to be there now. I would like you to be there sometimes, though," Ash says softly as he rubs my side and a contented peace comes over me.

We lie in silence for a few moments before Nate says, "Hey, if we have the others there next time, maybe we can get a cock in her ass and mouth, too."

The three of us burst into laughter, and I don't think I've ever been happier in my life. I fall into a blissful sleep, sandwiched between two of the most beautiful men I know.

Chapter 17

Lexi Is Broken...

I wake on Monday morning still cuddled between Nate and Ash. They're both asleep, and my head is on Ash's chest, with his arm over my back, while Nate also has his arm over me, his hand resting on Ash's stomach. Nate's cock is hard against my ass, Ash is stiff against my stomach, and I can't help but smile as I think about last night. My pussy aches from being stretched the way it was, and the feeling is deeply satisfying.

I kiss Ash's chest and soak in the feeling of being here with them. I'm acutely aware that I have to go to Black Lilac this morning, but I really don't think I can after the interview last night. It'll only cause more trouble at the store if I do. I can't get to my phone at the moment, nor do I want to, but I'll need to message Jenna and tell her that I won't be in today.

Eventually, Ash stirs, and his eyes flutter open. He blinks a few times, then looks down at me. "Morning."

"Hi." I can't stop the smile that comes to my face. "How are you feeling this morning?"

"I won't lie. I feel a bit weird," he admits.

"It was a pretty intense scene. That's normal. You're probably still having some sub drop."

"It's not entirely that." His eyes flicker past me, and I assume he's looking at Nate. "We've been friends for so long. I don't want this to change things or screw that up."

"Has getting involved with me done that?" I raise an eyebrow at him.

"Well, no, but—"

"Logan wouldn't lie. If he says he's okay with it, it's because he means it." I move up to kiss Ash softly. "But just go at your own pace. You don't ever have to do that again if you don't want to," I promise. "Or you can do it every night if that's what you want."

Ash chuckles and kisses me again. "I love you so much, Goddess."

"We're not full-time yet, Ash," I tell him.

"I know. But can I call you that, anyway? It feels weird when I call you 'baby' now." His cheeks flush pink as he says it.

I smile at him and nod. "Okay. When we go full-time, you'll do that anyway, and I prefer calling you 'sweet boy,' too," I admit.

Ash looks incredibly pleased by this, and I kiss him again, then rest my head back on his chest.

"It's so weird suddenly being a Domme." I snort with laughter. "It's even weirder liking it."

Ash kisses the top of my head. "You're as surprised as I am."

"What made you invite Nate to bed last night?" I place my hand over Nate's, where it still rests on Ash's stomach, and stroke his soft skin.

"I felt like complete shit after the interview. I knew it would be a good distraction." He looks over at Nate and gets a sweet smile on his face. "He was really nice about it and said he didn't have to come to bed with us if I didn't really want him to."

"What did you say to that?" I ask.

"He said, 'Come to bed with me if you want my mouth wrapped around your cock or don't. Either way, I'll get to fuck Lexi,'" Nate says with a laugh, and I jump because I wasn't aware he was awake.

I roll over to face him as Ash joins his laughter and grin at him. "You didn't want to miss out on that, I assume?"

He reaches between my legs to stroke my wet clit and says, "Something like that. Morning."

"Morning," I say before I kiss him.

As we kiss, Nate pushes a finger into my tender pussy, and it's uncomfortable. I break our kiss to groan aloud as I shake my head.

"My pussy's actually really sore this morning. I think I need some time to recover from having two cocks in me."

Even as I say it, my pussy throbs at the memory, but Nate removes his finger with a smile at me. "Of course."

He kisses me, and I put my arms around his neck to kiss him back. Ash gently strokes my back and side as I do, then rolls me back to him to kiss him as well.

When our kiss ends, I flop onto my back and give them a cheeky grin as I indicate between the two of them. "Now it's your turn, isn't it?"

They look at each other for a few seconds, then Ash leans over me and kisses Nate. His lips part, and Nate slips his tongue into Ash's mouth as he places his hand on the back of Ash's neck. My heart beats faster, and my breathing quickens as I watch them. I'm so excited for them to explore this new thing together.

When they break apart, Nate grins down at me. "Are you happy, Sexy?"

"Yup. You two are hot as fuck. I approve of getting to see you do dirty things together," I tease him.

I squeal as he grabs me and pulls me on top of him. His hand is firm on my ass, pressing my body against his hard cock as he stares at me with his beautiful blue eyes.

"I'm sorry, did you want to get fucked this morning after all?" he jokes. "Because your ass isn't sore, is it?"

He squeezes my flesh, and I groan as my pussy aches. Nate kisses me again, then trails kisses along my jaw to my ear.

He nips my earlobe with his teeth and tugs it gently as I moan, then he says in a low growl, "Maybe we could see if you can fit two cocks in your ass, too." I pant for breath as I imagine it, and Nate rubs his hand over my ass before grabbing it again. "I'd love to be in your ass with another cock in there, too. I don't even care whose it is. Ash, Logan, Dante, any of them would be fine."

"My whole downstairs area is sore, I'll have you know"—I cringe at him, then grin—"and I can barely fit Ash in my ass as it is," I point out, and the guys both laugh.

Nate looks over at him and grins. "I look forward to taking on the challenge of Ash's cock one day."

"It's here anytime you want it," Ash says, stroking his erection.

"Oh, I want it." Nate continues kneading my ass with one hand as he reaches down to take Ash's cock with the other. "I might not be ready to take it in my ass yet, but I definitely wouldn't mind having you blow down my throat."

Ash grins at him. "Well, I'm not going to stop you."

I kiss Nate, then roll off him as Ash sits up in the bed while Nate moves down to his cock. He wraps his lips around it with a groan from Ash. I get onto my knees and press my lips to Ash's.

He wraps his arms around me, and we kiss for a while before he breaks our kiss to moan as he looks down at Nate. "God, that's fucking good."

I turn to see Nate with his lips all the way at the base of Ash's cock as he uses his hand to play with Ash's balls. He's also using his spare hand to stroke his own cock as he sucks Ash.

Nate pulls his head off Ash with a gasp for air before grinning at me. "Want to help me out here, Sexy?"

"I'm hardly going to say no."

I move next to him, and he angles Ash's cock toward me. I take him in my mouth and suck him, using my hand to stroke him as I do before I let Nate have another turn. He kisses me first, thrusting his tongue into my mouth while he strokes Ash's cock before he returns to sucking it after our kiss.

We pass Ash's cock back and forth between us for a long time. Whenever I think Ash might be close to coming, I spend longer with his cock so that I can ensure he doesn't get too close before

Nate takes over. Despite the fact I'm so sore, I desperately want to fuck one of the guys, and my pussy is drenched.

Eventually, I move back to kiss Ash again and watch as Nate focuses on bringing him to orgasm. I revel in the sounds that both men make. The room is filled with the sounds of their hot, panting breaths, along with groans of ecstasy. Ash moves me up to take one of my breasts in his mouth and reaches between my legs to rub my clit.

He smiles at me and murmurs, "You're so wet, Goddess."

I feel guilty because I totally forgot to Domme him this morning, so I smile back at him. "Yes, I am, sweet boy. I'm going to have you make me come after you've blown in Nate's mouth." He groans, and I smile at him. "Do you like having Nate's mouth on your cock?"

"Yes," he pants for breath.

"Why don't you tell him, then?"

Ash stares down at Nate. "You're so fucking good at that, Nate."

He lifts his head but continues to pump Ash's cock with his hand as he grins at him. "I'm glad to hear it. Your cock is amazing, and getting to blow you is so good."

I lie next to Ash and kiss him as I spread my legs and rub my clit while I enjoy the show as Nate places his mouth on Ash's cock again. I'm in ecstasy and eager for the moment when Ash will come down Nate's throat.

I bite my lip as Ash groans, "I'm coming, Nate."

Nate continues moving for a few seconds before he clamps his lips around Ash's cock, and it jerks in Nate's mouth.

"Yes. Fuck, yes, Nate."

Nate's Adam's apple bobs up and down, and I moan softly, knowing that he's swallowing Ash's cum. He pulls his head back and swirls his tongue around the head of Ash's cock, licking up the last few drops of sticky fluid there.

They're both panting for breath as they stare at each other in awe. I think my heart might explode from the amount of love and satisfaction that I get from them enjoying each other.

Nate moves wordlessly over me, though, and my eyebrows raise. He places a hand on either side of my breasts and holds them together before pushing his cock between them. He moans as he fucks my breasts, and I open my mouth for him to slip the tip of his cock between my lips every few thrusts.

He leans down and kisses Ash as he fucks me. I watch as much as I can out of the corner of my eye, and when their kiss ends, Ash moves over my breasts. He takes one in his mouth and swirls his tongue around my nipple, causing me to moan.

"Yes, boy. Oh god, yes. Come kiss me."

He moves up and kisses me. I almost come when I can taste his own semen on his tongue. There's something about it having come from Nate's mouth to mine via Ash that is wildly erotic.

Ash turns away from me so I can only see the back of his head and don't know what's going on until Nate groans, "Oh, fuck. I love my cock being in your mouth while I'm fucking Lexi's tits."

It drives me crazy to know this is happening even though I can't see it. Nate moves his hands up to thumb my nipples while he thrusts into the valley between my breasts, and Ash makes a muffled groan. I reach between my legs to rub my clit again, and it takes barely any time for me to come because I'm so aroused by it all.

My body shakes as my orgasm hits, and Nate grins down at me. "Mmm. I love watching you come, Sexy." He waits until my orgasm has passed, then looks at Ash. "Hold her breasts for me, Ash, but stay where you are."

Ash places his hands over Nate's, and Nate gets a quick sweet smile on his face that melts my heart before he moves his hand out from under Ash's. Ash maintains the pressure on my breasts, and Nate continues to thrust between them, but he places his hand on the back of Ash's head and pulls his mouth right down to the tops of my breasts. His breath is hot on my flesh as Nate fucks me as well as Ash's mouth. Nate bites his lip and looks down at us with pure lust in his expression as he fucks us both.

He pants for breath as he says, "I'm going to come, Ash. If you don't want to swallow my load, now's the time to move."

Ash does nothing as Nate thrusts forward a final time and holds his cock in his mouth. He's absolutely glorious to watch, his muscles tensing as his cock jerks between my breasts, and I know he's coming down Ash's throat. The hand on the back of Ash's head is so tense I can see the whites of his knuckles, but as his orgasm passes, his hand relaxes, and he strokes Ash's head softly. All three of us are panting for breath, but I catch the sound of Ash swallowing, and it's one of the most erotic things I've ever heard.

Nate pulls his cock back and rests back on his heels at my side as he smiles at us. "Holy fuck, that was good. How did you like swallowing your first load of cum, Ash?"

"It doesn't taste that great," he says, and both Nate and I burst into laughter.

"No, it doesn't," Nate agrees. "I still think it's hot as fuck doing it." He smirks at Ash. "It's even hotter when it's you doing it to me, though."

"I'll definitely do it again sometime," Ash says, sounding amused.

I haven't forgotten that I told him he'd have to make me come once Nate did, so I put my best Domme voice on and say, "No rest for the wicked. Your mouth needs to be used one more time this morning, sweet boy. Don't put your tongue or fingers in my pussy because it's sore, but I want you to kiss it better by making me come."

I spread my legs wide, and Ash moves down to position himself between them. I doubt I'll be able to last long because my clit is so sensitive now, but I'm excited by making him get me off as our final act this morning.

Nate watches as Ash buries his face in my pussy before asking, "Do you like that, Sexy?"

"Yes, I really do," I moan as I reach down and stroke the back of Ash's head while he eats me out, reveling in the pleasure he gives me. "He's such a good boy."

"I thought it was hot watching the other guys Dom you, but I'm not gonna lie, this is just as fucking hot."

"Maybe you're more into kink than you realize. You could just be a voyeur." I grin at him.

Nate laughs and shakes his head before he places his lips less than an inch away from me, his bright blue eyes staring into mine as he murmurs, "Maybe, but maybe not. I definitely like being involved."

He presses his lips against mine and slips his tongue into my mouth, exploring my mouth until he breaks our kiss, and I'm left breathless and dizzy with lust. He trails kisses down my chin and neck to my breasts. I almost come when he bites my nipple, but I manage to keep my orgasm at bay, not wanting this to end.

Nate swirls his tongue around my nipple and tweaks the other between his forefinger and thumb, driving me wild before continuing his path. I moan in anticipation as he reaches my pubic bone. Each kiss brings him closer and closer to the place where Ash is working on my clit.

When he finally makes it there, he and Ash share the task of eating me, and I'm fucking gone. I watch their tongues on my clit, on each other's tongues, and when Nate grabs Ash's head and pulls his face to his so they can kiss properly, he doesn't fail to continue stroking my clit.

I'm so close to coming, and I can barely hold off now. I don't let it hit me because my instruction to Ash was for him to make me come, and if I come for Nate, it would be unfair to punish Ash.

I manage to say through panting breaths, "Ash has to make me come, Nate. I told him to."

"Huh?" Nate's fingers freeze on my clit as he breaks their kiss to give me a dazed look.

"I gave Ash an instruction, and I don't want to have to punish him because you made me come instead."

Nate blinks at me, then turns to Ash as he indicates to my pussy. "I'd better let you do your job, I guess."

He moves up to kiss me again before lying down next to me

and pulling me into his embrace. We watch together as Ash returns to his task, and it isn't long before I'm shaking against Nate when Ash makes me come.

"Yes, sweet boy. Make me come. Fuck yes. Oh, god." I'm not sure if he'll keep going, so I tell him through panting breaths, "You can stop now." He lifts his head to look at me, and I smile at him. "Come kiss me, boy."

He moves up to me, and I pull him into my arms to kiss him. I can taste myself on his tongue, and I'm on a total high, so happy in my post-orgasm glow. We lie together for a while, and none of us speaks as the sound of panting breath slowly fades into normal breathing. Nate and Ash's bodies are warm against me, and I reflect on what has happened since last night.

Like with Logan, I think I'll leave them to figure out what they want to be, but I want them to know that, so I say, "Just so you know, whatever you guys want to be or not be, you have my blessing. I know you probably already know that, but I wanted to make it clear."

"Like crystal." Nate chuckles and kisses the top of my head. "Good to know."

"Thank you, Goddess."

I get butterflies at Ash's use of my new nickname and turn his face up to kiss me again before we fall back into silence. Eventually, I sigh because I know that even though I'm not going to work today, I need to let Jenna know and be sure that she's going to be able to open the store.

"We should get cleaned up," I tell the guys.

When we get to the shower, Nate washes himself under one of the showerheads while I start to wash Ash under the other. He finishes quickly and kisses me before he turns to Ash. He hesitates for a moment, but Ash snakes his arm around Nate's waist and pulls him to him. I drop to my knees to wash Ash's legs but also to hide the satisfied smile that I can't help from coming to my face.

"I'm going to go see Logan. I'll see you guys later," Nate says before leaving the shower.

I continue washing Ash and then quickly clean myself when I'm done. After we're dry, I kiss him and hold him in my embrace before taking his hand to lead him back downstairs to his bedroom.

As we leave the bathroom, I ask, "How are you feeling?"

"Good. Still a bit strange. I thought I would feel different after I did sexual stuff with a man, but I don't. Is that weird?"

I look up at him and smile. "I don't know. It might be something to talk to Logan and Nate about, but you're still you, no matter what you do in the bedroom. Nothing you do sexually will change that."

"Interesting point," he says in a thoughtful voice. "Society certainly seems to think sex has some power to change people."

"Yeah, well, society can get fucked," I scoff, and Ash laughs. "I mean, it's a new experience you've had, but it doesn't change who you are as a person any more than eating a new flavor of ice cream or going skydiving or performing at a concert." I shrug because it's true and point out, "You're still the same Ash as yesterday. You're just Ash who has given and received head from Nate and knows what that's like. Carnal knowledge. Before, you could only imagine what it was like, but now you know that's the only difference. The core of who you are as a human being is the same."

He's silent as we make our way down the stairs, but when we reach the bottom, he says, "Thanks, Lexi."

"Anytime." I smile up at him. "I should be thanking you for including me. Although, maybe I wouldn't have a broken vagina today if you hadn't."

Ash snorts with laughter as I push open the door to his bedroom. While he gets dressed, I find my phone and send a message to Jenna. As Ash pulls on his shoes, she replies that she's fine to open the store and understands why I feel it's better to stay away today, which is a weight off my mind.

I take his hand again as we make our way to the kitchen and hand my phone to him. "Here, sweet boy. You can carry my phone since you have pockets and I don't."

"Yes, Goddess." He slips my phone into his jeans pocket and

then shakes his head. "Do you know how hard it is for me to cope with my Goddess being naked all the time?"

Given everything that's going on in our lives, I'm surprised by the end of this sentence and burst into laughter. "You're going to have to take that up with Logan, I'm afraid."

"What's he going to have to take up with me?" Logan asks as we enter the kitchen, where Logan is currently cooking bacon.

"Most immediately, whether you're making breakfast for everyone or just yourself like an asshole," Ash says with a grin.

"Calm down. I'm making it for everyone," Logan laughs. "Do you have time for breakfast, Lexi?"

"I'm not going to the store today. Jenna is going to handle it. I just can't face it, and it'll only be worse for them if I go in."

Logan nods. "Makes sense. So what else did you need to take up with me, Ash?"

"Oh. How hard it is for me that my Goddess is naked all the time."

Logan's eyebrows raise for an instant, then he clears the surprised look from his face and grins at us both. "Well, that's between you two. I like looking at my toy and having it accessible at all times. If I get to torment a second sub in the process, all the better, to be honest."

"Who hurt you, Logan Ballantine?" Ash asks with a grin.

Logan looks Ash up and down, then smirks at him. "Just consider yourself lucky I'm only a backup Dom. I can think of plenty of ways I could have fun with you."

Ash chuckles, and I say, "I might have to hit you up for ideas sometime, Sir."

"More than happy to help, Alexandra," he says in a husky voice. "Come here."

I let go of Ash's hand and walk over to Logan. He flips the bacon in the pan with a silicone spatula as I do, and I wait next to him. He turns to me and smiles as he uses a piece of paper towel to clean it.

"Bend over the bench, Alexandra."

I gasp and do as I'm told before Logan smacks my ass with the spatula. I gasp and jump at the stinging pain. The spatula is hot, but it's not a burning pain, just hot enough to remind me that he's spanking me with something he's using to cook our breakfast, and I'm turned on by this knowledge.

He smacks my ass again, then asks, "Do you like seeing your Goddess getting spanked with a spatula, Ash?"

"Yes," he admits, and I can hear the arousal in his voice.

Logan brings the spatula down on my ass again and says, "Take note, Alexandra. Sometimes spanking is just for fun. Are you enjoying this?"

"Yes, Sir," I gasp as he hits me again.

My pussy aches to be filled, and I'm so wet that I'm sure I'm going to make a mess on the chair when I sit down to eat breakfast…*if* I can sit down.

"I heard you took two cocks in your pussy last night. Is that true?" he asks.

"Yes, Sir."

He reaches down with his spare hand and rubs it through my wet slit. "So wet and ready for fucking. Too bad they broke my toy. As soon as it's mended, I'll make good use of it."

He rubs my clit just long enough to get me to a high level of ecstasy, then rubs my ass softly with his hand instead. He flips the bacon again, cleans the spatula, and spanks my ass three more times before he grabs my hair and pulls me upright with it.

He yanks on it to force my face upward and makes me look at him. "Good girl, Alexandra. I'm very satisfied with you, can you tell?"

He pushes me to my knees, and my face is right in front of his crotch. His cock is stiff in his sweatpants, and it's so hard that I can even see the outline of the head against the fabric.

"Yes, Sir."

"I'm going to play with you later, but I need to finish cooking for now. Go see Dante and Nate. They're in the dining room."

We leave the kitchen, and as we near the dining room, Ash

whispers, "Jesus christ, that was fucking hot."

"You're telling me." I grin at him.

"I mean, I always thought them Domming you was hot, but now it's like I can imagine you doing it to me, and it's a million times hotter."

"Carnal knowledge," I tease him as we enter the dining room.

Dante and Nate are sitting at the table, which has been set for breakfast, drinking juice while they talk.

"Morning, Honey," I say as I approach Dante.

I let go of Ash's hand and wrap my arms around his neck from behind.

"Good morning, Angel. Did you have a good night?"

I kiss his cheek and sit next to him, adjusting my position because my ass hurts as Ash sits at the spot next to me. "The best."

"I'm glad to hear it. I was just telling Nate that we're going to Lewis' office today and meeting Isaac there. He thinks we should proceed with a lawsuit against Cassie in tandem with the criminal case. Make it clear who's in the wrong without making any kind of statement. He's going to consult with Hades as well, of course."

A million butterflies tumble around my stomach at the thought of suing Cassie. It makes sense, and it does send a statement to the world that we believe she's in the wrong. The thought of airing it all in a trial is sickening, though.

"I'm not going to work today, so I can come with you guys."

"I know. Nate told me." Dante leans over and kisses me. "Have you given any more thought to stepping back from the stores a little?"

"Maybe." I sigh. "I can't deny that my presence there at the moment is probably doing more bad than good."

Logan appears with a platter of breakfast food, and as we eat, I think about what Dante suggested.

"Can I have my phone, please?" I ask Ash.

He nods, then puts his fork down to pull it out of his pocket and hand it to me. The screen is full of the usual notifications, and I sigh. I send a message to the chat I have with the managers and ask how the stores are doing this morning, so it doesn't seem like I'm just checking up on Jenna.

There's a notification about a call from my dad, and my heart pounds in my chest. He left me a voicemail, so I press the button to play it and lift the phone to my ear to listen.

"Hi, Lexi. Can you please call me to talk?"

My heart pounds in my chest, and I don't know what my face looks like, but Nate frowns at me and asks, "What's wrong?"

"My dad called me, and he wants to talk. I guess I'll call him back after breakfast."

Chapter 18

. . . and Her Heart Hurts

My nerves only get worse throughout breakfast. I don't know if my dad has changed his mind already, and a tiny part of me hopes for that, but I'm not optimistic. It's possible that Sophie has talked him around, though. By the time I'm sitting in one of the armchairs in the living room to call him, the nausea is so bad that I'm sure I'm going to puke. I press the button to call him and can barely breathe as I wait for him to answer.

"Lexi?" he answers my call, but his tone gives nothing away.

"Hi, Dad," I say with a sigh. "You wanted to talk?"

"Yes. What is going on with you? We saw that interview last night and some of the disgusting things you've been doing."

My heart splinters at the word 'disgusting.' I can't even bring myself to be angry because the sadness I feel is all-consuming, and tears start to fall.

"Please don't call me disgusting, Dad," I ask quietly.

"What word should I use, Alexandra? You've told us how you're living your life, and now the entire world knows because you yourself were recorded telling someone that you 'fuck four men,' or whatever it was. You were caught red-handed cheating on Ashton's girlfriend."

"We didn't *cheat*," I object.

"What were you two doing on that recording if you weren't having sex?" he demands.

I hate this. I hate that he heard that recording. I hate that he doesn't seem to want to hear what I have to say. That he's believing someone else over the word of his own daughter.

"*They were already broken up*," I practically yell. "Do you even care about knowing my side of the story, or are you just going to go off the word of someone like Cassie?"

"I'm going off *your* word. You told us these things yourself last week. What are you doing with your life, Alexandra? Where did I go wrong in raising you? Your mother would be so ashamed of you."

There is nothing left in my chest but a bleeding wound, and I can barely speak through my tears, but I croak out, "Don't bring Mom into this. That's not fair."

"Well, she would. We raised you to have morals, but you seem to have scrapped those. I can't believe that Dante is really okay with this. He's always seemed to have a level head on his shoulders."

I can't take this. I can't take the judgment. Not of me, and especially not of Dante, who has been the most amazing and supportive husband I could ever have asked for.

"I'm not having this conversation. I just can't, I'm sorry. Goodbye, Dad."

"Alexan—"

His voice is cut off as I pull the phone away from my ear and hang up the call. I burst into a loud wail as the things he said to me really sink in. The comment about my mom hurts the most. I wish she were here more than anything, but there is that fear that she might have treated me the same way if she had been here.

My head is in my hands as I sob when someone picks me up and sits back down with me in their lap. I don't even need to look because Dante's embrace is so familiar to me. He holds me tight while I cry and strokes my head gently.

I turn to bury my face in his chest and cry until my eyes hurt. I'm exhausted, have a headache, and don't have any tears left. Finally, I lift my head and sniff a few times as I look into Dante's chocolate brown eyes.

"I'm sorry, Angel."

"You didn't do anything," I point out, then sniff again. I have to wipe a few fresh tears from my puffy eyes as I whisper, "He said Mom would be ashamed of me."

Dante's expression turns thunderous. "How dare he? They'd been divorced for years before she died. As if he has any authority to talk about what she would or wouldn't think. He only brought up Debra to make you feel like shit."

"Maybe. If he did, then it worked. I feel like fucking shit."

Dante pulls my head down to kiss me and then cuddles me again before whispering into my hair, "I love you, Angel."

"Thank you," I murmur.

I don't know how long he holds me before saying, "Go sit with Logan, Angel. I think he's upset and needs a cuddle."

"Okay."

I kiss Dante, then stand and walk over to Logan, who looks perfectly fine but concerned. He's sitting on the sofa next to Nate and Ash, who also wear expressions of concern for me.

Logan holds his arms out, and I can't help but laugh as I sit on his lap. "I'm told you're in need of a cuddle."

"Definitely. I'm very upset," he says with a smile.

He wraps his arms around me, and it's soothing. I rest my head against his chest and close my eyes as I listen to his heartbeat. Logan strokes my back, and his skin is warm against mine as I start to relax a little.

"Christopher," Dante snarls behind me.

My eyes immediately snap open as I sit up and spin around to stare at Dante.

"Don't you fucking *dare* speak to my wife the way you did today." He's silent for a second. "I don't give a shit what you think, to be honest, but *she* does. If you ever speak to her the way you did today, I'll come over there and make sure your jaw is wired shut long enough for you to learn to stop being a judgmental asshole."

My mouth drops open because Dante rarely gets angry, and he's always been on very good terms with my dad. He's certainly never threatened him with physical violence before.

"Go right ahead. I'm seeing my lawyer today, so I'll make sure to mention it. An assault charge would be worth making it one hundred percent clear to you that you are *not* to talk to Lexi like that. Make no mistake. I mean *every* word. If I find her crying because you've treated her like shit again, you *will* regret it."

He hangs up the call without listening further or saying anything more and hurls it across the room at another armchair. It hits the back of the armchair but bounces off the seat and onto the floor. He glares at the phone, breathing heavily as he does.

"Dante?" I say quietly into the stunned silence that follows.

He whips his head around to glare at me before his expression immediately softens, and all of the wind goes out of his sails.

"I'm sorry, Angel. I fucking hate him for this," he spits.

I sigh and walk back over to sit on his lap again. I wrap my arms around his neck and look into his eyes.

"I love you, but you can't assault my dad. Okay?"

"I can if he pulls this kind of shit again."

I shake my head at him. "No." I gesture to the guys behind me. "We all need you. I don't want you in some jail cell for beating up my dad. Despite the awful shit he said to me, I do still love him. He's my dad. So I don't want you to hurt him."

"Hmph," Dante snorts.

"I'm not a masochist, though. I'm not going to have anything to do with him unless he apologizes. If he never does that, then I will never speak to him again. I'm not going to let him treat me like crap just because he's my dad."

Dante's jaw is still tight, but he nods. "Fine. That makes sense."

I look around and find my phone stuffed down the side of the armchair from before, so I unlock it and write a text to my dad.

I'm blocking your number. Do not contact me again unless it's to apologize. I'm leaving Sophie unblocked, but I cannot stress enough that I will block her number if you use it to contact me for any reason other than to apologize for the hurtful things you said to me. I still love you, Dad. I wish it didn't have to be like this. I wish you could be the kind of loving and understanding parent that I wish I had to support me through this.

Tears are falling again as I type out the message, but I go into his record on my phone and block him as soon as it shows as sent. I follow it by blocking him on the few social media platforms we're connected on. It's strange, and it hurts so much, but I feel a tiny bit better once I know the only contact he can have with me is through Sophie.

While I'm on social media, I happen to catch another article quoting the Reddit user throwawayimnotdumb. I go to the site and find the profile, then sort the comments on their profile from oldest to newest. They signed up last week, and I can see the first one they made, which was quoted in the article I read. There's a thread about that same article, and they commented on it.

Yes, that was me. I meant it. I don't think they cheated, but she's definitely with all of them.

A wave of nausea hits me as I read it. I hate it so much because it's obviously someone we know. Someone we trusted enough to confirm it. We didn't do it in as many words with many people, but I all but confirmed it for Jasmine. She'd be able to speak with this kind of authority. I look at the next reply, made over the weekend, on a thread talking about how we haven't made any statements.

They've told people. Cassie's not lying. She is about some stuff, though. Lexi's gross, but she didn't cheat with Ash, except on Dante, I guess. But no, he didn't cheat on Cassie with her.

Someone asked them how they know this stuff and proved that to the site that quoted them in the article.

I don't want to out myself. The site promised I would be anonymous, but I proved it to them. I've had contact with the band, and that's all I'll say.

They said they've had contact with the guys, which makes me wonder if maybe it's someone in Isaac's office. I know Isaac wouldn't say anything because he makes a lot of money off the guys, but maybe one of his employees overheard something.

The last two comments are on a thread about the interview from last night.

What people are forgetting is that Ash dated that model after Cassie. It doesn't matter what she says. She wouldn't be living with him to walk in on them. They broke up months ago. She would've come out then.

Their initial comment has thousands of upvotes and replies, but when someone responded to ask if they thought all of it was a lie, the person responded to them.

No. They've told people. She's with all of them. That part's true. As disgusting as that is, I just don't think the cheating with Ash on Cassie bit is true. It doesn't make sense, but I'm not exactly going to ask for clarification.

My blood runs cold when I read the last line. Is it someone we're still in contact with? Is it Jasmine? It does sound kind of like Jasmine, and she could contact us but wouldn't ask for clarification. Then again, neither would any possible person we've trusted so far.

The guys are talking about the meeting we're going to with the lawyer, and given everything that happened with my dad, I don't want to bring this person up right now. I lock my phone and set it aside, kind of hating its existence and the things that it has done to me today.

After a while, Nate asks, "Why don't we play pool?"

The guys agree, and as we head upstairs to Nate's pool table, Logan snakes his arm around my waist. "Do you want to put some clothes on, Alexandra?"

"Maybe. We'll be going out soon, anyway, and I'm out of commission at the moment," I say as a laugh escapes my lips.

Logan laughs and kisses me. "Okay, get some clothes on and meet us upstairs. You can even wear underwear if you want to."

"So magnanimous," I say, affecting a shocked tone.

"Of course. I'm well known for my magnanimosity—that doesn't sound right. Is that a word?"

"It is now, I guess."

I'm laughing again as I peel off from the group to get clothes from Dante's room. I love that even when I'm as stressed and upset as I have been today, the guys all still have the ability to make me laugh.

I pull on a floaty purple Serenity dress and head back to the living room to grab my phone, but it's not there. I frown and figure that one of the guys must have taken it, so I head upstairs, following the sound of their voices to the pool table.

I find Logan and Dante having a game while Ash and Nate sit on stools at the side of the room with beers in their hands.

"Did one of you grab my phone?"

"Me, Goddess," Ash says and pulls it out of his pocket. "You told me you wanted me to carry it."

I'm pleased that he followed my instruction so well and stride over to kiss him. "Thank you, sweet boy. I appreciate that. This dress has pockets, so I can take it now."

He hands it over, and I catch sight of a message from Vera on the screen, so I check the chat. Everything seems to be fine at all three stores, so I thank them for letting me know and put my phone away.

Ash gets me a beer, and I sit and talk to him and Nate as we watch the game. When Dante wins, Ash takes over from Logan, who comes to sit next to me.

He grins at Nate and me, then pulls his phone out and shows us the screen. "Your strap-on is out for delivery, Alexandra."

"Ooh. That's exciting," I gasp. I turn to smirk at Nate. "As much as I would love for you to destroy my ass, I'm just too sore today, but I can always destroy yours tonight if you think you can take it."

He takes my chin in his hand and says, "I'll do my best. I'm more than ready for you to fuck me."

He kisses me, our tongues intertwining as he does, and my excitement over the idea of fucking Nate tonight eclipses my worries about everything. At least for now. We spend hours playing pool, and when Logan goes to take delivery of a package, I bite my lip and look at Nate, imagining him bent over in front of me.

The bodyguards arrive after lunch, and we travel in one car with Darren and Shane Stuart, Nate's bodyguard, to Lewis' office in time for our appointment at two. The other bodyguards follow us in another black SUV and escort us inside amidst a crowd of paparazzi who followed us from the apartment.

I cling to Dante's hand, leaning into him and not daring to even look at any of the other guys. I'm very aware that this is the first time we've all been seen together since the news leaked.

"Is it true you're all sleeping with Lexi?" someone calls.

Nobody even says that we're not making any comments. We stay silent as we follow the bodyguards through the crowd. The office door feels as though it's a million miles away.

"Why are you seeing a lawyer? Are you going to sue Cassie?"

I grit my teeth and keep my eyes forward.

"Nate! Did you actually fuck Lexi during the 'Heavenly Promises' music video shoot?"

I keep looking straight ahead, but I dare to dart a glance at Nate behind my sunglasses. His body is stiff, and his jaw is tense, but he keeps his mouth shut.

"How many men can you handle at once, Lexi? Do you take all four in one go?"

I fight against the shame that threatens to overwhelm me. Even if they don't publish this question, everyone here knows it was asked. Our bodyguards can hear it. I squeeze Dante's hand tightly and fight to give no sign of how much they're upsetting me.

It's a struggle by the time we make it safely inside, but not before they've asked many more variations of the same intrusive questions. As soon as we're out of sight, my body starts shaking because everything hits me at once.

Dante wraps me in his arms and murmurs soothing words of comfort. We all agreed that I wouldn't go anywhere near the other guys or even really talk to them anywhere someone could see us. So even though he doesn't say anything about the other guys, I know that when he tells me how much he loves me, he's reminding me about them, too.

Isaac arrives, and we wait about five minutes before we're taken into a meeting room. Lewis sits at the head of the table, and he greets us with a smile as we take seats around the table.

"Welcome, gentlemen and Alexandra. It's good to see you again."

"Thanks for meeting with us, Lewis," Isaac says. "Hades is going to courier their statement about the interview." He looks at his watch. "It should arrive soon. They're releasing it at three. So, obviously, we need to talk about our options regarding Cassandra Foster and what our best legal path forward is for the guys. Obviously, any statement we make will be in consultation with Hades PR, but we want to make sure that the guys are covered legally."

Lewis launches into a legal breakdown of the definition of blackmail and the laws around recording people in California. A lot of it is the same information that I've heard secondhand from the guys.

"It can take anywhere from one to two years to get to trial, and it's separate from the criminal case that the state may bring against her. The other benefit is that through the discovery process, we could uncover evidence that gives more evidence to the state for their criminal case." He pushes his glasses up on his nose and gives us a reassuring smile. "We can go for a larger scope in a civil case because we're not bound by the same rules. They have to have a certain amount of evidence to even bring charges. But anything we find in discovery is fair game, which is why I strongly suggest you bring a civil suit against her."

It's all very overwhelming, and Lewis runs us through the

timeline, warns us about how draining depositions can be and says that we shouldn't make a decision today but should talk privately with Isaac first.

I'm already exhausted when there's a knock on the conference room door. I look up at the clock, and it's two forty-five already. Hades will be sending out their statement about the interview in fifteen minutes.

"Come in," Lewis calls.

"Sorry to interrupt, Sir, but the courier is here for Mr. Meade, and he needs to sign for the documents."

"No worries." Isaac gives her a friendly smile and then tells us, "I'll be back in a minute."

I trace a pattern on the boardroom table as we wait for his return. Logan and Dante are talking quietly, but I just watch the hand on the clock that hangs on the wall ticking by the seconds until Isaac comes back.

He takes his seat again, then opens a yellow envelope to pull out the documents inside. As he begins to read, a deep frown comes across his face, and he looks up at Lewis. "I think you need to read this."

"What?" he asks, his eyebrows flying up.

Isaac strides over to him and hands him the documents as he asks, "Is this legal?"

As Lewis reads the document, a cold knot of dread forms in my stomach. Something very, very wrong is happening. I can tell. Isaac heads back to his seat, his mouth set in a grim line.

There's silence in the room for about thirty seconds, then Lewis looks at Isaac. "You don't have their original contract here, do you?"

"I'm not in the habit of carrying it around with me, and neither are they," he says with a bout of mirthless laughter. "Someone from my office can send a digital copy over to you, though."

"Please do. I'll look over it, but I doubt there are any loopholes. Recording contracts are generally watertight."

“What’s happening?” Dante asks, looking between Isaac and Lewis.

Isaac heaves a deep sigh and says, “Hades is dropping you under the morality clause in your contract.”

Epilogue

Ass To Mouth Is Not A Safe Sexual Practice

Logan is still wearing the trousers and collared shirt he wore to the meeting this afternoon, but he strips me of my clothes as soon as he ascertains I'm still up for sex with Nate and him tonight.

"Come with me to your room, Alexandra."

I follow him upstairs, my body flushed with heat as arousal and excitement take me over. He opens the door and leads me to the center of the room.

"Kneel here and wait for me."

"Yes, Sir," I breathe as I take my position.

He tilts my face up and bends down to capture my lips with his. His tongue makes its way into my mouth, and I take in the taste of him before he breaks our kiss, straightens up, and walks away.

I don't know how long I wait for him, but by the time the door opens and he appears again, I practically have to pant for breath.

"Good girl waiting so patiently for me," he says in a low, sexy voice when he returns.

He sets something on the dresser at the side of the room, then strides over to me.

"Nate's going to join us soon." He puts his finger under my chin and tilts my face up to look at him. "In the meantime, I think I'll enjoy you while we wait." He gives me a smile and asks, "How do you want it tonight, Alexandra?"

He's stressed. I can see it behind his expression, and I know that he probably needs the distraction tonight as much as I do. I'm frustrated that I can't take a cock in my pussy, but the knowledge that I'm going to fuck Nate before the night is done sends a shot of arousal darting throughout my body.

I also know what I want, so I tell him, "Rough, Sir."

"What should I do with you, though?" He raises an eyebrow at me.

"Anything you want, Sir," I say in a breathy voice.

"It was a rhetorical question, Alexandra. If I wanted you to answer, I would've asked you directly." He reaches down and twists one of my nipples painfully. "I'm going to use the paddle on you for that."

Logan moves around behind me and fists his hand in my hair as he yanks me to a stand. The pain in my scalp causes me to gasp, and I stumble as he pulls me over to the side of the room before he pushes my torso down on the padded spanking bench.

"Climb onto it, Alexandra."

I climb onto the bench and straddle it before leaning down so I'm on all fours on the padded knee rests, with the raised central section pressing against my torso. The bench is on tall legs, so I'm looking at his chest when Logan walks in front of me. He picks up the paddle hanging on the side of the equipment, along with other implements used for impact play, and shows it to me.

"I'm going to spank you, then I'll facefuck you. If Nate isn't here by then, I'll keep finding ways to use you, toy."

I don't answer, and my anticipation grows as Logan moves behind me. I have to pant for breath, and my pussy is drenched. I get no warning before the paddle comes down roughly on my right ass cheek, and I squeal at the sudden pain. He spanks me roughly, and I lose count of how many times he hits my ass, but I'm so far gone into arousal that I can barely focus. All I care about is Logan and whatever he's going to do with my body next.

He uses his hands to spread me apart, and the cold room air hits my heated pussy. "You're so wet." He slides his hot, wet tongue up my slit, and I groan. "And so tasty." He does it again, this time swirling his tongue around my clit before he removes his face. "Do you want to come, Alexandra?"

"Yes, Sir," I moan.

He flicks his tongue across my clit, and I can hear the amusement in his voice as he says, "I'm sure you do. I'm not sure why you thought I would let you. You can come after both Nate and I have been satisfied."

I moan in ecstasy as Logan brings me right to the edge of orgasm. The pleasure is intense, and it takes every ounce of willpower that I have to stop myself from tipping over the edge as Logan uses his tongue on my clit to bring me painfully close. He does this three more times before he stops, and I pant for breath, lost in a daze of lust.

"Get down, Alexandra."

I climb down from the spanking bench, and Logan's cock is hard in his trousers. He shoves me down to my knees in front of him, and I groan softly because I fucking love it when he's rough with me.

"Look what you do to me." He takes my chin in his hand and holds it in place. "Can you see?"

"Yes, Sir."

"I don't think you can."

He takes a step closer and pushes his stiff cock against my face. Something about him rubbing his crotch against my face with his trousers still on drives me wild. He really is using my body tonight, and it's fucking amazing.

Still holding my chin in his hand, he uses his other one to unbuckle his belt and drop his trousers and briefs to the floor. His cock springs free and immediately hits my face because it's so close.

I gasp, and Logan takes that as his cue to push his cock past my parted lips.

He takes my face between his hands and thrusts his cock roughly into my mouth, fucking me until I'm gagging on his cock. He holds his cock down my throat until my eyes water, then pulls back, and I have time to gasp for breath before he does it again. He does this four or five times, and tears stream down my face.

"Safety light check?" he asks.

I have to pant for breath before I admit, "Yellow."

"Good girl," he says, sounding pleased with my honesty, and his praise adds to my arousal. He fucks my mouth this way two more times before he pulls his cock out and says, "I think I'm done with your mouth, for now, Alexandra. I'm going to get your cock on you, and then I'll go find out what's taking Nate so long."

He pulls his trousers up and struggles to do them up over his erection, then grabs my hair and pulls me up to stand with it. He wraps my hair around his hand, holding it tight as he moves behind me. He pulls me back against him, his cock hard against my ass, His free arm wrapped around my waist, holding me tight against him.

"Are you still sore, Alexandra?"

"My pussy is, Sir," I admit. "My ass isn't as bad tonight as it felt this morning."

"Do you think you can take my cock while you fuck Nate?"

"Yes, Sir. If you're not too rough."

He pulls my hair back, forcing me to look up at the roof, leans down to kiss my exposed neck, then asks, "What makes you think I would be rough?"

He slides his hand up from my waist and twists my nipple painfully. I cry out at the pain, and Logan holds me in this position.

"You didn't answer my question, Alexandra."

My brain is foggy with lust, but I manage to say, "You're being rough tonight, Sir. I was just warning you about my ass."

He moves around in front of me, his hand still wrapped in my hair, and I find myself looking into his eyes.

"Good girl. I like that you're advocating for yourself. Knowing your limits is a good thing. I'm proud of you for how well you've been doing that tonight." He lowers his face to mine and kisses me, exploring my mouth with his tongue before he pulls his head back and grins at me. "I'm giving you time to recover physically, but I'm enjoying finding other ways to use my slut toy's body."

I moan softly, and Logan grins. He reaches between my legs and rubs back and forth along my drenched pussy.

"You like being used, don't you?" he murmurs.

"Uh-huh," I manage through panting breaths.

He finally lets go of my hair and kneels in front of me, holding my hips as he buries his face in my pussy. I moan and have to brace myself on his shoulders as the onslaught of pleasure overwhelms me. I'm so close to coming when he stops that I've lost all control, and I make noises of mewling disappointment as my orgasm fades away.

Logan chuckles and takes my hand to lead me back over to the chest of drawers, where he left the package he received today. He's already opened it, and in it is a harness with a dildo slightly bigger than the butt plug Nate's been using already attached to it.

Logan has me step into the harness, then tightens it on me, and I blink as I look down at the cock attached to me. I feel strangely powerful with it on, and when Logan drops to his knees in front of me and takes it in his mouth, I think I might die.

I thrust my hips back and forth slightly into his mouth, and he reaches up and grabs my ass, kneading my cheeks with his hands as he blows the strap-on.

He pulls his mouth off it and grins up at me. "Do you like your cock, Alexandra?"

"Fuck. Yes. I can't wait to use it on Nate, and I really want to use it on Ash, too," I admit.

Logan stands and kisses me before he smiles at me. "It's yours. You can do with it as you wish. I've got a few bigger dildos for Nate to work up with before he takes mine. If Ash wants to take a cock in his ass, I suggest you do the same with him. Now, wait here. I'm going to go find Nate."

"Yes, Sir."

I watch as he walks away, cock stiff in his trousers as he turns toward the door. I stare down at the strap-on, barely able to believe this is going to happen. I reach down and wrap my hand around the shaft to stroke it.

I bite my lip as I run my hand back and forth on it, feeling the veins of the dildo and trailing my finger around the head of the cock. I can still see Logan on his knees in front of me, and my heart rate quickens as I remember him sucking me off. I imagine what it would be like to fuck his mouth with it instead and groan softly.

I have so many ideas for ways that I can use this, and when the door opens again, I stare at Logan and Nate in a daze.

"Nice cock, Sexy," Nate says as he strides across the room.

"Thanks," I manage to say through my increasing arousal.

He stops in front of me and kisses me passionately as he reaches between us to play with my breasts. He takes one in his mouth and looks up at me through thick lashes as I moan in satisfaction.

He continues to move down my body until he's on his knees in front of me, and he kisses his way onto the harness and then along the dildo before he pulls his head back to look at it.

"Okay, this is a good size," he comments.

"I figured it's a bit bigger than the plug you've been using, but not much," Logan says as he unbuttons his shirt. "I've got some bigger ones as well, so those should help you work up to accommodating me." He drops his shirt on the floor and smirks at Nate. "Good luck whenever you decide to try and take Ash. He's a big boy. I've had plenty of cocks in my ass, and even I would struggle."

"I do," I say with a laugh. "The first time he fucked my ass, I almost cried."

"You guys are scaring me." Nate cringes.

Logan crouches next to him and kisses him, reaching down to rub Nate's cock through his trousers as he does.

"You're not taking Ash's cock or even mine today, just Lexi's, and she's going to be very gentle with you." He smiles up at me. "Aren't you, Alexandra?"

"Yes, Sir. I won't hurt you, Nate."

Logan pulls Nate up to standing and wraps his arms around him as he kisses Nate again. He pulls Nate's shirt off over his head and unbuckles his trousers. Their mouths are connected whenever they can be as they both undress until they're standing there naked in front of me, stiff cocks pressed against one another as they kiss.

Logan has his hand on Nate's ass, pulling Nate firmly against him, and I absentmindedly stroke my cock while I watch them. My pussy aches with arousal, and my nipples are painfully stiff as they finally turn their attention back to me.

"Let's take this to the bed," Logan says in a husky voice.

He grabs a bottle of lube, and I take Nate's hand as we walk to the bed together. We lie on the bed facing one another, and he kisses me. It's strange having the cock I'm wearing between us and even stranger when Nate reaches down to stroke it.

"Why is that so hot?" I murmur as I watch him do it.

"You like watching me stroke your cock, Sexy?"

A dart of arousal zings through my body when he asks the question. Something is thrilling and exciting about having a cock and being able to fuck someone with it.

"Yes," I admit. "I can't wait to have it in your ass."

"Roll onto your stomach, Nate," Logan says in a low, sexy tone behind me, and I jump.

He rubs my back gently as Nate does as he's asked, and Logan looks at me.

"Start preparing his ass, Alexandra."

I kneel, straddling Nate's legs at his thighs, bending down to tongue his ass. He moans softly as I start by licking his perineum, and he groans when I reach his hole.

I gasp when Logan begins to give me the same treatment, and I'm lost in lust as I thrust my tongue into Nate. I reach around for the lube and pull my head back before I squirt some onto Nate. I carefully push a finger into him, and he groans when I do.

"Are you excited about this, Nate?" I ask him, and he groans again as he nods. "I am, too. I'm going to be the first person to fuck your ass."

I push a second finger into him, thrusting my hips in time with my fingers, and Logan matches my rhythm in my ass.

As he pushes a second finger into me, Logan asks, "What's your safeword, Lexi?"

"Pineapple, Sir."

"Will you call a color if it's getting too much?"

"Yes, Sir. I'll tell you if I get to yellow." I nod as I say it.

He leans down, still fucking my ass with his fingers, and says in a low, husky voice in my ear, "Good girl, Alexandra." I tremble at his words, and he chuckles. "Good girls get rewarded, and you've been a very good girl tonight."

I squirt more lube onto Nate's ass and fuck him with my fingers. It's strange that this is the goal tonight. Other times I've done this to Nate, Logan has always stopped me, or we've moved on to something else. Now, it's working up to me fucking his ass as the main act.

Logan doesn't instruct me to move on, so I don't. I continue using my fingers on Nate and loving the sound of his moans as Logan mimics whatever I do. When I add more lube, he adds more lube. When I slowly try pushing a third finger into Nate's ass, Logan does the same to me.

"Is that okay, Nate?" I ask when he groans.

"It's fine. A bit painful," he admits.

I'm frustrated that he's on his stomach because I know pleasuring him would help. "Can you get on your hands and knees for me?"

"Sure."

We adjust position, and I'm able to reach around and stroke his cock while I slowly fuck his ass with my fingers.

"Focus on the pleasure and try to relax," I tell him.

Nate moans, and I smile as his hole gets less tense around my fingers.

"There you go," I murmur. "I'm going to use my cock on you in a minute. Are you ready?"

"I think so." He swallows heavily.

I pant for breath as I continue what I'm doing for a while longer and add more lube to Nate's ass. Finally, I stop stroking his cock and pull my fingers out of his ass.

Logan does the same, and I turn to look at him. "Can you please help me keep him distracted while I do this, Sir?"

"Of course, Alexandra." He kisses me expertly, then moves his lips to my ear and whispers. "You're doing very well. I'm proud of you. Nate couldn't ask for someone better to be the first person to fuck his ass."

The combination of his praise and the knowledge that mine will be the first cock in Nate's ass makes me moan, and Logan chuckles as he plays with my breasts, teasing me as he pulls and tweaks my nipples, bringing me near orgasm before he stops.

I blink at him in a daze, and he grins at me. "Nate's ass isn't going to fuck itself, Alexandra."

"Yeah. I don't know what you two are doing back there, but I'm waiting very impatiently for Lexi to take my virgin ass."

I groan at the reminder, but Logan laughs and moves down to kiss Nate. "Your ass was virgin when Lexi first rimmed you, but you've had plenty of things in there since then."

"But not a cock yet." Nate sounds thoroughly amused and aroused.

"Not a cock yet, true. Lexi's about to fix that."

Logan moves under Nate and wraps his lips around Nate's cock. I take this as my cue to begin fucking him. I put a generous amount of lube on my cock, stroking it back and forth to make sure it's entirely covered, then spread his ass cheeks. I put some pressure against his hole with my cock, and Nate groans, but I don't know if that's from what Logan's doing to him or me.

I watch in fascination as my cock slips inside him. Nate gasps, and I freeze, holding myself with my cock only a few inches in.

"Are you okay, Nate?"

"Yes," he pants. "It's just…bigger than I expected."

Logan stops blowing him but continues stroking him as he says. "Lexi's cock is slightly bigger than the butt plug you've been using at its widest point, but her cock is the same thickness the whole way. You can take it, just focus on what I'm doing and try to relax."

Nate nods and says, "Okay. Keep going, Lexi."

Logan puts his mouth back around Nate, who moans in satisfaction, and I begin moving again. I only push in another half an inch, though, before I start pulling out. I do this for a while, pushing my cock in about two to three inches, then pulling out.

When I no longer feel any resistance from Nate, I push further in with each thrust. I revel in pushing my cock further and further into him, and I don't think I've ever felt more satisfied in my life than when I manage to bury myself in him.

I hold myself deep in him, the front of my thighs touching the back of his, and I pant for breath. "Fuck, yes, Nate. God, it's so good having my cock completely buried in your ass."

"It feels amazing. I love you fucking me, Sexy."

Logan takes his mouth off Nate and strokes him as he sits up to watch us. I take Nate's hips in my hands and begin to move in and out of him faster. I moan as I realize I really am fucking him now. We're both panting for breath, and Logan kisses him before he looks at me.

"I'm going to take your ass now, Alexandra. I'm going to fuck my toy while it fucks Nate."

"Yes," I pant, and thrust into Nate. "Sir," I finish as I pull back and then push my cock back in again.

Logan moves behind me, and I bury myself in Nate as I bend over a little to give him a better angle to get into me. Once he's in, we begin to move in sync together. With each thrust from Logan, I'm pushed into Nate. As I pull back, Logan pulls back and then thrusts into me again, forcing me forward.

This is absolutely amazing, and I manage to find a rhythm with Logan while also reaching forward to stroke Nate's cock. The room is filled with our grunts and groans, pants for breath, and the sounds of fucking. Every one of my nerve endings is on fire, and when Logan reaches around me to play with my breasts, I lose all control.

He kisses my neck, and I stop moving as my orgasm hits me. My body shakes, and Logan pulls and tweaks my nipples as I come.

"Fuck, Sir. I'm so sorry. Fuck. Oh my god, oh fuck," I cry and lean back against his hard body as the waves of pleasure rock mine.

I pant for breath when it passes, and Logan chuckles. "I'll have to punish you for that, Alexandra, but I do enjoy watching you come."

"I'm sorry, Sir," I say through panting breaths.

"Don't apologize to me. Apologize to Nate, who isn't getting fucked right now because you're a bad girl who came when she wasn't supposed to."

My cheeks heat, and I'm just as turned on by him telling me I'm a bad girl as I was when he told me I was a good girl.

"I'm sorry, Nate."

"What are you sorry for, Alexandra?" Logan demands.

"I'm sorry for stopping when I was fucking you because I had an orgasm." Embarrassment floods through me, and I'm so aroused that my pussy aches with desire.

"It's f—"

"I'm not sure you're truly sorry, Alexandra." Logan cuts Nate off and twists my nipple painfully. "Tell him how selfish you are for taking your orgasm instead of letting him come first."

I'm. Going. To. Die.

Just hearing Logan say the words sends me into the next level of ecstasy, and I know I need to make this good.

"I really am sorry, Nate. I was so selfish letting myself come around Sir's cock instead of fucking you like a good girl. I'm a bad girl and deserve to be punished, but not until I've given you and Sir the orgasms you're entitled to. I need to remember that I'm here to be used, and I'm not allowed an orgasm unless Sir tells me that I can have one."

The only sound in the room is our heavy breathing. I'm absolutely positive that if either of these men were able to access my clit right now, I would break into a million pieces at once the second they touched it.

"Jesus fucking christ, Logan," Nate says. "You and the fucking orgasm denial all the time. Poor Lexi can't even come in peace."

Logan laughs and twists my nipple. "She knows why I do it. Don't you, Alexandra?"

"Yes, Sir," I moan through the painful pleasure.

"Tell Nate why."

Logan releases my nipple and strokes it softly with his thumb as I answer, "Because my orgasms are better when I wait. Holding them off makes them more intense. That's why sometimes I can't do it because I'm so high that I can't stop it anymore."

"Good girl," Logan murmurs. He grabs my earlobe between his teeth and pulls, causing me to moan before releasing it, and he adds, "But now you don't get another orgasm tonight, no matter how good a girl you are. I suggest you remain my good girl, though, or there will be further punishments, and you won't like them."

I shiver, and goosebumps appear on my arms as I nod dutifully. "Yes, Sir."

"Now fuck Nate's ass with your thick cock like a good girl."

I take Nate's hips and begin moving in and out of him again. Logan finds his rhythm with me, and we move together as one, him fucking me and me fucking Nate. It isn't long before I'm back in a heightened state of arousal, but I focus on giving Nate pleasure, desperate not to come again.

It's almost a relief when Logan grips my hips so tightly it hurts and buries himself in my ass as he empties his load. He holds himself there, panting for breath before he pulls out, stands up, and walks around, so his cock is next to my face where I'm on my knees fucking Nate.

"Clean my cock, Alexandra."

Heat floods to my cheeks. I don't normally do ass to mouth, and Logan knows it, even though it's not a hard limit. I open my mouth and take his cock in it, feeling overwhelmingly aroused as I do.

Logan takes my chin in his hand and looks down at me. "Bad girls do dirty things, Alexandra. While you clean my cock, think about how bad you've been and how you can be better next time."

I almost fucking come just from his words. I suck his cock clean. The taste is mostly of lube mixed with cum and isn't particularly pleasant, but being used by Logan drives me wild. The taste is long gone by the time Logan pulls his cock out of my mouth and smiles at me.

"When bad girls take their punishments as well as you do, they become good girls again. Get your cock out of Nate, Alexandra."

I pull myself out of Nate, and he groans as his ass is emptied. Logan moves around to kiss him and looks into his eyes.

"Was that good, Nate?"

"Fuck, yes. Holy shit. I can't wait until it's your cock in me."

Logan smiles and kisses him again. "Me, too. Want to fuck my ass now?"

"Hell. Yes."

Logan turns to me and says, "I'm going to remove your cock, Alexandra."

He undoes the harness for the strap-on, and I feel strangely weird when it's gone. The air in the room is cold on my heated pussy, and I'm aware of how easily accessible my clit is now.

Logan grabs the lube, moves to the end of the bed, and bends over it before saying, "Come get me ready for Nate, Alexandra."

I eagerly move around behind Logan, tonguing his hole and fucking him with my fingers while making sure to use plenty of lube because I know how big Nate is. Nate moves next to me, stroking his cock and playing with my breasts. I'm just relieved he doesn't touch my clit because I'm wound so tightly that I'm sure I'm going to explode.

"He's all yours," I tell Nate when I can easily fuck Logan's ass with my fingers.

"I'm led to believe we share him," he jokes, and I laugh as I pull him close to me to kiss him.

Nate places his hands on my ass and pulls me hard against his stiff cock, his tongue exploring my mouth until he breaks our kiss.

"Mmm. You're so fucking hot," he murmurs.

"I know," I say with a cheeky grin.

Both of them laugh as Nate positions himself behind Logan. Nate pushes his cock into Logan's ass, and Logan groans when he does.

As Nate begins fucking Logan, Logan says, "Come lie on the bed in front of me, Alexandra. I want to eat your pussy while Nate fucks me."

I gasp and swallow before quickly saying, "Yes, Sir."

Logan lifts himself up, and I climb onto the bed to position myself underneath him and spread my legs wide.

"Isn't this a good view, Nate?" Logan says as he trails his finger up and down my wet slit.

Nate looks down at me, eyes full of lust, and nods. "The best view. You going to make her come?"

"Not if she knows what's good for her," Logan says in a warning tone.

He pushes my legs even wider apart, causing a slight pain as he does before he lowers his head to my pussy. He's always been amazing with his tongue, and tonight is no exception. I'm in such ecstasy watching Nate fuck him as he eats me that tears come to my eyes from the exquisite pleasure of trying to hold my orgasm at bay.

I'm so close, and it's so difficult that I'm on the verge of calling yellow when Nate grunts, "I'm going to come."

He empties himself in Logan's ass, and it's only a few more moments of painful pleasure before Logan lifts his head and looks at me. His face glistens with my juices, and he has a dazed look of lust on his face.

"Good girl, Lexi."

He drops down again but rests his head on my stomach and cuddles me. I stroke his head with my hand, and Nate smiles as he looks at us, rubbing his hand over Logan's ass.

I'm in complete bliss. I'm floating on a total high as Nate finally pulls out of Logan, and Logan picks me up to take me to get cleaned up. Nate follows us to Logan's bathroom, and while Logan washes me, Nate cuddles me and showers me with kisses. I'm held by one of them at all times while they clean themselves, and Logan holds me for a long time, wrapped in a fluffy towel, when we get out of the shower.

He picks me up and carries me to his bed. Even though I'm well and truly capable of walking the twenty feet to get there, I love feeling secure in his arms. I snuggle up to him, resting my head on his chest as Nate cuddles into me from behind.

"How are you feeling, Lexi?" Logan asks in a soft voice.

"Too good to be true," I murmur, and both men chuckle.

"Did you like fucking Nate with a strap-on?"

I smile and nod. "Yes. Having a cock is weird and awesome and made me feel oddly powerful. Is that what it's like having one all the time?"

I expect them to laugh at me, but Logan looks past me at Nate and shrugs. "I suppose so. I've always had one, so I don't really think twice about it."

"Well, you should. Fuck. If I had a cock, I'd spend all my time masturbating. I'd play with it all day, every day."

Nate does laugh this time. "That was basically me from the ages of thirteen to seventeen."

"You pronounced twenty-nine wrong," Logan says with a smirk, and Nate hits his arm.

A comfortable silence falls, and I revel in the warm coziness of being wrapped up between these two men.

"Was I too rough with you tonight? How is your ass?" Logan asks and rubs it softly.

I smile and shake my head. "No. I love it when you're rough and before you ask, being told to apologize was one of the hottest things ever."

Logan's chest rumbles as he laughs and kisses my head. "Good to know."

"I could do with an orgasm, though," I grumble.

Nate kisses my neck and says in an amused tone, "Didn't you selfishly have one while you were fucking me?"

"Well, yeah, but I want *another* one," I sulk. "I got all worked up again."

Logan laughs and kisses me softly. "Tell you what, Alexandra. I'll let Nate give you an orgasm tomorrow morning. I'm nice like that."

Exclusive Sneak Peek for Wicked Freedom

"Are you excited?" Heather asks as we walk down the hotel corridor with our bodyguards trailing us.

"To say I was 'excited' would be the understatement of the year." I grin at her.

"Well, I thought I should take you today while you've got the chance. It's almost better than if I'd taken you last time because everyone will be there today, and you'll be able to see clothes actually being made."

I shake my head. "It's so bizarre. I can't believe I'm going to *Serenity.*"

"I'm going to let you get away with saying Serenity's name like that, but only because sometimes even *I'm* blown away by the place," she teases me.

We head downstairs and into a black SUV with our bodyguards, but as we leave, some paparazzi take pictures of the car we're in.

"Ugh. It was better last time when they had no idea I was here."

Heather wrinkles her nose. "Yeah. It sucks. As soon as you're safely hidden away, they won't be able to bother you."

"You'd think it would be old news by now." I roll my eyes. "I mean, I knew it would never *really* be old news for us."

Heather cringes. "I hate to say it, but it's never 'old news' for any of us. We get past it, but for them, it's something to bring up in every article or when they want a reaction out of you." She gives me a cheeky grin and adds, "All I'll say is that I don't recommend slapping a reporter. Might want to pass that one on to Dante."

"Hey, he only threatened to hit a guy that one time."

I laugh but remember that technically, it was twice. I haven't heard from my dad, and this knowledge saddens me, ending my amusement abruptly.

"What a time, though. 'Keep my wife's name out of your *fucking* mouth.'" Heather fans herself dramatically. "Okay, Daddy."

Heather calling Dante 'Daddy' promptly distracts me from my thoughts, and I burst into laughter, then smirk at her. "Dante's normally so calm, and I was freaked out when it happened, but in hindsight, it's definitely hot that he's so protective of me." I smile as I think about the beautiful man I married. "He always has been. I couldn't ask for a better husband."

"He must be very self-assured being in the position he's in."

I nod and then shrug. "He knows I love him. The guys all love each other in different ways, but since we're all happy, that's all that matters." I can't really explain how some of our relationships work because it's not my place to divulge them, so I say, "None of us would want to deprive the others of happiness."

"I get it. Harrison and I are monogamous, but we both love Sebastian, Hayden, and Gabriel like family. Closer than family, actually," she amends. "Bands are weird. You get all these insular experiences together that kind of end up cutting you off from most of the people in your lives."

"Yes!" I exclaim. "Because, like, your cousin doesn't understand what it's like to have complete strangers giving an opinion on the top you wore to work last Wednesday."

"And your bestie at work doesn't understand why you don't like listening to the latest Cruise Control album because it's all about your breakup," she says with a laugh. I give her a quizzical look, and she says, "Ariana. Her best friend at her old job was a massive fan."

We spend the rest of the drive to Serenity listing out more and more bizarre aspects of our lives that we just take for granted these days. We laugh so hard we have tears in our eyes, and I wonder if our bodyguards think we're insane.

I've gotten a lot more comfortable around Darren lately. One, because I've spent more time with him, and two, because I found out he signed an NDA before he started working with us. So I'm a lot more confident he's not the person leaking information about us online.

When we reach Serenity, Heather cringes as she looks out the window. "Dammit. I should've known they'd guess where we were going."

I follow her gaze and sigh when I see a crowd of paparazzi out the front of the building.

Callum parks the car and turns to look at us. "Are you ready, Mrs. Fletcher?"

"Sure, Cal. No time like the present."

The bodyguards push the crowd back from the car before they open the door, and I follow Heather out into the fresh air. They manage to keep about a foot of space around us in a circle, but they can't stop the questions being called out to us.

"How long are you guys in Chicago, Lexi?"

I have zero desire to give them information about our travel plans.

"Heather, did you give Lexi tips on how to juggle multiple men?"

I dart a glance at her, but her face is perfectly impassive, and I remember that she's been dealing with this kind of shit for a long, long time now.

"Is there any truth to the rumors you're pregnant?"

I'm not actually sure who they're asking, but neither of us responds either way. We're coming close to the entrance to Heather's business, and I couldn't be more relieved.

"How many men did you sleep with last night, Lexi? On a scale of one to four?"

The question doesn't even make sense, and I have to resist the urge to roll my eyes. Callum yanks the door to Serenity open, and

I follow him and Heather inside. As it closes behind us, a final comment is called out.

"It makes sense that you two are friends. You're both known for being cheaters."

I'm in the lobby of Serenity, but I feel sick to my stomach as the familiar shame from a paparazzi run-in hits me. Heather's receptionist is looking at us, and I remember that she was once tasked with deleting nasty comments about me off the internet.

Heather sighs and puts her arm around my shoulders. "Forget those assholes, Lexi Sullivan. Welcome to Serenity."

Acknowledgments

This book wouldn't be what it is if it weren't for the people that supported me along the way.

Mum – Let's not talk about chapter one or two or four or six or seven or nine or ten or eleven or twelve or thirteen or fourteen or sixteen or seventeen. How's about those chapters three, five, eight, and eighteen, huh? Weren't they interesting!

Beate – Remember in the last book when I said there was only one last reverse harem to go? Baaaaaaaaahahahaha. That is all. I'm sorry.

Julia – Weeeeeell, poop. Another person who I promised I would write April's book next. Sorry about that!

Siân's Smut Party – I'm just going to put you all in one group from now on. Julia only got a separate one this time because she was owed an apology! Thanks for being there any time of the day or night to read my filth and give feedback. I can't thank you all enough.

Natalie – Lewis keeps asking me every night when we'll be having our next play date with Dean. Now that this book is finished, we should get on that!

Dignity Mesh Survivors – Sorry you haven't heard from me for months. Here's a metric fucktonne of smut as an apology! Thanks for being so absolutely epic for so many years. I love you guys. We should go back to the hot springs sometime soon.

Michelle – I apologise in advance for the way you're going to sound even more like you're having an orgasm when you read this book aloud. Also for the wholeass fourth book you're going to have to moan your way through. I mean…I haven't written it yet, but I'm just assuming.

All my advance readers – Thank you so, so, so much to all of my wonderful advance readers. I love that you're willing to read my work and give me your honest thoughts on it. I love the messages I get to discuss the books and how many of you are willing to spread the love by sharing my teasers and stuff. Team Cruise Control rocks!

Mark and Lorna Reid – I'm so sorry that you'll be getting this book so ludicrously late. I'm sorrier still for the last-minute title change, but Wicked Freedom is just so perfect for the final book in the series, and Wicked Screwed is just so perfect for this one. No. More. Preorders. Except Hayden's, of course, since that's already up. I'm so grateful to you both for everything you do to make my books far more amazing than I could ever manage. I hope the house move is going well. I know things freaking suck sometimes, but hopefully, some fucker has a rainbow somewhere for you.

Damien – Thanks for everything. Sorry I've been so absent basically all of this calendar year. This book is finally done now. The pressure is gone. I love you, and I love the boys, and I couldn't do this without you.

My readers – If you're reading this, thank you for being here on this author journey with me. I hope that you enjoyed this book. I didn't predict writing a book with so much smut that I couldn't tie up the series in three books. I'm assuming book four will be the final one. I think it will be. Even at over sixty percent smut, I should be able to finish it!

About the Author

Siân Ceinwen lives in Western Australia with her husband and two sons. She grew up with a love of telling or writing stories for her friends to read and enjoy.

Wicked Screwed is the third book of the 'four-book trilogy' about the members of Wicked Stallion.

If you enjoyed this, please share it with your friends, and please write a review on Amazon or Goodreads.

It would really be appreciated, as this helps more people to discover the book. Reviews assist with the algorithms used by these platforms to display books, so every little bit helps indie authors to get noticed.

You can also join Siân on TikTok, Facebook, or Twitter for all the latest news on the Something Wicked series of novels.

Printed in Great Britain
by Amazon

83279021R00173